"I thoug[ht] taken me i[...] to make love..."

The timbre of his voice deepened as he grew bolder. "It was you I wanted that day, and I want you even more desperately now."

His lips parted slightly as he lowered his head, and Dana knew she should flee but his arms encircled her with such a tender embrace she wanted only to stay. Such a desire was impossible for more reasons than she could count, but as his mouth covered hers she could recall none of them. She raised her hand to his shoulder, then wove her fingers in the tawny curls at his nape to hold him close. Without ending the kiss, he pulled her down onto the soft spring grass at the edge of the stream.

His touch was light as he began to trace the luscious swells of her figure...

➤

THE REVIEWER'S CHOICE

Also by Phoebe Conn

☆

Beyond the Stars
Hearts of Gold

PHOEBE CONN
BY LOVE ENSLAVED

WARNER BOOKS

A Warner Communications Company

WARNER BOOKS EDITION

Copyright © 1989 by Phoebe Conn
All rights reserved.

Cover art by Pino Daeni

Warner Books, Inc.
666 Fifth Avenue
New York, N.Y. 10103

A Warner Communications Company

Printed in the United States of America

First Printing: November, 1989

10 9 8 7 6 5 4 3 2 1

BY LOVE ENSLAVED is dedicated to my two handsome sons, Jeff and Drew, whose Swedish blood allows them to proudly claim a Viking heritage.

CHAPTER I

Denmark, Early Summer, A.D. 882

Dana brushed the tears from her lashes, but the harder she tried to suppress her laughter, the more impossible it became. Her aunt's flustered irritation at her mirth only served to amuse the flame-haired beauty all the more. Finally she raised her hand in a graceful appeal for mercy.

"Please, Aunt, no more."

"But every word is the truth," Grena insisted indignantly. "None of our women can resist the man." Turning to her sixteen-year-old daughter, she urged her to speak. "You tell them, Berit. Perhaps they will believe you even if they think I am merely spinning fanciful tales to keep them entertained."

Barely able to contain her own amusement, the vivacious blonde spoke in a breathless rush. "Jørn bought the Celt thrall only three days before he left on the summer voyage with Uncle Haakon. He had no time to observe the problems the man from Erin would create or I'm certain he would never have left us with such a troublesome burden."

With marked skepticism, Dana glanced at her mother. Jørn was her Aunt Grena's eldest son. At nineteen he had a well-deserved reputation for being not only irresponsible but reckless as well. He was also so self-centered that Dana doubted he would have cared even if he had known how

1

difficult the new slave would make things for his widowed mother.

Berit correctly interpreted the silent exchange passing between Dana and Berit's Aunt Freya, but she knew her brother's faults too well to take offense and hurriedly continued. "The Celt has caused no end of turmoil, and truly there's not one of our female servants who isn't enamored of him. They are either shirking their work to sneak out to the stables to see him, or fighting among themselves over which of them is his favorite. While it is amusing to see them making fools of themselves over him, when their work goes undone we're the ones who suffer."

"Is he handsome?" Dana inquired with playful curiosity. "Or merely possessed of such remarkable stamina he can satisfy all your girls?"

When Berit blushed deeply at the indelicacy of the question, her mother responded for her. "He's a surly brute, but I suppose some might find him handsome. As for his ability to satisfy a woman, that's part of the problem. He'll have nothing to do with any of them, but his disinterest only serves to make the girls all the more bold."

"How can that be true?" Freya leaned forward to look directly at her younger sister. The day was warm, and the four women were seated beneath a massive oak whose leafy branches shielded their lovely fair complexions from the brightness of the sun's rays. "With so many eager women, how can you be certain he wants none of them?"

"I have ears as well as eyes, Freya." Annoyed that her sister would question her judgment, Grena paused only long enough to adjust the half-dozen heavy gold bracelets encircling her right wrist before she resumed her attempt at gaining sympathy. "None of the girls is happy. Brendan seems to hold all of them, as well as our family, in contempt. I'd sell him tomorrow, but Jørn said he was an extraordinary horseman, and all the men who would be willing to pay the price I would have to ask are away, just as our men are."

While she was as greatly amused by the amorous antics of Grena's servants as Dana, Freya knew her sister had come to her expecting help with her problems rather than merely unbridled laughter. Since the thrall couldn't be sold, there appeared to be only one other option. A gracious woman, Freya was not reluctant to offer it, but she thoughtfully consulted her daughter first.

"Dana, can you imagine any of our servants chasing this poor man so shamelessly?"

Instantly comprehending the import of her mother's question, as well as her reason for asking it, Dana's smile vanished. Freya had been ill with a recurrent fever the past winter, and since she had yet to fully regain her strength and vitality, she relied heavily upon her eldest daughter to manage the duties she had formerly handled with ease. While Dana was happy to spare her mother every bit of work she could, she didn't want to see her take on the responsibility for an obnoxious slave just because Grena was unable to control her household properly. Pampered and spoiled, first by her parents and then by a generous older husband, her aunt solved all her problems simply by thrusting them onto others. Dana would not insult her aunt by saying so to her face, however, so she offered an objection she knew would be readily understood.

"Father hasn't kept thralls in years. Don't you think he would be very displeased if we began taking in Grena's?" she asked pointedly.

Freya's delicately arched brows rose slightly at the mention of angering Haakon since she knew the possibility was an extremely good one. Despite that threat, she could not turn her back on the sister she held so dear. "You know your father expects us to make our own decisions when he's away. Just let me worry about his reaction when he comes home in the fall. For the time being, we need only concern ourselves with Grena's dilemma."

Not pleased to have what she knew was sound advice cast aside so casually, Dana turned away to watch her younger brother and sister, who were playing nearby with Grena's twelve-year-old twins, Olaf and Hrolf. The children's happy laughter rang out over the blossom-filled meadow as they chased the lambs through the tall grass that extended clear down to the sandy shoreline.

The island of Fyn was not only beautiful, but it was also blessed with fertile soil and a mild climate. Though she had never traveled more than a few miles from her family's farm, Dana knew it had to occupy one of the most perfect spots on earth. She took a great deal of pride in her home, as did her mother. Yet, while her mother's health was still delicate, Dana didn't want a troublesome thrall any more than Grena did. Why couldn't her aunt see that she was thoughtlessly taking advantage of her sister's love? Was she simply as selfish as Jørn?

When she reluctantly forced her attention back to the conversation at hand, she was embarrassed to find Grena waiting impatiently for her response to a question she had not heard. "I'm sorry, did you ask me something?"

Grena dared not criticize her niece for being inattentive when she needed her help so urgently, but her tone was cool and her diction crisp as she repeated her request. "Will you come for Brendan tomorrow? When not pestered by overeager females, he has shown himself to be a good worker, and I'm sure he won't cause you any trouble. Then when Jørn comes home, he can decide what to do with the man. After all, Brendan is his property, so the problem is rightfully his."

Knowing that was merely another convenient excuse for Grena to avoid taking responsibility for what went on under her own roof, Dana had to force down a bitter response before giving a polite one. "If the matter is decided, then yes, I'll come for the man in the morning."

"Don't come alone," Berit warned immediately, her blue eyes bright with the imagined peril of so foolhardy an action.

"Don't be ridiculous," Grena scolded her daughter crossly. "No thrall is so stupid as to attack his mistress, and whatever Brendan is, he does not lack intelligence."

"But he is irresistible to women," Freya reminded her sister in a teasing jest. "That is reason enough not to send Dana alone."

Grena laughed. She knew her niece to be an extremely independent young woman who had stubbornly resisted the charms of the fine men who had courted her, so surely she would have no interest in a common slave. "Will you accept Jarald's proposal this fall, Dana? You must know there are many young women who would not only be honored but thrilled to wed so handsome and successful a man.''

Dana suddenly felt as uncomfortable as her aunt had when they had made light of her domestic problems. She knew mentioning Jarald had been Grena's way of putting her in her place, but while crude, the tactic had worked. She had used the slowness of her mother's recovery from her lengthy illness as an excuse to avoid Jarald's attentions all spring, and she knew he was nearly at the end of his patience with her. He was as forceful and determined a man as her father, and he was used to getting his own way. On several occasions he had made it plain that he intended to make her his wife, but she had felt only suffocated by his commanding presence and not in the least bit flattered or pleased that he had chosen her. That he would be away trading until autumn, as her father, older brother, Svien, and Jørn were, had provided a much needed respite from his overbearing personality, and she was far more delighted by his prolonged absence than she had ever been by his frequent visits.

Rising to her feet, Dana tactfully avoided replying to her aunt's question. ''The fall is months away. Right now I need to see what's keeping Moira with our refreshments.''

''Weren't Moira's parents also Celts from Erin?'' Berit asked with a sudden burst of the enthusiasm which marked all her actions. ''Maybe that's what Brendan wants, a woman of his own kind.''

That suggestion was so intriguing, Dana hesitated before turning away. Moira was so totally devoted to Freya that they had not once stopped to consider that the quiet girl might want a husband. Seeing the same realization dawning in her mother's eyes, Dana decided to wait until they were alone to discuss Moira's future. That Brendan was a slave was a problem, of course, but an ambitious man could earn enough to buy his freedom in a year's time, and Grena had said he was a good worker.

Hiding her smile, Dana lifted the skirt of her flowing silk chemise to the level of the loose-fitting sleeveless tunic worn over it and hurried toward the house with a spritely step. She would have to thank Berit later for proposing such a charming way to turn Brendan's stay with them into an advantageous one.

After her cousin had left them, Berit swiftly grew restless. She toyed with the end of her long blond braid as her mother and aunt began discussing their younger children. Uninterested in their conversation, she rose and leaned back against the stately oak. Hoping the true reason for her curiosity would not be suspected, she scanned the farm's well-kept grounds and numerous buildings, seeking a glimpse of her cousin Erik.

Of course Erik was not a full cousin, but it wasn't the peculiar manner in which they were related that intrigued her. When she and Dana had been children, they had often tagged along behind Erik, Svien and Jørn. Now her brother and Svien had gone trading with Haakon while Erik, who was two years Svien's senior, had been left behind. She knew how badly the slight must have hurt him, for it made it plain as never before that, while Svien was Haakon's heir, Erik was a bastard who would inherit nothing.

Born to a slave before Haakon's marriage to Freya, Erik had been raised with his father's legitimate children. His mother had died shortly after his birth, and Freya had cared for him as though he were her own. This was not an uncommon practice among wealthy men like Haakon, and some men even acknowledged their bastard offspring, giving them an equal inheritance. But not Haakon. For as long as Berit could remember, her uncle had regarded his first-born son with a cold aloofness that bordered on a cruel disdain. Since the man had ceased keeping slaves and had been faithful to his beloved wife, there were no other illegitimate children who shared the taint of Erik's birth.

Despite his lowly status, Berit believed Erik still loved his father, or perhaps it was Freya he loved, and his affection for her kept him on Haakon's farm. Whatever the reason, at twenty-two he seemed to be content to work as his father's falconer. That demanding task kept him busy, and he no longer had the time to entertain the younger children.

Berit hoped Erik would bring them their horses later, for she would consider their visit wasted if she did not even catch sight of the young man. Just the hope of seeing him had filled the day with a sense of excitement she had not expected. Since she had known Erik for as long as she could remember, she did not understand why his friendship would be more valuable now than it had been when she was younger.

Seeing Dana returning with Moira bearing a heavily laden tray, Berit resumed her place at her mother's side, but she was hungry for something she couldn't name, something far sweeter than the honey cakes Freya always served. Sighing wistfully, she made herself comfortable, grateful that her companions could never guess the improper nature of her thoughts.

Unlike Freya's children, Erik was dark rather than fair, but he had his father's violet eyes. He not only trained Haakon's regal birds of prey, but in his father's absence he also attended to the farm's needs. He had noted Grena's arrival, but since she had never displayed Freya's warmth toward him he had not gone out of his way to greet her. He was soon sorry for that show of pride when he realized too late that Berit was with her mother and the twins.

He had always had a special fondness for the pretty blonde. She had been a delightfully happy little girl who had made no secret of her affection for him despite her mother's attitude. He had been amazed when Berit had not grown up gradually as Dana had. During one of her visits to Haakon's farm she had been a playful child, and on the next her budding figure had made it plain that she was rapidly becoming a woman.

Even as that thought brought a smile to his lips, Erik was disgusted with himself for allowing his mind to wander so far afield from his duties. It did not pay to be inattentive around the falcons, for that could result in a serious injury. Nevertheless, he made certain that when Grena was ready to depart, he was there to help her mount her horse.

Unlike her painfully thin sister, Grena was a full-bodied woman who appreciated a boost to reach her saddle, but she gave Erik only a brief word of thanks before turning her mare toward the gate. That move discouraged any response he might have cared to make, but her daughter did not follow her example. Berit was as lithe as Dana, although not as tall, and while she could have mounted her mare as easily as her brothers leapt upon their ponies, she waited for Erik to reach her side.

"Have you been so busy all morning with your birds that you didn't have even one minute to spend with us?" she inquired with a saucy smile which she hoped would make him think she was only teasing, when her words clearly revealed how disappointed she had been not to have had his company.

A rakish grin spread across Erik's finely chiseled features as he recognized Berit's flirtatious greeting for what it was. "Expertly trained falcons are every bit as demanding as a beautiful woman, Berit. Did you really expect me to have the time to sit in the shade and chat with you?"

His point made in a charming fashion, Erik bent over and laced his fingers together to provide the lively young woman with a convenient step. Berit laid her hand on his shoulder as she placed her tiny foot in his hands. In an instant she was seated on her mare's back, but her eyes had never left his face.

"No," she replied sweetly, still attempting to keep the mood light, "but if you truly wished my company, you could come calling at my home."

Erik patted her thigh, then remembering that she was no longer a child he could pet with such open affection, he jerked his hand away as though he had been burned by the inviting warmth of the smooth flesh beneath her flowing garments.

"Don't tease me," he cautioned, his voice deepening as he forced himself to be stern. "You know your mother would set the dogs on me if I ever came anywhere near you or your farm."

His unexpected taunt brought a bright blush to Berit's cheeks because she knew it was undeniably true, and that pained her. She cared not at all what the circumstances of his birth had been, but since she could think of no way to encourage him to visit her without revealing more than she dared, she offered no such invitation. Deeply embarrassed by his rebuke, her lips formed a bewitching pout. She murmured no more than a hasty farewell, then tapped her heels against her mare's flanks and quickly followed her mother through the gate with the twins following close behind.

Erik had only briefly glimpsed Berit's expression, but he had witnessed a disturbing array of emotions: frustration, anger, and the same sense of hopeless rage he often felt, although he was uncertain of exactly what had upset her.

Dana had seen, if not overheard, the parting conversation between Berit and Erik, but his resulting frown was too deep for her to think he would wish to discuss it. He was such a good-natured young man, she hoped Berit had not said something thoughtless and insulted or hurt him.

"Erik," she called as she approached him. When she had his attention, she explained the errand that would take them to Grena's the next morning.

"What?" Erik's dark brows came together in a harsh line as his frown deepened into a hostile scowl. "Haakon refuses to own thralls. How could you and your mother have forgotten that?"

"Please don't misunderstand. We've not bought the man," Dana hastened to explain, but when Erik still failed to respond favorably, she revealed the true reason Grena had asked them to take the man temporarily.

In spite of the darkness of his mood, Erik began to chuckle. He was a handsome man, and a smile made him all the more so. "I find that a difficult tale to believe, but now I am too curious not to go with you."

"Good, because I don't dare risk going alone since the danger is so great I might also be tempted to seduce him," Dana responded with a sparkling laugh. She reached up on her tiptoes to kiss his cheek, for she loved Erik as dearly as she did her other two brothers. "Let's pretend we have no idea why he's being sent here. I imagine the poor fellow will be grateful for a chance to rest if Grena's women have pestered him so relentlessly."

"I'll not say a word," Erik promised with a sly grin. As he returned to his chores, he laughed time and again over the prospect of meeting a man so many women were eager to possess. But then he began to wonder if Berit had found the Celt slave attractive too.

Late that afternoon, Dana joined her mother when Freya awoke from her nap. She sat down on the edge of her bed, and taking advantage of the privacy afforded by the cozy sleeping chamber, she was eager to discuss their favorite maid. "Moira is twenty. Don't you think we ought to be giving some serious thought to finding her a husband?"

Freya covered a wide yawn with a pale hand before nodding in agreement. She found it difficult to shake her desire for more sleep. "Yes, I most certainly do. She is such a dear little person, I don't understand how I could have been so remiss."

Dana was delighted to find her mother's interest in Moira's future was as keen as her own. It would provide a welcome diversion, for she knew her mother spent far too much time dwelling on the aftereffects of her long illness. Freya had recently celebrated her thirty-seventh birthday, but Dana still thought her mother beautiful. Her golden-red hair was as glossy and curly as her own, and her flawless complexion was unlined. Only her eyes looked different. They had once sparkled with the fiery brilliance of sapphires, but now her gaze held only a compelling sadness that frequently moved Dana to tears.

She knew her mother had tricked her father into thinking her more fully recovered than she truly was so that he would leave for the summer. They were a devoted couple, and Dana could not bear to think how deep her father's pain would be should he return home to find the wife he adored more frail than when he had left her. The winters in Denmark were not harsh, but should Freya fall ill again, Dana knew she would not survive to see another spring.

Forcing such sad thoughts aside, she pressed on with their discussion. "Let's not say anything to Moira until we've all had the opportunity to get to know Brendan well. The fact that they share a common heritage won't mean anything if they don't like each other."

Making no effort to hide her smile, Freya offered a perceptive observation. "That's true. She might dislike him every bit as much as you dislike Jarald."

Dana pulled back slightly. "It's not that I dislike him," she denied unconvincingly. "It is just that, well, I find him a difficult man to like. He talks about nothing but himself, which I know most men do, but with him it always seems more of a fault than with others."

Freya reached out to pat her daughter's hand. "Jarald has many fine qualities which perhaps you are still too young to see, so I don't want you to dismiss him too hastily. You know you needn't marry a man you don't love. Your father and I would never ask that of you. We Danish women are fortunate in that we may divorce a poor husband quite easily, but that is no reason to enter into a marriage with haste. If nothing about Jarald pleases you by the coming spring, then I'll ask your father to tell him to pay his calls elsewhere. I know Grena would be very pleased to have him court Berit. Do you think she likes him?"

"Berit's only sixteen, Mother, and Jarald must be thirty at least, perhaps closer to thirty-five. He ought to court Grena rather than her daughter."

Freya found that suggestion, while sensible, quite amusing. "Jarald is not the type of man to marry a widow and take on the responsibility for another man's children. He is far too proud for that."

Dana nodded, hoping her mother would let the matter drop. Since she had been troubled ever since she had found her half brother in a dark mood that afternoon, she asked about him. "What's going to happen to Erik, Mother? Where will he be able to find a wife?"

Immediately taking that question to heart, Freya sighed unhappily. "We love Erik, so I'm certain other women will too. None of your friends would have him, of course, but that doesn't mean he couldn't successfully court a girl of modest means. A girl from a small farm would think him a wonderful husband, I'm sure."

"He is so busy here. When does he have time to travel the countryside calling on farmers in hopes they have marriageable daughters?"

"Yes, finding such a young woman will be the problem, but Erik is young yet and I doubt he has given any thought to taking a wife. Let's worry about Brendan and Moira first, and see if we can't make a match there." Freya paused as her ten-year-old daughter, Thora, peered in the door. "Come join us, baby."

A precocious child, Freya's youngest was a delightful imp who thoughtfully did not tax her mother with her own boundless energy. "I heard Moira say you're taking a thrall from Grena. Won't father be furious at us for that?"

"Now, how did Moira hear about Brendan?" Freya asked Dana in dismay.

"I've no idea," Dana assured her. "I've said nothing about the man to anyone but Erik, and surely he would not gossip with the servants."

"Oh, don't be silly," Thora exclaimed as she crawled over the end of her mother's bed. "Erik talks with Moira all the time. I think they're lovers."

"Thora! Shame on you," Freya scolded, but her laughter kept her from sounding cross.

Dana gave her little sister a hug. Each had inherited her mother's golden-red hair and her father's deep violet eyes, but their personalities were distinctly their own. "I wish you had joined us earlier, Thora. I think perhaps we have been worrying over matters that have already been decided."

"What matters?" Thora asked as she eluded her sister's grasp to reach her mother's lap.

Freya greeted her daughter with a welcoming embrace, but quickly released her. "I'll explain later, but it's Erik I need to speak with now. Will you please go and get him for me?"

Thora responded with a prompt refusal. "Not if you're going to be angry with him."

"No, baby, I'm not angry with him, merely curious. Now run find him for me so we'll have time to talk before supper."

When Thora returned a few minutes later leading Erik by the hand, Dana quickly rose from her mother's bed. "I'm sure you two would appreciate some privacy," she explained as she winked at her half brother and escorted her little sister from the room.

Having no idea why he had been summoned, Erik hoped Freya had not become so weak she needed to be carried out to the main hall where they took their meals. "What do you need?" he asked anxiously.

"You are like a son to me, Erik," Freya began, but then, delighted by her topic she smiled eagerly.

"Freya?" While Erik was happy to find that the woman who had been the only mother he had ever known wasn't as ill as he had feared, he didn't understand why she was so amused. "Have I done something wrong?"

"No, of course not," Freya assured him before taking a deep breath in an effort to begin again in a more serious manner. "I just wanted to ask you a question. You know Moira is very dear to me. Since her parents are dead, I feel it is my responsibility to find a husband for her. You are quite young to marry, but if you hope someday to make her your wife, please say so now."

Erik was so shocked by the suggestion he didn't know how to reply. Moira was small and dark, probably as petite as his mother had been. He thought her a sweet girl and they were friends, but she was very shy and he could not even imagine taking her for his wife. He wanted someone with the spirit of the Danish women he knew. While he thought his red-haired half sisters as beautiful as their mother, he longed for a pretty blonde like Berit. Even though he knew she was beyond his reach, he would not deny that he hoped to wed someone exactly like her.

"No!" he replied angrily, barely able to force the word over the painful surge of emotion that filled his throat. His well-defined features were contorted in a mask of hopeless confusion at the absurdity of her question. "I know Moira would have me, but can't I hope to do better?"

As deeply shocked by his response as he had been by her question, Freya tossed her blankets aside and rose to embrace him. "Forgive me, Erik, I never meant to make you think I thought less of you than I do of my own sons. I have money of my own. Whenever you are ready to take a bride, I'll see you have her price."

As the compassionate woman drew him into her arms, Erik buried his face in the softness of her curls, but he was far too proud a man to weep at the generosity of her offer. He had never had reason to consider the fact that he would be expected to give both his bride and her family sizable gifts which would be theirs to keep should their marriage fail, while he would have to return her dowry. It wasn't only money he lacked, however, but a heritage he could ask a woman to share and pass on to their children. Freya had forced him to confront that issue as he never had before, and he didn't like what he had found. Placing his hands around her tiny waist, he stepped back. He made a heroic attempt to smile, but failed.

"I don't want Moira, nor is there anyone else I can hope to marry now, but thank you for wanting to help me. You have always been so kind to me and I love you dearly for it. Save your money for yourself, or the others. I won't have any need of it."

Knowing she had upset him badly, Freya let Erik go without argument, but she was thoroughly depressed by their encounter and promptly returned to her bed. The only arguments she and Haakon had ever had were over the cool indifference with which he regarded his eldest son. That she could now foresee disagreements aplenty over Erik's future darkened her mood even more. Even if Haakon had never loved his firstborn, she would not deny that she did, and she wanted to see Erik have the happy life he deserved.

When Dana entered her room a short while later, Freya would not violate Erik's confidence by explaining what had transpired between them and greeted her coolly. "Thora is an imaginative child. There's nothing between Erik and Moira so please don't embarrass him by mentioning that we thought there might be. Just go and get Brendan in the morning, and if he proves to have an agreeable personality, we'll arrange for Moira and him to have the opportunity to get to know each other."

Dana could readily discern there was far more to her mother's conversation with Erik than the frail woman was reporting, for she had obviously been badly upset by it. Her face was flushed and the threat of tears were plainly in her eyes. Whatever could have happened? Dana wondered. "You know I love Erik too. If there's anything wrong—"

"That will be the end of it, Dana," Freya interrupted sharply. "We'll talk of him no more."

Since her mother seldom gave such explicit commands, Dana respected her wishes and left to summon Moira to help her dress. As she prepared for the evening meal, she couldn't stop wondering why her mother's mood had changed so suddenly. Erik would know the reason why, of course, but since she had been forbidden to ask him what had happened, she would not. Still, if the subject of marriage came up between them, she would most definitely encourage her half brother to talk.

CHAPTER II

The following morning both Dana and Erik were so lost in their own thoughts that they were halfway to Grena's farm before they realized they had failed to bring along an extra horse for Brendan to ride home on. While they laughed at that oversight, neither could believe the other hadn't had the presence of mind to remember such an obvious detail.

Chagrined, Erik dismissed the problem as one of no consequence. "Let's have him follow us home on foot. It's not too long a walk."

"No," Dana argued persuasively. "That would be a poor way to welcome him to our home."

In the teasing tone he often used when they were together, Erik dismissed that comment as utterly ridiculous. "He is a thrall, dear sister, not an important guest we must impress."

While that was true, having a thrall on their farm would be such a novelty Dana was not at all certain how they should treat the man. But she did not want to get off to a bad start. She knew some masters treated their slaves well, but many more did not. From what she had observed, her aunt was neither cruel nor kind, but merely indifferent to her hapless slaves' welfare.

Dana had never inquired about the reason for her father's preference for staffing his farm with freemen. Haakon was not the type of man whose authority could be questioned on any matter, let alone the manner in which he chose to run his home. He was an affectionate man, a loving father, but also one who insisted upon strict obedience to his commands. She had never defied any of his rules, and could not even imagine a situation which might lead her to do so. The very thought of crossing so determined a man made her shiver with dread. She was the very best of daughters, and had never caused the man she both admired and feared a moment's worry.

Until now, she thought with a painful stab of guilt, but since the decision to bring Brendan to their farm had not been hers, Dana decided her only choice was to make the best of the situation and have confidence that her mother would be able to soothe her father's temper as she always had. That happy thought brought a smile to her lips. Haakon might be able to strike terror into his children's hearts with an angry glance, but her mother had always loved the man far too much to fear him.

Turning her thoughts to the problem at hand, Dana knew it was only common sense that a slave who was well treated would be a more willing worker than one who was abused, and she made up her mind to treat Brendan as fairly as possible. She would not make him walk to her home on his first trip there.

"Grena has horses aplenty. We'll just have him borrow one."

Complaining of fatigue, Freya had not left her bed that morning, and Dana didn't know whether it had been Grena's visit that had taxed her mother's small store of strength or her conversation with Erik later that afternoon. The pensive redhead peeked at her half brother's expression and, finding him equally preoccupied, she made a sincere request rather than pester him with questions.

"No matter how difficult Brendan proves to be, we

needn't trouble my mother. Let's agree to handle him ourselves."

Devoted to Freya, Erik was happy to oblige. "I understand. She'll hear no complaints from my lips, and I'll see the servants don't bother her either."

"Thank you. I don't know what I'd do without you, Erik. There is so much to be done each day, and although I try my best to see everything runs as smoothly as it always has for Mother, I fear I'm not nearly as good at it as she is."

Surprised by the confession, since Dana had a confidence well beyond her seventeen years, Erik reached over to give her shoulder an affectionate pat. "You're doing beautifully. Freya has merely had more practice at running the farm than you, that's all."

While Dana was certain the compliment was undeserved, she was grateful for it as Erik's approval meant a great deal to her. But it was the agonizing slowness of her mother's recovery rather than maintaining the efficient routine of the farm that weighed most heavily on her mind. Her fourteen-year-old brother, Soren, provided no help at all, for he did little other than complain endlessly that he was old enough to have gone trading with his father, while Thora's incessant curiosity and seemingly limitless energy often landed her in trouble. Summers were never completely free of care with her father and older brother gone, but as Dana reviewed her many problems, she hoped with all her heart the time would pass quickly this year.

Seated at the gate, Brendan grabbed up the small bundle containing his meager possessions and leapt to his feet when he saw two riders approaching. When they came close enough for him to make them out clearly, he found it difficult not to gape like a witless fool, for he had never dreamed such a striking pair would come for him.

It was the young woman's bright halo that captured his attention first, but as she drew near he discovered that heavenly glow was an illusion created by the rays of the morning sun being reflected off her golden-red curls. Never had he seen a woman with such a glorious shade of hair, for it rivaled even the vibrant colors of a sunset for beauty.

Kissed by the sun with each turn of her head, the glossy tresses fell in a cascade of ringlets that reached clear past her waist.

As his glance strayed to her face, Brendan was even more awed to discover her remarkable hair merely complemented delicate features of exquisite perfection. Her flawless skin was the pale golden shade of rich cream and her lashes were so long and thick that they veiled the color of her eyes, but he imagined they must be as clear a blue as the summer sky.

The astonishingly lovely young woman was dressed in a pale pink chemise topped with a loose tunic of deep rose whose hem was decorated with a wide band of gold braid. Her garments were easily the finest he had ever seen. The chemise was plainly silk and the tunic of whisper-light wool, and although he dared not reach out to touch it, he knew the beautifully woven fabric would have the softness of a sparrow's breast.

The twin brooches that secured the tunic to the front of her chemise were gold, and the keys suspended from the right one showed her to be the mistress of her household. Brendan thought her very young for that much responsibility, but she carried herself with an unmistakable pride that convinced him she was fully capable of handling it.

He knew she must possess wealth beyond measure if she chose to ride in such costly attire. As if her appearance were not dazzling enough, she seemed to have selected her mount to complement her outfit, for she rode astride a dapple gray mare whose flowing white mane and tail had been decorated with pink satin bows trailing long streamers. She presented a vision of such incomparable beauty it was all Brendan could do to wrench his gaze away and turn toward her companion.

Her escort appeared to be in his midtwenties, as Brendan was. While his kirtle and breeches were of dove-gray wool rather than brightly colored like the young woman's regal attire, his garments were as handsomely tailored as those Brendan had once owned. The man was quite handsome, but dark for a Dane. That puzzled the slave, as did the fact that his features, while definitely masculine, in some faint way resembled the woman's, leading him to think they were kin despite the sharp contrast of their coloring.

Struck speechless by the magnificence of the pair, Brendan swallowed hard in an attempt to overcome his dismay. With effort he adopted his usual fierce mask of disdain and straightened his shoulders proudly. He didn't care how attractive or rich these two were. They were still Danes, and that was reason enough to despise them. He prepared himself to hate them most thoroughly, as he had all the others who had claimed to own him.

"I am ready to go," he announced clearly.

While he had been observing her with a rapt glance, Dana had been every bit as impressed by Brendan's appearance as he was by hers, but for completely different reasons. She knew the Celts had once been a proud race, and from the looks of this man she did not think those days were long past. She was also surprised to find him fair-haired and blue-eyed, as were most of her countrymen. While his hair was overlong, and his cheeks and chin darkened with several days' growth of beard, she thought that with more care to his appearance he might prove remarkably handsome.

He stood just over six feet tall with a lean yet muscular build that his snug-fitting kirtle and breeches displayed in unseemly detail. It was no wonder Grena's women thought him attractive, she mused silently, for his own clothing left so little to her imagination he might just as well have been standing before her nude.

When he raked his fingers through his hair in a futile attempt to keep it off his forehead, she realized he probably did not own a comb and instantly forgave him for looking so unkempt. That her aunt could have allowed him to remain in the same wretched attire in which Jørn must have bought him sparked her anger. Grena did not lack for anything, so it was inexcusable that she had not treated this man far more kindly than she obviously had.

Pointing to his cloth-wrapped package, Dana inquired sympathetically, "Is that all you have to bring?"

Brendan shrugged, not knowing how she expected him to reply. He considered himself fortunate to have an extra set of clothing. Did this elegant creature expect him to have a wagonload of belongings?

Seeing his confusion, Dana feared he did not speak her tongue nearly as well as his brief greeting had made it seem. "Whenever you do not understand me, you must say so," she explained with exaggerated care. "It will save us both many a problem."

While Dana's advice was well-intended, Brendan reacted as though it had been a gross insult. "I am not stupid," he replied in a voice more suited to yelling across a noisy barnyard than to conversing with a fine lady. "You needn't treat me as though I were an ignorant fool."

Grena had referred to him as surly, and Dana now understood why. How the man had twisted her question into grounds for a heated argument she didn't know, but she would not respond in kind. Rather than tell him she expected far better of him, she decided to wait until they had returned home, where she could also make his duties clear.

Continuing as though he had not spoken rudely, Dana's voice was soft with an inviting, musical lilt. "Saddle a horse while I tell Grena we are here. Do not keep us waiting, for we are needed at home." Urging her mare past him, she dismissed the disheveled slave with a slight nod.

Rather than run to follow her orders, Brendan was so intrigued he remained at the gate to watch Dana approach her aunt's home. She rode with a graceful ease he knew came from an innate skill rather than merely a desire to impress others, and that angered him all the more. He was disgusted with himself for not giving the good impression he had intended, but in his present wretched state he doubted it would have been possible with such a well-bred young lady. Grena had not told him why he was being sent away, merely that he was leaving that morning. In the past his situation had always gone from bad to worse, but now he wondered if his luck had finally changed, for surely the serene red-haired beauty would have a fine farm and many slaves. He would probably have little work to do.

When Brendan stood transfixed, studying Dana with an insolent gaze of which he did not approve, Erik quickly lost his temper. "Can you ride?" he asked caustically.

"Of course I can ride!" Brendan exclaimed proudly as he wheeled around to face the dark-haired stranger.

"Do not make the mistake of believing Dana's sweetness covers a weakness of character or a lack of resolve. When she tells you to do something, do it immediately, not after you have daydreamed half the morning away. Now go get a horse and be quick about it," Erik commanded firmly.

Brendan's eyes narrowed slightly, for he was sorely tempted to yank the arrogant man from his horse to demonstrate just how little he liked taking orders. Since that was a show of pride he knew from bitter experience he could ill afford, he turned away and sprinted toward the stables, but he mouthed a silent string of obscenities all the way.

When Dana entered her home, Berit greeted her warmly, but as her cousin began to chat with her mother, the enterprising blonde slipped by them and hurried outside. In spite of her disappointment with their conversation the previous day, she was hoping that Erik had been the one to accompany her cousin. Seeing that he was, she waved excitedly. He returned the eager gesture by raising his hand in a lazy salute, and again disappointed her by remaining at the gate.

As she often did, Berit had dressed in blue. She had chosen a pale shade for her chemise, with a deep azure tunic whose vibrant color made the clear blue of her eyes dance with a bright sparkle. Knowing her garments were especially becoming gave her the courage to approach their handsome visitor.

"Good day," she called out as she hastened across the distance which separated them, hoping that by the time she reached Erik's side she would have thought of some pressing subject for them to discuss.

Sorry that she had not reacted to the lack of enthusiasm in his greeting and returned to her house, Erik slid down off his horse, then took the precaution of giving the sleek black gelding a quarter turn so their conversation could not be observed by curious eyes. "Good day," he responded, and taking her hand, he lead her around behind his mount.

Thrilled to find that he thought such discretion necessary, Berit hoped they might share a closeness which would merit it. "You see, you had nothing to fear. We've not set the dogs on you." That he still held her hand pleased her enormously, but when she gave his fingers an affectionate squeeze, he broke the clasp instantly.

"That's only because your mother doesn't know that I'm here." Erik had meant to keep his mood as lighthearted as hers, but when he tried to think of another teasing comment to make, his mind went completely blank. Berit was looking up at him with so adoring a gaze he was badly embarrassed. She looked as pretty and fresh as the summer morning, but he would not pay her compliments when he dared not encourage the affection that would be impossible for them to express.

When Erik said nothing more, but continued to regard her with a perplexed stare, the silence between them swiftly grew to an uncomfortable length. Desperate to continue their conversation, Berit said the first thing that came into her mind. "Where's Brendan? Wasn't he waiting out here for you?" Alarmed that the slave might have run off, she turned to look across the meadow that bordered the path.

Assuming her curiosity meant that she admired the man, Erik had difficulty speaking. "He's just a thrall, Berit, and not worthy of your notice," he instructed harshly, inflicting the same pain on her she had unknowingly caused him.

Shocked by the undeserved rebuke, the lithe blonde began to back away. "I'll notice whomever I please," she informed him with a careless toss of her long braid.

Despite being ill-groomed and poorly clothed, Erik had suspected Brendan would be a handsome man were his situation not so bleak. The slave possessed a fine physique, but Erik knew his own build was impressive too. He caught himself then, for he had no right to be jealous where Berit was concerned. Nor would he compare himself to a thrall. "Go back to your house," he ordered gruffly.

Berit could not imagine what had come over the young man. She knew he had once considered her company most amusing.

"Erik?" Berit whispered in a breathless sigh. When he stubbornly continued to ignore her, she turned her back on him and hurried toward her house, but just as she reached the door Danǎ and her mother came through it.

Dana had tarried only long enough to tell Grena her sister wasn't feeling well, and now she was anxious to be on her way. She didn't notice Berit's pained expression as she brushed her cheek with a farewell kiss.

"I should have put chains on Brendan," Grena remarked absently. "Do you want me to do it now?"

"Chains?" That offer was one Dana found so repugnant she was actually sickened by it. "No, with Erik's help I'm sure I'll have no trouble with him." Before her aunt could question her judgment, she hurriedly mounted her mare and rejoined Erik, who seemed not to have moved in the time she had been gone.

"What's keeping the man?" she asked, but before Erik could offer an opinion, Brendan rode out of the stable astride Jørn's bay stallion, whom he had named for the god Odin's marvelous eight-legged horse, Sleipner.

That was so audacious a choice, Erik could not help but laugh. "You told him to saddle a horse, but you didn't forbid him to take Jørn's."

"I didn't realize I should have to," Dana responded in amazement. She was used to giving orders to servants who were eager to do her bidding. Brendan had just made it obnoxiously plain that she could not expect such respectful obedience from him. She had not wanted to take the responsibility for him initially, and now she resented having to do so all the more. She glanced back toward her aunt, wondering for an instant if chains weren't exactly what Brendan needed to remind him of his place, but she couldn't bring herself to ask for them.

"Careful," Erik warned under his breath. "This may not be the best place to reprimand him."

Agreeing that she would be wise not to create any sort of a scene under Grena's watchful gaze, since she would never hear the end of it, Dana did not speak as Brendan reached them. Her expression assumed a bored nonchalance, but inside she was seething.

Expecting to have his action questioned, Brendan had a ready excuse even though he was not asked for one. "The stallion needs the exercise, and I am the only one here who can handle him.''

Delaying the tongue-lashing the defiant slave deserved, Dana waved good-bye to Berit and Grena and turned her mare toward the path home.

Brendan followed at what he considered a respectful distance, but he longed to issue a challenge for a race. Equally eager to run, Sleipner tossed his head, sending his flowing ebony mane flying, but he kept the lively animal's speed in check. He knew that Grena called at her sister's farm often, so he knew she could lead Sleipner home on her next visit, but he hoped there might be an opportunity to race the fine animal before then.

As their journey progressed, Brendan's thoughts soon strayed from the thrill of racing to the woman traveling ahead of him. Each time she turned to speak to her companion, shimmering waves of light radiated down the length of her curls, capturing his interest anew. Her profile was as splendid as a full view of her face, and his lurid imagination painted vivid pictures of the slender body her flowing garments concealed.

He knew her breasts would be full and tipped with pert nipples of the palest pink. Her waist would be impossibly tiny, and the flesh of her flat stomach satin smooth. Her legs would surely be slim perfection, and he longed to feel her wrap them tightly around his hips. He was startled by thoughts that grew far too erotic to continue in broad daylight, and with a great force of will he focused his curiosity on the dark-haired man riding at Dana's side.

He did not behave as though he were her husband, but that some enormously wealthy Dane undoubtedly did have that honor nagged at Brendan with a haunting sense of frustration he couldn't subdue. Dana was attractive, but many of her accursed kind were. He knew that the devil himself could assume pleasing forms when he chose. He would have to dismiss her beauty as only another of the endless torments he had been made to endure since he had been taken captive.

While Grena's farm had obviously been prosperous, Brendan's first glimpse of Dana's home impressed him far more. The main house, while one story, was long and wide, and he thought in addition to the kitchen and large hall all Danish homes contained, this one must have several other rooms as well. Clustered nearby were quarters for servants, a bathhouse, privies, and the storehouses whose keys Dana wore. Then came buildings housing a smith's forge, barns to store hay for the winter, a byre to shelter cattle, a stable, and pens for sheep.

In front of the farm grew a home field which he was sure had been heavily fertilized to insure the production of the finest hay. It was walled with turf to keep out animals, but he could see the grass-filled meadows where their herds grazed just beyond. In the other direction were plowed fields to furnish crops of barley, oats, and wheat. Every building was in excellent repair, and what servants he saw were industriously attending to their chores. Dana might be young, but his respect for her grew as he considered how well she obviously managed the running of her home.

When they reached the stable, Dana dismounted quickly, then waited for Brendan to leave Sleipner's back. She then handed him her mare's reins. "You'll see to the horses first. They need to be cooled down, then watered, groomed, and fed."

As Erik stepped up to her side, she relaxed slightly, hoping Brendan would be smart enough to behave well, since she had a man with the strength necessary to enforce her orders clearly ready to back them up. As they had made their way home, she had asked her half brother to find the poorly clad slave some clothes that fit and a place to sleep, but she thought he might first have a more pressing need.

"Are you hungry?" she asked.

"No more than usual," Brendan replied flippantly.

Dana stared at him, and annoyed by the ambiguity of his response, she made no further attempt to hold her temper in check. "I do not want you here any more than you wish to be here," she informed him coldly. "Until Jørn comes home you will follow my instructions and make yourself useful or I will lock you up until you beg me to allow you to work. When I ask you a question, I expect a straight answer. Since you've given me no idea whether or not you're hungry, I will assume that you aren't and I won't bother to offer the food that I would have provided.''

As she spoke, Dana watched Brendan's gaze grow dark and threatening, but she was too disgusted by the hostility of his attitude to be in the least bit intimidated by him. ''If you're not clean-shaven in time for the evening meal, and haven't cut your hair and dressed in the clothes I've asked Erik to provide, then you won't eat at that time either.

''I expect you to give Erik the same respect you are going to begin giving me this instant or he will be free to punish you in any manner he sees fit. If you have any questions, then ask them now, as I've no more time to waste on you today.''

Brendan knew Erik had warned him, and he was sorry now that he hadn't been wise enough to realize how hot-tempered Dana was. When he failed to respond, she took a step closer, as though daring him to speak. He was so shocked to find her eyes were not the blue he had expected but an exotic violet in hue, he could not even recall what he had been asked.

Erik had seen the same look of rapt fascination on the faces of many men. Brendan was completely bewitched by his half sister's beauty. Since he had no desire to stand there for as long as it might take for the slave to gather his wits, he took charge of the situation. ''I will take care of Brendan, and if he has any questions he can ask them of me.''

Dana nodded, grateful as always for her half brother's willing assistance. She thanked him. Then, eager to see if her mother was feeling better, she dismissed Brendan from her mind. She started toward the house, but she had not taken more than two steps when she heard the slave mutter something in a most uncomplimentary tone and she wheeled around to face him.

''Are you not man enough to curse me to my face?'' she asked accusingly.

His bitter insult had simply slipped out, and while it had been in his own tongue rather than hers, Brendan couldn't deny that she had understood its meaning. He had called her the foulest of names, which he definitely thought all Danes deserved, and now he fully expected her to make him pay for it. When Erik tapped him on the shoulder, he turned without thinking and walked right into a punch to the jaw so fierce he was stunned, and staggered backward.

Not about to let Sleipner and the other two horses get into the middle of the fray, Dana jerked their reins from Brendan's hands and pulled the animals out of Erik's way. While clearly he had caught the Celt by surprise, she didn't object to the way he was handling the man. In her view Brendan had asked for the beating he was taking when he dared to call her what had to have been a hateful insult. Clearly the slave was not only arrogant, but too stupid to keep his thoughts to himself as well.

While those same two faults registered instantly in Brendan's mind as Erik struck him again, he refused to accept any abuse without fighting back. He blocked the next punch thrown at him, then drove his fist into Erik's solar plexus. In the next instant they were scuffling in the dirt while Dana struggled to keep the three high-spirited horses under control.

Drawn outside by the commotion, servants came running from all directions, and the blacksmith grabbed the reins from Dana and pulled the horses away. She was tempted to leave then herself, but knew she had to remain to see that Brendan was sufficiently punished. He and Erik were nearly the same size, but the hostile slave fought with a vicious zeal that shocked her and she feared he might soon gain the advantage. Not about to allow that to happen, she grabbed the back of his kirtle to pull him away from her half brother, but the worn fabric was so thin the garment ripped all the way down the back.

An astonished gasp went up from the surrounding crowd as the torn kirtle revealed a savage pattern of long scars crisscrossing the slave's back. Distracted by that sound, Brendan glanced over his shoulder to find Dana staring down at him with a look of such horrified disbelief he knew he was in even worse trouble than he had been when the fight had begun. Jarred by this realization, he released Erik with a rude shove and scrambled to his feet. He tried then to pull his kirtle back into place, but discovered it was ruined and yanked it off instead. His chest heaved as he tried to catch his breath, but the gaze he directed at Dana was as defiant as ever.

Erik also got to his feet and began brushing off his clothes. While in his view the fight had been a draw, he knew Brendan might have gotten the better of him had it continued. He didn't understand his sister's anguished expression until he noticed the slave's badly scarred back. That Brendan had once had so brutal a master provided a clear explanation for his belligerent attitude, and it was thus difficult for Erik to remain angry with him.

"Go on back to work," he directed the bystanders with a ready smile. "Our dispute is settled." With a few more words of encouragement, the crowd of curious servants dispersed and Erik, Dana, and Brendan were again alone.

Dana knew she would have to take some action immediately to discipline the troublesome slave, but having no experience with owning human beings, she was at a loss for just what to do. She knew she dared not let him see her confusion, however.

"I'm sure you deserved the beating that left you so badly scarred, and if you don't apologize immediately for insulting me, I will take great delight in giving you an even worse whipping myself."

Caught by surprise, Erik's eyes widened in amazement, for he could not imagine Dana being so cruel. The defiant tilt of her chin convinced him she was completely serious in her threat, though. "Well, go on, apologize," he urged the man he had just fought, not nearly so eager to see Brendan's back again cut to shreds as she appeared to be.

Brendan wadded his torn kirtle into a tight ball as he tried to decide what to say. Since he knew it had been a mistake to speak his opinion of Dana out loud, he had no choice but to sacrifice his pride and apologize, but he thought a beating might prove less painful. "I, that is, I—"

"Yes?" Dana folded her arms across her chest and tapped her foot impatiently. Seeming to have a will of its own, her glance strayed from Brendan's intense frown to the pulse beating wildly in his throat and then swept slowly over the powerful contours of his upper body. His broad chest was covered with a thick mat of hair a shade darker than the untamed curls she'd ordered trimmed. That handsome accent to his muscular build narrowed to a thin line as it crossed the flatness of his belly. Her gaze followed that enticing trail as it disappeared at his waistband, but when her inquisitive stare reached the prominent bulge outlined so impressively by the tightness of his breeches, she shook her head slightly to clear her mind. She didn't understand why it was so difficult for her to get along with him.

She dropped her hands to her sides. "I will not wait all day for an apology," she prompted coolly. "Erik, bring me the whip we use on the bull."

Erik took a step away, but only to hide his smile. Haakon would have skinned any man alive who turned a whip on one of his animals. He understood immediately that Dana's threat was not one she meant to carry out, but he appeared to go along with it. He didn't think they even owned a whip, but knowing if they did it would be in the stable, he headed toward the wide double doors.

"Wait!" Brendan called to Erik. He swallowed nervously, then forced himself to speak in a calmer tone. "I am sorry," he began hesitantly, trying to sound sincere even though he wasn't. "I spoke without thinking. I did not mean to offend you." He paused then, hoping Dana would accept the effort at an apology, but when she appeared by her silence to want still more, he lost his temper again. "Do you want me on my knees?"

"Of course not, but it is remarkable you are still alive when you have not one bit of sense," Dana replied with a thoughtful frown. Truly, she didn't understand why a slave possessed of such enormous pride hadn't provoked a beating that would have left him dead long ago.

While she didn't believe for a second that he was really sorry he had insulted her, she saw no point in calling him a liar to his face. "You are much too thin," she criticized instead. "Erik, I want you to get him some food, and force him to eat it if you must, but I won't have him looking as though he's being starved while he's here." Hoping Brendan would now refrain from making remarks about her behind her back, she turned toward the house and was greatly pleased when she reached the door without hearing him utter a single word.

CHAPTER III

When Brendan had seen to the horses, Erik took him to the neatly kept dwelling he called home and heated the porridge that had been left over from breakfast. When the slave ate it all eagerly, he offered several slices of bread and a thick wedge of cheese, then tried unsuccessfully to hide his dismay as Brendan gobbled them down with the same ravenous appetite.

"Didn't Grena feed you?" Erik asked as he debated with himself the wisdom of offering still more.

Brendan washed down the last bite of cheese with a long swallow of ale before he replied, "I was fed."

"Obviously not recently." Erik shook his head, as perplexed by the slave as his half sister had been. As he searched his mind about what to do with him, he had a sudden inspiration and decided to teach the man to behave more politely with the same techniques he used to train his falcons. He would be kind but firm. He then realized Dana had been very clever to threaten to withhold Brendan's food if he did not improve his appearance by nightfall.

Taking a seat beside him on one of the long benches which provided seating in his home, Erik cleared his throat and began to speak in an effort to make Brendan's situation clear. "While a farm this size might be expected to have as many as thirty thralls, Haakon prefers to hire freemen and owns none. You'll be here only until he returns home, but you'll be treated well as long as you give us your best."

Brendan looked away, not caring to hear a lecture on the

joys of hard work, but when Erik paused he glanced toward him. "Haakon is Dana's husband?"

When Erik did no more than regard him with an amused stare, Brendan finally noticed his eyes were the same unusual violet color as the redhead's. That made him all the more curious. "What is Dana to you?"

Certain their conversation was going to be more lengthy than he had anticipated if Brendan persisted in asking such irrelevant questions, Erik leaned back against the wall and crossed his arms over his chest. He had no desire to make a friend of the slave, so he made his answers brief. "Haakon is Dana's father and mine as well. While my mother is long dead, Dana's is alive, but she hasn't been well. Freya is a dear woman, and neither of us will allow you to disrupt her convalescence. Should I even suspect that might happen, I will lock you up in one of the storehouses until Jørn returns. Now I'll loan you clothes, and a razor. Do you want me to cut your hair, or will you do it yourself?"

Insulted by the implied criticism of his appearance, Brendan rose to his feet and picked up the change of clothes he had brought with him. "I have other clothes," he pointed out sullenly.

Erik regarded the slave's hostile stance with a cool stare. "You are a fool to be so stubborn when I'm trying to help you. If what you brought fits no better than what you are wearing, we'll use the garments for rags."

Brendan straightened his shoulders proudly. He knew his clothes fit poorly and were far from new, but they were all he had. "If you give me clothes now, what happens when Jørn comes home? Will I have to give them back?"

"As on all farms, the women here weave and fashion the fabric into clothing. Your garments will be tailored for you, and we won't expect you to return them, as we'd not send you back to Jørn naked. For the time being I will lend you some clothes of mine, but you needn't return them either."

Brendan continued to grip his small parcel possessively. "I want to keep my things too."

"Fine." Thinking that their discussion was as successful as it was likely to be with Brendan in so obstinate a mood, Erik rose to his feet and went to the end of the house's single room to open the chest where his garments were stored. He sorted through his kirtles until he found one that was a trifle large. Then he searched for a pair of breeches he would not miss. Since he could not hope Brendan owned wearable undergarments, he provided those too.

"Where did you sleep at Grena's?" he called over his shoulder.

"In the stable. I kept the straw clean."

"I'm sure you did." Erik broke into a wide grin as he remembered Dana's story about the slave's remarkable success with women. He preferred to keep a far closer eye on the man than Grena had, and he would not allow him to set up residence in the stable, where any women who cared to visit him could come and go as they pleased. When he turned around to face him again, his mind was made up.

"I have ample room for you here. At breakfast I can tell you what I expect of you each day. I take the evening meal in the main house, but I'll have food sent over for you to eat here. Our servants are a good lot, but I don't want you to mix with them. They all have their own duties and you'll have yours. Is that clear?"

Before he replied, Brendan surveyed the neatly kept interior of Erik's house. He knew the benches which lined both walls were also used for sleeping, and he couldn't deny that he would be more comfortable there than in a drafty stable. He was not used to being treated kindly, however, and he didn't understand why Erik was being so generous. Surely it was some sort of devious trick.

"Do you snore?" he asked suspiciously.

"No," Erik insisted, startled that Brendan seemed to consider him a poor companion when he was willing to share his quarters with a slave. "You have a strange way of looking at things, but I think in time you'll learn not to ask such insulting questions. Now, do you want me to cut your hair or not?"

"Have you no barber here?"

"Yes, we do, but he also shears the sheep. Do you want him to cut your hair or will you take your chances with me?"

Erik's hair brushed his collar. It was dark and thick,

without the slightest hint of curl. Brendan's hair was also thick, but curly, and he did not think it was too long. "Why must I cut my hair?"

"Because Dana said you must to eat tonight. Of course, if you'll not be hungry by then, or in the morning either, then let it go."

Since that was no choice at all, Brendan reluctantly gave in. "All right, you cut it, but not any shorter than yours."

"Come outside," Erik directed, and grabbing a comb and pair of scissors, he followed Brendan out the door. There was a stool at the side of the house, and once the slave was seated, Erik began to comb and snip with a confident hand.

Brendan watched the mounting pile of severed curls lying on the grass and feared he might soon be bald. "You're cutting off too much!" he protested angrily.

"Hush, I've just begun."

Brooding over this latest misfortune, Brendan didn't hear Thora sneaking up on them until she greeted Erik. He jerked his head up and looked around to find a beautiful little girl who resembled Dana so closely he knew they had to be sisters.

"Is Erik any good at this?" he asked, for he had found children were often more sympathetic to his plight than adults, and far more honest.

Thora pursed her lips thoughtfully as she walked around the two men. After studying Brendan's appearance quite thoroughly, she offered her opinion. "I think not."

Certain she was right, Brendan leapt to his feet. "Isn't that enough?"

"Sit down," Erik commanded firmly. "And you'll keep your opinions to yourself, Thora dear."

When Brendan reluctantly resumed his seat, Thora shook her head sadly. "You must cut his hair with the wave, not against it. I can show you how."

Erik had thought he was doing a splendid job until Thora had pointed out why he wasn't. Since he realized instantly that she was right, he readily relinquished the task. "All right, you do it." Handing the slender child the comb and scissors, he stepped back out of her way.

Brendan was sorry he had spoken up, for he doubted the

little girl knew what she was doing either. As she stepped around to trim the hair over his ears, he noted the intense concentration of her expression and did not complain again, but he knew it would probably take months for his hair to grow out sufficiently for him to look normal again.

"How old are you, Thora?" he asked with an enticing sweetness, as eager to distract himself from the ordeal he was undergoing as he was to hear her answer.

"I'm ten, Soren's fourteen, Dana's seventeen, and Svien's twenty. Now be still."

Amused rather than silenced, Brendan continued his quest to learn more about the family on whose farm he now resided. "What about Erik here, don't you know how old he is?"

"He's twenty-two," Thora added as an afterthought.

That surprised Brendan, for the dark-haired young man's manner was so serious he had judged him to be several years older than that. "What about Dana's husband, how old is he?"

"She has no husband yet, but she soon will," the talkative child confided.

"How soon?" Brendan asked, her answer suddenly more important to him than he cared to admit.

"I'm not supposed to gossip," Thora replied with an impish toss of her long red curls.

Before Brendan could think of another way to phrase the same question, Thora announced she was finished and handed the comb and scissors back to Erik.

"Well, how does it look?" Brendan asked as he got to his feet and brushed off his bare shoulders.

Thora answered before Erik could, as always speaking with the voice of authority despite her tender years. "If you would only shave and put on a kirtle to hide those ugly scars you might even be called handsome."

When Brendan laughed at her comment, Erik got his first glimpse of the man's smile. His grin was wide, showing off even teeth of a dazzling white. It was no wonder women sought his company, but Brendan's questions had made it plain he wasn't interested in meeting any servants here. Since he knew Dana did not even like the man, Erik wasn't worried, and he bent down to give Thora a loving hug before sending her on her way.

As Dana drew her mother's door closed, she paused to rest her forehead against the intricately carved wood. She tried to tell herself she hadn't really lied to her, but she knew she had stretched the truth shamelessly. She had succeeded in giving Freya the impression that while Brendan's manners were a bit coarse, he was going to do whatever work they assigned him quite willingly. She had then misled the woman even further by encouraging her to continue to think him a fine prospect for Moira.

Thoroughly embarrassed by such inexcusable behavior, Dana hoped she could keep her mother from ever discovering what an obnoxious person Brendan truly was. With that thought in mind, she hurried into the main hall, where half a dozen women sat weaving fine woolen cloth at looms propped against the walls.

"I beg of you," she greeted them in a conspiratorial whisper, "not a word of the fight Erik had with the thrall is to reach my mother's ears. He won't be with us long, and I don't want my mother's rest disturbed by tales of his antics."

"Yes, mistress," the women murmured softly, but after they paused to exchange knowing smiles, none seemed eager to return to her weaving.

"What's the man's name?" asked the youngest.

"It's Brendan, but I trust you will have no reason to speak with him," Dana cautioned firmly. "I plan to see that he is kept busy working, and hope that the time passes swiftly until he's gone."

That she had not come near to satisfying the weavers' curiosity didn't occur to Dana, and she hurried on through the hall to the kitchen at the far end of the house. Because someone would have to be responsible for taking Brendan his meals, Moira seemed the perfect choice, but when Dana explained this, the shy girl shrank back in fear.

"I caught only a glimpse of him as he struggled in the dirt with Erik, but I would rather you sent one of the others, a man perhaps, than me."

Dana first cautioned the girl never to mention the fight to her mother, and then resting her fingertips on Moira's narrow shoulders, she attempted to win her cooperation. "Brendan is a Celt. He is from Erin, as your parents were. Naturally he is confused about being sent here, but I am certain in a few days he'll be far more agreeable. You might even find that you like him."

"I do not think so, mistress."

Since she spent most of her own time avoiding men's attentions rather than cultivating them, Dana did not try and convince Moira she would enjoy Brendan's company. Instead, she merely smiled. "You needn't be afraid of the man, and to prove that, I'll go with you tonight. I'll need to see if Brendan followed the directions I gave him before he has his supper anyway."

Mollified for the time being, Moira smiled shyly. "As you wish, mistress."

Soren's duties were to recover stray cattle and sheep and to see all the farm's fences and walls remained in good repair. When he returned his horse to the stable that afternoon, he saw Sleipner in the last stall, and having always wanted to ride his cousin's stallion, he seized the opportunity without any thought of the consequences. That the horse was far too high-spirited for a fourteen-year-old boy to handle did not occur to him. He saddled the bay quickly, and rode out of the stable at a full gallop, eager to see how fast the elegant animal would go.

Brendan had just finished shaving when he and Erik heard Soren ride by the house. The thunderous pounding of Sleipner's hooves echoed inside the small dwelling with an ominous rhythm that alarmed them both. When Erik rushed outside to see who was being so foolish, Brendan followed right behind him.

When the slave saw Jørn's horse disappearing from sight, he thought immediately that the magnificent mount had been stolen and feared he would be blamed for bringing him there where it could happen. "That was Jørn's horse!" he exclaimed excitedly. "Who could have taken him?"

Erik had seen a glimpse of blond curls and had recognized the rider instantly. "It's Soren, Dana's younger brother. I'll have to go after him."

Brendan ran along beside him as Erik entered the stable. "That black gelding you rode this morning is no match for Sleipner. Haven't you another horse with more speed?"

Erik had already grabbed his gelding's bridle, but he recognized the truth of Brendan's words. Haakon's stallion was grazing in the adjacent pasture, but he had never ridden him. "Haakon owns a fleet stallion, but he never allows anyone else to ride him."

"What if his son is thrown and badly hurt, or if Sleipner is injured and must be destroyed?" Brendan forced him to consider. "Wouldn't he call you a fool for not borrowing his horse to prevent it?"

Erik could not imagine his father's wrath being any more violent upon hearing of those tragedies than if he learned his stallion had been ridden. That was expressly forbidden, and he dared not disregard his father's wishes for any reason. "I'll ride my own mount," he announced without the slightest doubt that that was the only choice he had.

Brendan could not understand Erik's reluctance to ride the farm's swiftest horse. He cared not at all what happened to Soren, but he wouldn't allow any mishap to befall Sleipner. "Where is this stallion?" he demanded.

Erik waved him aside as he ran to his horse. "Sky Dancer's in the pasture, but I'll not ride him."

Too eager to protect his own skin to worry about angering a man he had not met, Brendan gave up the attempt to influence Erik and grabbed the most ornate bridle from the hooks by the doors. Once outside the stable he circled the building in a lively sprint, hoping that Haakon's stallion would be grazing nearby. When he saw the white horse, he thought him aptly named, for his alabaster coat had the snowy appearance of the clouds overhead. Knowing such a fine animal would be able to race the wind, he vaulted the wall and whistled as he approached him.

As a small child, Brendan had discovered he had a way with horses, and this was a talent he relied upon often. He called to Sky Dancer, speaking in a low, friendly tone that instantly piqued the animal's curiosity. The stallion eyed the blond man suspiciously, not recognizing his scent, but apparently attending to his rhythmic flow of words, the horse did not bolt when Brendan reached him. In one fluid motion the confident slave slipped on the bridle and sprang on his back. Having no time to waste in opening the gate, he urged the stallion to a gallop, and the horse cleared the wall surrounding the pasture in a majestic leap with nearly a foot to spare. As they sped by the stable, Brendan saw Erik just emerging, leading the black gelding, but he didn't bother to wave.

Erik screamed a vile curse, for he knew he would be in far more trouble for allowing the slave to ride Sky Dancer than if he'd had the courage to ride the spirited white horse himself. He leapt on his gelding's back, then jabbed his heels into the horse's sleek black hide. He doubted they could overtake his father's stallion, but he was determined to give it his best try.

The exhilaration of riding Sleipner was short-lived when Soren found the stallion had taken the bit firmly between his teeth and would not obey his frantic tugs on the reins and halt. The boy had meant to go only for a brief ride, not to streak clear across the island of Fyn, but he began to fear the horse would not stop until they had reached the sea. Although he pulled with all his strength on the reins, he could not subdue the fleet-footed animal's innate desire to run. He could do nothing but hang on and hope Sleipner would grow tired and come to a halt of his own accord.

Brendan soon had Sleipner in sight, and he could easily discern from the helpless bobbing of his rider that the animal was running out of control. When the horse veered off the path to cross a nearby meadow, Brendan urged Sky Dancer to put an even greater effort into the chase. When the stallion responded, they began to close the distance between them.

Soren saw the succession of stone walls in the distance and knew while Sleipner might clear them all, he probably wouldn't. He clung to the speeding horse, his heart pounding in his chest in time with his mount's thundering hoofbeats, and he shut his eyes tightly as they reached the first wall. He felt a surge of power as Sleipner's feet left the thick grass, and in the next instant he was nearly thrown forward over the horse's head when the spirited stallion's hooves returned to earth. When the ground did not rise up to smack him in the face, he peered ahead cautiously, only to find the second wall mere seconds away. Tears streamed down his face as he imagined himself lying in the dirt, a heap of badly broken bones, and he again closed his eyes. The wind stung his cheeks, making Sleipner's progress seem all the more swift, and Soren uttered a wild scream of terror as the stallion's feet left the ground for the second time.

Not realizing that only paralyzing fear kept Soren in the saddle, Brendan began to think the boy might be a better rider than he had first thought. He had no business to ride Jørn's horse, however, and that was Brendan's sole concern. He could not overtake Sleipner as he gathered speed to leap, for that might cause the horse to break his stride and fail to clear a wall, resulting in a disastrous fall for both horse and rider. Instead, he would have to come alongside the runaway stallion, leap the next wall with him, then force Sleipner to run parallel to that barrier until he could reach out to catch him. It sounded like a good plan to him, and while he had no way to explain it to Sky Dancer, he had found the white stallion remarkably responsive and did not doubt the horse would follow his unspoken commands.

They were nearing the third wall when out of the corner of his eye Soren caught a glimpse of Sky Dancer's glossy white coat. While he couldn't imagine who had had the audacity to ride his father's horse, he took heart in the fact that help was so near. Not wanting to embarrass himself by falling now, with a brave effort he kept his seat as Sleipner cleared the third wall with another effortless leap. When Sky Dancer's rider headed them off, then reached over to pull the reins from his hands, he opened his mouth to shout a hearty thanks until he saw his rescuer was a bare-chested stranger with the meanest expression he had ever seen.

Brendan slid off Sky Dancer's back the instant he had brought Sleipner to a halt. He then pulled Soren off the sweat-soaked bay and, kneeling in the grass, turned the boy over his knee and commenced to give him the spanking he deserved for riding his cousin's horse without permission.

By the time Erik reached them, he had punished the reckless boy to his satisfaction and released him. Soren then stood sobbing pathetically and rubbing his bruised behind.

While Erik knew Soren had gotten exactly what he deserved, he did not understand how Brendan could possibly have thought that he had the right to reprimand him. Even though he had no experience with slaves, he was certain they were never allowed to strike their master's children. He didn't know whether he was more angry with Brendan or Soren. While his half brother had already taken the beating he had earned, he would not let Brendan escape without equally harsh punishment. Erik was not a man to make rash judgments, though, and he decided to wait until he had returned home to talk the matter over with Dana. Then he would take whatever action they deemed best.

Glaring down at them, his violet eyes flashing with purple sparks of rage, Erik delivered a scathing rebuke. "You are both equally guilty of willfully endangering the lives of valuable horses, and that is inexcusable. Since neither of you may be able to walk when I finish with you, get home as best you can. I will deal with you when you get there." Without dismounting, he circled Sky Dancer and Sleipner, grabbed up their trailing reins, and led them away to find a way out of the meadow that did not require the horses to leap the walls a second time.

Brendan still thought he was in far less trouble than he would have been had Sleipner been injured, and he hurriedly climbed over the wall to begin what he knew would be a long and tiring walk. "Hurry up," he called over his shoulder, "or we won't get back to your farm before dark."

Soren brushed away the last of his tears, but he didn't budge. Danish boys were considered men at twelve, even if they remained at home several more years, and his father had always encouraged him to display a bold spirit. He doubted Erik would have punished him for riding Sleipner if this slave had not interfered.

"Who are you to give me orders?" the boy shouted hoarsely. At first he had not known who the abusive man was, but once he had seen the scars on his back, Soren knew he had to be Jørn's thrall. He was sick of taking orders not only from his mother, but from Dana and Erik too. He wouldn't allow a slave to talk to him in so abrasive a manner.

Brendan did not turn to reply, but kept right on walking. He certainly didn't want the company of the spoiled brat he knew Soren had to be. The boy could walk home alone, for all he cared, and he would refuse to take the blame if he got lost on the way.

When Brendan didn't wait for him, Soren didn't know what to do. He was still shaking from the fright of his wild ride and ready to cry again at being made to walk home. He had expected Erik to be happy that he was safe rather than angry because he had ridden Jørn's horse, since Jørn would never have to know about the incident.

Nothing ever went his way, Soren grumbled to himself as he started over the wall. If only he could have gone with his father, then he could have shown everyone he could do a man's work. Why did he have to be left behind as though he were a child when he was nearly grown? Reciting his oft-repeated complaints about the way he was treated, Soren followed Brendan home, but he trailed at a distance so he didn't have to speak to the man again.

Dana's eyes smoldered with fury as she listened to Erik's account of how Brendan had dared to ride Sky Dancer to overtake Soren. "I would send him back to Grena's at first light, but I know my mother would never allow it, since she won't go back on her word to her sister. We can't let her hear about this, though. Oh, Erik, what are we going to do?" the distraught redhead asked with an exasperated sigh. "We can forbid Soren to ride for a good long while, but his crime is a small one compared to Brendan's. Do you think he actually wants me to whip him? Is he so perverse he enjoys pain?"

"That's something I'd not considered, but yes, I think if any man could relish pain, it would be he." Erik was leaning against the gate, his eyes scanning the path for the first sign of Soren and Brendan's return. "If he were one of the servants, I'd fire him and send him away this very afternoon. Since we can't get rid of him so easily, we will either have to whip him or lock him up. Which do you want to do?''

Dana paced up and down by his side, her expression as dark as her thoughts. "Grena never should have asked this favor of us."

"The problem is that she didn't ask us. She asked Freya. Unfortunately, we are the ones who are faced with the disagreeable task of handling the man. I won't make the mistake of going after him again with my fists when we are so even a match, but we must think of a suitable way to punish him because I'm afraid we are going to be forced to use it again and again."

Since that was so likely a possibility, Dana suggested a novel way to discipline the man. "Frankly, I'd like to chain him naked in Grena's yard and let her women have their fill of him, since he seemed to find their attentions so distasteful."

"Dana," Erik chided with a low chuckle. "That is fiendishly clever, but the man has to stay here, remember?''

While she was reluctant to abandon her idea, Dana knew he was right. "It's plain from the scars on his back that a whipping doesn't improve his attitude. As angry as I am with him, there's too great a risk I might beat him to death anyway, so I suppose we'll have to confine him in one of the storehouses." She turned to look at the row of buildings nearby, wondering which to choose.

"We can't keep him in the one with food, for that would be like putting a mouse in a sack of grain. It will have to be one of the others," she mused aloud.

"Since Haakon has taken most of the furs for trading, why not use the one for storing furs?" Erik suggested.

"What are the chances he will set it on fire?"

"With himself locked inside? Not likely."

Dana continued to pace, wondering if merely confining Brendan would be harsh enough treatment to inspire him to become cooperative. When no more attractive strategy had occurred to her by the time he and Soren arrived, she showed no reluctance to punish him despite her misgivings about the effectiveness of her plan.

When Soren began to complain of being mistreated, Dana quickly silenced him and sent him inside, promising to deal

with him later in private. She then turned her full attention
to Brendan. The haircut and shave had improved his appearance enormously, but she tried to ignore his good looks.
After all, it was his behavior to which she objected. Still,
the fact he was even more handsome than she had first
imagined proved an unwelcome distraction.

"Do you have something to say for yourself? I can't
imagine that you will have an excuse for taking my father's
horse after Erik told you no one is allowed to ride him, but
perhaps that is only because I am not eager to break every
rule I hear."

Brendan thought the color which anger imparted to Dana's
cheeks was wonderfully attractive, but he knew she wouldn't
enjoy hearing such a compliment from him. "Since I am the
one who rode Sleipner here, I am responsible for him until
he is returned to Grena's stable. Because I knew I could not
overtake him on any other mount, I had no choice but to
take your father's."

"No choice?" Dana scoffed. "That's utter nonsense. We
have many swift mounts."

"But none as swift as Sky Dancer. Erik told me so
himself," Brendan contradicted. "You should be thanking
me for catching up to your brother before he was thrown
instead of criticizing how I did it. Is Sky Dancer more
important to your father than a son's life?"

Erik knew that would depend on which son was endangered.
He turned the full force of his anger on Brendan. "First you
were concerned about Sleipner, and now about Soren? You
are a liar who cares about nothing but yourself. A thrall who
will not obey his master is worthless, and that's exactly
what I'll tell Jørn when he returns home."

Fearing a shouting match between Erik and Brendan
would quickly produce blows, Dana stepped forward to take
charge before Brendan could respond with the bitter retort
she was certain was already on his lips. "You will come
with me, Brendan. I think perhaps a few days of solitude
will do you good. You obviously need time to reflect on
your actions since coming here so that you can improve
them."

Brendan continued to return Erik's hostile stare. He didn't

understand why Dana gave the orders rather than her brother when Erik was five years her senior. He wondered if the whole family behaved as strangely as these two did. Truly, they did seem to have been more worried about the white stallion than Soren, and he decided Haakon must be the worst of fathers to have produced such sorry children who cared so little for each other.

"You will come with me," Dana repeated before turning away. As they walked to the building, she removed the key to the storehouse where furs were kept from her brooch. Once unlocked, the door swung open on well-oiled iron hinges to reveal the paneled interior. There were shelves from floor to ceiling, but there were no more than two dozen furs resting on them now. With the door closed, no light and little air entered the storehouse, but she was certain Brendan would not suffocate. Someone had left a bucket lying nearby, and she gave it a push with her foot to roll it inside.

"I'll see that someone comes to escort you to the privy occasionally, but you may use that bucket if they are late."

Only a narrow beam of the late afternoon sunlight lit the smallest of the farm's storehouses, and while Brendan had no desire to enter, he would not let Dana see his hesitance. He marched through the door and turned to face her, his expression still one of cocky defiance.

"How long am I to stay here?" he asked.

"That depends on how long it takes you to mend your ways. Take off your breeches," Dana ordered brusquely.

Brendan was certain he couldn't possibly have understood her. "What did you say?"

"You heard me. Take off your breeches. They don't fit, and I'm going to throw them away. I told you you had to cut your hair, shave, and wear clothes that fit if you were to have supper. You're still in the ill-fitting breeches you were wearing this morning, so do not expect anything to eat tonight. Now hand them to me. I have three brothers, so I can assure you I will not faint at the sight of an unclothed male."

Brendan clamped his teeth together so hard that his jaws began to ache, but he didn't reach for the button at his waistband. While he had never mixed with any of his master's other slaves or servants, he had been lover to more than one mistress, and while he hated what Dana was, he couldn't deny that he found her haunting beauty impossible to ignore.

Thinking an attraction as powerful as the one she exerted over him must be returned, he spoke in a seductive, honey-smooth whisper. "What is it you really want, Dana? If it's me, then we can strike a bargain. If you'll take me for your lover, I'll follow each of your orders gladly."

At that astonishing offer, Dana's mouth dropped open, but in the next second she recovered her senses. "How dare you!" she screamed, the fury of her temper now impossible to control. She stepped inside the storehouse, grabbed ahold of his waistband, and just as she had anticipated, the worn fabric of Brendan's breeches ripped as easily as his kirtle had. She had expected him to be wearing linen drawers, and when she discovered he wasn't, it was too late to regret the haste of her actions because his breeches were already ruined.

That the flame-haired young woman would take it upon herself to strip him naked jolted Brendan as badly as his outrageous proposition had shocked her. When she had stepped close, he had been enveloped in the enticing fragrance of her perfume. It was a heady scent that flooded his mind with exotic images of the Orient. As one of her flying curls grazed his bare chest like a silken whip, the exquisite sensation provided a further assault on his beleaguered senses. The touch of her fingers as they brushed across the newly exposed skin of his hips sent a flame of desire curling through his loins that brought the immediate physical reaction he thought she should have anticipated, but he made no move to cover himself or turn away.

"Isn't your effect on me proof enough that I'd make you a good lover?" he taunted invitingly.

Despite her boast, Dana had not realized there was such a vast difference between a man who was merely nude and one who was fully aroused. That Brendan seemed so proud of himself revolted her thoroughly, but she refused to show it. Her gaze raked over him in a fiery wave that would have blistered the skin of a lesser man before she turned away and went to the door. His torn breeches in her hand, she called to him as she stepped through it.

"You have proved absolutely nothing, and I'll make no bargains with you. If you can't mend your behavior, then you'll remain in here until the summer's end." She slammed the door shut before Brendan could offer another of his obnoxious remarks. Her heart was beating wildly and her hands shook so badly that she fumbled with the lock. Her cheeks burned with a bright blush of embarrassment. She didn't see how she could ever release Brendan from his makeshift prison, no matter how good he promised to be.

CHAPTER IV

Dana flung what was left of Brendan's breeches on the trash heap as she ran toward the house, but before she reached the door she knew that was the last place she ought to go. How could she turn away the questions which were certain to come her way if she bolted through the door like a wounded bird frantically trying to outrun a hungry cat? She was far too distraught to provide a coherent excuse for her agitated state, and she would never be able to make polite conversation.

Realizing that sorry fact, she made an abrupt turn, then slowed her pace as she walked to the oak tree at the edge of the meadow where she had first heard Brendan's name. Had it only been the previous afternoon?

"Impossible," she hissed through clenched teeth, her temper still simmering. Brendan had caused far more than one day's worth of trouble. She leaned back against the old tree, taking comfort in the strength which had allowed it to weather more than fifty winters. She closed her eyes for a moment, but almost instantly Brendan's mocking grin came to mind and she shook her head, trying to banish his image. When she opened her eyes, she was surprised to find Erik standing in front of her.

"Oh, Erik," she began apologetically. "I'm afraid I've made things even worse for us."

Dana did indeed look worried, but Erik doubted that what she feared was even possible. "Nonsense," he exclaimed with a broad grin. "You made the right choice in locking up Brendan. If a few days of nothing but his own company doesn't turn him into the most obedient of thralls, then we'll just lock him up again, and again if need be."

Dana licked her lips anxiously, silently debating the wisdom of sharing the shocking terms of the ludicrous bargain Brendan had offered, but she swiftly decided against it since that revelation would only enrage Erik as much as it had her. "You'll have to take him some clothes," she stated instead.

Erik reached out to grab a low-hanging limb, draping his arms over it as a comfortable support while they talked. "Yes, I gave him some. He didn't have time to put them on before he went off after Soren."

"It was the horse he was after," Dana reminded him. "I think I should take the stallion back to Grena's in the morning. With any other horse, I'd just wait for Grena to fetch him when she comes to see Mother, but I don't want to give Brendan any other opportunity to use the animal as an excuse to make trouble."

"He can scarcely cause any trouble where he is now," Erik pointed out with a teasing grin. As far as he was concerned, their problems with Brendan were over for the time being, and he wanted to simply forget the man.

Dana looked away quickly, not about to admit the slave had managed to do just that with his despicable bargain. "All right, I'll wait a day or two. Grena is sure to pay us another call soon."

Dana was naturally high-strung, but as Erik studied her preoccupied frown, he feared Brendan had upset her more than he had first realized. "No, you're right. We ought to make certain that Sleipner is returned while Brendan is confined. I'll take the stallion back to Grena's in the morning. That will be one less problem for you to worry about.''

"I hate to have you miss working with the falcons two mornings in a row,'' Dana remarked considerately. "I ride nearly every day, I can go to Grena's as easily as anywhere else.''

Knowing her point was well-taken, Erik hesitated a moment before making up his mind, but when he had he stated his plans firmly. "I'll take the falcons out at first light and then see to the horse.'' He knew his offer was a reasonable one, but he also had the nagging suspicion that his eagerness to return Sleipner might just be an excuse to see Berit again. That was ridiculous, of course, as he could scarcely encourage tomorrow the friendship he had rejected today, but the haunting memory of Berit's stricken expression as he had rebuffed her attentions had made him feel guilty all day.

"Erik?" Dana prompted, thinking the obstreperous slave was the cause of his pensive frown. "You'll have to take Brendan the clothes right away.''

"Why? He's not going anywhere.''

"I did promise someone would take him to the privy.''

"I can't trust that task to one of the servants,'' Erik realized instantly. "The belligerent oaf might harm one of them. I'll see to him myself after supper.''

"Just remember to take him the clothes so he doesn't get cold. It would be just like him to fall ill and die on us.''

Erik couldn't help but laugh at that dire prediction. "Not even Brendan is that obstinate, Dana. He'd not die just to spite us.''

Dana's lovely violet eyes narrowed as her gaze swept over her handsome half brother's amused expression. "Oh, yes, he is, and I don't want Jørn coming to me demanding I pay him what he spent on the man.''

"All right, I won't forget the clothes, but there must still be enough furs handy for him to keep himself warm until I get there.''

Dana had completely forgotten about the furs remaining in the storehouse and now felt very foolish she had stopped for even one instant to consider Brendan's health. "I'm sorry, I didn't mean to sound like a shrew.''

Erik leaned forward to plant a light kiss on her cheek. "You never do, dear sister, never."

While she feared that wasn't true, Dana returned his kiss without argument, and the problems Brendan presented solved for the moment, they discussed Soren's punishment and decided to forbid him to ride for a week. As always, Erik's level-headed sensibilities calmed Dana's frayed nerves, and she felt up to returning to the house when they parted a few minutes later. She realized Erik had such a soothing effect on everyone. He was a very competent young man, and while Brendan had provoked him to anger, she was certain the obnoxious slave would have the same disastrous effect on any other man.

Taking a deep breath, Dana promised herself she would not lose her temper again. No matter what disgusting thing Brendan said or did, she would not react with anger. Instead, she would remain firmly in control of her emotions. She was the mistress and he was the slave. She would not forget that fact nor allow him to disregard it either.

With her family seated on either side of the hearth located in the center of the long room, Freya could not help but cast frequent glances toward Haakon's empty place at her side. As master and mistress of the home, they normally shared one of the wide benches placed between the four central posts which supported the roof. Ornately carved, the columns marked not only the center of the house, but the heart of the family as well.

Freya missed her husband terribly, and not simply at mealtimes but at every hour of the day and night. She missed the sound of his deep voice and hearty laughter, and longed to again feel the exquisite sensation of his loving touch. They were so close a couple that when he was away she felt only half alive. As a young bride she had learned to focus her attention on her children when Haakon traveled, and that was exactly what she did this night. When she found not only Soren, but Dana and Erik unusually quiet, she encouraged Thora to talk about her day.

The vivacious ten-year-old finished spreading butter on a thick slab of bread as she began an enthusiastic account of how she had given Brendan a haircut. "His hair is every bit as thick and curly as yours, Soren, and he hates having it trimmed as much as you do. It was a good thing I happened along, since Erik was making such a mess of the job he would have left the thrall nearly bald."

Erik opened his mouth to argue, then thought better of it. "You're right, Thora. I'm a poor barber, it seems."

Freya took a sip of ale and then set her tankard upon the small table which had been placed in front of her bench to hold the evening meal. "I should have told you to stay away from the man, baby. What's done is done, but I don't want you talking with him again. I'm sure he's no fit companion for a young girl, so just stay out of his way. It's not your fault, Erik, I know Thora is always underfoot, but you must keep Brendan too busy working to have any time to chat with children. What did you plan to have him do tomorrow?"

When Dana dropped her spoon with a loud clatter, Erik knew she had been as badly startled by the question as he was. "It will take me a few days to decide what he does best."

"From what Grena told us, he is an expert horseman. Isn't there plenty of work for him to do around the stable?" Freya inquired with a curious glance. Her lashes were as long and thick as her daughters', and her face was now so thin her eyes were her dominant feature.

"Well, yes, I suppose there is," Erik was forced to admit. When Dana gave him an encouraging nod, he continued with a forceful show of confidence. "I think I'll release the stable boys to work in the fields and turn their work over to Brendan. That will give him more than enough to do."

"Good. For as long as he's here I want him to earn his keep," Freya instructed with the quiet competence which marked all her actions. "After we have finished breakfast in the morning, bring him to me. I didn't feel up to speaking with him today, but I'm certain that I will tomorrow."

Dana exchanged a stricken glance with Erik before she hurriedly attempted to change Freya's mind. "I really don't think that's wise, Mother. Erik and I can handle the man. You needn't trouble yourself over him. His presence here really doesn't merit your attention. He's already insufferably arrogant. If you give him any of your time, he'll be so flattered it will make him even worse.''

Surprised not only by Dana's opinion but also by the fervor with which she had expressed it, Freya glanced at the other members of her family to see if they shared it. She found Erik's expression equally determined, but then he and Dana usually agreed. Soren was bent so low over his plate his nose was in danger of becoming coated with gravy. The fourteen-year-old's silence puzzled her, but she found it preferable to the stream of complaints he usually made during supper. As for Thora, her violet eyes were alight with mischief.

''I like Brendan,'' the lively girl announced when her mother looked her way. ''I don't see how you can say I can't talk to him when you haven't met him. Maybe you'll like him too.''

''Mother's right, Thora,'' Dana insisted in the same emphatic tone she had just used with Freya. ''We know almost nothing about Brendan. We can't trust him like we do our servants. He might try to befriend you in hopes you'll help him escape.''

''That's silly. Fyn is an island,'' Thora remarked with a giggle. ''He can't escape.''

''Let me put it this way, Thora,'' Erik said, swiftly coming to Dana's aid. ''I plan to keep Brendan too busy to talk with anyone. If you pester him with questions, then he won't get his work done and I'll have to punish him. If you like him as you say you do, then you'll spare him that pain and keep away from him.''

Thora knew Erik didn't make idle threats, and rather than waste her breath arguing with him, she grabbed up her freshly buttered bread and took a savage bite. She continued to glare at her half brother as she chewed, letting him know that while he may have gotten the last word for the moment, she wasn't ready to concede the fight.

That the conversation about the slave had become so heated only served to whet Freya's curiosity about him. ''Soren, you've not said a word. Don't you have an opinion about Brendan?''

Soren looked up then, his blue eyes smoldering with fury.

"I despise the bastard!" he shouted, and shoving aside the small table upon which his dishes sat, he leapt to his feet and stormed out of the hall.

A deathly silence descended upon the long room, for the servants tidying up the kitchen had also heard Soren's curse and were as deeply stunned by it as his family. They all knew Erik's heritage and Soren's outburst was an insult and a shocking breach of manners.

"I'm going to kill him!" Dana swore as she rose from her seat, but Erik reached out to catch her wrist.

"Soren has been in a disagreeable mood ever since Haakon left. He didn't mean anything by that," the persuasive young man insisted as he coaxed the volatile redhead back down into her place.

Freya sighed sadly, fearing she had caused a regrettable scene when it should have been obvious to her by his dejected pose that Soren was in no mood to contribute anything positive to the evening. What little appetite she had had was now gone, and she wanted only to go to her room and rest for the coming day.

"I really must speak with Brendan in the morning, Erik," Freya insisted as she rose from her place. "If he has stirred up such deep resentment after only one day with us, I don't dare let another go by without meeting him."

Feeling utterly defeated, Dana sank back against the thickly padded bench as she watched her mother move away. Freya had always been graceful, but now she was so thin that her flowing garments floated about her as though borne by an unseen breeze rather than being suspended from her narrow shoulders.

"I don't know whom I dislike most at this moment, Soren or that despicable Celt!" Dana whispered under her breath.

"Soren," Thora spit out the name, as always ready to offer her opinion.

Erik and Soren had never shared the closeness he and Svien did. Indeed, Soren admired neither his elder brother nor his half brother. He was simply jealous of them and envied the independence their advantage in years had given them. Since each had his own work, Erik seldom spent any time with Soren, which he was certain only added to the strain that existed between them. Still, he knew the boy had not meant to insult him as well as Brendan.

"Soren's moodiness is a minor problem, Dana. Forget him. In the morning I'll see Brendan behaves himself so you needn't worry about him either. Now let's finish this stew. It's quite the best meal we've had all week."

Dana watched Erik and Thora finish the tasty dish down to the last drop of gravy in the bottom of their bowls, but she didn't take another bite. All she could think of was Brendan's mocking grin, and the prospect of facing him again so soon was almost more than she could bear.

As Erik approached the fur storehouse, he could hear Brendan singing to himself. While the words of the song were in the slave's own tongue, it was obvious from the lighthearted nature of the tune that the Celt was having no difficulty keeping himself amused. He had not expected the man would be weeping over being confined, but still Erik was not pleased to find him distracting himself with so pleasant a diversion.

When Brendan heard the key being turned in the lock, he sprang to his feet and took a firm grasp on the bearskin he had wrapped around his waist. Thinking it must be Dana returning to bid him good night, a surge of exhilaration coursed down his spine and he let himself hope she had realized his bargain would be beneficial to them both. He broke into a wide grin at the delicious nature of that possibility, but when he saw Erik standing at the door, his expression became a disappointed frown.

When Erik first peered into the storehouse, he thought Brendan must have discarded his breeches in preparation to sleep. When he saw no sign of them he realized why Dana had been so insistent about his taking the Celt some clothes; and he began to chuckle.

"What do you find so funny?" Brendan inquired in a sarcastic snarl. Knowing few men could project an air of dignity while wrapped in a bearskin, he straightened his shoulders proudly in an attempt to do just that.

"I warned you not to underestimate Dana's wrath. The

next time you fail to curb your insolence she may take more than your breeches.''

Brendan took a deep breath and held it. He wasn't certain what Erik was threatening, but since he didn't think he really wanted to know, he hurriedly changed the subject. ''If you've come to take me to the privy, let's go.''

The days were lengthtening with the arrival of summer, and Erik had no desire to parade the half-naked slave through the twilight when his state of undress would be readily observed. ''I brought the clothes I showed you earlier. Put them on first.''

Since he knew no matter what lay ahead that he would be better off clothed than wrapped in a fur, Brendan didn't argue.

Erik leaned against the doorjamb and crossed his arms over his chest as he waited. He wasn't surprised to find the Celt as well-endowed below the waist as he was above, but he couldn't help but wonder just how much of the handsomely built slave Dana had observed.

''The knife Dana carries is as sharp as her tongue. You mustn't provoke her again,'' he advised calmly.

Brendan noted that the direction of Erik's glance was focused squarely on his crotch, but he had never heard of anyone castrating a slave. He did not wish to be the first to suffer that misfortune, however. Pretending not to understand Erik's remark, he sat down to put on his boots and fasten the laces on the leggings he had been given. When he got to his feet, he waited for Erik to move out of the way, then walked along beside him to the privy the servants used. When he came out, Erik marched him straight back to the storehouse, but then paused at the door.

''Freya wishes to speak with you in the morning. If you succeed in impressing her favorably, I'll let you work in the stable tomorrow and provide all the food you can eat. If not, well, then you'll just have to spend the day in this small, dark storehouse with perhaps a scrap of bread. The choice is your. Make it a wise one.''

Bristling under the unwanted advice, Brendan sought more information than Erik had given. ''I thought you said Freya was ill.''

"No, I said she hasn't been well. There's a difference."
When Brendan nodded, Erik was glad he understood. "She
is dearly loved by us all, and you must treat her with all the
respect and courtesy you possess. Since we have seen none,
I can only hope you will learn how to behave by tomorrow."

"I thought it was Dana you wanted me to please." That
was exactly what Brendan wanted to do too, although not in
the way Erik would imagine.

"Dana will be satisfied with your behavior if Freya is,"
Erik informed him coolly. "Good night." As soon as the
slave had crossed the threshold, Erik closed and locked the
storehouse door. He wasn't certain he had made any impression on the man, but he hoped Brendan had sense enough to
do what was in his own best interests.

Dana had stepped outside for a breath of air before
preparing for bed, and while neither Erik nor Brendan had
seen her as they walked across the yard, she had seen them.
In Erik's clothes, Brendan resembled a Dane so closely she
had not immediately recognized him. Then she had been
filled with shame over the flutter of excitement that had
caused her heart to skip a beat when he had first come into
view. She had repeatedly told herself that Brendan's appearance was totally irrelevant, and she knew she was right. He
might be bright, attractive, and clearly possessed of a great
deal of courage, but that didn't make up for the vileness of
his nature. That memory of his suggested bargain brought a
renewed flush of anger to her cheeks, and she hurried back
inside before Erik escorted him back to the storehouse, for
she did not want to suffer the torment of watching the
graceful pride in the impossible slave's long stride a second
time that night.

Immediately engulfed in darkness, Brendan fumbled with
the buttons on his new shirt, and succeeding in freeing
them, he then yanked it off over his head. He lay the light
woolen garment on the closest shelf so it wouldn't get
wrinkled while he slept. Then realizing he didn't want to
sleep, he began to pace the narrow space near the door.

Two Norsemen and three Danes had claimed him as their

property before Jørn, and while he had hated them all equally, he had never found himself in so confusing a situation as his present one. While Erik was not truly friendly, he had displayed none of the outright meanness Brendan had seen so often. Nor could he truthfully describe Dana as cruel, and he would not deny that the fire of her temper intrigued rather than repelled him.

It would be quite a challenge to tame a woman with her spirit. He longed to possess not only her shapely body, but to hold her heart in the palm of his hand. He made a tight fist then, as though he had already accomplished that impossible feat and could crush both her spirit and emotions in one masterful gesture.

He knew such thoughts were dangerous, and yet they were only thoughts. What harm could they do when he had nothing better to occupy his mind? He would reside on Haakon's farm all summer—surely that was time enough to win any woman's heart. He had learned that both she and Erik held Haakon in such high esteem that they would not disregard her wishes no matter how dire the situation. Now it seemed Freya might be feared too, or was it merely love that made them want to please her, as Erik had said? Whatever the reason, neither of them would take any action without first thinking of the consequences. That might be seen as a strength by some, but in his view, it was a weakness he planned to use to his own advantage.

Dana might fight the prospect of taking him for a lover, but he was confident it was only a matter of time before she succumbed, for he had seen the keen interest in her eyes earlier despite her attempt to hide it. If he were truly clever, he would soon have not only a magnificent mistress, but his freedom as well. That thought was so pleasant that when he removed the rest of his clothes and stretched out on the bearskin, he fell asleep instantly and had the most amusing dreams the whole night through.

CHAPTER V

Dana had never thought of herself as a coward, but when Erik was ready to bring Brendan into their home she chose to sit some distance away from her mother, discreetly screened by the women working at the looms. She was far too curious about what might transpire to leave the house as Soren had, but she didn't want to provide the contentious slave with another opportunity to insult her. She wanted only to listen without being drawn into the conversation she feared could not possibly go well. She trusted her mother, however, to handle the man without losing her temper. When she heard the door open, she leaned back into the shadows, but her senses were keenly alert.

Erik had insisted that Brendan wash and shave again that morning before meeting Freya. Preferring to be clean, the Celt had not argued since it was always to his advantage to look his best when he met a new mistress. He could not help but wonder what sort of woman Freya might be, but he hoped she was not nearly so easily provoked to anger as her eldest daughter.

As they entered the hall, they passed first through the area where the meals were prepared. Brendan attempted to ignore the tantalizing aroma of freshly baked bread, but it taunted his senses with poignant memories of home. The gnawing hunger with which he had awakened had yet to be assuaged, and while he rebelled inwardly at the crudity of Erik's tactics, he had to admit they worked. After going nearly a full day without food, he feared he would have little resistance no matter what Freya demanded of him. He was willing to agree to perform the most menial of chores provided she would give him a good meal.

Before Erik led Brendan into the hall, Freya had been concentrating on making the tiny stitches necessary to fashion a new hood for one of the falcons. When she heard the men approaching, she lay the piece of glove-soft leather aside and looked up into the bright blue eyes of a far more handsome young man than she had been led to expect. Grena was wrong, she thought to herself, for any woman would find Brendan attractive, not merely a few. He had not only a pleasing appearance, but also a powerful build which conveyed the unmistakable impression of both strength and courage.

His features, while definitely masculine, were so finely sculpted that it was immediately apparent he was no peasant who had been dragged from his fields in Erin to till those of her homeland. No, this was no humble farmer, nor was he a mere stablehand who possessed extraordinary skill with horses. He was someone else entirely, and greatly intrigued, she wanted to know precisely who and what he was.

As soon as Erik had introduced the remarkable slave, Freya began to question him. Her voice was light, enticing rather than commanding a response, just as Dana's had been the first time she had spoken to him. "From where do you come, Brendan, and what do your people do there?"

Freya's golden-red curls were drawn back into a knot at her nape and caught the same bright blue ribbons she had used that day on Thora's hair. Her silk chemise and sleeveless wool tunic were as fine as the garments Dana wore, and Brendan glanced around quickly, hoping to find the young woman nearby. When he saw only Thora and half a dozen servants looking his way, he could scarcely hide his disappointment. He had been certain that Dana would have been anxious to see him again.

Disgusted with himself for overestimating the fiery young woman's interest in him, Brendan turned his attention back to Freya. That she and Dana resembled each other so closely had given him something of a start when he had first entered the long, wide hall. Freya was also a beauty, but a very fragile one, while Dana's vibrant good looks glowed with the bloom of health.

Frowning slightly, he tried to recall what it was Freya had asked him, and as a result his expression mirrored the curiosity in hers. It was plain to him where Dana had gotten her long dark lashes, since Freya had them too, but in her case they framed eyes of a clear blue rather than a haunting violet. Her features held the same sweet perfection as her daughter's, and he was relieved to see no evidence of the underlying tension which erupted so easily into fits of temper with Dana. His immediate impression of Freya was one of graceful tranquillity.

Brendan's glance swept over the soft folds of Freya's loose-fitting garments, noting they failed to disguise her far too slender figure. Her hands were resting lightly in her lap, displaying the well-manicured nails of a lady who did nothing more strenuous than an occasional bit of sewing. Her fair skin was translucent, allowing the network of blue veins crossing the backs of her hands to easily show through. He drew in a deep breath as he wondered why Erik had lied to him. Freya was not recovering from an illness. She looked to him as though she was slowly sinking to her death.

"Where I am from matters not at all now that I am here. As for my people, I'll not speak of them with you," he stated firmly.

While disappointed in his refusal to provide information about himself, Freya did not insist. It was obvious to her that he was a man of great pride, and she assumed that, like Haakon, once he had taken a stance on an issue he would not change it. "Grena told me you are good with horses. Is that true?"

Brendan shrugged slightly. Then, realizing by her question she must know nothing of Soren's wild ride and how he had come to the boy's rescue, he glanced over at Erik. The dark-haired young man nodded, urging him to respond. "Some say that I am," Brendan admitted modestly. He smiled slightly then, wondering what he could get from Erik in exchange for his silence. What would Freya do if she learned Soren had ridden Sleipner? Surely she would not be pleased, since Erik and Dana had been so upset by it.

Naturally observant, Freya watched what she considered an evil glint fill Brendan's gaze and, growing cautious, decided to bring the interview to a close. "My husband takes a great deal of pride in his horses, Brendan. You must give them excellent care or his anger will know no bounds. Strive to avoid that."

After only one day, Brendan was thoroughly sick of the way everyone shook with dread at Haakon's name. Was there not a single member of his household who was not terrified of the man? He saw Thora out of the corner of his eye, and wondered if maybe the bright-eyed child might be the only one who wasn't. Before he could assure Freya that no one had ever complained about his work, his stomach rumbled so noisily that everyone in the hall heard it, and several laughed.

Rather than being embarrassed or annoyed, Freya was relieved to suddenly have an excellent excuse to dismiss the unusual thrall. "Erik, it's plain this man is hungry. We can't expect him to work without hearty meals to sustain his strength. See that he has all he wants to eat, and then show him what must be done."

"I'll see to it immediately," Erik replied eagerly, equally relieved that they were being sent on their way before Brendan had created some type of unfortunate scene.

As Erik turned away, Brendan hesitated to follow, for while he never talked about himself, he sensed how greatly his reluctance to do so had disappointed Freya. Seized with a sudden inspiration, he dropped to his knees in front of the soft-spoken woman. Grabbing her hands, he brought them to his lips and covered her palms with a flurry of adoring kisses. "Bless you for your kindness, mistress. It will not go unrewarded."

Freya was so shocked by this totally unexpected display of gratitude she sat staring at the top of Brendan's bowed head for a long moment before she had the presence of mind to withdraw her hands from his. He had nearly flung himself across her lap in his eagerness to thank her, and when she recovered from her initial astonishment, she was quite touched by the spontaneity of his display of devotion.

She reached out to pat his fair curls lightly, thinking she must have badly misjudged his attitude. "Get up, Brendan. Have something to eat and then see to our horses' needs. That's all I've asked of you."

Brendan wiped away a nonexistent tear as he rose to his feet. Uncertain if he could keep from laughing out loud, he kept his head bowed as he followed Erik out of the hall, but as soon as they had stepped out into the sunshine he broke into a wide grin.

"What did you expect to gain by behaving in so outrageous a manner?" Erik asked as he gave Brendan's shoulder a hearty shove, which nearly knocked the slave off his feet. "I wanted you to be civil, not to worship Freya as though she were a goddess!"

"You told me only to please her," Brendan contradicted. "You didn't say how to go about it."

Erik let out a moan which closely resembled a menacing growl, but he didn't strike Brendan again before starting toward his house. "Come on. I'm too busy to argue with you. You must eat and get to work. I want the stables thoroughly cleaned inside and out and each of the horses groomed."

"Sky Dancer too?" Brendan asked as he swaggered along behind him.

"Of course!" Erik shouted over his shoulder. "Just don't ride him again, ever."

Brendan knew Erik was too angry to strike any bargains now, but the thrall thought that after a day to consider how best to better his situation, he would have a most intriguing deal to offer by nightfall.

Had Brendan scanned the hall before leaving, he would have seen Dana peering around from behind a loom, her mouth again agape with wonder at the absurdity of his behavior. What idiotic scheme was the man up to now? she asked herself as she rose and went to join her mother. Had he given up on seducing her in favor of ingratiating himself with Freya? Had the man no sense of honor at all?

Freya picked up the scrap of leather to continue sewing, then had to lay the half-finished hood aside and wipe her palms on her tunic to remove the last traces of moisture from Brendan's fevered kisses. "I don't understand why Soren has taken such a dislike to that man. He seems agreeable enough to me. More than agreeable really, if we disregard his reluctance to confide anything about his past."

"I thought you would like him once you met him," Thora exclaimed happily.

"Let's not form our opinions until after we have seen a sample of his work," Dana offered wisely as she slid into the place at her mother's side. "He may only be trying to fool us into thinking he's a willing worker when all the while he may try and sleep away his days in the hay."

"He is not built like a man who shirks his share of the work," Freya mused thoughtfully. "I doubt he will prove to be lazy."

Dana doubted that too, although she suspected Brendan would be likely to devote himself to plotting ridiculous schemes calculated to embarrass them all rather than to doing any useful work. Soren had left early that morning, and she suddenly found remaining in the house as impossible as he had.

"I think I'll go for a ride. Do you want to come with me, Thora?"

"Shouldn't we wait until Brendan has had time to eat so he can saddle the horses for us?" the little girl inquired as she joined her mother and sister on the long bench.

Dana had forgotten that Erik planned to assign the stable boys work to do elsewhere. "Of course, we'll wait a while longer." She sank back into the cushions, disgusted she would have to rely upon the very man she wanted to avoid to provide the mount she required.

After Brendan had eaten a breakfast Erik considered sufficient for three men, he had him saddle Sleipner and his horse, Shadow, and leading the black gelding, he started out for Grena's. He enjoyed riding the spirited bay for a change, but the lively animal demanded his full attention and he had no chance to think of anything witty or charming to say to Berit before he arrived at her home.

Erik turned over Jørn's horse to the stable boys, but then remained by the low structure to tighten his gelding's cinch in preparation for the trip back home. That provided him with the opportunity to surreptitiously observe the yard and gardens, but there was no sign of Berit anywhere about, and he had to face the unfortunate fact she would have no way of knowing he was there if he did not announce himself.

While he was not truly worried Grena would set dogs on him, he was certain she would not make him feel welcome. He felt he owed Berit an apology, though, and wanting to speak with her more than he wanted to avoid Grena's indifference, he led his horse over to her house. Ulla, an elderly servant, soon answered his knock, but he declined her invitation to enter and instead asked her to convey the message to Grena that he had returned Jørn's stallion from Freya's.

When the old woman had closed the door, Erik wondered if Berit would even care that he was there. Fearing that she wouldn't, he felt increasingly foolish waiting around in hopes she would appear. When the wait grew uncomfortably long, he finally gave up the effort as useless. He turned away, but just as he raised his foot to the stirrup, the door opened again.

Berit looked out, but she didn't smile when she saw Erik about to mount his horse. "Thank you for returning Sleipner. I never ride him, but I'm sure our mares would soon miss him."

Despite the teasing nature of her comment, there was a wariness in her glance that he had not seen before, and Erik, knowing he was to blame, felt a sharp stab of guilt. Rather than swing himself up into the saddle, he took a step toward the house. He had come to apologize, and now that he had the chance, he blurted it out.

"You have always been as dear as a sister to me, Berit. I'm sorry if what I said to you yesterday seemed needlessly cruel. I didn't meant it to be."

Sufficiently intrigued to risk speaking with him again, Berit stepped out the door and pulled it closed behind her. "Brendan means nothing to me. How could you have even imagined that he did?"

His accusation had been motivated by a searing flash of jealousy, not reason, but Erik couldn't admit that. "He's a handsome man," he pointed out instead.

"We had so much trouble with him I really didn't notice." Berit moved another step closer to her violet-eyed visitor. Wayward strands of his shiny, dark brown hair dipped down low over his right brow, and she longed to reach up and push them back into place but restrained that impulse as doubtlessly unwanted. He had forced her to realize they were no longer children who could touch without causing comment, and that was a loss that saddened her.

"You may have been like a brother to me once," she began softly, "but not anymore."

Berit was regarding him with a level gaze, her manner sincere rather than flirtatious, and Erik realized he was dangerously close to getting himself in trouble again. He noted the wisps of honey-blond hair that framed her face and provided a delicate accent to the sparkling blue of her eyes. Her nose had a slight upward tilt that fit the vivaciousness of her personality perfectly. Her lower lip had an inviting fullness that promised her kisses would be delicious, but forbidding himself to dwell on such a tantalizing sight, he lowered his glance only to find that the pert upward thrust of her breasts showed clearly through her lightweight wool tunic. There seemed to be no place he could focus his gaze without becoming far too aware of the abundance of her charms, and he feared he was becoming so distracted that their conversation would go no better than it had the previous day.

"Berit," he begged hoarsely. "Don't do this to me."

"Do what?" the pretty blonde inquired innocently. "Ask you to think of me as a woman instead of a sister?"

"Yes." Erik took a step backward, but when Berit took another step forward he bumped into Shadow and had to stand his ground. "Brother and sister is all we can ever be." Yet the thoughts that filled his mind as he looked at her were anything but chaste. He wanted to reach out and gather her into his arms, to cover the silken smoothness of her pale golden skin with more kisses than she could count. Not to do so took all the self-control he possessed.

While Berit assumed Erik had meant his words to sound convincing, he had failed to sway her. A delighted smile lit her face with happiness and she shook her head emphatically. "You are no brother to me, and I don't believe that's what you truly want either. I seldom ride, but if you'll tell where it is you'll be taking your falcons tomorrow, I'll meet you there."

Unable to think clearly with her standing so close and the subtle fragrance of her perfume clouding his mind, Erik tore his eyes away from hers. Her request was a bold one, but he couldn't deny it was enormously appealing. He couldn't bring himself to scold her again for putting her desires into words simply because he dared not do the same. She was only sixteen, but he was twenty-two, and concentrating on that fact, he forced himself to act like a man who was totally in control of his emotions even though that was a long way from the truth.

"The falcons will be molting soon and won't be training, so what you suggest is doubly impossible."

When Berit frowned slightly, Erik knew she was about to argue and he refused to provide her that chance. Giving in to the love he had always felt for her, if only for a second, he bent down to place a feather-soft kiss on her lips, then he abruptly turned away. In an instant he was seated astride his sleek black horse, and from that lofty perch he could speak with far more confidence than he felt. "I've asked you not to tease me before, Berit. Please don't do it again. We can't meet tomorrow or any other morning. The risk is simply too great."

Berit reached out to grab Shadow's bridle before Erik could turn away. "What risk? I'd never tell."

"The risk is that we would fall in love, but be forbidden to marry. I could never bear that pain, and I won't inflict it on you. Now good day."

Erik wrenched his mount free of her grasp and urged him into a brisk canter that swiftly carried him across the yard and out onto the path that led home. He didn't look back, but Berit remained where she stood until he was no longer in sight.

The disheartened blonde let out a mournful sigh as she turned around, but when she found her mother standing in the doorway observing her with a darkly menacing scowl, she did her best to display her most dazzling smile. She was certain Grena couldn't have seen Erik kiss her, so she didn't understand why she looked so troubled.

"Just what did you and Erik have to discuss for so

long?'' Grena asked without responding to her daughter's friendly smile.

"We were talking about horses." Why that subject had come to her mind she didn't know, but it had sounded plausible enough to her, so she elaborated on it. "He thought we might want to breed Sleipner to some of their mares, but I told him that's something for Jørn and Haakon to decide."

"Why would Erik be talking to you about such things?" Grena asked suspiciously.

"Well, I suppose the thought occurred to him when they had Sleipner at their farm last night. Sky Dancer is a better stallion than Sleipner, though, isn't he?" Berit was sorry now she had not said they were talking about falcons, since she knew her mother had little interest in the elegant birds of prey.

"Yes, he is a splendid animal, while Sleipner seldom lives up to Jørn's boasts. Is that all Erik said to you?"

"He wished me a good day. Did you want to speak with him? I wish you had said so. I would have told him to wait a moment."

"No, I've nothing to say to Erik." Grena's frown had failed to lift, however. "See that you don't either, as it will only encourage him and we don't want that."

Berit wanted to argue that she would never want any man's attentions more, but knowing that declaration would only serve to make her mother even more suspicious than she appeared to be already, she shrugged as though Erik meant nothing at all to her. "I seldom see him anymore, Mother, and he treats me as though I were still a child, so you needn't worry about him."

Grena continued to regard her lovely daughter with a thoughtful stare. Erik was quite handsome, and with all the wealthy traders gone, Berit would have no young men calling on her until the fall. "I intend a fine marriage for you, Berit, and your reputation must be above reproach. You are not to speak with Erik again unless Freya sends him here with a message."

"Yes, Mother," Berit replied, but she had no intention of honoring that promise. She had never enjoyed riding as much as Dana did, but she decided instantly that was an interest she ought to cultivate since it would provide an excuse to visit Freya's farm often, and with luck she would see Erik every time she was there. Surely, in time he would want to meet with her alone. That possibility was so exciting she couldn't look her mother in the eye as she stepped by her. Fortunately, Grena was so preoccupied she didn't notice Berit's delighted smile.

When Dana called his name, Brendan was so startled he nearly drove the tines of the pitchfork he was using through the toe of his boot. He wheeled around and found her standing at the stable door. She was silhouetted by the morning sun so he could make out nothing but her shapely form. That she had come looking for him pleased him enormously, until she spoke.

"Thora and I are going riding, and we need you to saddle our mounts. You know which horse is mine, and the sorrel pony in the next stall is hers."

As the redhead turned to go, Brendan stifled his anger long enough to call out to her, "Wait!"

Dana paused, still holding the front of her tunic as she prepared to take another step. "Is there something you don't understand?" Having come to the regrettable conclusion she would have to deal with Brendan on a daily basis, Dana had decided she would speak with him only when she had a specific task for him to perform. Otherwise she would pretend he did not exist.

After leaning the pitchfork against the wall so he would not be tempted to spear her with it, Brendan walked to the end of the stable. While he worked, he had again been telling himself that Dana was a pagan beauty with the blackest of hearts, but once he could see her delicate features clearly his resolve to despise her wavered dangerously. He could think of only one thing when he looked at her: how glorious it would be to feel her naked body pressed close to his.

"Do you ride without an escort?" he asked incredulously.

"Neither of us is in any danger of being thrown," Dana assured him.

The sunlight had again given her glossy red hair a halo's bright gleam, and dazzled by that splendor, Brendan had to take a moment to explain his concern. "I've seen you ride, so it's not your skill which I'm questioning, but the wisdom of riding alone. Are there never any travelers on the roads, strangers who might wish you harm?"

Amused, Dana responded with a throaty laugh, certain his remark was based on something other than concern for her safety. "You are the only dangerous stranger on Fyn, Brendan, and as long as you attend to your duties here, I will feel safe." His glance turned cold, but that didn't bother her in the least. She preferred his hatred to the scathing heat of his unbridled lust. As a scowl contorted his mouth into a fierce grimace, she noticed for the first time that a thin scar crossed his upper lip midway to the left corner. Probably the result of a punch to his mouth he must surely have deserved, she mused silently.

"I waited until you had finished eating to ask this of you," Dana pointed out in the same emotionless tone she had used when first addressing him. "Do not keep us waiting any longer than necessary." She turned her back on him and disappeared around the side of the stable, giving him no opportunity to reply.

"The bitch!" Brendan again swore in his own tongue, repeating the insult that had started the fight with Erik the previous day. He would saddle her horse all right, but he was tempted to cut the cinch nearly through so it would break during her ride and spill the haughty flame-haired beauty in the dirt, where he thought she belonged.

"I don't think I should ask Moira what that word means," Thora announced solemnly.

His attention drawn to the shadows at the door, Brendan cursed himself for not having noticed Dana wasn't alone. "No, you shouldn't," he agreed. "Who's Moira?"

Thora followed as Brendan walked back to the stall where Dana's dapple-gray mare stood. "She's one of our servants, and her parents were from Erin so she speaks your tongue."

"I thought I was the only thrall here."

"You are. Her parents earned their freedom before she was born."

"She was born here then?" Brendan thought Dana's mare a beauty, but expecting her to have the same disagreeable temperament as her owner, he was pleasantly surprised when she stood quietly as he swung her saddle up on her back. Adorned with ribbons as was the horse, it had been easy to recognize which saddle and bridle Dana used.

"Yes. Does that matter?" Thora stepped out of Brendan's way as he moved on down the aisle to her pony.

"Yes, for she will have no memories of my home." Not wanting to think of his own memories growing faint before he was able to win his freedom and return home, Brendan abruptly changed the subject. "What's your pony's name?"

"Rascal," the little girl responded with a giggle. "My father named him."

"Did he?" The sheer playfulness of the name amazed him. Was it possible Haakon had a charming side? he wondered. "Why is everyone so afraid of your father? Does his sword never leave his hand?" Brendan's tone was teasing, but he thought it more likely he could inspire Thora to provide some useful information about Haakon than anyone else, and he wanted to be prepared to meet him.

Thora cocked her head as she gazed up at the handsome slave. "What does it matter to you? You belong to Jørn, not him."

Brendan was astonished the little girl had been clever enough to cut him off as coldly as he had her mother. She had been too bright to fall for his ploy and he wouldn't insult her by attempting it again. "I was just curious since I'll be here all summer." He had Rascal saddled in a few minutes, and Thora took the reins from his hand, bounded up on the pony's back, and rode him out of the stable without speaking to him again.

"Amazing child," he murmured softly. He would have to remember to watch for her before he spouted off again about her sister.

By the time Brendan led Dana's mare from the stable, his temper had cooled. He found the perplexing beauty waiting in the yard, and clasped his hands to provide her with a convenient step to reach her stirrup. After a slight hesitation, she lay her hand on his shoulder and placed the toe of her boot in his palms. Even encased in leather it was plain she had tiny feet, and her leggings were so snug they didn't hide the elegant shape of her calf. She was dressed in pale green that day, and her garments were lightly perfumed with the exotic scent he immediately recalled from their encounter in the storehouse. What sweet torture, he thought to himself, but the moment passed all too swiftly.

Once comfortably seated astride her mare, Dana reached out to take the reins from Brendan. He did not simply hand them to her, however, but first brought her palm to his lips and brushed it lightly with a kiss. As shocked as her mother had been by such unexpected affection, her reflexes were far more swift, and she immediately jerked her hand free. "You are undoubtedly the most contemptible man ever born!" she hissed under her breath so Thora could not overhear.

Brendan flashed a wicked grin. "I can only beg your forgiveness, but after the aromas of the stable your perfume was too enticing to resist."

"It is not my perfume which is the problem, but your arrogance!" Dana jabbed her heels into her mare's flanks and bolted out of the yard at a speed so swift Thora had no chance to keep up.

Knowing she had missed something, the little girl turned back to look at Brendan, but he just waved and wished her a pleasant ride before returning to his chores with a smile he couldn't hide. He would settle for arrogance for the time being. At least it showed something about him had touched Dana, and he considered that a good start.

CHAPTER VI

When Erik arrived home, he found Brendan seated in the pasture where Sky Dancer and half a dozen brood mares were grazing. Checking the stable to make certain the slave had cleaned it, he complimented him before issuing a reprimand.

"The stable has seldom looked better, but you should be grooming our stock, not merely admiring it."

Brendan rose to his feet with a lazy stretch. He had removed his kirtle to enjoy the warmth of the sun, but donned it again before walking over to the wall where Erik stood. "They need an opportunity to get used to my scent, and it's always wise to observe horses in order to understand their temperaments before working with them."

Knowing that each animal did indeed have its own unique personality and quirks, Erik nevertheless appeared skeptical. "Just what have you learned this morning?"

Brendan casually leaned back against the wall. "Sky Dancer is naturally protective of his mares, but he has a very good disposition in addition to speed. It's no wonder your father is so proud of him. These mares are all equally fine, as are the horses you use for riding. I've not had time to observe the yearlings or two-year-olds, but if Sky Dancer sired them all, I've no doubt they are outstanding animals too."

"Yes, they are," Erik agreed with justifiable pride. "Haakon sells any that don't measure up to his high standard. Two of the mares should foal soon. The gray is Freya's horse, Light of Dawn, so you'll need to keep a close eye on her. Her last foal was sickly and didn't live. I'd hate to see that happen again, but I'm more worried about the mare. Freya would be heartbroken if we lost her."

Brendan pursed his lips thoughtfully, wondering if this wouldn't be a good time to propose a bargain. Being a daring individual, he decided it was. "You don't let bad news of any kind reach Freya's ears, do you?" he asked slyly.

The change in the Celt's expression alarmed Erik, and he grew wary. "As I told you, she's very dear to me. It's quite natural that I'd want to spare her grief."

"Of course," Brendan concurred. "So she knows nothing about what happened yesterday, does she?"

"There was no reason to upset her with tales of your

disobedience, if that's what you mean," Erik replied sarcastically.

"Nor of her own son's?"

Unwilling to justify his actions to a slave, even a strong and clever one, Erik drew himself up to his full height before speaking. "What Dana and I wish to confide or conceal is none of your business."

"I happen to think that it is," the Celt contradicted as he turned to face Erik squarely. "I understand that Freya isn't well enough to manage this farm, but why do you let Dana give the orders? You're not only several years older, but a man. Why isn't the greater authority yours?"

When Erik's violet eyes narrowed to menacing slits, Brendan was grateful for the wall that separated them, but he didn't back down. "Just hear me out. I think you and I can strike a bargain that would be advantageous to us both. To enhance your position, I'll do only what you tell me, and conveniently forget Dana's orders. That will make you look forceful while she'll appear incompetent. I'll also go along with you to make Freya believe the life here is placid, even if that's not the case, but I'll expect certain favors in return."

Erik immediately struck Brendan with a vicious back-handed blow that caught the startled slave on the right cheek and nearly knocked him off his feet. "You'll get meals as long as you work. That's the only bargain we'll ever have," he informed the badly bruised man in a threatening hiss. "Now see to my horse first, and then all of the others as you were told to do."

Brendan slumped against the wall as the dark-haired man strode away. The acrid taste of hatred boiled up in his throat. It nearly choked him, and he spit in the dirt, disgusted that he had not made the defiant gesture in Erik's face.

It took a moment for Brendan's anger to subside enough for him to think clearly, but even then he still didn't understand what he had done wrong. A lifetime of experience had taught him that selfishness was a common human failing. As a handsome youth he had discovered most women wanted skilled lovers who praised their beauty even if it was merely a convincing lie. It had taken him slightly longer to understand that what men craved most was power and prestige.

On Haakon's farm those rules didn't seem to apply, and he was becoming increasingly more confused as a result. Dana's reaction to him had been hostile in the extreme. She was not attracted to him as women usually were. On the contrary, she seemed to take a great deal of pleasure in despising him. While only that morning he had had high hopes that she would eventually change her view of him, he now had his doubts.

And Erik had to be daft. That was the only explanation Brendan could imagine regarding Erik's refusal of a bargain that would have afforded him control over his father's farm. His pride aching as badly as his battered cheek, Brendan completed his chores, but he moved without a trace of the ambition he had felt earlier.

In order to avoid speaking with Brendan, Dana left her mare tethered outside the stable after her ride. She insisted that Thora do the same with Rascal. It wasn't until that evening when she escorted Moira to Erik's house that she saw him again.

She had intended to introduce the thrall to Moira, and then leave so she could truthfully tell her mother that the pair had met. The change in the slave's appearance was so disturbing, however, that she completely forgot why she had accompanied Moira on her errand.

When Brendan opened the door and found Dana and a young serving girl bearing a heavily laden tray, he moved out of their way but not before Dana had seen his right cheek was badly bruised and his eye nearly swollen shut. He had had only a few slight cuts and scrapes after his last fight with Erik, but she was amazed that he appeared to be the loser in this fight. As the only slave on their farm, she had not considered how one of the servants might take advantage of him or abuse him, but that appalling possibility occurred to her now.

"Tell me who hit you, and I'll see they're punished immediately. You needn't follow the orders of anyone but my mother, Erik, or me. If someone else thinks they can make you do their work, I'll tell them just how wrong they are before your supper has had time to cool."

Rather than reply, Brendan took a deep breath and held it a long moment. He already knew Erik and Dana kept things hidden from Freya, but they were seemingly not all that open with each other. He was in no mood for intrigues that night. "I'll survive," was all he said.

Moira set the tray by the hearth, where the meal would remain warm, then returned to the door. Being so near Brendan frightened her, and she stole only a quick glance at him before whispering, "Excuse me," as she slipped past Dana and hurriedly returned to the main house.

Moira's exit didn't distract Dana, and she repeated her demand. When Brendan again refused to provide a name, she tried another approach to learn the identity of his assailant. "Just because you and I don't get along is no reason for you to protect someone who's been mean to you. Are you afraid if you tell me who did that to you, they'll do something worse tomorrow? You needn't worry. I'll send them away tonight. We've plenty of servants. We don't need one who has nothing better to do than mistreat you."

"I'm not afraid of him," Brendan finally announced with a faint smile. He had not expected Dana to be angered when what he had suffered was really only a small fraction of the abuse he was used to taking. He couldn't help but hope her reason was a personal one. His spirits soared at that possibility. "I didn't think that you cared what happened to me," he murmured in an invitingly husky tone as his gaze locked with hers.

Dana clenched her fists at her sides, steeling herself to ignore the insolence of his glance. "You're a valuable piece of property, so I have no choice but to care about what happens to you until I can hand you back over to Jørn," she informed him flippantly, but when his slight smile vanished she recognized instantly that she had hurt him. The man was exasperating in the extreme, but she had not thought he possessed any feelings. That he clearly had surprised her. It also made her far too aware of him as a man who possessed a full range of emotions, and she didn't like that feeling one bit. Reminding herself she had meant to speak with him only when she had a specific task to assign him, she returned to the original subject of their discussion.

"Let's not argue. Just tell me the man's name, and I'll send him away tonight. That will keep anyone else from bothering you."

"I can take care of myself," Brendan insisted stubbornly, his hopes that she might come to care for him dashed. It was now obvious she put him in the same category as the animals on the farm, and his only value was in his price. "You needn't trouble yourself about me," he continued, adopting his oft-worn sneer.

"Must you be so obstinate?"

"In this matter, yes."

As he approached his house, Erik overheard the last of Dana and Brendan's conversation. He stepped up to the door and quickly satisfied his half sister's curiosity. "I hit him, Dana. He insulted me, and I made him pay for it. There's nothing more to it than that. Now come, we must hurry. Freya is waiting supper for us."

When Erik took her arm to escort her to the evening meal, Dana looked back over her shoulder at Brendan. He was watching her with a puzzled stare she didn't quite know how to interpret. All she did know was that finding him battered had been strangely disturbing, but she could not imagine why.

"What did he say to you?" she whispered to Erik.

"Nothing that I'll repeat."

Understanding precisely how difficult Brendan could be, Dana let the matter drop. They hurried into the house and were delighted to find Freya feeling well enough to suggest they entertain.

Once everyone had been served freshly caught codfish that had been steamed to perfection, Freya began to make plans for the coming week. "Is there time to invite Grena's family to go out with you for one last day of hunting with the falcons, Erik? Her twins enjoyed it so much last year. Since their father's death, they've had few opportunities to go on a hunt. Berit and Dana can watch the children so you aren't distracted. Why don't you take Brendan too? I'm certain it would be helpful to have another man along."

"I'll be there," Soren pointed out sullenly. "I can take care of my cousins better than a thrall can."

"Of course you can, my darling," Freya instantly agreed. "But I want you to enjoy the day without having to worry about being responsible for the others."

Mollified by his mother's considerate comment, Soren devoted his energies to consuming his supper while Erik and Dana exchanged a meaningful glance. Each thought the day of hunting would be fun, but neither was pleased by the prospect of taking Brendan along or of allowing Soren to ride again so soon.

"Let's plan the hunt for the day after tomorrow," Erik suggested, attempting to share Freya's enthusiasm. "With Light of Dawn and Spring Blossom ready to foal, I'd rather Brendan remained here."

"I can't recall the last time we had a foal born during the day," Freya remarked thoughtfully. "Let's wait until the morning of the hunt and then decide what to do about him."

"As you wish," Erik agreed reluctantly. When Thora suggested she and Dana ride to Grena's the next morning to deliver the invitation, he was sorry he had not volunteered first, but then quickly thought better of the idea. The less he saw of the delectable Berit, the easier it would be to pretend she did not exist. Plans for the hunt and talk of the delicious meal that would follow took up the remainder of the evening, and it wasn't until he returned to his house that Erik again thought of the slave who would be there.

Brendan had expected no more than bread and water, and when he found his supper tray contained a fine meal he was too delighted to question why. He ate slowly, savoring each bite of flaky white fish, tangy morsel of cheese, and crusty slice of bread. There was a bowl of berries too, and cream to pour over them. He had not eaten such a delicious meal in a long while and had just finished when Erik entered.

Now certain it had been unwise to quarter the slave in his house, Erik was sorry he had not arranged to move him elsewhere. Because he had neglected to do that, he promptly made his feelings plain. "You'll sleep under my roof only as long as you can keep your thoughts to yourself. Is that understood?''

The Celt nodded. He knew it had been a grave mistake on his part to expect the people here to behave as others he had known when their actions had been so unpredictable. He simply did not know enough about them yet to better his position. As he contemplated the fact that he was living in Erik's house, wearing his clothes, and undoubtedly had been given a meal as fine as the one served in the main house, he knew he should be satisfied with his situation for the moment, but inwardly he rebelled. He would be satisfied with nothing less than total freedom.

"I meant only to help us both," he offered apologetically, but he was simply confused rather than being truly sorry for insulting him.

Erik found the comment very amusing. "Offering to stir up trouble between Dana and me is scarcely what I'd call help." As he removed the hay-filled mattress that was stored beneath one of the benches during the day, he explained why. "Have you no brothers or sisters that you love? Would you be pleased if someone tried to pit one of you against the other?"

Brendan rose to help Erik arrange his mattress, and when he was tossed blankets and a feather-filled quilt to make his own bed on the bench on the opposite side of the room, he thought again that he should be grateful for what he had, but he wasn't. "Not all families are like yours," was all he cared to contribute to their conversation.

Erik waited a moment, but when Brendan offered no information about himself, he doubted he ever would. "I'm going out for a walk. I'll see you in the morning. I hope tomorrow will be better than today."

"So do I," Brendan murmured to himself as Erik left. He had worked hard all day, and was relieved not to be ordered to do more. He soon went to sleep, but he had no dreams of lovely redheads that night.

Dana shared a sleeping chamber with Thora, but while the little girl fell asleep as rapidly as she always did, Dana's thoughts were far too troubling to allow her to rest as easily.

Her insomnia began when she allowed her thoughts to wander to the summer's end. Her father and Svien would return home, but that pleasant prospect was swiftly overtaken by the realization Jarald would be coming home then too.

While she had always found her mother's advice valuable, Dana was certain Freya's estimate of Jarald's good points was too generous. As she saw it, the man had nothing but wealth to recommend him, and while she knew many young women would consider that enough, she did not. Oh, he was pleasant to look at, she had to give him that. His hair was very blond and his eyes an attractive sea green. He was tall, and while he was heavyset, there was nothing soft or effeminate about him. On the contrary, his manner was most definitely masculine, but she just didn't like the man. In her opinion he was loud, coarse, and rude, hardly the qualities she, or any intelligent woman, would admire in a husband.

Dana tossed and turned, tangling her long legs in her quilt as she wished Jarald and her father weren't such close friends. The likely possibility their friendship might come to an abrupt end when she refused to become Jarald's wife frightened her. If Jarald didn't accept her decision graciously, the two men might even become the bitterest of enemies. That would lead to terrible strife between their families. If that happened, it would be entirely Jarald's fault, not hers, although Dana knew she would be called fickle and given all the blame. She hoped Jarald would not want her for his wife if she did not love him, no matter how enthusiastic he had been about the match, but the more she thought about his reaction, the more apprehensive she became.

She realized that she should have told him how she felt before he left, she mused regretfully, so that he would have had the entire summer to get over her rejection. She didn't think she could possibly stall him until spring, as her mother had suggested. There was no point in even making that effort, as it would only prolong the ordeal of his visits and not save him a moment's suffering when her opinion of him would never change. It would be far better to tell Jarald the truth when next she saw him so he could expend his energies courting some other young woman who found him more personable than she did.

That painful matter finally settled in her mind, if not in fact, Dana rolled over on her stomach and propped her chin on her crossed arms. She was looking forward to going hunting with Erik, and even if her mother made them take Brendan along, she doubted he would ruin the day. They could leave him with the horses, or assign him some other chore so he would not only make himself useful but also stay out of their way. That was undoubtedly the best way to handle the man.

With two notable exceptions, she thought Brendan had gotten along better that day than on his first with them, so with any luck his behavior would continue to improve. He had too aggressive a manner and that was disconcerting. Perhaps all the men from Erin were so forward with women, but she could not believe he didn't know a slave had to treat his mistress with more respect.

The sudden memory of the feel of his lips caressing her palm made Dana's whole hand tingle. That surprising sensation puzzled her because at the time she had wanted only to punish him for taking such a shocking liberty. Now, in retrospect, the gesture did not seem so terribly unpleasant, merely inappropriate. Even if her plan to speak with him only about chores hadn't been a complete success, she had lost her patience with him only once that day, and that was a marked improvement over their bitter confrontations yesterday.

She laughed softly to herself. If she practiced speaking to Brendan without provoking heated arguments, perhaps by the time Jarald came home she would be able to refuse his proposal so diplomatically he would not feel more than a tiny twinge of disappointment. When a wide yawn interrupted Dana's reverie, she realized her problems were nearly solved. Gradually she drifted off to sleep.

On the morning of the hunt, Erik was relieved to find Light of Dawn and Spring Blossom grazing placidly, with no sign that birth was imminent in either mare, but he was disappointed to have thought of no other excuse to exclude Brendan. The slave might prove helpful, but there was also the more likely chance he would cause a disturbance that would ruin everyone's fun. More importantly, Erik didn't want the handsome Celt around Berit, despite her reassurance that she cared nothing for the man.

Freya studied Erik's uncharacteristic frown and totally misread its cause. She had come outside when Grena's family had arrived, and slipped her arm around her stepson's waist as she whispered so they would not be overheard. "I'm so sorry, Erik. I should have spoken with you privately before I suggested inviting your cousins to come today. I didn't realize this might not be as enjoyable for you as it will be for them."

Erik hastened to reassure her that was not the case. "We all discussed it together, Freya, and if I'd not wanted to take everyone hunting I'd have said so then. I'm just trying to decide how far away I want to go today, that's all." He smiled then, bathing her in the warmth of a captivating grin that immediatley convinced her of the truth of his words.

Unfortunately, Erik found himself at a disadvantage when the gracious woman relieved him of the burden of the last-minute preparations for the outing so he could attend to the falcons. When he had the magnificent birds of prey ready to depart, Brendan had already been told to saddle a horse to accompany him, and Erik had to resign himself to the fact he could not leave him behind.

Grena never ran out of conversation and was looking forward to spending a restful day with her sister while their children were occupied elsewhere. When Brendan moved by her to carry the last of the baskets containing food for a midday meal, his appearance had improved so greatly since he had left her home that she didn't recognize him.

"Who is that man? I don't recall seeing him here before today," she asked with an appreciative glance which raked over the handsome slave as she took in the width of his broad shoulders and the lean perfection of his superb build.

"That's Brendan, Mother," Berit explained happily. "He's just cut his hair and put on new clothes is all. I'll admit he looks far better, but not so different I'd not have known him."

Chagrined by so silly a mistake, Grena blushed deeply,

but she didn't take her eyes off Brendan as he worked to secure the baskets to the back of his saddle. "Are you certain you're taking along enough for the boys to eat? You know how often they complain of hunger."

"They'll be too busy to eat, Mother. Don't worry about them. Besides, we want them to be hungry enough to enjoy supper tonight." Berit kissed her mother and aunt farewell, then mounted her horse and took her place beside Dana, who was already seated astride her beribboned mare.

When Freya had told Brendan he would be needed that day to watch the children and assist Erik, he hadn't believed his luck. He had replied he would be happy to watch the children all day long, but he hadn't mentioned that he was grateful for the chance to see that Dana came to no harm either.

His eye was no longer swollen, and the bruise on his cheek had faded to the point it resembled a smudge of dirt, and Freya hadn't noticed it. He had planned to lie had she asked him about it, though. Even if he hadn't been able to interest Erik in a bargain, he knew he ought to go along with everyone else and protect Freya from worry. During their two conversations, her sincerity and sweetness had been so genuine he had found it impossible to dislike her. That troubled him more than his desire for Dana did. He could rationalize his interest in her beautiful daughter, but to admire a Danish woman for her kindness struck him as a foolish weakness he might soon come to regret.

As everyone got ready to leave, Brendan was grateful that Erik hadn't needed any help with his three falcons, as the thrall had never trusted the regal birds. Their wickedly hooked beaks and sharp talons signaled danger so clearly he skirted their three-sided enclosure each time he left Erik's house. To avoid damage to their feathers, the falcons were not kept in cages. Instead, they sat atop perches out in the open, held in place by a leash attached to the jesses, the leather straps fastened to their legs. Ingeniously connected by a swivel, the birds could move about without becoming entangled in their leashes, but they could not fly away.

Because they were traveling some distance, a cadge was used to transport the falcons. Consisting of a wooden frame worn over a cadger's shoulders, it provided a comfortable perch for the birds and enabled the falconer to take more than one bird into the field. In an effort to involve Soren in the sport as more than a spectator, Erik had asked him if he would like to be the cadger that day, and the boy had beamed with pride as though the chore were an honor. Erik chuckled to himself as their small procession left the farm, for he had found a way to not only make Soren walk, which was his punishment for riding Sleipner, but also to make him enjoy it.

Erik led the way with two of his father's hunting dogs and Soren and the falcons behind him. Then came Dana and Berit riding side by side, while Thora preferred staying back a way with the twins because they always let her join in their games. Brendan brought up the rear, but he was enjoying not having to work at physical labor and didn't consider being last demeaning. The day was warm, and while his mount was a fine bay gelding, he wished more than once he could have ridden Sky Dancer again.

Erik turned often to glance over his shoulder at Soren, and each time, his half brother waved and smiled. I will have to give him more of my time, Erik thought to himself. While the lad had shown no interest in the falcons before that day, the majestic birds clearly had his full attention now, and that would be a good place to start. Hoping to find pheasant, Erik led the hunting party well past the boundary of the farm, through the cool depths of the adjoining woods, and out into an open meadow.

Once everyone had dismounted and Soren had placed the cadge on the ground, Erik motioned for them to come close and be silent as he issued a stern warning to Grena's twins. "It's been a long while since our last hunt, and I don't want you to forget that the falcons are not merely pretty pets who like to strut and sing. You must not touch them, nor distract them in any way. First, the dogs will find the pheasants nesting in the grass. When they take to the air, I will send up one of the falcons to make the kill."

Brendan moved up close behind Dana and watched as Erik pulled a thick leather gauntlet on his left hand. He then stepped over to the cadge and unfastened the swivel and leash from one of the peregrines. Relishing the coming kill, she stepped up on his padded wrist, her long-clawed, yellow feet taking a firm grip as his thumb closed over her jesses. He turned so the bird would face into the morning breeze, and it ruffled her feathers softly. Her breast was beige with a soft pink tinge while her back, wings, and tail were a dark brown that would appear black once she took to the air.

Confident the bird was eager to fly, Erik sent the dogs out, and as predicted they soon flushed a plump pheasant. As her quarry struggled into a clumsy flight, Erik removed the falcon's hood and immediately her dark eyes adjusted to the brightness of the morning sun. He cast her off, and she soared into the air, a vision of deadly grace as she rose higher and higher. She circled for a moment, then drew in her wings and plunged toward the earth, diving for the hapless pheasant and an inevitable kill.

Fascinated by the falcon's beauty and prowess, Dana didn't realize Brendan was standing so near until he whispered softly in her ear, "Falconers train only female birds because they are far better hunters than males. Do you suppose the lust for blood is part of every female's nature?"

Startled not only by the sound of his voice but also by the impertinence of his question, Dana turned slowly to face him. Erik had loaned him a pale blue kirtle that day, and it not only complemented his dark tan, but enhanced the sapphire sparkle in his eyes as well. A playful smile tugged at the corners of his mouth, but she was not amused. As always, he was far too sure of himself and actually seemed to be enjoying baiting her. She had already planned her strategy for dealing with him, however, and did not react angrily.

"Be careful, Brendan," she warned in a lighthearted tone. "Or some of the blood spilled here today may well be yours." When his taunting smile became what she considered a lewd grin, Dana turned her back on him before he could reply. She could feel his presence like the warmth of a winter cloak, but she pretended not to notice and did not move away.

Brendan was quite pleased with their exchange until he recalled Erik had mentioned that Dana carried a knife. She was again dressed in green that day, and the flowing tunic that covered her chemise was open at the sides, allowing a glimpse of the narrow leather belt that encircled her waist. Did she truly wear a knife suspended from it? He licked his lips as he decided that before the day was over he would satisfy his curiosity on that point and, he hoped, several others.

CHAPTER VII

While Brendan drank in the marvelous fragrance of Dana's perfume and fought against the nearly overwhelming impulse to slip his arms around her waist and draw her back against him, Dana continued to give Erik her full attention, as though the most distracting man she had ever met were not standing so close he was undoubtedly treading on her hem. Completely unaware of the silent interplay of emotions taking place at her side, Berit was hanging on Erik's every word, fascinated by the ease with which he handled the falcons.

He called each by her name, his voice soft and yet commanding as he released them in turn to take to the sky. There were small brass bells affixed to their jesses so they could be found should they stray, but none did. They flew with the effortless ease of their kind, gliding on the wind currents, circling their prey, and then swooping down, their talon-tipped feet outstretched as they overtook their hapless quarry with unerring accuracy.

"How did you teach them to relinquish their prey?" Berit asked in a breathless whisper as the last bird to fly returned to Erik's padded wrist.

Pleased to see by her rapt expression that she was

genuinely interested, Erik readily explained. "It's a matter of trust. The falcon learns she will be well rewarded for her work, so she has no fear of going hungry. You must remember this bird is an eyas, one taken from the aerie when she was newly hatched, as were the others. I trained them to hunt as they do, and these three were all apt pupils. A hawk of passage is caught during its migration and tamed. That's another challenge altogether."

"I'm sure it is," Brendan remarked with bitter irony. "It's always more difficult to tame an animal that has tasted freedom."

Erik frowned slightly, but he did not scold Brendan for speaking out of turn. He merely nodded to concede the point and then asked if anyone else would like to don a glove and send the falcon up to hunt. When Soren immediately volunteered, he gave the boy some additional instruction and then allowed him to take charge of the bird. He had wisely chosen to have the most docile of the three fly last, so an accident would be unlikely, but he again stressed the need for caution, as her talons were as sharp as the others'.

Soren had hunted with Eric before, but not recently, and he had not recalled it being such a thrill. When the falcon was again in the air, he knew he would never be happy until he had one of his very own. "Could you take me to where you caught these, Erik, so I could find one to raise?"

"Would you like that?"

"Oh, yes, very much," Soren enthused as he watched the falcon flying overhead.

Erik glanced toward Dana, and seeing her encouraging smile, he agreed. "I'm afraid we would be too late to find a bird of the right age this year, Soren, but we can start to look for one early next spring if you're still interested."

His gaze firmly glued to the soaring falcon, Soren nodded vigorously. "Oh, yes, I'll still want one."

Neither Thora nor the twins shared Soren's sudden love for birds of prey, and they were content to watch the hunt without taking an active part. The sport was exciting, the time passed quickly, and soon the sun was high overhead, signaling the morning's end.

"We've enough pheasant to feed the whole household,"

Erik remarked proudly as he slipped the hood over the head of the bird that had just landed on his wrist. He bent down to return her to the cadge and fastened her leash before straightening up. "Let's all move over into the shade of the trees and have something to eat."

Rather than bump into the thrall, Dana remained in place until she heard Brendan move away. She knew he had been talking about himself when he had mentioned the difficulty in taming animals that had tasted freedom, and she was glad Erik had accepted the comment so graciously. Brendan had then stood silently at her back for the remainder of the hunt, but how could she have forgotten that she had intended to tell him to stay with the horses?

Not about to let the man confuse her thinking any further, Dana chose a place where the grass was thick for their picnic, and Soren brought the cadge into the shade nearby. With their hoods covering their eyes, the falcons thought night had fallen and slept contentedly.

Erik spread out a blanket to sit on, and Brendan brought over the baskets of food. He moved out of the way as Dana and Berit took their time to arrange the picnic meal attractively while the children complained they were much too slow. With good-natured playfulness the pretty women ignored their younger siblings' comments until they had everything prepared to their satisfaction.

They had brought cheese, dried fish, bread, and fruit for what had been planned as a light snack, but as the children sat down it was clear they planned to make a full meal of it. Erik poured ale for the young women and himself, and buttermilk for Soren, Thora, and the twins. He then leaned back against the oak which shaded their blanket, content to wait for the ample meal they would have that evening. With that same thought in mind, Dana and Berit took only a piece of fruit to enjoy with their ale.

When everyone had begun to eat, Dana looked up just as Brendan turned away and started toward the horses which had been left at a distance to graze on the succulent grass encircling the trees. She had succeeded in putting him out of her mind for the moment, but now she was overwhelmed with guilt. He hadn't asked for anything, nor had he made any pointed remarks about being left out. As a thrall, he was probably used to eating whatever scraps he was thrown, but unlike the hunting dogs which lay at Erik's side, he had not been content to wait for such meager fare.

"Erik," Dana whispered anxiously, "what should we do about Brendan?"

Brendan was by that time seated on the far side of the horses, so Erik saw no reason to whisper as he answered her question. "We'll just give him whatever is left."

"If the boys don't slow down, there might not be anything left," Berit teased as she winked at her brothers. At twelve they were almost as tall as Soren, and their appetites were as hearty as their mother had predicted.

Dana noted how rapidly the bread and cheese were disappearing, and instantly came to a decision. She gathered what she considered an adequate portion for a man, and since there was no extra tankard, she refilled her own with ale.

"What are you doing?" Erik asked incredulously.

"Brendan's not caused us any trouble today, so there's no reason why he shouldn't be given something to eat." Dana didn't give Erik time to object. She rose to her feet and started off toward the slave as though she routinely carried him his meals.

Brendan was looking the other way. He didn't really know what he had expected from Dana and Erik, but simply being ignored certainly wasn't it. After enduring three wretched years of slavery, it still hurt to be treated with such casual indifference. He had once had so much, and he would never grow accustomed to having nothing. It was worse to be reminded so forcefully that he was an outsider in a land he despised. The sadness of his situation ate at him with a gnawing pain which overcame whatever feelings of hunger he might have had. He didn't care if he didn't eat until midnight. He didn't care at all.

When she reached him, Dana was discouraged by the bitterness of Brendan's expression, but having brought him something to eat, she could scarcely turn around and walk off without giving it to him. "Brendan," she called softly.

Astonished to have his solitude interrupted, Brendan leapt

to his feet. When Dana held out the tankard and the cloth bulging with bread and cheese, he was absolutely dumbfounded. He took them from her very carefully so as not to spill a drop or crumb. He wanted to reach out and hug her for realizing he was hungry too, but his hands were full and prevented such an unbridled show of gratitude.

Dana watched a look of wonder replace the one of stunned disbelief that had first crossed Brendan's features, and began to laugh. "It's only some bread and cheese. I've not brought you an entire banquet."

"It's not what you've brought, but that you cared enough to do it," Brendan confided softly, and his glance shone with triumph, as though he had won some important concession from her.

Dana was certain the conceited Celt had again read more into her gesture than was there, but she didn't want to argue about it. "The children will be finished soon. Keep an eye on them so they don't become lost in the woods." She turned away then and hurried back to the others, knowing Brendan would have undoubtedly boldly invited her to sit down with him had she remained any longer.

His mood greatly improved, Brendan again made himself comfortable and enjoyed what he swore was the most delicious bread and cheese he had ever eaten. By the time Soren, Thora, and the twins were scampering about, he had finished eating and had quenched his thirst with ale. In an ebullient mood, he remained close to the children, who were playing a spirited game of tag, but Dana was never out of his thoughts. The beautiful young woman had again confused him completely, but he hoped before too much longer he would understand her better than she understood herself.

As they continued to sit together. Erik was grateful for Dana's presence, for she kept the conversation flowing smoothly without the awkward pauses they had experienced when he and Berit had spoken alone. The two young women were a delightful pair, witty and sweet, and he enjoyed sitting between them so much that he was completely relaxed and in no hurry to return home. Just hearing the bright sparkle of their laughter and watching the prettiness of their smiles made his day complete.

Berit toyed with the end of her braid as time and again her gaze lingered on Erik's face. He had a slight cleft in his chin, and she couldn't help but wonder if her thumb wouldn't fit that indentation perfectly if she reached over to draw his mouth to hers. She had not forgotten that he had kissed her good-bye the last time they were together, and she hoped he would take the same liberty that day.

Dana was also enjoying the beauty of the afternoon, but she grew increasingly aware of the intensity of the glances that were passing between her cousin and her half brother. Berit had always been flirtatious, but she seemed even more so that day, while Erik's wide grins and deep laughter continually encouraged the blonde to be coy. They might have grown up together, but Dana was quite perceptive and noticed the difference in the way Berit and Erik treated each other now.

She envied them their enjoyment of what appeared to be a budding romance, but at the same time, she knew that Grena was unlikely to think Erik a proper suitor for her only daughter. If the two were merely flirting to pass the time on a lazy afternoon, that was one thing, but if it was an indication of feelings that were far deeper, she feared they would face many problems to solve. She recalled Jarald, and her blissful mood was spoiled. She excused herself to go check on the children, who had all disappeared into the woods, although their laughter could still be heard.

"I know the boys won't come to any harm, but I want to make certain Thora isn't trying too hard to keep up with them," Dana explained as she rose to her feet.

Erik shaded his eyes as he looked up to gauge the position of the sun. "Wait. We ought to be going soon. I'll go and get them."

"No, sit still, I'll do it." Dana waved as she started off in the direction from which the last boisterous shouts had been heard. She was eager for a bit of exercise to clear her mind of thoughts of Jarald and her regrets for the unwanted romance she had been foolish not to discourage from the very beginning.

Unable to believe her luck, Berit watched Dana enter the trees before she turned back to face Erik. "Did you plan this outing today so we'd have a chance to be together?" she asked, an impish sparkle dancing in her eyes.

Erik stared at his pretty companion, amazed she would make such an assumption in light of the subject of their two disastrous conversations at her house. "No," he denied. "This was Freya's idea."

"Really?" Berit licked her lips suggestively as she moved closer to his side. "That was very sweet of her."

"Berit," Erik pleaded with a low moan as she leaned closer still. He knew he ought to get up and start gathering everything so they would be ready to go when Dana returned with the children. His body, however, refused to obey such a sensible command.

Berit reached out to caress his cheek, and knowing exactly what she wanted most, she dropped her hand to his shoulder and pulled him forward. "Come here," she whispered seductively. Their lips met, and she sighed softly, immensely pleased to feel him slip his arms around her waist rather than draw away.

Erik thought himself pitifully weak where Berit was concerned, but for the moment he wanted only to enjoy himself. He savored her first kiss, and then another, and soon the taste of her was so delicious he had lost count of how many times his lips had received a sweet response from hers. Her perfume was a delicate floral fragrance that blended perfectly with the fresh scents of the sunlit afternoon, and he began to worry that he might never have his fill of her enticing affection.

Dana followed the sounds of the boys' voices and Thora's high-pitched giggles. They were running to and fro, still playing tag as they dashed in and out of the trees. She called out to them, but they were so absorbed in their game they didn't hear her.

Brendan didn't hear Dana either, but when he caught sight of her approaching, he hid behind a tree. While he hadn't joined in the children's games, he had been enjoying watching them and was in a decidedly playful mood. When the lithe redhead reached his hiding place, he stepped out and caught her hand.

"I didn't have a chance to thank you properly for providing me with one of the most splendid meals I've ever had the privilege to eat," he began with a ready grin.

While he had startled her, Brendan's mood was so lighthearted Dana was neither frightened nor offended. "You must have had some very bad meals then," she responded at the same time she tried to withdraw her hand from his, but he didn't release her. Instead, he not only tightened his grasp, but drew her near.

Brendan watched as Dana's lashes fluttered slightly. She had the most incredibly lovely eyes he had ever seen, and he knew the rest of her delectable body was just as beautiful. He dared step no closer, for his desire for her would have been shockingly plain if he pressed against her. "Don't forbid me to repay you in the only way I can," he ordered firmly, but his smile was charming rather than threatening.

Enveloped in the warmth of his easy embrace, Dana had only a split second to decide she liked Brendan's smile ever so much better than his frown. His mouth covered hers, and when she tried to protest, his tongue slid between her lips to muffle the sound. He kissed her the same way Jarald always had, with a fierce possessiveness that both appalled and repelled her. Rebelling against such unwanted domination, she reached for her knife, but Brendan's hand locked around her wrist before she could free it from its sheath at her belt.

"I'm too valuable to kill," he scolded as he released her from the near suffocating kiss, but he continued to grip her hand tightly. "How could you have forgotten that?" Brendan's expression was far from charming now. He was staring down at her, a scornful sneer twisting his handsome features into a mask of hatred.

"How dare you be angry with me?" Dana exclaimed. "How dare you?"

Brendan considered the question absurd. "I only wanted to kiss you. You needn't have tried to kill me," he shouted right back at her.

"I was not trying to kill you!" Dana shrieked, and then fearing the children would overhear their argument, she lowered her voice to a discreet, if still belligerent, whisper. "You are not supposed to kiss me, and most especially not like that."

"What angered you most? That I kissed you, or the way that I did it?" Brendan relaxed his hold on her wrist, but when she only glared at him he didn't release her. "Must I wait until you want to kiss me to learn what you like?"

"That will be an exceedingly long wait," Dana hissed through clenched teeth. "It's time to go. Call the children."

The sharply voiced order was like a slap in the face, and Brendan reacted just as negatively. "Call them yourself. I'll see to the horses." He dropped her hand and turned away, but the sound of a scream stopped him cold. Certain it was Thora who was shrieking hysterically, he sprinted off toward the sound.

Dana grabbed her flowing tunic to keep from tripping over the hem and followed right after him. Brendan ran with the same fluid coordination that marked all his motions, and while she couldn't begin to keep up with him, fortunately they didn't have far to go.

The more talkative of Grena's twins, Olaf, saw Brendan dashing toward them and ran to meet him. "Thora climbed a tree to hide from us, and now she can't get down. Soren went up after her, and that's when she started screaming. She's afraid he'll drop her if he tries to carry her down."

Brendan was glad to see that Soren cared enough about his little sister to make such an effort, but it was as obvious to him as it was to Thora that her brother wouldn't be strong enough to bring her down the tree safely. They were perhaps fifteen feet off the ground, a distance he knew must seem enormous to the stranded child. "Come down, Soren, and I'll go up and get her."

Soren opened his mouth to argue, but when Thora began to wail even louder, he was so insulted he gave up his attempt to rescue her. "You stay put, you hear?" he told the frightened child before swinging himself down to a lower branch.

When Soren reached the ground, Dana drew him into an affectionate hug before scolding him. "You were supposed to keep an eye on your sister. What happened?"

Soren mumbled the same explanation Olaf had given, then pulled free of Dana's arms. His face showing disgust at the situation his little sister had gotten herself into, he went over to stand beside the twins.

"Don't worry," Brendan boasted confidently to Dana. "I'll bring her right down."

"Wait, I'll go and get Erik," Dana insisted, and she reached out to grab Brendan's arm.

"I can do it," the slave assured her. He brushed her hand away, and with an agile leap he started up the tree.

By the time Brendan reached her, Thora's screams had lessened to mere whimpers, but tears were still streaming down her cheeks. Her resemblance to Dana was so striking he couldn't help but wonder if she had also been such an adventuresome child. Deciding she must have been, he reached out to pat Thora's knee sympathetically, wishing all the while that he might someday have such a good excuse to touch Dana.

"Don't cry, little one. Do you think you can put your arms around my neck so I can carry you down on my back?"

Thora sniffed loudly before she spoke. "Yes, but I should have been able to get down all by myself."

"Going up is always easier than getting back down. I don't know how many times I got stuck up in a tree before I discovered that."

"You got stuck in a tree?"

"Had to sit there all night one time." Brendan kept talking, embellishing his tale as she clasped her tiny hands around his neck. Taking a firm grip on her arm so there was no danger that she might fall, he continued to recount the horrors of that unfortunate night until he at last reached the ground.

Erik stepped up to take Thora, but the spirited child insisted on having Brendan carry her back to the horses. Pleased that she felt so secure with him, the slave looked back over his shoulder and called to Dana, "You can thank me later for saving your sister's life."

Because she knew exactly how he would like to be thanked, Dana's cheeks flooded with a bright blush. "Come on, boys, let's go,'' she called brightly, and hoping they wouldn't notice the depth of her embarrassment, she quickly followed Brendan.

When Soren and the twins had walked by them, Erik bent down to give Berit one last kiss. He had never thought merely kissing a woman could be so enjoyable, but he was grateful Thora's screams had interrupted them before he had been tempted to lead the affectionate blonde any further.

Berit, however, thought it a terrible shame that she had had so little time alone with Erik. Brightening at the thought of the evening that lay ahead, she slipped her arm through his and took care not to trip and fall as they left the woods.

When they returned home, Dana cautioned the children to keep Thora's mishap a secret from her mother and aunt. Then she and Berit entered the house to help with the preparations for supper. Soren and Erik busied themselves with the falcons, and Brendan was left to care for the horses. He loved roasted pheasant as much as the rest of them, but after his latest argument with Dana, he wasn't sure she would send him any supper, let alone some of the scrumptious game bird.

Dana, however, had no way to deprive Brendan of a fine meal without revealing that the arrogant slave had kissed her, and she was far too embarrassed to admit that. She had to bite her tongue when Berit described to Grena what a help the Celt had been in supervising the children that day. Dana knew Brendan was very helpful at times, but in her opinion he continually created far more problems than he solved.

"You're not sorry that he's here then?" Grena asked Freya, her expression tinged with a hint of doubt.

"Why, no," the delicate woman assured her sister. "He's a very agreeable sort. He's been no trouble at all."

Dana couldn't bear to hear another word of praise for the slave she considered insufferably conceited and demanding. She moved into the kitchen to watch the pheasants roasting on the spit and saw that half of the first one was placed on Brendan's tray. Again insisting Moira carry his meal, she left the house determined to introduce the petite servant properly that evening. Unfortunately, when they reached Erik's house, they found it empty.

"Wait a moment, Moira," Dana insisted. "Maybe Brendan hasn't finished grooming the horses. You wait here while I check the stable."

"I'm needed in the house, mistress," Moira complained apprehensively. She was relieved to find the Celt gone and didn't want to have to wait for him to appear.

"Wait here," Dana commanded firmly as she hurried out the door. She made her way to the stable, but when there was no sign of Brendan inside, she walked around to the back to check the pasture. At that point, she was happy to find the tall blond man standing out with the horses, but before she could call to him, she saw one of the mares sink to her knees. Even from that distance she was certain it was Light of Dawn.

Alarmed, Dana dashed to the gate, flung it open, then slammed it shut behind her and ran through the tall grass to her mother's mare. The gray horse raised her head and gave a feeble whinny when she recognized Dana, but clearly the horse was in pain. Kneeling by her side, the redhead patted her neck with long, reassuring strokes.

"I know it's best to leave the mares alone when they foal, but Light is so precious to us I don't want to take any chances with her."

Brendan watched Dana's graceful gestures, wishing all the while she would show him that same kind of tender concern. "I'll stay with her all night if I must," he assured her. "You can go on back to your guests."

Dana turned to look up at him. "You've watched many a birth?"

Brendan nodded. "A great many."

Dana cast a worried glance over the gray mare. She thought it likely Brendan would know what to do should anything go wrong, but still she couldn't leave. "No, I want to stay. Your supper is waiting for you. Go on back to Erik's and eat. Introduce yourself to Moira, and tell her I said it was all right for her to go back to the house."

Dana had dismissed him again, given him a carefully worded order just as she would a servant, but Brendan refused to go. "My supper can wait." He knelt by her side, and while he did not want to see the mare suffer unnecessarily, he hoped they could pass the entire night together. "How many foals has this mare given you?"

Dana was too distracted to realize Brendan had not done as she had asked. "Dawn's Kiss, my mare, was her first." She hesitated a moment, counting in her head. "There were three others, then the one we lost. That makes this number six."

"She knows what she's doing then," Brendan remarked softly, but he didn't like the way the mare looked either. Her labor had been under way when he had come out to check on her and Spring Blossom, but he had no way of knowing when it had begun.

As they remained side by side, so close their shoulders were touching, Dana found Brendan's presence more comforting than she had thought possible. Rather than pester her with his usual taunts, he spoke only to Light of Dawn, his voice low and soothing, and the mare actually seemed to grow more calm.

"I think she likes you," Dana remarked hesitantly.

"Horses always do," Brendan replied with a shrug.

Dana turned slightly to peek at the Celt through the fringe of her half-lowered lashes. The sun was still hovering on the horizon, and there was light enough for her to see his expression clearly. It was his enormous confidence that was so unsettling, she thought to herself. He was his own man, regardless of the fact Jørn owned him. Jørn, of all people, she scoffed silently, for the handsome thrall had far more intelligence and initiative than his owner any day. Because that had to be an intolerable situation, she couldn't help but feel guilty despite the fact she had had no hand in the transaction that had made him her cousin's property.

As they waited in the meadow, her attention remained more focused on her companion than the mare, but Dana knew his status was not something they could safely discuss. When Jørn returned, she would ask if he planned to allow Brendan to earn his freedom, and if he didn't, well, she would just have to convince him that he would have to allow it. If for no other reason than she simply couldn't bear to think of Brendan causing owner after owner the same endless problems he had caused her, she wanted him to have his freedom. That she might have a more personal interest in him was not something she dared admit.

With a sudden lurch, Light of Dawn struggled to her feet, but when she tried to take a step, she nearly fell. Brendan gave Dana a hand to pull her up, then pushed her aside out of his way. "Something's wrong," he advised with a frown.

"Go and get Erik then."

"No, I don't think there's going to be time." With the mare standing, Brendan had no difficulty examining her, and just as he had feared, the foal was in the wrong position, with the forelegs bent back rather than extended. "Take the mare's head and talk to her so she doesn't get frightened."

"Just what are you going to do?" Dana grabbed Light of Dawn's mane. She couldn't see from where she stood, yet she had no doubt Brendan meant to assist the horse.

"I'm just giving nature a bit of a help, is all," Brendan called as he struggled to push the foal back far enough to allow him to straighten out the forelegs. The head had been in the right position, and once he had realigned the forelegs, the birth proceeded rapidly. Tiny hooves appeared first, then a soft white nose.

Brendan removed his kirtle to wipe off his arms, and allowed the mare to do the rest of the work without further assistance. The horse stood until the withers had appeared, then lay down to expel the rest of the snow-white foal. With Dana kneeling by his side, Brendan used his stained kirtle to dry off the foal, whose legs appeared far too long for his diminutive size, but his eyes were bright as he took his first look at the world.

"Isn't he a beauty?" the Celt exclaimed proudly.

Dana wanted to agree, but tears choked her throat and she could only nod.

"What's the matter?" Brendan inquired. "Didn't you want another stallion as fine as his sire?"

Dana used the front of her tunic to dry her tears as she tried to explain, "I always cry," she sobbed. "Every last time. Lambs, calves, puppies, watching all our animals being born always makes me cry.''

Brendan leaned over the newborn colt to pull the tearful redhead into his arms. Cuddling her cheek against his bare shoulder, he felt the same sense of wonder and joy that had overwhelmed her, but he only wanted to shout with glee rather than weep as she was. He closed his eyes for a moment, savoring the softness of her flowing curls as he stroked her hair lightly. For one brief moment he thought the world perfect and didn't hesitate to whisper his request.

''Show me how you like to be kissed,'' he murmured as his lips caressed the damp curve of her cheek.

As entranced with him as he was with her, Dana lifted her lips to his without a moment's hesitation. She raised her hand to his nape to keep his mouth molded to hers as she opened her lips slightly. Displaying the grace of the most practiced temptress, she slid her tongue between his lips, and with a captivating insouciance created the most memorable kiss he had ever received. It was filled with the delicious flavor of true affection and left him breathless when all too soon she drew away. Brendan could only stare at her in awestruck silence when he saw by the bright color in her cheeks that the emotional splendor they had just shared had also affected her deeply.

Dana had been stunned, for Brendan had just shown her a gentleness she had not suspected he possessed. The colt stirred then, eager to get to his feet, and the loving mood which had enveloped them came to an abrupt end.

''I've got to go and tell the others,'' Dana exclaimed as she rose to her feet. ''This has been such a perfect day, and Mother will be thrilled to know Light of Dawn has given us such a sturdy colt.''

Brendan watched the flame-haired beauty who had just captured his heart race across the pasture with light, dancing steps, and prayed he would be able to find his voice by the time she returned with her family. He didn't know how it had happened, but even though he despised the Danes, he feared he had just fallen in love with the prettiest one he had ever met.

CHAPTER VIII

That night Brendan listened to Erik flip-flopping on his mattress like a fish out of water, and easily surmised the falconer was no more able to sleep than he was. In his case, it was the persistent memory of Dana's luscious kiss that was keeping him awake. He couldn't help but wonder if Erik might not be thinking about a woman too.

"Is Berit your betrothed?" he asked when his curiosity got the better of him and he could no longer keep still.

"What?" Erik replied in a harsh gasp, both dismayed and alarmed at being asked such a personal question.

"You heard me." Brendan stretched out on his back and placed his hands behind his head to make a comfortable pillow while they talked. "Berit's very pretty. She seldom takes her eyes off you, and she often stands close enough to rub up against you. I didn't see you trying to discourage her either."

Realizing he had been holding his breath ever since Brendan had first spoken, Erik exhaled slowly. He hadn't thought their behavior as indiscreet as the slave described, but obviously it had been. If Brendan had noticed, then what about the children? If they had noted that Berit's affection for him was readily returned, wouldn't they soon be teasing them about it? Or worse yet, telling their mothers?

"Berit's my cousin," he answered noncommittally.

"More than one man has married an attractive cousin," Brendan observed smugly.

Again Erik had no ready response. He could not deny that he wanted the delightful blonde, but wanting and having were two entirely different things. He had not even dared hope there might be something more than friendship between them until Berit had made it so shockingly plain that she craved much more.

"She's only sixteen," Erik reminded himself aloud.

"Is that your only objection to her?"

Objection? Erik groaned inwardly at the ridiculousness of that word. How could any man object to a young woman as loving and sweet as Berit? He could as easily object to the warmth of a summer day, or the vibrant beauty of wildflowers, or the magnificence of a falcon in flight.

"I'll not answer your questions," he snapped angrily. "Go to sleep."

Brendan smiled to himself, certain he had discovered something important about the man whose house he shared. "Jørn is hot-tempered too. If he suspects you have taken advantage of his sister's affections, you might need help to defend yourself."

Erik was out of bed before he stopped to analyze the comment. He halted then and stood with his fists clenched at his sides. "What are you threatening? That you'll tell Jørn I'm bedding his sister if I don't give you what you want?"

"You're bedding the girl?" Brendan sat up, as startled by the remark as Erik had been by his. After all, Berit was Erik's cousin, and he had not thought even Danes would sink to seducing their own kin.

"No!" Erik shouted angrily. "And if you think you can threaten me with such a vile lie, we'll settle the matter outside right now."

While Brendan was usually quick to defend his honor, he remained seated on his makeshift bed. There had been a time when he would have threatened anything to get a crust of bread, but not now, not here where the people were kind. It was difficult to explain why, even to himself, but he had no desire to fight Erik ever again.

"You misunderstood me," the Celt began with deliberate care. "I meant that I would take your side, not that I would carry tales."

"Another of your ridiculous attempts to help me?" Erik scoffed. "Like your offer to make Dana look inept?"

"I'll admit that was a mistake," Brendan readily confessed,

but he would not explain what constant floggings and mistreatment did to the soul. He had learned to survive by playing the members of a large household off against each other, and if that method no longer worked, then he hoped he would soon discover another.

His house was dark, and Erik could see only Brendan's dim silhouette. The slave's voice was low and soft, conciliatory rather than belligerent, and suddenly his anger seemed totally misplaced. Erik knew it was bitterness over his fate that was tearing him apart, not worry over what Jørn might do. When he spoke, his voice had a hollow ring, even in his own ears.

"My mother was a thrall. I'm Haakon's firstborn, but a bastard, and of no consequence to him. Because of that misfortune, Grena will never give Berit to me, so nothing can come of what we feel for each other. Forget whatever it was you think you saw. That's all you need do to help me."

"So that's why Dana runs things?" Brendan inquired hurriedly, wanting to keep Erik talking now that he had revealed such an important point about his heritage.

"Yes. There's no reason for me to give orders to anyone but you. I'm employed here as a falconer, nothing more."

"You're wrong," Brendan was quick to argue, for everything he had seen convinced him Erik was a respected member of Haakon's family. "Dana relies on you, Freya as well. Berit adores you. Don't think less of yourself than those women do."

"I've never relied on a thrall for advice, and I'll not begin now," Erik cut him off rudely. He returned to his bed and yanked his quilt up over his ears to drown out any other unwanted comments the Celt might wish to make. He didn't want to talk about himself, not with Brendan nor anyone else. A multitude of women might love him. So what? The only person whose opinion mattered was Haakon, and all he had ever gotten from his father was contempt.

Disappointed that Erik had ended the intensely interesting conversation when he was still so eager to talk, Brendan lay back down, but his mind wasn't ready for sleep. He couldn't help but think how different he and Erik were. He didn't care what people called him, when it was only what he thought of himself that truly mattered. Clearly Erik didn't share that view. Brendan had fought him, though, and knew Erik possessed an admirable toughness not only of body, but of spirit as well. Erik was the type of man he would choose for a friend, if he ever wanted a Dane for a friend, which was highly unlikely.

As Brendan slowly began to relax, his thoughts again filled with haunting visions of Dana. That was another difference between himself and Erik, he decided. His intentions were not in the least bit noble. He simply planned to seduce the woman he desired the first chance he got, and as often as he could thereafter.

Grena's family had stayed the night, but Berit was still so excited she lay awake long after she had joined Thora and Dana in their sleeping chamber. The ten-year-old was on her right, her supple body curled up in a tight ball as she slept, while Dana, who was on Berit's left, was tossing restlessly.

"Can't you sleep?" the blonde asked, hoping her cousin would also be in a talkative mood.

"I think I'm too tired. It was a long day," Dana murmured softly.

Taking the remark as encouragement that her cousin would like to chat, Berit hurried on in a breathless rush. "Dana? How does Jarald kiss? Is he so good at it you never want to stop?"

Amazed by so unexpected a question, Dana rolled over to face Berit, then propped her head on her hand. "No, that's not how I would describe it at all."

"Well, what's it like then?"

Dana frowned with concentration as she forced herself to remember an ordeal she would sooner forget. "It's more like being suffocated beneath a sack of grain."

"You don't mean it!" Berit hid her giggles behind her hand so as not to wake Thora.

Dana sighed sadly, "I'm afraid that I do. Jarald has nearly shattered my ribs with his bear hugs, and having to endure his kisses is the worst torture I can imagine."

"You'll not marry him then?"

"No," Dana announced firmly. "I've decided to tell him

so as soon as he returns. It's been a mistake to keep him waiting for my answer.''

"He's very rich," Berit reminded her.

"Yes, and it's a good thing he is, as that's the only reason a woman will want to marry him," Dana quipped, but she was still worried the man's reaction to her rejection might be a violently hostile one.

Berit didn't want to talk about wealth, since Erik had none. Besides, she had a far more fascinating topic in mind. "Do you ever wonder what it will be like to make love?"

"Never," Dana revealed with a shudder. "Just kissing Jarald sickened me."

"But you've decided not to marry Jarald, so you needn't think about him. Aren't you curious about what it will be like? I asked my mother, but she told me I'd just have to wait until I'm married to see. Has Freya ever described it to you?"

It was plain to Dana that Berit had spent a great deal of her time considering the subject, while she had always done her best to suppress all thought of it herself. Her parents seemed well-suited and happy, but all the men who had courted her had been so aggressive in their efforts to impress her she had only been frightened by their affection rather than aroused by it.

"No, my mother has never said anything about making love. I imagine she considers it too private a matter to discuss."

Because Berit knew her aunt's gentle sweetness well, she thought Dana's observation was probably true, and quickly dismissed Freya as a possible source of information. "Would Erik tell you if you asked him?" she inquired softly. "You and he are so close. Do you suppose he'd tell you about it, and then you could tell me?"

"Berit," Dana scolded in a whisper. "Erik is very dear to me, but he would be horribly embarrassed if I asked him such an intimate question. Besides, he's a man, so he could provide only his view of it and not a woman's."

"Do you suppose he's made love to many women?" Berit wondered aloud.

"I really don't know, but I doubt it. He has a far more

serious nature than either Jørn or Svien. They're the ones who are always being teased for carousing and chasing women, not Erik.''

''But he's with them sometimes.'' Berit pulled the quilt up to her chin as the depressing thought of Erik making love to another woman filled her heart with dread.

The sudden change in Berit's mood wasn't lost on Dana, but she didn't want to pursue their conversation any farther. Erik was a grown man, and she trusted him to know what limits to set with Berit. As for herself, somehow she had forgotten herself completely and had kissed a slave. The shame of that action was almost more than she could bear, but it didn't come close to erasing the pleasure she had felt at the time.

''Good night,'' Dana murmured.

''Good night,'' Berit replied. A single tear slid down her cheek as thoughts of Erik overwhelmed her with sorrow. Just as Dana had said, he was a very serious individual. He was reserved, and cautious too, but he had kissed her that afternoon with a reckless abandon that had been totally unlike him. She had kissed him first, though. He had not been the one to initiate the affectionate exchange.

As she lay contemplating what the future might bring, Berit soon realized she would be wise never to discuss the difficulties of their situation with Erik. He would only insist it was an impossible one, as he had before, but he seemed no more able to recall that than she once they had begun to kiss. What if they were to make love? Berit knew without a moment's doubt that he would never abandon her were they to become lovers. But with his reserve, it would be up to her to make that happen. She fell asleep with that challenging thought in mind. She might not know exactly how to go about it, but she was determined to seduce Erik, and soon.

During the night, while everyone slept, Spring Blossom's foal was born. The tiny filly was gray rather than white like her newly born half brother, but she showed the same fine lines and excellent promise. Dana went out to see the new foal when she bid Grena and her cousins good-bye, and quickly returned to the house where she showed a sudden interest in weaving she had never before displayed.

Freya did not work on the large looms making cloth, but she did enjoy doing tablet weaving to create the narrow decorative braid used to adorn the hems of their garments. It required the use of a small square board or bone plaque that could be picked up and worked upon at idle moments. Dana had always admired her mother's skill at the craft, and had decided she ought not to waste another day before perfecting her own technique at the art. Besides, remaining indoors meant she would not have to face Brendan until after their kiss had become a faint memory.

When Dana did not ask him to saddle her mare that morning, Brendan assumed she was tired after the previous day's excitement and had decided not to ride. She was quite slender, and while she did not appear to be delicate, he thought she was wise not to overextend herself. He was disappointed when Moira came alone to bring him his evening meal, but he thanked the shy girl graciously so as not to show it.

It was not until Dana failed to appear the second morning that he began to suspect something was amiss. Thora came out to the stable often to visit the new foals, and since he had brought her down from the tree, she now regarded him as a friend. While he had never had any success gaining information from the charming child, he decided to give it another try now that she was more relaxed around him.

"You're not riding again today?" he asked with a ready grin that belied his true purpose.

"No, Dana's busy making braid for a new gown, and Mother won't let me go alone. She might let me go with you, though. Shall I ask her?"

Brendan was replacing a worn leather strap on a bridle, and shook his head. "I'm supposed to work, and that would be play. I doubt she would think it a good idea." He watched the little girl out of the corner of his eye as she patted the two foals and cooed softly to them. It was like looking into the past and seeing Dana at an earlier time. Thora had a delightful personality all her own, but her features and coloring mirrored her sister's too closely for him not to think of Dana each time he saw her.

"Is this new gown of Dana's for a special occasion?" he inquired in an offhand manner.

"No, I don't think so. It's not for her wedding, if that's what you mean." Thora came close to watch as Brendan completed his work on the bridle. "I know you like her. All the young men do."

Brendan had not realized he was being so transparent, but as usual Thora had understood the intent of his question. "She is almost as pretty as you are, Thora. Why wouldn't I like her?"

Amused, the red-haired child laughed at his compliment. "It will do you no good. She's going to marry Jarald when he comes home. He's very rich. His farm is a fine one and he owns a great many thralls. He's been begging Dana to marry him for two years now, so she can't keep him waiting much longer."

That was not the kind of news Brendan had wanted to hear. He had been enchanted by Dana's kiss, but it had not occurred to him until that very instant that another man had taught her how to bestow such generous affection. What had happened was painfully obvious to him then. Dana had merely been toying with him. Just as a wealthy man might amuse himself with a comely slave, she had seized the opportunity to enjoy a passionate moment with him.

Brendan's finely chiseled features hardened with defiance as he realized Dana must be avoiding him because she now regretted being so free with her affections. He had been misused in countless ways, but surely to trifle with his emotions was the worst possible offense. In his opinion, for a man to use a woman was his natural right, but for the reverse to happen was an outrage!

"Brendan?" Worried by the change in his expression, Thora spoke in an apprehensive whisper. "What's wrong?"

Brendan turned toward the inquisitive child, the flames of his hot temper now under control and his gaze curiously blank. "Nothing's wrong, little one. Dana's a rare beauty, and she ought to have a rich husband. I imagine you will have one too."

"Well, I certainly hope so," Thora replied, and with a toss of her bright red curls she went skipping back to the house.

In the days following the hunt, Erik thought of little but Berit. In many ways she was as pampered and spoiled as her mother, but he did not think her feelings for him were insincere. She was simply very young, and to her, love was so glorious an emotion she was blind to its many complications.

He knew he had never had as innocently optimistic a view of the future as she had, for he had learned at an early age that life contained far more painful disappointments than carefree bliss. He had never wallowed in self-pity, though, and he refused to do so now. As always he would accept what could not be changed and bravely hide his sorrow.

When it came to loving Berit, Erik considered their pitifully few options and decided he ought to speak with Grena soon. He would ask to make Berit his wife, Grena would refuse to allow it, and their brief romance would end. It would be painful, but not nearly so agonizing as it would be should they continue to delude themselves into thinking they might share more than one sunlit afternoon. With a great deal of effort he finally convinced himself that this was not a cowardly approach, but the only honorable one.

While Erik devoted both his days and nights to pondering his romantic dilemma, he was not unaware of how Brendan spent his time. Since his arrival, the slave had exhibited an astonishing amount of initiative. He did not have to be constantly reminded of what needed to be done, as the stable boys had. In fact, Erik was frequently amazed to find his orders had already been carried out before he had given them. The horses were all beautifully groomed and the stable as clean as the day it had been built. Erik found Brendan's independence so admirable a trait that he began to regard him with a growing respect, and the strain which had existed between them as thrall and master lessened considerably.

Because he did not want to see such hard work go unrewarded, Erik soon arrived at the same conclusion Dana had: Brendan was both intelligent and ambitious and ought not to belong to a reckless fool like Jørn. While he discussed his plan with no one, Erik decided that if Jørn refused to allow Brendan to earn his freedom, then he would persuade Freya to loan him the money to buy the slave so he could set him free himself. He said nothing to Brendan to encourage his hopes when he could not guarantee the man a bright future, but Erik no longer reacted to his questions with the short-tempered disdain he had once shown. They saw each other only briefly in the morning and evening, but their conversations no longer ended in arguments. At times they were even quite friendly.

As the days passed, Brendan noted the improvement in Erik's manner, but as before he suspected it was a trick of some kind to enable the man to manage him more easily, and so Brendan remained on his guard. Each morning he waited for Dana to come ask him to saddle her mare, and when she continually failed to appear, his frustration grew to nearly unbearable proportions. He could not walk unaccompanied into her house to look for her, so he had no choice but to wait for her to again come to him. When, after a week, he could no longer bear the insult her failure to continue her daily rides clearly had to be, he asked her half brother if she were ill.

"Why, no, Dana's in perfect health. She's probably just been spending her time with her mother, and Freya hasn't been strong enough to ride since last summer." When Brendan did not appear satisfied with that answer, Erik gave it more thought. "Dana and Thora ride fairly often. If not in the last few days, then they'll probably go out tomorrow or the next day. You're right to be concerned about their horses, though. Turn them out in the pasture so they can get some exercise on their own."

Brendan had not been worried about Dawn's Kiss and Rascal, however, but about how cruelly Dana was snubbing him. Freya was frail; he knew that. Could Dana suddenly have become so devoted a daughter she never left her mother's side? No, the timing was no coincidence. Dana was avoiding him, and that was not a slight he would forgive.

Erik had seen that very same look of defiant anger cross Brendan's features too often not to recognize it, and with a moment's reflection he thought he understood the cause of the slave's troubled mood. "Dana's a young woman of remarkable beauty and charm, but you mustn't allow yourself to fall in love with her. She's one woman you can never have, and the sooner you accept that fact the better off you'll be."

They had been preparing for bed, but Brendan was far too restless to sleep. "I will accept nothing!" he blurted out as he started for the door. "You may meekly accept your lot in life without trying to better it, but I never will." He stomped out of the small house, and certain Erik trusted him enough not to follow, he started out on what he knew would have to be a long walk to cool his temper.

Erik was stunned by Brendan's words, but he had struggled far too long to gain what status he had to consider himself meek. On the contrary, he thought himself unusually strong-willed. He might have let his feelings for Berit cloud his thinking, but Brendan's impassioned insult had made him realize it was pointless to avoid facing up to what had to be done, and he vowed to visit Grena the very next day.

The more immediate problem was Brendan's surly attitude, and Erik would not allow him to speak to him in such a rude fashion. He followed him out the door, and seeing the slave had not gone far, he took off at a run and tackled him around the waist with a mighty leap. The two men landed in the dirt, fists and insults flying as thick as the dust that swirled around them.

Too evenly matched in size and mood for one to gain the upper hand, they fought until they finally grew exhausted enough to realize neither had created the frustrations that had made the other so short-tempered. Fortunately, neither was badly hurt before that moment arrived.

"You must learn to keep your ridiculous opinions to yourself," Erik warned with a satisfied chuckle. Brendan was a strong brute, and he was confident that by again fighting him to a draw he had proved himself to be anything but meek. After scrambling to his feet, he extended his hand to help the brawny slave rise.

Brendan grasped Erik's hand for the instant he needed to leap to his feet, then broke the contact between them immediately. He gave a hoarse laugh as he dusted off his kirtle and breeches. "I am wearing your clothes, and it is your fault they are so dirty."

Erik regarded the disheveled Celt with an amused stare. "You are so close to my size I told Freya to have her seamstresses use my measurements for your garments. They should be ready soon. Perhaps that's why you haven't seen Dana. Maybe she's been too busy sewing the buttons on your new clothes to go riding."

While the sweetness of that thought nearly overwhelmed him with longing, Brendan knew Dana couldn't possibly be doing anything of the kind. "Your opinions are far more ridiculous than mine. Must I hit you again to convince you to swallow them?" he asked, all playfulness gone from his tone.

"I'll say whatever I please," Erik replied without growing angry. "It's late and I've too much to do tomorrow to continue our fight." He returned to his house with a confident stride, but he still had no hope things would turn out well on the morrow.

Brendan hesitated a moment, then followed Erik back inside. Any other man would have whipped him for being so insolent, but Erik liked to settle things with his fists. It was an odd approach to take with a slave, but Brendan could not deny that he liked it, since it gave him a chance to defend himself. What a strange place this was! he thought, as he did so often.

"Erik?" He cleared his throat.

"What is it now?" Erik yanked off his kirtle quickly so he could keep his eye on his companion.

"Meek was the wrong word."

Because he knew that was as close as the Celt would come to making an apology, Erik clapped him on the back and wished him a good night. His knuckles were scraped, his hands ached badly, and his body was covered with bruises from the slave's hearty blows, but he felt too tired to complain about the pain and had no trouble falling asleep.

* * *

Not wanting to involve Freya or Dana in his mission, Erik did not reveal the purpose of his errand before leaving for Grena's farm. He practiced what he had to say as he rode along, polishing his speech until it sounded painfully sincere, but he couldn't bring himself to prepare any sort of a response to the terse rejection he was bound to receive. He would just have to listen silently, no matter how coldly Grena refused him, and then turn and leave.

Too restless to remain indoors, Berit had been out gathering berries off the vines that grew along the path to her home. When she saw a rider approaching, she moved out of his way, until she recognized the dark gleam on Shadow's coat and knew it must be Erik. She ran forward then, berries flying from her basket, but she was too happy to notice how many she had spilled.

One look at Berit's radiant smile and Erik completely forgot the purpose of his visit. In one fluid motion he pulled Shadow to a halt, slid down from his back, and drew the breathless blonde into his arms. "Oh, how I've missed you," he sighed in the second before his lips touched hers.

Berit flung her basket aside, spilling the last of the berries into the path as she threw her arms around his neck. "And I have missed you even more!" she exclaimed when he gave her a chance to draw a breath.

Berit had eaten as many of the succulent berries as she had picked. Her lips were stained with the deep red juice and her taste was delicious. Erik had kissed her a dozen times before he could bear to draw away. He glanced down the path, but none of the field-workers, nor anyone else, was in sight.

"Come on, we must find a secluded place to talk." He took her hand and, leading Shadow through a break in the vines, made his way to a stand of trees where they could sit and the horse could graze unnoticed.

Berit wanted to discuss only one topic: how dearly she loved him. She covered his face with kisses, then reached for the buttons on his kirtle.

Erik caught her hands, but he did not want to hurt her feelings and spoke softly. "I meant talk, Berit. I could kiss you forever, but we must talk first."

Adopting what she hoped was a suitably rapt expression, Berit sat back and waited for him to begin. The morning sun cast copper highlights on his hair that made the sharp contrast of his cool violet eyes all the more appealing. "How can I listen?" she teased. "When you are so very handsome, I can think of nothing but how much I love you."

"Would you find me less distracting if we sat back to back?"

"No, I don't think so," Berit revealed with a bewitching smile.

The spontaneity of her mood was infectious, and Erik drew her across his lap, where he could hug her tightly as they talked. His plan to ask for her and then accept Grena's refusal suddenly seemed so ludicrous an option he did not know how he could have deluded himself into thinking it was his only choice.

Brendan's words came back to him then. Perhaps he had been meekly accepting his lot in life, but with the enthusiasm of Berit's love for encouragement, he would not pursue such a hopeless course any longer. There had to be some way he could make her his wife, and he would just have to be clever enough to find it.

"Freya offered to give me the money I will need to marry the woman of my choice, but she didn't even suspect that might be you. She might refuse to give me the money now; I haven't asked her to find out. We both know your mother thinks you are far too good for me, so she may ask so exorbitant a bride-price that I will never be able to raise the sum."

"Erik," Berit interrupted, as always not interested in talking about practical matters when they had so few opportunities to be alone. "I'll simply refuse to wed anyone else, and you know that I can't be forced to marry against my will. My mother can ask any amount that she wants, but when she realizes all she will ever get for me is what you can afford to pay, she'll not forbid the match."

Encouraged by the determined set of the lively blonde's chin, Erik was inclined to believe her prediction. He still saw complications, however. "Freya isn't well enough to argue with your mother, Berit. If Grena wants to be stubborn, then you and I will have to stand up to her all by ourselves.''

''Dana will take our side. Svien too,'' Berit argued. ''Jørn will want to see his only sister happy, and you are one of his closest friends. He'll help us too.''

''Yes, Dana will be on our side, but I want this matter settled before Svien and Jørn return, so don't count on them.''

Berit snuggled against the hollow of his shoulder as she considered his words. She was certain what he really meant was that he wanted their marriage arranged before Haakon came home. ''Are you afraid of what Haakon will do?'' she whispered apprehensively.

Erik paused a long moment before speaking his fears aloud. ''Not in the way you think, but he might forbid Freya to give me the money since he doesn't consider me one of his family. She would defy him, but that conflict would hurt her badly. It might cost her what little strength she has, and if she falls ill again—''

Berit turned to face Erik when he could not continue. ''I understand. Our love mustn't cost Freya her life, but I'll not give you up, Erik.''

Erik raised his hand to her cheek, caressing her fair skin softly as he gloried in the love that shone so brightly in her eyes. She had grown up quickly, but he did not doubt for a moment that she was a woman who knew her own mind. Her delightful curves, fair coloring, and warm smile all conveyed a charming innocence, but she had an inner strength he had not even suspected she possessed until that very moment.

A slow smile played across his lips before he spoke, ''You'll not give me up? When did I become yours, Berit?''

The affectionate blonde lowered her glance demurely as she thought of a suitable reply, but when she looked up again, her eyes were dancing with mischief. ''On the day I was born, Erik, for I swear I have loved you my whole life.''

As his lips met hers in a lingering kiss, Erik could not recall a time when he had not loved her either. The love for a pretty child was far different from what he felt for the lovely young woman in his arms now, however. Their kisses grew more fevered, and he did not object when she slid her hands beneath his kirtle and drew it off over his head. He loved the feel of her hands on his chest and soon found himself wanting to caress her bare skin as well.

Her long tunic was easily cast aside, but he paused to release her hair from its confining braid before he reached for the ribbon at the neckline of her chemise. The sun was warm at his back, the only sounds those of birds singing in the trees overhead, and with each step he took toward total intimacy, Berit encouraged him to take two more. He did not recall flinging the last of his clothes aside, nor helping her out of hers, and once she lay nude in his arms it was impossible for him to think at all.

It was not the curiosity she had exhibited with Dana that had motivated the abandon of Berit's actions, but the sheer joy of love. She was too bright to have thought they could wed without first overcoming the objections to the stigma of his birth, but those objections would all be Grena's and not hers. She wanted the handsome man in her arms for her husband and did not hesitate to take him for a lover first.

Erik wound his fingers in the glorious cascade of Berit's honey-blond tresses as he paid her a well-deserved compliment. "Your hair is as beautiful as sunshine. You should always wear it falling loose like this, instead of in a braid."

"If it pleases you, then I will," Berit promised before drawing his mouth back to hers. She had never kissed another man, but she was certain his was the only affection she would ever want. When he lowered his mouth to the fullness of her breasts, she combed her fingers through his hair to press his lips closer still. While she had known nothing about making love, it was plain to her that Erik most certainly did, for his motions were smooth and sure, without the slightest trace of clumsiness. To enjoy what he was so thoughtfully teaching her seemed her natural right, when each new sensation was even more pleasant than the last.

Erik knew Berit was a virgin, but she was so wonderfully responsive he saw no reason to inhibit his own desire. He lost himself not only in her beauty, but in the warmth of her affection which enticed him to pursue what they had begun and promised endless satisfaction as a result. He traced each curve and hollow of her figure until he had committed it to memory. Then, delving deeper, he began the slow, rhythmic assault on her senses that would soon make her completely his.

Berit's whole body tingled with the warmth of desire as Erik caressed the smooth skin of her inner thighs, but when he eased her legs farther apart to reach the tawny triangle of curls nestled at their apex, her breath caught in her throat for fear he would draw away.

Sensing the depth of her need, Erik did not disappoint her, but used her body's own sweetly scented fluids to lubricate his path. "Don't hold your breath," he whispered. "You'll faint long before I'm through."

Berit tried to follow his directions, but the feelings his touch aroused were so new, and so exquisitely beautiful, she could not concentrate on anything as distracting as the need to draw a breath. She was aware only of a growing heat that seared within her loins. Like an open flame, it danced and leapt to ever greater heights until she feared she would be consumed and leave behind no more than a handful of ashes that would be scattered by the wind.

Erik's mouth covered hers, muffling a cry for release from passion's torment at the very moment he brought their bodies together with one deep, masterful thrust. He had timed their union perfectly, drowning the inevitable pain with wave after wave of rapture. He moved gently at first, but when Berit clung to him, eagerly accepting all he wished to give, he abandoned himself in the ecstasy of her love. The splendor poured through him, then echoed through her in throbbing tremors that gave him clear proof she had shared his joy in full measure.

"I love you," he whispered as he smoothed her tangled hair away from her face.

"And I love you," Berit replied, but until that morning, she had not truly realized how much.

CHAPTER IX

While Erik was initiating Berit into the delights of making love, Freya was observing her eldest daughter with a mother's experienced eye. Dana had been far too quiet of late, and she had also begun spending her days indoors. That was so unlike her that Freya was very concerned. Dana's recent solitary production of the delicate patterns used in tablet weaving also struck her as a further indication that something was amiss. After drawing her second child into her sleeping chamber on the pretext of examining some fine cloth stored in a chest there, Freya closed the door to assure their privacy.

"It's plain to me that something is troubling you. Erik has been preoccupied as well. If there's a problem with the farm, I'm no longer ill, and you needn't shield me from it."

"Why, no, the farm is running almost as smoothly as it does for you. We've had no problems." Dana had a clear conscience on that score, for the management of the farm was now the least of her worries.

Freya sat down on the foot of her bed and patted the space at her side. "I'm pleased to hear it, but I want you to sit with me awhile so we can talk about you. It's not like you to spend so many sunny days indoors. Won't you please tell me what's wrong?"

Too distraught to describe her predicament coherently, Dana swallowed hard and shook her head. She was alarmed by her mother's insightful questions, and rather than join her, she began to pace at the end of the massive bed that had been constructed for Haakon's impressive proportions. Her mother was perceptive, and also wonderfully sympathetic, but Dana could not bring herself to reveal that no matter how hard she tried, she could not force thoughts of Brendan from her mind. She had foolishly thought she could forget his kiss in a day or two, but with every hour the brief moment she had spent in his arms had become more vivid and her feelings of shame that much more intense.

With no hint from her daughter as to the cause of her obvious discomfort, Freya suggested the only logical possibility. "Is it Jarald? Are you still worried about marrying him?"

"Jarald?" Dana murmured the name in so distracted a fashion it appeared as though she had forgotten the man. Then realizing her mother would readily believe it was indeed thoughts of the seafaring trader rather than those of a handsome slave that gave her no peace, she agreed. Once she had begun to talk, her emotions swiftly ran away with her, for she was truly on the edge of despair.

"Why, yes, and I know I should never have tried to hide my anxiety from you, but I just can't do as you ask, Mother. I can't give him until spring to change my mind. I'll never come to love him, and it will be better if I tell him so when next I see him. What if he reacts very badly, though? What if he curses me and despises us all and—"

Freya rose to take her daughter's hand and drew her back to the bed to sit down. "You're making yourself ill over something that may never happen, my darling. Jarald has a temper, it's true, but how can he complain that you have refused him without making himself appear ridiculous to his friends? Men like to brag about their success with pretty women; they are loath to admit their failures."

Grateful for her mother's comforting advice, as well as the fact she had been so easily misled, Dana managed a faint smile. "I hope you're right, but—"

"No," Freya interrupted. "You must cease to worry about Jarald. It's always best to face problems squarely rather than allow yourself to be overwhelmed with dread, but in this case you have no choice about having to wait. Perhaps that's my fault. If you hadn't spent so much time with me in the spring, you would have been able to get to know Jarald better, and would have come to the decision to refuse him then."

Dana hugged her mother tightly. "None of this is your fault, Mother. You mustn't ever think that."

"Thank you, dear." Freya enjoyed her daughter's affectionate squeeze, then, seeking to lift her mood, changed the subject to a more lighthearted one. "I know Moira has been taking Brendan his supper. Does she seem attracted to him, or he to her?"

Dana's heart missed a beat at the mention of the slave's name, but she quickly recovered. "I've been so worried about Jarald, I really haven't noticed. I'll ask Moira what she thinks of him tonight."

Freya pursed her lips thoughtfully. "No, you must ask Brendan first if he finds her attractive. Moira is so shy, it would be cruel of us to encourage her to care for him if he has no interest in her. From what Grena said, he would not accept her women's attentions, but perhaps he has changed his mind now that he's here."

Knowing that her mother was right as usual, Dana nodded, even though the thought of speaking to Brendan chilled her clear through. Her mother might think problems should be faced squarely, but the attractive Celt presented a dilemma so unique she didn't think any proven approach would work.

Freya smoothed a long red curl away from her lovely daughter's cheek and gave her a sweet kiss. "It's a beautiful morning. Why don't you go for a ride? That will give you the opportunity to speak to Brendan. Taking an interest in a romance other than your own will do you good. Now go on, I insist you go out and enjoy the beauty of the day."

With Freya still offering advice about romance, Dana found herself being pushed out into the yard. Thora had gone riding with Soren, so she couldn't rely on her sister for the company that might keep Brendan civil. With a slow, measured step she approached the stable, but she doubted she could speak to the handsome slave when her heart was lodged so firmly in her throat.

After Thora had left with Soren that morning, Brendan had followed Erik's instructions and had turned Dawn's Kiss out in the pasture. When he looked up to find Dana standing at the stable door, he was annoyed that her mare was not in her stall. "Did you want to ride?" he called out as he approached her, his eyebrows knit in a forbidding frown. She was dressed in the pale pink and rose garments she had been wearing the first time he had seen her, and again her beauty took his breath away. Silently cursing his weakness for her, he stepped out into the light. "Well, do you want me to saddle your mare or not?"

Dana had feared she would be too ashamed to speak, but it wasn't humiliation that filled her cheeks with a bright blush. It was another emotion entirely. Her first thought was how handsome Brendan was. Even when he wore a scowl, his appearance was appealing. She had to clasp her hands behind her back to overcome the impulse to reach out and touch him. Despite the fact they had spent the longest week of her life apart, when she looked up at him, Dana felt the same sweet longing for more than one kiss that had caused her to flee his embrace.

"Would you please?" she finally managed to ask.

Brendan eyed the redhead with a skeptical glance before responding. He had expected one of her coolly voiced orders, not a politely worded request. "I'll have to fetch your mare," he explained. "Are you going alone?"

"No, I want you to come with me," Dana heard herself say, but she was more shocked than Brendan was by her boldness. She had berated herself repeatedly for encouraging the attentions of a thrall, but now that she had seen him again, she knew a slave was the very least of the things he was. Brendan was a remarkable young man in all respects, and it saddened her that she knew nothing whatsoever about him.

While nothing would please him more than to spend some time alone with the violet-eyed beauty before him, Brendan was so taken aback by her unexpected invitation he feared his imagination had supplied it. "You want me to accompany you?" he asked in an incredulous gasp.

"Yes, it will give us a chance to talk," Dana replied with growing confidence. "I'll tell Erik you were with me. You needn't worry he'll punish you if you don't have time to finish all your work."

"How kind of you," Brendan responded, but his tone

was still one of dismay rather than sarcasm. Even after he had saddled her horse and the bay gelding he had ridden on the day of the picnic, part of him doubted Dana truly wanted his company. An equally insistent part feared that she might want more than he cared to give a mistress who would ignore him for a week at a time.

Dana led the way as they followed the path toward the woods. She didn't want to go a great distance, only far enough to assure herself their conversation would not be overheard. Once they had reached the trees, she dismounted, let her mare graze, and waited for Brendan to follow her example. Too restless to choose a place to sit, she wandered about in a lazy circle as she encouraged him to talk.

"My mother asked you to tell us about yourself and your people, but you refused. I hope you'll feel more like talking now."

"You were there that day?"

"Yes. You might not have seen me, but I was there." Dana focused her attention on the tall grass beneath her feet, since she found it too difficult to think clearly when she looked at him.

Brendan leaned back against a beech tree, thinking back to that morning and recalling his disappointment when Dana hadn't been there. But now he knew she had been. A slow smile tugged at the corner of his mouth. She had wanted to see him, but hadn't wanted him to know. He had not thought her so coy, and it amused him to discover that she was.

When Brendan didn't speak, Dana risked a glance his way, but she didn't understand his sly smirk. It would have infuriated her at one time, but her desire to get to know him was sincere and she would not allow their conversation to deteriorate into an argument if she could possibly prevent it.

"I can appreciate your reluctance to speak," she continued in the same calm, sympathetic tone. "You had just met my mother, and there were too many curious servants nearby. Now we're alone, and I won't repeat what you say, not even to Erik and my mother if you'd rather I didn't."

Brendan had been surprised when Dana had not led him farther away from her home, since the edge of the woods struck him as a poor place for a tryst. He half expected Soren and Thora to come galloping by, or a field hand or two to come looking for a bit of shade in which to rest. The spot she had chosen was private enough for a talk, but little else. Could that possibly be all she wanted? That was so unflattering an idea, he instantly rejected it.

"Why are you suddenly so curious about me?"

"Does my interest seem sudden?"

"I have not seen you in a week, so it seems unlikely you are all that interested in me."

Dana found that an impossible accusation to deny, since it had been her unseemly interest in him that had kept her away. "My routine varies from day to day, and I don't always have the time to ride. If you've become bored, you should have told Erik you need more work to do. You needn't wait to speak with me."

"No thrall ever asks for more work," Brendan responded with a derisive snort.

Dana had paced so many circles she was growing dizzy and had to stand still for a moment. She bent down to pluck a small yellow flower from the grass so she would have something to contemplate other than Brendan's perpetual frown while they talked. When they had last parted, he had been smiling. How could she coax that marvelous expression from him again without surrendering to the desire she dared not acknowledge? she wondered silently.

"I had hoped we would be able to talk, Brendan, not argue. I don't even know how old you are, or from what part of Erin you come. Won't you please tell me something about yourself? At least enough so that I can begin to understand you?"

Brendan waited for Dana to look at him, but she seemed fascinated by the blossom she held. He could think of only one reason for her to ask him to reveal such personal information: the desire to bind him to her with an emotional tie that would make him all the easier to exploit. In that moment he despised her as deeply as he had ever hated anyone.

"I am an expensive piece of property. You said so yourself. There's nothing more you need to know about me," he replied gruffly. He moved away from the tree, their conversation over as far as he was concerned.

Dana did look up then. Brendan had taken a step toward her, but the gulf between them had never seemed so wide. Instantly she thought of the servants at Grena's, and knew how devastated they must have been to find Brendan so cold. Tears filled her eyes at the realization she was behaving as badly as a servant with a crush on a slave, and she quickly blinked the telltale moisture away. It was plain Brendan had no interest in her, and she knew all too well she ought not to be so fascinated by him.

Rather than sacrifice any more of her pride, she straightened her shoulders and forced herself to behave like the competent young woman her mother had raised her to be. "Moira, the girl who takes you your supper, is a Celt. She's my mother's personal maid, and we would like to find her a husband. We thought perhaps since you are—" But Dana found it impossible to continue as she watched Brendan cross the distance between them in two long strides.

"Is that why you brought me out here?" the outraged slave shouted in her face. When Dana's eyes widened in alarm and she seemed unable to speak, Brendan grabbed her arms and shook her. "Is that all you want from me? You want a husband for your mother's maid?"

His fingers dug into the tender flesh of her upper arms, and this time her tears spilled over her lashes, but Dana was too torn by her own emotions to react with anything except shock at this forceful show of his. It was the unexpected tenderness in their last kiss that had melted her natural reserve, and she had failed so completely in her attempt to rekindle that same mood in Brendan that she felt more lost than she had during the week she had avoided him.

"Moira is very dear to us," she mumbled hoarsely through trembling lips. "I did not mean to insult you."

Brendan's eyes narrowed to menacing slits as his glance swept her face with a look of scathing disgust. "Insult me!" he snarled. "You've done far worse than that. As a thrall, my children would be born thralls as well. I'll not be used like Sky Dancer, as a stud to service your maid. I'll not give life to children who would have no future!"

"You can earn your freedom," Dana managed to whisper.

"That's not for you to decide. You don't own me. Have you forgotten that?" When she didn't reply, Brendan continued his fiery rebuke. "Is this why you and Erik have been so kind to me? Just so you could make me part of your breeding stock?"

"No," Dana denied emphatically, horrified he would make such an outlandish assumption, but she could see he didn't believe her. Unable to bear another instant of the hatred that seeped from his every pore, she shut her eyes tightly and turned her face away. She knew she ought to scream at him to unhand her, and slap his face soundly too, but she was too hurt by his angry accusations to respond in kind.

Brendan held the weeping beauty at arm's length, his expression still filled with loathing. But he was as disgusted with himself as he was with her because he still wanted her. Why hadn't she brought him out to the woods to make love? Why hadn't she wanted him for herself rather than a favorite maid? His rage was nearly blinding, and he was tempted to take what he knew she would never willingly give. A slave did not rape his mistress and live, however, and his life was far more precious to him than it would ever be to her. He released her then with a rude shove, knowing the desire to humiliate her as she had him by suggesting he marry another woman was far too dangerous to pursue.

"You're a heartless pagan bitch, and if you ever ask me to do anything more than care for your horses, I'll spit in your face!" he shouted in a final fit of temper. He hurried to his horse, and once in the saddle, he pushed the gelding to a near flying gallop and rode back to the farm without once looking back to see if Dana were following.

Once alone, Dana sank to her knees, unable to understand how she had aroused such virulent hatred in a young man she had wanted so desperately to get to know. The bitterness of their encounter had left her so thoroughly sickened she began to retch. Tears poured down her face as she tried to regain her self-control, but it was a long time in coming. She had not dreamed Brendan's reaction to a possible marriage with Moira would be so negative or she would never have brought up the subject. "Never," she whispered dejectedly. "Never."

Knowing she could not go home in such a sorry state, Dana curled up at the base of the beech tree Brendan had used for a backrest and hoped she would feel well enough to sit a horse before nightfall. Again overcome with feelings of shame and guilt, she tried to think of some way to relate what had happened to her mother without revealing a single word of the truth.

Gradually the morning gave way to early afternoon, and after considerable reflection, Dana came to the regrettable conclusion that she should be grateful for having inspired Brendan's hatred, no matter how unintentional the result. She had always found him attractive, but the tension his arrogant conceit created between them was more than she could sanely endure. What did it matter that in an unguarded moment he had kissed her sweetly? She was still the daughter of a proud and wealthy Dane who expected her to marry a man who could provide the same pleasant life she had always known.

"At least Jarald would never abuse me," she murmured softly to herself as she rubbed her bruised arms. Perhaps that was what her mother had meant about the man having qualities she did not fully appreciate. Jarald was loud and boisterous, but he wasn't cruel. If she gave it more effort, maybe she could even convince him to channel his enthusiastic affection into a more tender form of expression. As her usual confident manner slowly returned, she tried to reconsider Jarald, but time and again the voice of her heart wondered why the only passion she aroused in Brendan was hatred.

Brendan did not calm down sufficiently to consider the most probable result of his actions until long after he had turned the bay gelding out into the pasture. Most masters would whip a slave for raising his voice, and he had not only yelled at Dana but manhandled her too. He could already feel the sting of a whip ripping the scarred flesh off his back, and the longer Dana took to return home, the more certain he became she was planning even more fiendish tortures.

Erik had warned him she would cut him, but would she go so far as to render him less than a man? He broke out in a cold sweat as he realized a woman with Dana's temper might do just that. Would it be cowardly to run, or wise? Sick clear through that he had so little control over his fate, he went out to the farthest pasture and sat down to await Dana's return. At least he would see her coming and would have a head start if she had a knife in her hand rather than a whip.

Before Berit left for home, she washed hurriedly in a nearby stream and took care to dress as neatly as she had that morning. Amid lingering farewell kisses, Erik had rebraided her hair and helped her to pick a basketful of berries. Despite their combined efforts to restore her appearance to normal, she had been gone far longer than usual, and was afraid her mother would be suspicious no matter what excuse she gave. Her first glance at Grena's worried expression did not reassure her either. After attempting to smile innocently, although she felt far from innocent now that she and Erik had become lovers, she popped a succulent berry into her mouth.

Grena watched her daughter cross the yard, and went forward to meet her. "You've picked more berries than we can possibly eat tonight. Were you so lost in daydreams you didn't realize what you were doing?"

"Is this too many?" Berit asked in surprise. "We all love berries and cream, so I was afraid this basket wouldn't hold nearly enough."

"That's more than enough." Grena studied her daughter's face and was alarmed to find her cheeks flushed. "You've gotten too much sun," she scolded crossly. "A woman's skin should be fair, not tanned as deeply as a field hand's."

Rather than reply, Berit ate another scrumptious berry. She now understood her mother's reluctance to discuss making love, for the pleasure was nearly indescribably sweet, but she thought Grena should have at least told her it was something she would enjoy.

Grena saw a subtle change in her daughter's expression. It was not merely the color in her cheeks that brought that realization either. Berit might lack her cousin Dana's remarkable beauty, but she had a lush prettiness Grena knew most men would find irresistibly appealing. The problem would be to save that valuable asset for a suitably wealthy man. Slipping her arm around her daughter's waist, she led her toward the house, where she intended to have a lengthy discussion about possible husbands. Berit was still quite young, but attention would soon be coming her way, and Grena wanted to make certain her daughter knew exactly which men to encourage and which to ignore.

Berit found her mother's comments not even faintly interesting since she had already chosen a husband for herself. She sat without interrupting, though, appearing to be seriously considering each name suggested, but all the while she was counting the hours until she would see Erik again.

Erik arrived home in such high spirits he didn't think it odd Brendan was sitting idle in the pasture where the two-year-olds grazed. Certain the Celt was observing them for a purpose, he walked out to talk with him.

Brendan saw Erik coming and hurriedly got to his feet. There was still no sign of Dana, so he knew the man hadn't come to punish him, but he was apprehensive all the same. As Erik drew near, he saw by his ready grin that he was in too fine a mood to berate the farm's lone thrall. On another day he would have called out and asked what good news he had, but now he held his tongue.

"Has Dana been gone long?" Erik asked when he reached Brendan's side.

Hoping to discuss horses, Brendan had trouble finding his voice. "Longer than usual, but she hasn't been riding for a while." In truth, Brendan didn't understand where the redhead was when he had expected her to waste no time in coming after him.

Erik frowned impatiently. "I need to talk with her as soon

as she returns. Watch for her and send her over to my house.'' He turned then to look at the three fillies and two colts grazing nearby. ''What do you think of this lot? Do they look promising to you? Thora has nearly outgrown Rascal, and I thought perhaps one of the fillies might make her a good mount.''

Brendan had worked with the two-year-olds before that day, and so he was able to offer an intelligent comment despite his muddled thinking. ''They are all very gentle, which is surprising for foals allowed so much freedom.''

''Haakon makes pets of them all. They are handled from the day they are born so they aren't man shy.''

Brendan tried to concentrate as Erik described his father's techniques for training horses, which surprisingly didn't sound all that different from his own. His mind kept wandering, however, and his glance continually swept the path that led to the woods to watch for Dana's return. He even toyed with the idea of relating his side of their argument in hopes of winning Erik's sympathy, but he already knew Erik would take his half sister's side against a slave any day and didn't waste his breath in such a futile effort.

Despite his ebullient mood, Erik couldn't help but note Brendan's distress. It was so unlike the Celt to fidget nervously that he finally had to comment on it. ''What's wrong, Brendan?'' There was a faint bruise on the slave's chin as a result of their fight the previous night, but he didn't think the man was harboring any hard feelings over it.

Brendan turned to face Erik, as dismayed as he had been by Dana's request that he confide in her. They were not friends, regardless of the fact they shared a small house, and he couldn't find the words to describe his latest confrontation with Dana. ''I saw a slave beaten to death once,'' he blurted out instead. ''I don't believe the man actually meant to do it. He was just so angry he couldn't stop whipping him until it was too late.''

Erik stared at Brendan's pained expression, then nodded sympathetically for it was plain the Celt was greatly disturbed by the memory. ''Was this the same man who whipped you?'' When Brendan replied with a distracted nod, he continued, ''He was not a Dane, I hope.''

''No, a Norseman,'' Brendan heard himself say.

Erik spit in the dirt. ''Well, what can you expect then?'' He followed his unhappy companion's glance, and was delighted to see his half sister approaching. ''There's Dana at last.'' He turned away, his perplexing conversation with Brendan forgotten as he hurried across the verdant pasture to meet her.

While he knew he would be expected to take care of Dawn's Kiss, Brendan remained where he stood. With his heart in his throat he watched Dana ride into the yard, where Erik ran to meet her. He swung her down from her saddle, and the two stood with their heads together, conversing with an excitement Brendan could readily discern. While he couldn't tell what they were discussing at that distance, he knew Dana had to be describing the disrespectful way he had treated her, and tiny rivulets of sweat began to trickle down his back.

He was no coward, but he knew she was going to hurt him badly. As hot-tempered as she was, she might even leave him crippled. She had threatened to whip him herself, and being beaten by a woman was a humiliation he had never before had to suffer. He knew he could have taken it had Grena used a whip on him, but not Dana.

Overcome with dread, he looked up at the cloudless sky and repeated the same prayer he had said every night for the last three years, ''Please, God, give me the strength to survive long enough to get back home.''

When he looked back at the couple in whose hands his fate lay, he was shocked to find them gone. Dawn's Kiss stood at the end of the stable where Dana always left her, but her flame-haired mistress was nowhere in sight. She had gone for the whip—he just knew it—while Erik was probably fetching a rope to bind his hands to a tree.

Brendan took a deep breath and held it. He had lived through one nightmare after another, but nothing to compare with this. ''Let Erik do it,'' he prayed aloud. ''Just let Erik be the one to do it. He won't kill me, and Dana surely will.''

CHAPTER X

When Erik ran out to greet Dana, she was relieved to find him so eager to talk that he failed to note that her mood upon returning home had been a very somber one. He insisted she come to his house, where they would not be interrupted, and grateful for a distraction to help her forget her latest clash with Brendan, she went prepared to give him her full attention.

Once Dana was comfortably seated and provided with a tankard of ale, Erik found it difficult to begin. Finally he chose to confide only as much of the truth as he dared reveal.

"I want Berit for my wife, Dana. I know it's preposterous, so you needn't tell me that, but she loves me too and is more than willing to become my bride."

Astonished, Dana stared at the half brother she held so dear, unable to provide any sort of a response to his announcement for a long moment. "Preposterous" was not nearly strong enough a term to describe what he had suggested, but she would not insult him by quibbling over his choice of words. Instead, she took a fortifying breath and let it out slowly.

"Does Grena have any idea of your intentions?"

"No, not yet. I wanted to talk with you and Freya before going to her."

Relieved by that, Dana took a sip of ale, and then another, but the refreshing beverage failed to soothe away her initial dismay. "You know what she's going to say: that she didn't raise Berit to live in a falconer's hovel."

Erik cast an anxious glance around his one-room home. "Are you calling this a hovel?"

"No, of course not. It's a very comfortable house, but I doubt you have the space to store Berit's clothes, much less her other possessions." Seeing Erik's stricken expression, Dana reached out to catch his hand and pulled him down by her side.

"All I mean is that Grena will have a lengthy list of reasons why you are an unsuitable mate for her daughter. We'll have to anticipate them so we can counter them forcefully. Had you planned to begin clearing land for your own farm?"

"Well, no, I'd not thought that far ahead, but—"

"You simply must, Erik." Relishing the prospect of tackling so difficult a problem which would require weeks if not months of diligent effort to solve, Dana threw herself into the planning with an enthusiasm that amazed her half brother.

"There will also be the problem of gathering the money for Berit's bride-price. I know you're well paid and thrifty, but do you have enough saved to satisfy Grena and set up housekeeping as well?"

Erik shook his head. "I haven't nearly enough, but Freya has offered to help with a loan. You know Grena's main objection to me will not be one of money, though."

Dana set her tankard aside so she could grasp both of Erik's hands in hers. "You are a fine man, Erik, and you know none of us will allow her to insult you."

"That's exactly what I'm afraid of, that this will turn into a battle that will leave Grena not speaking to any of us, and your dear mother sick, as a result. If I could think of any way to save Freya what will surely be a wretched fight with her sister, I'd gladly do it."

Dana felt a momentary twinge of shame that she had not considered her mother's feelings before he had mentioned them. "Let's not tell my mother yet. Why don't you begin clearing land and building your house first? Brendan complained to me only this morning that he's growing bored, so he ought to enjoy felling trees. Soren is always asking to be treated like a grown man so there's no reason why he can't be put to work. There's time before the fall harvest for the field hands to work for you, too."

"And how am I to pay them?" Erik inquired with a knowing grin.

"You won't have to, we're already paying them and they'll work wherever we tell them to."

"I had hoped that you'd help me, Dana, but I hadn't dreamed you would be so willing." The warmth of Erik's gratitude shone brightly in his earnest glance.

"But I love you. How could you have thought I'd be otherwise?" Dana and Erik had always found it easy to exchange affection and she went into his arms to give him a loving hug. "Don't you think my idea is the best? That you ought to have some land cleared, and a house built before you announce you want Berit for your wife? You will have a home and a means to support her then, and that will counter two of Grena's most serious objections."

Erik shook his head ruefully. "I always thought I was practical, but you've seen things so much more clearly than I. I wish I had spoken with you before I talked to Berit, because now it's going to be very difficult for her to wait."

"You are an exceedingly practical man, Erik, but no one in love ever thinks clearly, do they?"

"I guess not," the dark-haired young man admitted sheepishly. "Do you have a suggestion for what I might tell Freya to explain my sudden desire to start my own farm?"

Giving his request careful consideration, Dana licked her lips thoughtfully before replying. "You're twenty-two. That's certainly old enough for a man to begin thinking about the future. It's only natural that you would want a farm of your own so that you'll be able to support a family. If my mother has already offered a loan, you must have discussed marriage with her, so I doubt she'll be all that surprised."

When Erik recalled that particular conversation with Freya, he was disconcerted to think how recently marriage had been an extremely remote possibility. That made what he and Berit wanted to do seem hasty and ill-advised, but he knew in his heart that fate had meant them to be husband and wife.

"You're wrong. She'll be completely surprised, and especially so when she hears it's Berit I plan to wed."

While Dana feared he was right, she didn't want him to worry about her mother when surely it was Grena who would present the greatest obstacle to his plans. "It may take her awhile to accept the idea, but she loves you as dearly as I do, and she's sure to give you her support. It's too late to go out riding again today, but at supper this evening you can tell everyone you've decided to clear land for a farm of your own. Then tomorrow we can take Thora and Soren with us and decide just where it ought to be."

Elated by their discussion, because it allowed her to focus on problems other than her own, Dana left Erik's house knowing that while they had many a difficult challenge ahead, she would do all in her power to assure him the happiness he deserved. With a wistful sigh, she hoped one day the same blissful happiness would find her as well.

Brendan spent one of the most wretchedly miserable afternoons of his life waiting for Dana to come for him. When she had not appeared by nightfall, he began to fear she was waiting until her younger brother and sister had gone to bed to spare them what he was certain would be a horribly gruesome scene.

He sat alone in Erik's house, valiantly attempting to gather the courage to withstand whatever lay ahead, and when Moira appeared with his usual ample supper tray, he seized the opportunity to find out all he could from her.

"Stay with me awhile," he invited in Gaelic, but his grin was shaky.

Moira handed him his supper, but she kept her gaze demurely focused on the tray. "No, I mustn't tarry, or I'll be missed."

She had replied in their native tongue, but her accent sounded peculiar to Brendan until he realized she had probably had scant opportunity to practice their language if she had spent her whole life among Danes. Feeling like a condemned man, he had no appetite and set the wooden tray aside.

When he turned back to face Moira, he recalled she was

such a shy young woman that he had never actually seen her face clearly. Her hair was a rich chestnut brown that fell loose over her shoulders, partly concealing her features like a carelessly worn veil. Curious, he reached out to tilt her chin up so he could get a good look at her face.

To his surprise, Brendan found Moira's blue eyes quite attractive. Her nose was a trifle long and her mouth a bit too wide, but he thought if she had a livelier personality and smiled often, those slight flaws would go unnoticed. She was no more than five feet tall and seemed almost childlike compared to Dana, who stood even with his shoulder. He stopped himself then from any further comparison between maid and mistress, for Moira excited not the slightest bit of desire within him, while a mere glimpse of Dana from afar set his blood aflame.

"You're a pretty girl, Moira. You ought to tie your hair back so men can see that," he began in an inviting tone.

The quiet maid's eyes widened in alarm, for no one had ever said she was pretty. That so well-built and handsome a man as Brendan might think so unnerved her completely. "Thank you," she finally managed to mumble.

"As Freya's maid, you must overhear most of the conversations in the main house," he continued smoothly.

Moira nodded, far too awed by him to respond more freely.

"What are they talking about tonight? Have you heard them mention me?"

Brendan's smile was so warm, his charm easily overcame Moira's reticence to speak. "No, Erik wants to clear land and build a house. They have been talking about that for hours."

Mystified by that revelation, Brendan found it impossible to believe. "Dana hasn't said anything about me? Are you certain?"

"She never talks about you," Moira insisted, not realizing how insulting her remark sounded. "Now I must go."

Brendan made no effort to detain the petite maid when her comments had made no sense at all to him. Why would Erik want to build another house when there was nothing wrong with the one he had? As for tending a farm, he had thought

Erik was only interested in raising falcons. And what of Dana? he wondered impatiently. He had expected her to be far too angry with him to want to discuss anything other than tearing him limb from limb. As always, he found the actions of the Danes on Haakon's farm impossible to comprehend.

The tantalizing aroma wafting from the bowl of stew on his supper tray captured his attention, and he sat down and began to eat. It would be impossible to keep up his strength without food, and he still feared he would need every last bit of stamina he possessed.

When Erik returned to his house for the night, he was still smiling happily. He hummed softly to himself as he undressed and fell asleep promptly, leaving Brendan to wonder how long he would have to wait for the punishment Dana was sure to inflict. She was so high-strung he had not realized she possessed the patience to make him wait for a whipping. He had not thought her so cruel as to make him suffer the torment of a long wait, but now he had proof that she most definitely was.

As Dana dressed in shades of cream and beige the next morning, she realized with a pang of conscience that the approach she had advised Erik to take was a devious rather than a straightforward one, but she soon shook off any sense of guilt. She told herself there was a vast difference between facing problems squarely and barging headlong into trouble totally unprepared. She was merely trying to help Erik overcome Grena's objections to him.

When they were ready to begin their explorations, Erik helped Dana mount Dawn's Kiss. Brendan was standing outside the stable and gave Thora a boost to Rascal's back, but Dana took care not to even glance in his direction for it would have been far too painful. Forcing herself to think only of her half brother's future, she rode through the gate displaying the easy confidence she always showed on horseback. Brendan had disrupted enough of her summer, and she was determined to see he did not do so ever again.

The preoccupied Celt stood with his hands on his hips, his glance dark as he watched the small riding party depart. The last time this foursome had gone riding together, he had been invited to go along, and he wasn't pleased at being left behind that day. He looked up at the sky, hoping to sight dark rain clouds that would soon drench them all, but the sky was clear and the gentle breeze free of the scent of rain.

How he was supposed to attend to his chores when he knew he had a whipping coming he didn't know. Dana couldn't have forgotten about punishing him. Was she merely too busy to bother with him now? After her ride, would the thought of watching him bleed be more appealing to her? Hearing his name, he wheeled around to find Freya and Moira walking his way. Not wanting his expression to give away the hopelessness of his mood, he forced himself to smile, but was only partly successful.

Freya gestured toward the stack of clothing in Moira's arms. "I meant to send these things over to you last night. Erik said you and he were the same size, but I told my women to cut your kirtles a little more generously through the shoulders. If you don't find them comfortable, then they can rip out the seams and try again. The breeches can also be altered, so don't feel you must wear them if they prove too snug."

Dumbfounded, Brendan took the two pairs of breeches and four kirtles from Moira, unable to do more than stare at the handsomely tailored garments in shades of blue, brown, and gray. Made of lightweight wool, they were the first new clothes he had been given in three years, and that they were such fine ones made accepting them graciously all the more difficult. He didn't want to take gifts from Danes. He wanted to throw the clothes in the dirt and tell Freya what he thought of her daughter, but instead he clutched the garments as possessively as he had the pitiful rags he had brought with him from Grena's.

"Is something the matter, Brendan?" Freya asked considerately. "We've not forgotten your undergarments. Is that what you're thinking? They should be finished by this afternoon."

Although overwhelmed by her generosity, Brendan finally found his voice. "I did not expect so much," he murmured softly.

"We're very pleased with your work, and when Erik said

you needed clothing, I was happy to provide it. Now why don't you go put those things away? Moira and I want to see the new foals, but we didn't mean to interfere with your routine.''

Brendan waited until Freya and her tiny maid had disappeared around the back of the stable before he started for Erik's house. He could not get over the fact Freya had again spoken to him as though he were a valued servant who had been with her family for many years rather than as a slave who would be spending only a few months in her care. She was so kind, he thought it a great pity her eldest daughter had inherited her remarkable beauty but none of the gentle sweetness of her ways.

While Soren had learned at an early age that Svien would inherit their father's farm, he had also been told his brother would give him a generous amount to compensate him for his share so that he could acquire property of his own. That tradition kept a family's holdings intact rather than divided from one generation to the next, but it had always rankled him that he was not the firstborn.

Erik's sudden announcement that he intended to clear unclaimed land and build a house had surprised them all, but Soren found it particularly troubling. What if Erik's land proved to be better than any he could find when he got ready to go out on his own? Being the second son was bad enough, but to have a half brother who was also competing for the remainder of the island's land was doubly unfair. He rode along, his expression as downcast as his mood, for while he knew Erik had never presented any competition for his father's love, land was a different matter altogether.

Turning back often to glance over his shoulder at Soren and Thora, Erik correctly guessed the cause of the boy's frown. His vow to spend more time with Soren had been a sincere one, and he slowed Shadow's pace until the boy reached his side.

"I thought we might begin looking for land for you today too, Soren. It will mean we'll have to clear a larger portion of the forest, but if you're willing to help me, then I'll do all that I can to help you."

As Dana listened to Soren's enthusiastic response, she

could not help but admire Erik's thoughtfulness. He was a remarkable young man, one who always had time to acknowledge the needs of others, and was never selfish about his son. Was Jarald's character as admirable? It took her little time to ponder that question, for nothing she had ever seen Jarald do or say led her to believe he gave a moment's thought to anyone but himself.

Of course, when it came to selfishness, she could not imagine a worse bully than Brendan. He was not only selfish, but obnoxious, arrogant, and demanding too. She had promised herself she would not dwell on the Celt, but somehow he had managed to invade her thoughts again. That was the only subtle thing about the slave, she mused silently—the way his distractingly handsome image crept into her mind no matter how hard she fought to keep him away.

Wanting to make the best choice of lands, the riding party covered ground they had ridden over for years but had never stopped to analyze. Haakon had a protected harbor and docks for his ships, but the shoreline adjacent to his offered nothing in the way of natural harbors for his sons to claim. Soren was certain Svien would allow them to use the docks when they became his, but Erik knew that day might be many years away. Because Haakon had never taught him how to sail, nor taken him on any voyages, Erik knew he ought not to count on the man sharing his docks with him.

"When neither of you owns a ship, is having a harbor all that important?" Dana inquired playfully.

"Yes, I think it is," Erik insisted, and as usual he had a valid reason for his opinion. "If we are choosing land for generations to come, we ought to choose it wisely."

"I'm sorry, I didn't mean to make light of your efforts," Dana responded immediately. "It's only that the meadow where we had our picnic is so lovely I'd claim that land and worry about a harbor later."

Erik couldn't help but smile broadly at that suggestion, for it was such a good one. To build a house on the spot where he and Berit had first allowed their feelings for each other free rein was wonderfully appealing. Drawing Dana aside, he whispered his request. "Would you do something for me? Tomorrow I'll tell Soren I'm too busy to look at land. Would you go to Grena's and invite Berit to go riding? I need to talk with her and let her know what we're planning."

"Of course," Dana agreed. "I'll be happy to help. Just tell Brendan to saddle my mare, and I'll go first thing."

"Thank you." Erik bent down to brush her cheek with a kiss. Then, seeing that Soren and Thora looked tired, he suggested they start for home.

The next morning Dana was relieved to find Dawn's Kiss saddled and waiting, but just as she reached the mare, Brendan suddenly stepped out of the stable to confront her. "It's been two days," he announced hoarsely. "Whatever hateful thing you plan to do to me, I want to get it over with now."

While Dana was accustomed to his frown, Brendan's expression held more than disgust that morning. He looked dead tired, as though he had been under a terrible strain, and since she had done her best to avoid him, she couldn't imagine why.

"I don't know what you're talking about. I'm planning only to ride over to Grena's to see Berit, and that doesn't concern you." While her voice was steady, Dana blushed slightly at the thought of her part in arranging a romantic rendezvous.

"How long are you going to make me wait?" Brendan asked in a threatening whisper.

"Wait for what?" Dana asked innocently. He was wearing one of his new kirtles, and the soft blue-gray shade made the vivid sapphire of his eyes all the more attractive. "I've told you more than once to ask Erik for whatever you need."

Brendan then moved so close he forced Dana back against the side of her mare. "I know you, Dana. You must still be seething after what I called you the other day. Why haven't you already punished me for that insult? Do you intend to wait a few more days, hoping I'll think you've forgotten so when you finally bring out your whip the torture will be all the worse?"

He had called her a heartless pagan bitch. The problem was she did have a heart, one that pounded quickly each time he was near, but until that instant Dana had not understood just how thoroughly he despised her. Her first impulse was to reach up and touch his cheek because she dared not draw him into an embrace. Yet it was plain that her touch would merely revolt him, and she left her hands at her sides.

Scarcely knowing where to begin to refute his ridiculous allegation, she summoned all the tact she possessed. "The only tortures you'll suffer over our misunderstanding will be of your own making, Brendan. I have no plans to punish you for what you said when the fault was mine. You have every right to your privacy and needn't have answered my questions. I didn't realize how our interest in finding a husband for Moira would sound to you either. I'm so sorry you've worried needlessly over this, but I am neither heartless nor cruel and I've no desire to cause you any pain."

Brendan's startled gaze swept Dana's expression, searching for evidence she was the liar he knew she had to be, but all he found was a stunning sincerity that made him feel like a complete fool. He had done little since they had parted but imagine how she would delight in humiliating him. To find she did not consider the violence of their last exchange worthy of a reprisal was almost more than he could believe.

He took a step backward as he fought the ridiculous urge to apologize. He wondered now if she would have suggested he marry Moira if he had answered her questions. Why hadn't he had sense enough to lie? He could have told her a dozen different stories, all equally heartbreaking, and all true. What would it have mattered that they were not his? He decided not to speak for fear he would make a bigger fool of himself than she must already think he was. Instead, he reached for Dana's hand. He brought it to his lips for a brief moment, and caressed her palm softly with a gentle kiss before releasing her. He then turned away, certain he would never understand her or his compelling need to try.

Dana closed her hand carefully, as though she could

capture Brendan's fleeting kiss and hold it for all time. That he had expected her to beat him was heartbreaking, but she was glad he had accepted her reassuring comments without the hostile response she was used to receiving from him.

Her mare turned her finely shaped head to glance back at her, and she realized that if she delayed any longer, Erik might think they weren't coming. Not wanting to be late, she led the eager horse over to the stump at the side of the stable door, where she could mount more easily, then left the yard at a brisk trot.

Fortunately, Erik's plan went smoothly, for Grena was delighted to allow Berit to go riding with a cousin she considered not only lovely, but levelheaded and wise. As soon as they had left her farm, Berit began to talk in a breathless rush.

"My mother tells me frequently that I should spend more time with you. She thinks you're going to marry Jarald, and she wants me to follow your example and flirt with his friends. I didn't tell her that you've no interest in the man, despite his wealth." Berit giggled mischievously, thinking that a marvelous joke on her mother. "Is Erik going to meet us somewhere?"

"Of course," Dana assured her. "I like your hair that way. It's very becoming."

Because Erik had asked her to wear her hair loose, Berit had begun tying her long honey-blond tresses at her crown with a ribbon and letting the back fall free. "Thank you. This is the way Erik likes it."

Dana regarded her cousin with a curious frown. "When did he see you wear it that way?"

"The last time we were together," Berit replied with a fetching blush. "I can't wait to see him again."

"He's very anxious to see you too." As they neared the wooded area that Erik had chosen for their rendezvous, he rode out to greet them, and Dana suddenly felt dreadfully out of place. The three of them had had such a good time at the picnic after the hunt, she had not dreamed she would feel so awkward, but when Erik gave Berit a long and enthusiastic kiss, she couldn't bear to remain with them.

"I know you two want to talk, and the day is so pretty I'd

rather ride. I'll meet you here later," she called out, and urging Dawn's Kiss to a canter, she hurried away.

Surprised by his half sister's rapid departure, Erik stared after her before dismounting and leading Berit's horse into the woods. "What did you tell Dana?" he asked as he reached up to encircle the blonde's waist and swing her down beside him.

"Why, nothing," Berit gasped in dismay. "How could you think that I would?"

Erik had not meant to upset his delightful companion, and he pulled her into his arms for another lengthy kiss before he spoke again. "You're not sorry, are you?"

"Sorry? Oh, Erik, you're making no sense at all this morning!" Berit cried out in a petulant moan. Wanting to recapture the loving mood they had shared when last together, she stood on her tiptoes to return his kiss. "Dana said that we would want to talk, but that's not what I want to do at all."

Erik intended to discuss his plans, but when Berit pressed her breasts to his chest and he felt her nipples grow taut, he found it impossible to think of anything other than making love. He needed no further coaxing to draw her down on the soft blanket of grass at their feet.

Berit gave a triumphant squeal as she slid his kirtle off over his head. "I like the fact you're dark. I always have. It makes you unique."

Erik knew he was unique in many important ways, but he didn't want to point them out now when she had meant only to pay him a compliment. "I like the fact you're fair," he murmured instead as he lowered his mouth to the curve of her throat. As before, her smooth skin was scented with a sweet floral fragrance that was as enticing as her generous affection. She returned his kisses with a child's enthusiasm for a new game, but he wanted her too badly to question the reason for her responsiveness.

Berit relaxed in Erik's arms, and yet she was never still. She raised her hands to ruffle his hair, then slid her fingertips down his back to hold him close. When he tugged on her tunic, she removed it quickly, then slipped off her chemise. By the time she had cast her linen shift aside, he was also nude.

They were screened by the lush canopy of leaves overhead, and the sun covered their sleek bodies with shimmering patches of light. They pleasured each other as they drank in the intoxicating sight of the other. Masculine strength and feminine grace, the lovers were soon entwined in an ageless clasp as they lost themselves in the stunning beauty they again created together.

As the pleasure swelled within him, Erik was certain Berit was unlike any other woman ever born, for she loved him with an unabashed delight that made him dare to believe for the very first time that he was the equal of any other man. Her glance was filled with playful affection, but her kisses promised undreamed-of ecstasy, and he wanted all she could give, and still more. He plunged deeply into the welcoming heat of her velvet core with a forceful rhythm, enthralled by a love more precious than he had ever hoped to find.

The rapturous bliss that swept through Erik filled Berit with a longing for fulfillment that grew ever more intense until at last it burst within her in a shower of splendor that sent her spirit soaring. Never had she expected making love to be so wildly pleasurable, and she clung to the handsome man she adored until the last tremors of joy they had shared had become no more than a lazy warmth.

"I don't ever want to go home," she breathed softly in his ear.

Erik raised himself up slightly, wanting to look at her as they talked, but the dreamy light in her eyes fascinated him, so he lowered his mouth to hers, wanting only to make love to her again and again until neither would ever want more. But he knew in his heart that day would never, ever come.

Not wanting to intrude on Erik and Berit, Dana rode a long way before turning around and retracing her path. When she came to the edge of the forest, she found them seated together, talking earnestly about the home they hoped to build. It wasn't until they rose and Erik kissed the pretty blonde good-bye that Dana noted how easily they went into each other's arms. There was nothing hesitant about their embrace, but instead it was a joyful celebration of love and life that made her heart ache with longing.

Afraid she might sound jealous of their happiness, Dana kept her thoughts to herself as she and Berit returned to her home. Berit was not in the mood to talk either, but her unusual silence didn't trouble Dana. She could understand how her cousin would want to savor whatever memories she and Erik had created that morning.

When they reached her home, Berit insisted Dana come in for something to eat. "My mother will think it very strange if you don't, and I don't dare let her suspect where I've really been."

While that was certainly true, Dana encouraged her cousin to be herself. "That you love Erik will come as a shock no matter when your mother finds out, but if you'll simply calm down, she'll not guess anything is amiss."

Berit placed her right hand over her heart. "I'll try, but that's why I need you. My heart is still beating as rapidly as when—" The lively blonde caught herself and demurely lowered her gaze. "As when Erik kissed me."

Dana regarded her cousin's appearance with a more thoughtful glance, and while Berit looked as pretty as when they had left to go riding that morning, the high color in her cheeks and bright sparkle in her eyes made Dana wonder just what Erik had done other than kiss her. "Were you two making love?"

"Dana! How can you ask me such a thing?" Obviously horrified, Berit turned to look toward her house and was greatly relieved her mother was nowhere in sight. Certain they would not be overheard, she replied more honestly, "You won't tell, will you? Promise me you won't tell."

Dana watched as huge tears formed in Berit's eyes, but she quickly reached out to pat her hand sympathetically. "Of course I won't tell. Your secret is safe with me, but I think Erik better get that house built as soon as he possibly can."

That the half brother who had always been so sensible had lost his head completely and become involved in a passionate love affair shocked Dana far more than she let

Berit see. Berit was a wildly romantic child, but Erik was a grown man! Taking her own advice, Dana discussed nothing more important than the mild summer weather while she enjoyed refreshments with Grena and her charming but secretive daughter. It wasn't until she rode home by herself that she realized just how deeply Erik had drawn her into their intrigues. She loved Erik and wanted him to be happy. She would not complain.

By the time she got back home, Dana was tired. When Freya again invited her into her sleeping chamber to talk, she would have much preferred to take a nap instead.

Freya's expression bore the same worried frown as during their last private conversation, but her concern was a far different one now. "I stepped out the door this morning in time to see Brendan place that adoring kiss in your hand. To say I was shocked that he would take such liberties with you does not even begin to describe my dismay. That you did nothing about it will only encourage him to display more affection the next time he has the chance. You are not leaving this room, Dana, until you tell me why you let him believe he has that right. I don't think I need remind you that if it had been your father who had seen what I did, Brendan would no longer be alive."

Because Dana knew that ghastly prediction might well be correct, fear encircled her throat with a suffocating grip. When it came to describing her complicated relationship with Brendan, Dana didn't even know where to begin. Her life had become a tangled web of deceit beginning with the hour they had met, but straightening her shoulders proudly, she decided another lie or two couldn't hurt her now, and she would not let anyone harm Brendan either.

CHAPTER XI

Attempting, for Brendan's sake as well as her own, to project a confidence she didn't feel, Dana sat down on her mother's bed and made herself comfortable before replying to Freya's startling accusation. "I think Brendan must have been badly abused before coming to us, Mother, because he reacts to our smallest kindness with an extraordinary show of gratitude. I'm so sorry you were upset this morning because I had merely thanked him for saddling Dawn's Kiss, and you saw how moved he was. Except for the fact he didn't throw himself at my feet, his gesture was no different than when he kissed your hands. I'm sure had Father been here that day, he would have been as touched as you were by Brendan's humility, not enraged by it."

Taken in by the calmness of her daughter's manner, as well as the reasonable nature of her explanation, Freya was deeply embarrassed by how quickly she had leapt to a shockingly erroneous conclusion. Going to Dana's side, she sat down and slipped her arm around her waist.

"Before you presume to predict your father's reactions, which is a grave danger in itself, you must remember that if he were, Brendan would not be. I think you might be right about Brendan, because when I gave him some new clothes yesterday, he appeared to be overwhelmed. The problem is he is young and very handsome. Had someone else observed him kissing your hand, they would also have been shocked. They might even have suspected he is your lover, and that's a risk you simply must avoid.

"Everyone knows our menfolk amuse themselves with

145

attractive thralls, but women are never permitted that same privilege. Your reputation would be irrevocably damaged should there be rumors about you and Brendan. Your father, or Jarald for that matter, would undoubtedly react to that disgrace by killing the Celt rather than investigating the source of the lie. I will have to speak with him about confining his expressions of gratitude to words.''

Dana dared not provide her mother with the opportunity to discover Brendan was not at all the man she had described him to be. ''No, I think I should be the one to do it,'' she insisted, ''because the problem concerns his behavior with me.'' When her mother didn't instantly argue, the relieved redhead pushed their conversation in a new direction. ''I did speak with him about Moira, but he has no interest in marrying while he is a thrall.''

''But he should be able to earn his freedom soon.''

''That would be true if he belonged to us, but he doesn't. I didn't dare promise him something so important as his freedom when I can't be certain Jørn will grant it. That would be cruel.''

Impressed by her daughter's insight, Freya's fears for her reputation were laid to rest and she let the matter drop. ''You're right, of course. We'll not mention marriage to him again, but it does seem that he would be perfect for Moira.''

Since Dana had done her best to make her mother believe Brendan was as mild an individual as their shy maid, she didn't dare contradict that opinion, but she knew Moira was no match for a man with the Celt's violent temper. Eager to be excused, she covered a wide yawn as she rose to her feet.

''Berit and I rode farther than we had planned today, and I'd like to rest awhile. Was there anything else?''

Freya found it difficult to recall when she had been Dana's age, but she was certain she had not been nearly so mature and confident, despite the fact she had married at sixteen and borne a son ten months later. ''No, but you must caution Brendan about his behavior at your first opportunity. Scandalous talk about what occurs between you two would be ruinous to you, but might well cost him his life. I think once he understands that danger, he will avoid touching you ever again.''

"He's bright," Dana reminded her mother. "He should have no trouble understanding what I mean." As Dana left Freya's sleeping chamber to go to her own, she carried a heavy burden of guilt for again having lied to her mother. She had had such good intentions in the beginning. She had wanted only to spare her mother the distress of Brendan's abusive ways. Somehow that noble cause had gotten completely turned around until it was now Brendan that she was protecting. What a ridiculous happenstance that was.

Brendan would surely laugh at her, if not far worse, for what she had done. She sat down on her bed and, thinking of him, rubbed her palms together slowly, creating the same subtle warmth as Brendan's kiss. It had been such a tender gesture, filled with the sweetness he let her see all too seldom. Now she would have to tell him she did not want to see it ever again, but she knew she would be lying to herself as well as to him.

Once assured he would not be whipped, Brendan had little time to contemplate how greatly he had misunderstood Dana's intentions, for that afternoon Erik took him out to the meadow where they had gone hunting and announced his plan to build a house there. The spot was attractive, the soil rich, and the perceptive Celt felt certain the man's sudden interest in farming had to be connected to his high regard for Berit.

Erik had brought two hunting dogs and one of his falcons, and as the bird soared above them, Brendan tried to make tactful comments. Because his impressions had never served him as well as he had expected with these Danes, he had begun to think what he saw were such tiny glimpses of their lives that he would never fully understand them.

"The summer is a good time to build a house," he finally remarked, hoping to inspire Erik to reveal why he wanted to begin the project.

Erik, however, was busy watching his falcon as he walked about judging the gentle slope of the meadow. "I want to make it large enough to begin with so that we don't have to add on to it later," he called over his shoulder.

"Have you ever built a house?"

Erik walked back toward him, his smile still as wide as it had been when he had kissed Berit good-bye. "No, but we employ others who have. It isn't difficult, although the work will be hard. I'm going to put the boys who handled the stable before you back to work there so you can help me out here. In fact, we probably ought to live out here while the construction is going on."

While it would not be the first time he had slept under the stars, Brendan's immediate concern was the distressing one that he would be unable to see Dana. The high-strung beauty had caused him nearly endless torment. Why would he want to see her? he asked himself accusingly. He knew the answer to that question, but he had found that wanting a desirable woman and getting along with her were two entirely different things. Because the possibility he had fallen in love with her was something it was painful to admit, even to himself, Brendan decided it would do him a tremendous amount of good not to have to be near her.

"I like that idea," he agreed enthusiastically. "It will save us the effort of going back and forth each day, and it will take us much less time to build your house."

"Have you any skill at carpentry?"

"I am good at everything," Brendan boasted proudly.

"Somehow I knew that you would be," Erik replied with a chuckle. Eager to begin work, as soon as the falcon had returned with a pheasant, he hooded the bird and left it perched on the back of his saddle. He had brought along two shovels, and after he had tossed one to Brendan, they began to dig up the lush wild grass to mark where he wanted his new house to be.

Berit's shoulder brushed Dana's as they peered through the leaves. Hidden by the dense foliage at the edge of the beech woods, the pretty cousins were observing closely as Erik, Soren, Brendan, and the dozen men working with them raised the last in the double row of posts that would support the roof of the new house.

"Just look how well they're doing," Berit exclaimed excitedly.

The men had been hard at work for more than a week,

first felling trees and then sheering away the branches to prepare the sturdy posts needed for construction. Dana knew Berit had every reason to be excited about the fine house Erik was building for her, but she murmured only a distracted word of agreement as she continued to give Brendan her full attention. While all the men had muscular builds, none of the others caught her interest. The Celt had been tan, but working without a kirtle had made his skin even more deeply bronzed. Yet even from a distance the sight of his badly scarred back made her shudder.

Dana had not seen Brendan since the morning he had demanded the whipping she had not planned to give, but knowing he thought her so cruel a mistress pained her still. As before, the time they had spent apart had not lessened the man's appeal in the slightest and Dana did not understand why. She had hoped seeing him again would put her restless heart at ease, but now she feared her weakness for him was an affliction from which she might never recover. Whether she saw him or not, thoughts of him filled her days with longing and her nights with indescribable torment. It was humiliating to admit that she found a thrall who despised her the most attractive man she had ever met. It made no sense, but it was not the practical side of her nature that ached with desire.

Erik was expecting them to arrive around noon, and when the men paused to rest after completing their task, Dana stepped out into the sunlight. As soon as Erik had seen her and waved, she turned back into the shadows. He would know Berit was with her, but it would have been far too dangerous for anyone else to suspect how he planned to spend his time while the others stopped to eat. That Soren might grow curious about his absence concerned them, but the youth enjoyed the company of the men with whom he had been working, and Erik hoped he would stay with them as he usually did.

Brendan had felt Dana's gaze long before she left her hiding place. Being watched created a curious sensation, an uneasiness he couldn't shake until he realized its source. He caught only a brief glimpse of the slender redhead before she vanished into the woods. She was dressed in the rose and pink garments he found so attractive, and he wished she had crossed the meadow to observe their progress up close.

When Erik left hurriedly, Brendan could not contain his curiosity, for it seemed unlikely the man would flash such a wide grin at the prospect of speaking with his sister. He thought it far more likely Erik was dashing off to meet Berit, but what would occupy Dana's time while those two were together?

The field hands helping with the construction were gathering in small groups to share a noon meal. Soren had already sat down with his back toward the forest, but the boy was not the one who gave him his orders, so Brendan didn't care what he thought. Hungry for something far more delicious than dried fish and cheese, he hesitated only a moment, and then, certain no one would notice his departure, he followed Erik into the woods.

The inquisitive Celt heard a woman's laughter floating through the trees, but it was too high-pitched to be Dana's so he didn't pursue the sound. Instead, he scanned the patches of sunlight dotting the forest floor and luckily caught sight of a rose-hued blur moving off to his right. Certain that had to the young woman he sought, he summoned the stealth of a born hunter and silently began to close the distance separating them. He had not gone far when it occurred to him that not only Erik, but also his desirable half sister might be meeting a lover, and he quickened his pace. If there was a man who claimed ownership of Dana's heart, then he was eager to get a look at him.

Unaware she was being followed, Dana wandered aimlessly through the woods. She stopped occasionally to pluck a wildflower or a deep red berry, but she was merely out for an enjoyable stroll and had no destination in mind. When she came to the stream that flowed into the meadow and would provide water for Erik's farm, she knelt down beside it to take a drink. Cupping the cool water in her hands, she sipped her fill before noticing Brendan's reflection hovering above hers in the sparkling water.

Certain his image was a trick played by her imagination, she turned around expecting to find herself alone, but Brendan stood right behind her. Water dripped off his curls and slid down the smooth planes of his bare chest, making it obvious he had stopped to wash off the dirt and sweat of the morning before confronting her. Such concern for his appearance struck Dana as absurd when she knew what he thought of her, so she decided he must have merely been trying to refresh himself, not impress her.

"What are you doing here?" she asked with a poise that belied her dismay.

Bending down beside her, Brendan scooped up a drink of his own. "I was thirsty too," he explained with a mocking grin.

Because he was already dripping wet, Dana thought his response unlikely. She tried to look away, to focus her attention on the bubbling stream, on the canopy of leaves overhead, or the carpet of new grass cushioning her knees, but her traitorous gaze swiftly returned to the sarcastic curve of Brendan's smile. She wondered again how he had gotten the thin scar that crossed his lip, but knew he would not reply to so personal a question and refrained from asking it. Looking at Brendan was like facing her worst nightmare fully awake, and silence seemed to be her only weapon when he twisted each word she spoke into an insult.

Brendan watched a shadow of apprehension fill Dana's glance, but he had not meant to frighten her. She had not reached for her knife, though. Her hands were resting lightly on her knees, and he considered that a good sign. "I know Erik is meeting Berit. Are you meeting someone too?"

"How could you know?"

Her question shocked Brendan as badly as his sudden appearance had startled her. He looked around quickly to make certain her lover was not approaching with sword in hand. When he found the surrounding woods still deserted, he turned back to face her. "You are very beautiful. Why shouldn't you have a dozen lovers if you want them?"

Exasperated that he would again mention the subject of lovers, Dana replied flippantly, "Whether or not I take lovers is no concern of yours."

"What do you mean, 'whether or not'? You just said you were meeting someone. Isn't he your lover?"

Thoroughly confused, Brendan couldn't recall exactly

what she had said, but he found her outraged expression so charming he began to smile. "If no one is coming, then I'll stay with you so you don't become lonely."

"No, that's not a good idea," Dana responded immediately. "You should go back to the others."

Thinking their argument might prove to be a lengthy one, Brendan made himself more comfortable by assuming a cross-legged pose by her side. "They're having something to eat and I doubt they'll get back to work before Erik returns. You need me far more than they do."

"Is there no end to your conceit?" Dana asked as she started to rise.

Brendan reached out to encircle her wrist with a firm grasp so she could neither escape him nor reach for her knife. "Is it conceit that makes me prefer to spend my time with you rather than them?" The wily Celt realized he had revealed more than he wished to with that question, but it was too late to take back his words.

His hand formed too confining a restraint for her to shake him off, so Dana made no attempt to struggle. Instead, she recited the speech her mother had instructed her to give. "You mustn't touch me, Brendan. It's not only disrespectful, but dangerous as well. My father will not tolerate even the slightest hint of gossip about us, and—"

As Brendan listened, he saw an intensity of emotion in Dana's violet gaze that was far different from that conveyed by her words. Being apart had done nothing to lessen his fascination with the stunning redhead, and her threats of a gruesome death at Haakon's hands failed to faze him. Although he doubted she would ever admit that she cared for him, her concern for his safety proved that she did. That was not nearly enough to please him, but it was a sign something more was possible. Impatient for that day to arrive, he offered what he considered a fine suggestion.

"If you were to meet me each time Erik meets Berit, how would there be any gossip for your father to hear?"

As Dana finally succeeded in wrenching her gaze from his, she wondered if all young men were such reckless fools. "Did you hear nothing I said? The thrill of an affair isn't worth your life, Brendan. Now let me go and hurry back to work."

Rather than being angered that she was again ordering him about like the slave he would never accept being, Brendan chose to comment on her first remark. "I'm glad to hear you already know that having an affair with me would be thrilling. It will save me the trouble of having to convince you of that." When Dana turned a truly murderous stare on him, Brendan broke out in hearty laughter.

"You must not think of me as a thrall, Dana, for I never do. I wasn't born one, and I won't die one either." Before she could point out that his opinion mattered not at all as long as Jørn's claim of ownership was considered valid, he had pulled her across his lap and covered her lips with his own. Caught off guard, she lacked the leverage to push him away.

While Brendan's embrace was a confining one, his kiss was feather-light. He longed to take her swiftly, to give free rein to the savage passion she always aroused within him, but he fought that impulse in hopes of winning a far more valuable surrender. He longed to tame the wildness of her spirit, to make her admit that accepting his affection would be worth risking any danger, even death. That was his goal, but Dana's heart was not a prize so easily won. Wise enough to realize this, Brendan finally had to admit defeat and bring his lingering kiss to an end.

Keeping her cradled in his arms, he kissed her delicately arched brows, her flushed cheeks, and then brushed her lips softly with his own. "The choice has always been yours, Dana. I cannot force you to take me for your lover. You must want me as badly as I want you."

Snuggled against his bare chest, Dana was certain she already did, but that was not something she dared admit. "You regard me with contempt one day, and then attempt to seduce me the next. You are the one who has no idea what he wants."

As Brendan looked down at her, reveling in the uniqueness of her rare beauty, he wanted to laugh again at the absurdity of her words, for he knew precisely what he wanted from her. The attraction that existed between them was too powerful a force to mistake for anything other than the obsession it was rapidly becoming.

"I know what I want," he vowed confidently as he regarded the lush curves of her figure with a boldly appreciative glance.

No stranger to the lustful admiration of young men, Dana rebelled as she had so often in the past. "It is not a lover I want," she explained with the same cool disdain she had frequently received from him, "but merely an obedient thrall."

For the first time Brendan began to suspect Dana might be more her father's daughter than her mother's. A woman with such fierce pride would never accept the domination of any man unless it was by her own choice. In her case, he thought only a king would possess the strength of will necessary to subdue her wildly independent nature. That thought brought a slow smile to his lips, for a king was exactly what he had been raised to be.

Despite her defiant words, Dana had made no effort to move off his lap, and he was pleased that even after he began to stroke her bright red curls she remained nestled contentedly in his arms. Like her concern for his welfare, her behavior now told him her feelings for him were far warmer than she would admit. The challenge was to fan that warmth into flames, however, and he was not a patient man.

"Jarald must be a clumsy brute," he whispered seductively, "if he has made you afraid of making love."

Dana risked peering up at him, then wished that she hadn't, for his expression was one of sympathetic concern rather than sarcasm. "Do you really expect me to reply to such a ridiculous comment?"

"Why not? Women often confide secrets to a lover that they would never share with a husband."

Dana sighed softly, then closed her eyes for a moment. "You are neither my lover nor my husband, so I'll share no secrets of any kind with you."

Brendan wound his fingers in her curls, and when his palm brushed her cheek he forced her to look up at him. "What am I then, Dana? What am I to you?"

Her gaze again captured by the stirring intensity of his, Dana stared up at the man who continually provoked an emotional turmoil the likes of which she had never known. What was he to her? What, indeed, for there seemed to be no word to describe the longing that filled her heart each time they were together.

"Why would you care what a pagan bitch thinks?" she finally asked, her taunt a deliberately hostile one.

That she would recall an insult he had hurled during a heated argument gave him a moment's pause, but Brendan was far too determined to possess her to give up his quest now. After releasing her hair, he reached for her hand, and bringing it to his lips, he kissed each of her fingertips tenderly before tickling her palm with the tip of his tongue.

"I thought you had taken me into the woods to make love. Surely you can understand how disappointed I was to discover what you truly wanted. I had every right to be furious then, for Moira is no substitute for you. You have both beauty and spirit, while, sadly, she has neither." The timbre of his voice deepened as he grew more bold. "It was you I wanted that day, and I want you even more desperately now."

His lips parted slightly as he lowered his head, and Dana knew she should flee as though her very life were in danger, but his arms encircled her with such a tender embrace she wanted only to stay. Such a desire was impossible, of course, for more reasons than she could count, but as his mouth covered hers she could recall none of them. She raised her hand to his shoulder, then wove her fingers in the tawny curls at his nape to hold him close as she welcomed his kiss with a graceful abandon. His response was a low moan from the back of his throat, and without ending the kiss he pulled her down onto the lush grass that blanketed the soil at the edge of the stream.

Brendan drew her so close his right hip and leg were resting on hers. Dana was dimly aware that he was cleverly blocking her access to her knife, but such a precaution was unnecessary, for the last thing she would ever do was harm him. His kisses were slow and deep, flavored with an adoring sweetness she readily returned. She would have been content to float forever on the cloud of desire that surrounded them, but Brendan had made it plain that he wanted far more.

The Celt's touch was light as he began to trace the luscious swells of Dana's figure. He soon slid his hand beneath her woolen tunic but swiftly grew impatient that her silk chemise and linen shift separated them still. He knew her flesh would be as smooth and flavorful as rich cream, and he longed to strip her bare so he could taste as well as feel her beauty. Moving away for an instant, he succeeded in lifting her tunic off over her head. The ribbon securing the neckline of her chemise came untied easily, and when he pushed the silken garment off her shoulder, the linen shift slipped out of his way to expose one perfectly formed breast.

Just as he had imagined, the tip was a delicate pink that flushed with a hint of rose as his fingertips teased it into a firm bud. Eager to deepen the thrill of his discovery, he bent down to draw that tantalizing morsel into his mouth, where his tongue could encircle the silken flesh with sensuous rings of praise. His joy increased as he felt Dana respond with a shudder of delight. Her hands moved over his shoulders, then down his back, gently tracing the raised patterns left by the whip before moving through the coarse curls covering his chest.

Brendan had never wanted any woman as badly as he wanted Dana. It was no longer the challenge to possess the fiery beauty that drove him, but a desire so deep it bordered upon madness. He clung to her, his lips returning to hers again and again before he peeled her chemise clear down to her waist. Discovering the cut of her shift was too narrow to allow the access to her breasts he craved, he simply ripped it open and buried his face between the kiss-swollen mounds.

The wildness of Brendan's passion inflamed her own, and had he been wearing a kirtle, Dana would have ripped it from him. With each kiss he gave, she wanted more. Never passive, she lured him on with breathless sighs and caresses that grew increasingly more bold until finally she slid her hands beneath the waistband of his breeches to ease them down over his hips.

Brendan scarcely needed such enthusiastic encouragement to make love to her, but he was grateful for it, all the same. He raised himself up on his elbows to look down at her, wanting to memorize the glow that passion gave her gaze, but as he leaned down to kiss her they heard Berit calling her name, followed by a sparkling burst of giggles that sounded much too close.

When Brendan gave a harsh cry of disappointment, Dana clamped her hand over his mouth to silence him. She had to struggle to catch her breath, but succeeded in doing so before he did. "Hush," she ordered in a frantic whisper. When he got up and pulled his breeches back into place, she looked down at her torn and disheveled garments and feared she must look as though she had been raped. Although her hands shook badly, she managed to pull her torn shift together and wiggle back into her chemise. She yanked her tunic over her head, then stood up and brushed off the blades of grass that clung to the deep rose fabric.

Brendan looked no better than she felt, and while they could still hear Berit calling her name, Dana couldn't bring herself to reply. "I am so sorry," she began.

"Don't wait for Berit to come back to see Erik. Meet me here tonight."

"Oh, no, I couldn't."

"You must!"

Dana ran her fingers through her curls and winced at the tangles. "No, that's impossible." What had happened to her mind? she groaned inwardly. She was bright. How could she have thrown herself at Brendan as she had? The man's touch had an indescribable magic and his kiss was divine, but that did not change the fact he was a thrall, and the pleasure they had shared was too dangerous to repeat.

Correctly reading the fear in her expression, Brendan reached out to grab her arms and pulled her close. "Tell Berit you fell asleep. That will explain how you look. Meet me back here tonight, or I will go to Grena and tell her exactly how her daughter spent the afternoon. You know what will happen to Erik's plans to wed her then."

"You wouldn't!"

Cleverly Brendan had not threatened Dana directly when he knew her love for her half brother would make a far better weapon. "Oh, yes, I would, and you know it too."

Dana's eyes filled with tears, but her terror failed to move Brendan. His expression remained fierce as he awaited her reply. She swallowed hard, trying to think of some way to change his mind. "It is too far," she finally argued. "You can't expect me to come all this way in the dark."

Brendan increased the pressure on her arms until pain filled her glance with dread, but still she would not agree to his demand. "All right. Meet me at the edge of the woods where we talked last week, but you must be there before midnight or I will make my way to Grena's. I want what you offered me so willingly this afternoon too badly to wait past tonight to have it."

Too late Dana realized her impulse to run had been the one she should have heeded rather than allowing her weakness for him to overrule her reason. She still had a choice, however. She could tell Erik what Brendan intended to do. She knew Erik would help her, but as she heard Berit calling her name again, that seemed like a terribly selfish way out of her dilemma, for Erik had more than enough problems of his own without her creating new ones for him. This was a mess she had gotten into on her own, and she would have to get out of it the same way.

"I'll meet you at the edge of the woods. You have my word on it."

Brendan bid her farewell with a bruising kiss. "I'll have far more than that, Dana. Don't be late."

When he released her, Dana walked away with all the dignity she could summon, but she had never expected the joy she had found in his arms to so quickly turn to dread.

CHAPTER XII

As they returned to Grena's farm, Dana and Berit provided a study in stark contrasts. Berit was relaxed, smiling radiantly as she talked about the home she soon hoped to share with Erik. Dana's features were etched with tension, however, for she was filled with a dreadful sense of foreboding that made attending to her ebullient companion's comments nearly impossible. When they reached Grena's, she again stayed to have refreshments with her aunt, but the effort to converse with the woman gave her a headache so severe that by the time she left she feared she might actually topple from her mare's back before reaching home.

Dana knew she had to meet Brendan that night. She simply could not risk jeopardizing Erik and Berit's future by defying him. She had absolutely no intention of submitting to his demand that they become lovers, though. They had not had sufficient time to talk after Berit had interrupted them, a happenstance for which she was supremely grateful, but talk was all she intended to do later.

While it was plain Brendan wanted her, and badly, she was positive he would want his freedom more. She would offer him that prize, with the two conditions that he make no further demands on her and that he also keep his silence about Erik and Berit's romance. To her it seemed like an excellent exchange, and one Brendan could not possibly refuse. How she would arrange the details of setting him free she was not certain, but she was confident she could accomplish it without revealing to either her mother or aunt the reason why it was imperative that she do so.

The day had taken on a seemingly interminable length by the time the distraught redhead retired for bed. To make matters worse, Thora was in a playful mood. Dana had hoped her sister would fall asleep as quickly as she usually did, but that night the ten-year-old giggled and talked far later than she ever had. When finally she did close her eyes, Dana was so relieved she did not immediately rise and prepare to leave, but instead remained in the bed they shared to silently rehearse what she wished to say to Brendan. By the time she was certain she had found the perfect manner in which to propose her bargain, the strain of the day had left her exhausted.

Thinking she would be wise to take a brief nap before meeting the wily Celt, Dana gave in to the irresistible urge to close her eyes and rest. Her bed was warm, and snuggled in the thick quilts, she felt the pain of her dilemma swiftly replaced with thoughts of Brendan that were both compelling and sweet.

The landscape of her dream was a moonlit shore. She was standing at the water's edge, watching Brendan swim toward her from far out in the shimmering sea. When he reached shallow water, he stood and began to walk toward her. The water streaming off his broad shoulders reflected the moon's radiant light, creating a glittering cape that hurled droplets of fiery brilliance with every step. He was nude, and the perfection of his powerful build gave him the mystical aura of a god, but it was his eyes that captured her heart with a gaze so piercing it burned clear through her, igniting an unquenchable flame of desire.

She stood transfixed, unable to greet him with more than a low moan before he reached her. He did not speak either, but merely inclined his head to brush her lips with a gentle kiss. The cool seawater dripping from his curls rolled down her cheek, leaving the salty trail of a tear. His lips were warm, enticing, inviting surrender, but when she reached out to enfold him in her arms his sea-bathed body was as cold as death.

Instantly reacting to the shock of that unexpected chill, Dana awoke with a start. Her heart was pounding wildly, and she knew that had she not awakened when she did she would have given herself to Brendan with the same mindless abandon she had displayed that afternoon. She was horrified that her desires betrayed her even in her sleep, but she soon shoved that disgrace aside when she realized she had no idea how long she had slept. What if it was past midnight and Brendan had already left for Grena's?

After leaping from her bed, Dana dared not waste any time changing out of her nightgown, but she donned her cloak and hoped the ample folds of the long woolen garment provided a modest enough covering. Barefoot, she tiptoed out of the house, then broke into a run as she crossed the yard. The moon was high overhead, feeding her fears that she would be too late to stop Brendan, but just as she reached the stable he tore around the corner astride Sky Dancer and nearly ran her down.

Brendan had waited at the edge of the woods long past the hour he had sworn to depart. Infuriated that Dana had not kept her promise to meet him, he had decided to insult her in return by riding Haakon's prize stallion to Grena's.

That he had come so close to trampling the stunning redhead horrified him, but he reached down to pluck her off her feet, and holding her tightly in front of him, he carried her back to the spot where they had agreed to meet.

The breath forced from her lungs by Brendan's confining grasp, Dana laced her fingers in Sky Dancer's flowing mane and tried to hang on rather than give in to the weakness that threatened to leave her in a helpless faint. To again be in Brendan's arms was terrible, and to be on Sky Dancer's back made that outrage all the worse. The magnificent horse seemed to find two people as easy to carry as one, for his stride was long and swift, but she could not ignore the fact that Brendan had again defied her wishes by choosing her father's stallion as his mount.

As they neared the secluded spot where Brendan had expected to find Dana waiting earlier, he loosened his hold on her waist and began to nuzzle the elegant line of her throat with light kisses. She was the most perverse of females, but her flowing cloak convinced him she had been on her way to meet him, and he would not waste the few remaining hours of darkness in criticizing her tardiness. He had spent the time they had been apart in nearly breathless anticipation, and he intended to claim the prize that had eluded him earlier without further delay.

That Brendan's mood would be so loving surprised Dana, but knowing she dared not accept any of his affection, she hastened to escape his embrace the instant he brought Sky Dancer to a halt. In the dark she misjudged the distance to the ground, stumbled, and lost her footing. Before she could scramble to her feet and back away, Brendan had slid from the white stallion's back, given him a whack on the rump to send him out of their way, and joined her on the grass.

Pulling her into a fervent embrace, he silenced her protests before she could voice them. The hours they had been apart dissolved in his mind, and they were again at the edge of the stream, allowing their passions free rein. Bathed in sunlight, Dana's perfume had teased his senses. Now veiled in a sensuous web of darkness, the exotic fragrance spurred his desire, driving him to put an end to the physical torment his need for her had made him endure all day. He paused to yank off his kirtle, then again captured her lips in a searing kiss that took her breath away.

Appalled that the amorous Celt was again wreaking havoc with her emotions, Dana tried to summon the anger necessary to break free of his enthusiastic embrace, but she failed miserably and her motions were so subtle they served only to arouse him to further heights. He then pulled her right hand down between them to rub the smooth surface of her palm against the hardened shaft of his manhood. What he wanted was shockingly plain, but Dana continued to fight a losing battle within herself, for she was loath to admit it was what she wanted too.

Even crazed with desire, Brendan recognized Dana's reticence to complete what they had begun that afternoon. She had not been the one kept waiting, however, and he had no intention of allowing the dawn to overtake them before he had had his fill of her charms. He wanted her nude, and eased the burden of his weight from her lissome body for the fraction of a second it required to pull her cloak and flowing nightgown off over her head.

"Brendan," Dana gasped as his lips left hers momentarily, but all too soon his hair-roughened chest was pressed against the lush fullness of her bare breasts and she could recall none of the speech she had so carefully prepared. His next kiss was flavored with the adoring sweetness he had shown her that afternoon, and she could no longer deny that she wanted him as badly as she had then.

Encouraged by the warmth of Dana's acceptance, Brendan relaxed his hold on her. He moved aside so he could caress the tender tips of her breasts with his hands and lips until he had coaxed a soft sigh of surrender from her, for he wanted their pleasure to be shared. Continuing that quest, he moved his hand over the smooth hollow of her stomach, across her hip, and then down the outside of a thigh that proved to be as long and shapely as he had imagined. After gliding over her knee, he traced the gentle curve of her inner thigh, slowly moving his hand higher until his fingertips brushed the triangle of curls he was certain would be as fiery a red as her flowing tresses.

Dana knew all hope of reasoning with him was already

lost, but she still tried to elude his touch as it grew increasingly more intimate. Brendan's response was a low chuckle as he delved even deeper into her welcoming wetness. She reached down to clasp his wrist, but then could not bear to push him away when his rhythmic touch filled her with longing for still more of the most exquisite sensation she had ever felt. She had never dreamed she could be so dreadfully weak, but, then, she had never allowed any man to take more than a hurried kiss she had had no desire to return. Brendan was like no other man, though, and the tenderness of his tantalizing touch had proved that in a way his words never could.

Brendan readily sensed when Dana became as desperate for them to become one as he. He was also clever enough to grab her wrists with one hand as he pushed his breeches down and shifted his position into the classic one for possession. He had never slept with a virgin, and when his first gentle probings revealed an inviting snugness, he pushed forward, seeking to make the pristine recesses of her beautifully formed body welcome the full length of his now throbbing shaft. It was not merely her flesh which resisted him, but Dana herself as well. She tried to pull back, but Brendan held her fast. He knew he could make up later for whatever pain he caused her now, and with a forceful lunge he put an end to her innocence and buried himself deep within her womanly core.

The first twinge of pain as her body refused to immediately accommodate his brought Dana to her senses. As swiftly as the deathly chill of his wet skin had ended her wonderfully erotic dream, her present torment shocked her into the full realization of what she was about to do, but there was no escape. Brendan held her too securely, and his weight kept her in place while he was able to move at will. With an insistent thrust, he swiftly claimed what should have been her husband's right, and robbed of the pride the gift of her virtue would have been, Dana felt only shame. She had blindly followed an unreasoning passion to its natural end and in doing so had selfishly betrayed her own honor.

Brendan lay still within her, fighting his own need for

fulfillment as he waited for the tension that filled his lovely partner to subside. He raised himself up slightly to speak. "It's no wonder that you were frightened. I imagine all women are the first time they make love, but you'll enjoy it the next time."

Fright did not begin to describe how Dana felt. She wanted to scream and bite and kick. No action seemed too desperate to her if it would make him stay away from her forever. To make even the slightest noise, she would need to draw a breath, though, and she felt incapable of doing even so little as that.

Because he could not recall ever finding Dana speechless, Brendan leaned down to kiss her. "You wanted me," he whispered persuasively. "Do not say that you didn't, because you did."

Oh, yes, she had. Dana could not deny nor pretend that she hadn't. That was the cause of her shame. Erik and Berit loved each other, but what did she and Brendan share? Nothing but a senseless passion that had robbed her of all sense of pride and self-respect. The man did not love her, and never would. They were as different as any man and woman could possibly be. Enemies, that's all they were, and what they would always remain.

Brendan was in no mood to talk, and because nothing he had said had made any impact on Dana, he lowered his mouth to hers and began to move his hips with a gentle rhythm, creating a pattern of thrusts that were alternately shallow and deep. He wanted her to respond with the wild delight he knew she possessed, but he was determined to take his own pleasure, even if she denied him the compliment of hers.

At first Dana felt only a cool numbness, but soon Brendan's motions brought an alluring warmth that enticed her ravaged emotions, then conquered her resistance, and finally yielded another joyous surrender. She clung to him then, wanting him, needing him, and the heat of her desire inflamed his until they were borne aloft on a dizzying spiral of rapture. It spun slowly, allowing their spirits to hover on a plateau of ecstasy where they remained entwined in each other's arms until the first bird nesting nearby sang to greet the coming dawn.

"I must go!" Dana whispered hoarsely, instantly shattering the bliss of their mood. They were surrounded by a shadowy mist, but once the sun had reached the horizon there would be too much light for her to return home safely. With the strength that had deserted her earlier, she shoved Brendan aside and rose to her feet. She grabbed up her nightgown and slipped it on over her head, then her cloak. She ran to get Sky Dancer, but Brendan blocked her way before she could mount him.

"Aren't you going to kiss me good-bye?" he asked as he raked his curls off his forehead. It had been a simple matter for him to dress as well, since he had not bothered to remove either his breeches or boots before their passionate encounter.

Thinking the request absurd, Dana looked away quickly. "There isn't time. I don't dare be late, and neither do you."

Insulted that she would again order him about after the intimacy they had shared, Brendan reached out to grab her arm and yanked her around to face him. "Are you ashamed of me? Is that it? You're ashamed because you gave yourself to a thrall?"

The teasing light that had filled his eyes only moments before was gone now, replaced with the hostile gleam she despised. "Ashamed of you?" she repeated distractedly. He was not only handsome, but bright and clever. No woman would be ashamed of a lover who gave the abundant pleasure he did. Forcing herself to look at him squarely, she told him the truth.

"I am ashamed there is no love between us. I can't forgive myself for that."

Brendan thought the continually perplexing redhead daft, for the overpowering attraction that flowed between them far surpassed the thrill of love, in his estimation. This was no time to argue the point, however, and he made no effort to do so. "Wait," he said instead. Going to pick up his kirtle, he hurried back and smoothed it out on Sky Dancer's back.

"This is not the morning for you to ride a white horse without a blanket."

Dana blushed deeply as he gave her a boost onto Sky Dancer's back, for she understood precisely what he meant. She had neither the means nor time to wash away the evidence of their passion, but she had no desire to leave telltale stains on the snowy white stallion's glossy hide. Taking a firm hold on the reins, she urged the horse past Brendan, but he called out after her.

"Remember, whenever Erik meets Berit, you will be with me."

Shocked by the demand, Dana turned back to give him a withering glance, but she did not refuse to meet him. She would only talk with him the next time, though. She promised herself that. With a flick of her reins she encouraged Sky Dancer to gallop toward home, never once recalling that riding the splendid horse was forbidden.

When she reached the stable, Dana led Sky Dancer out into the pasture and quickly removed his bridle and Brendan's kirtle. That the pale blue garment bore dark stains proclaiming the loss of her virtue didn't surprise her, but she didn't have time to either launder or burn it now. After hanging the stallion's bridle on its hook, she wadded the borrowed kirtle into a ball and hid it beneath the straw in Shadow's stall. The gelding was on the far side of the woods with Erik, so she doubted the stable boys would bother to clean his stall, and she could retrieve the kirtle later after she had decided what to do with it.

She dashed across the yard, then reentered her house on tiptoe just as she had left it. She heard the clang of a pot lid from the kitchen, and grateful to have escaped the notice of an early-rising servant, she returned to her sleeping chamber. With a rag and a pitcher of water, she removed all traces of Brendan's possession from her body, if not her mind, sprinkled herself liberally with perfume, then returned to bed. Having rested only briefly all night, she was asleep almost instantly.

In midmorning Freya dashed into her daughters' room. Thora was already up and outside playing, but it was Dana she needed to see. "Wake up," she cried as she gave the young woman's shoulder a frantic shake.

That she had overslept was obvious from her mother's worried frown, but Dana needed a moment or two to recall why. Then, mortified by the memory of the way she had spent the night, she sat up quickly and shoved her long curls out of her eyes. "Yes, Mother, what is it?"

"The stable boys just found one of Erik's kirtles in his horse's stall. It's stained, and I'm terrified something awful has happened to him."

Dana was stricken with sharp pangs of guilt as she watched huge tears well up in her mother's eyes, and she hastened to ease her fears. "I'm sure nothing's wrong. Neither of the stable boys is particularly bright. They've probably found an old kirtle that Erik had used as a rag to clean his saddle. Give me a few moments to dress and I'll speak with them."

Freya dried her tears on the back of her hand. "I hope you're right, but the kirtle didn't look old, and I'm sure it's stained with blood. What if someone attacked Erik? He might have been seriously hurt, and the culprit dragged him away. I've already sent one of the boys out to the new house to see if he's there, but I'm dreadfully afraid he won't be."

Dana had hoped to find a way to allay her mother's fears, but now she was more worried Erik would recognize the kirtle with the suspicious stains as one he had loaned to Brendan. Would he then accuse him of loitering around their house and stable at night? Would he be clever enough to guess she was the one the handsome thrall had come to see?

That wretched possibility forced her to take immediate charge of the potentially disastrous situation, and Dana rose from her bed. "Let me see the kirtle. If Erik was badly hurt, it ought to be torn or slashed full of holes. Is it?"

"Well, no, I don't think so."

Dana followed her mother out into the main hall, and after briefly examining the kirtle, she dismissed the slight stains as insignificant. Not wanting anyone else to have the opportunity to look at it closely, she handed the soiled garment to the woman who did their wash and told her to launder it immediately. "I think we used that as a rag the night Light of Dawn's foal was born. Obviously it got mislaid rather than washed.''

Feeling very foolish, Freya sat down and shook her head sadly. "Of course, why didn't I realize that myself?"

Dana bent down to give her mother a kiss on the cheek. "The fault is mine. I should have been up, and then I would have been the one to handle this. Your mistake was a natural one since you seldom visit the stable and have no idea what might be found there."

"But I thought Brendan was very good at keeping the stable neat," Freya remarked with a puzzled frown.

"I thought he was too," Dana agreed, easily telling another lie, "but obviously he has his faults. Now I think I'll get dressed before Erik arrives so I don't have to speak with him in my nightgown."

Dana didn't draw a deep breath until she reached her room. She hadn't been thinking clearly that morning or she wouldn't have carelessly left the evidence of her indiscretion where anyone could find it. Too much had happened in too short a space of time. That was the problem. Things were happening much too fast, and she would have to slow them down, but before she could take any steps in that regard, the situation grew more complicated as Grena arrived with Berit and the twins.

Dana emerged from her room to find Freya disclosing the morning's stressful incident to her sister and niece. While Grena dismissed Freya's concern for Erik's possible injuries with the usual lack of regard she showed for the young man, Berit's ghostly pallor made her feelings all too plain. Grabbing her cousin's hands, Dana pulled her to her feet.

"Let's go outside. The day is too lovely to spend indoors." Not waiting for her mother and aunt to follow, Dana laced her arm in Berit's and drew her out through the kitchen and into the yard. "Nothing's happened to Erik," she confided, "but it soon will if you don't make more of an effort to hide your feelings when his name is mentioned."

"Your mother said it was all a misunderstanding, but I couldn't help but worry about him still. I didn't expect to see him this morning, and now knowing that he'll come home—"

"Berit," Dana cautioned sternly, "you must treat him as you always have. Now let's go sit out under the oak tree and pretend we've nothing on our minds but passing a pleasant day."

Brendan had not had the option of sleeping late, and was at work stripping branches from a tree they had felled that morning when the stable boy arrived looking for Erik. After speaking with the dark-haired Dane briefly, the boy had waited for him to saddle Shadow, and the pair had then departed at a gallop.

Not liking the looks of what appeared to be a hasty summons home, Brendan planted his ax in the tree trunk and sat down to think. It did not surprise him that most of the other men followed his example and ceased working too, for Erik had left no one in charge in his absence.

The muscular Celt's first thought was that Dana had sent for Erik, but he refused to torture himself with the imagined horror of a whipping, as he had the last time he and the willful redhead had parted angrily. He had had all morning to contemplate the sorry fact that nothing had changed between them, despite the incredible beauty of the night they had shared. The darkness of her parting glance had convinced him of that. He had obviously expected more than a woman with her pride would give, but that she had mentioned love had confused him completely. His life was already in her hands. Would she not be satisfied until she had his heart as well?

He would truly be her slave then, but he would not succumb to that humiliation. No, he would never admit what he felt for her was love. Were they in his land rather than hers, then it would not matter what pretty promises he made, but here it most certainly did. Because Dana had never beaten him, he knew she would not do so now. Indeed, how could she punish him without revealing knowledge about herself she would not want anyone to know?

If Dana had not sent for Erik, then who had? he wondered. Was Freya ill or had Grena discovered he and Berit were in love? Brendan was full of questions, but sadly he could do nothing but wait anxiously for Erik to return with the answers.

When Erik arrived home, he swung down off Shadow and walked over to greet the women seated beneath the oak that shaded a good portion of the yard. With forced nonchalance he included Berit in the brief greeting he gave her mother. Then he bent down to kiss both Dana and Freya with his usual show of affection.

"As you can see, I have come to no harm," he assured Freya with a wide grin.

Before Freya could repeat the cause of her unfounded hysteria, Dana offered her explanation for the stained kirtle. When Erik appeared puzzled, she rose gracefully and took his hand. "Come with me. I'll show you the garment is an old one you no longer wear." Just as she had earlier with Berit, Dana led him away from the others before he had a chance to object.

Once they had turned the corner of the house and were out of both sight and earshot, Erik pulled his lovely half sister to a halt. "It doesn't matter what the others think, but I want the truth, Dana. I remember Brendan was wearing an old kirtle of mine the night the foal was born. He made quite a mess of it, as I recall, but he washed it and he's worn it several times since."

Because she knew Erik would recognize the garment in question, Dana didn't even attempt to convince him it was another that had been found. Instead, she demanded the unquestioning loyalty she had always shown him. "You must accept the tale I told as the truth, Erik, even though you know that it isn't. I have done all that I can to help you and Berit. What I ask in return is your silence."

Erik frowned slightly as he tried to make sense of her request, but the obvious conclusion was so outlandish he refused to believe it. "If Brendan was here and left his kirtle behind, he must have come to see a woman. That he is fascinated with you is plain whenever you two are together, but surely you would never sneak out to the stable to meet a thrall." He paused then, waiting for her to confirm that assumption, but Dana did no more than lift her chin proudly.

"Dana!" he gasped, horrified to realize the impossible was true.

Dana would not reveal that Brendan had threatened Erik's chance for happiness with Berit, nor would she excuse her behavior by admitting she found the thrall's affection irresistible. That she had disillusioned Erik completely was obvious in his pained glance, but she was far more disappointed in herself.

"If you despise me for this, it will break my heart," she said softly. "But even if you do, you must keep my secret."

In an attempt to control his frustrated rage, Erik turned away for a moment, but he swiftly realized Brendan was the one who deserved his anger, not the half sister who had shown him so much love. Turning back toward her, he reached out to draw her into his arms. "Do you want him dead?"

Erik's embrace was warm and comforting, nothing like Brendan's demanding hold. "No, I don't want him to come to any harm. I hope to set him free and send him home by the summer's end. We can forget that he ever existed then."

Erik doubted such forgetfulness would be possible where Brendan was concerned, but he gave Dana a fond squeeze before releasing her. "If that is what you want, then I'll help you all I can. But Dana, I could never despise you."

Grateful for that sweet promise, Dana kissed his cheek, then again took his hand. "Let's go back to the others. Berit was as worried about you as Mother. Won't you stay with us awhile before you leave?"

At the mention of Berit's name, Erik began to smile. "For a little while, yes. I will enjoy that as much as she will."

As they rounded the corner of the house, they saw the three women they had left behind talking excitedly with one of the shepherds, and curious to learn what had happened, they hurried to join them.

Sighting Erik, Grena immediately gave him a harsh command. "My boys have taken Thora out in a boat. They've gone too far, and you'll have to go out and get them."

Erik shrugged helplessly as he looked toward Freya for advice. "I don't know how to sail."

"Soren does," Dana interjected quickly. "You go and get him and any of the men who are helping with your house who can sail, and we'll wait down by the docks. With any luck, the children will be back before you return."

Erik wasted no time dashing for his horse, but by the time Dana, Berit, and their mothers had walked down to the docks, the small boat the children had taken was no longer in sight. Grena began to complain bitterly about the wildness of her twins, but Dana ignored her and offered her mother what comfort she could. The day had begun so poorly, she could not help but be as terrified as Freya about how it might end.

CHAPTER XIII

Dana was not at all surprised to see Brendan among the half-dozen men returning with Erik and Soren. She knew him well enough to be convinced that, if there were an adventure to be had, he would be the first to volunteer.

"Do you know how to sail?" she asked with what she hoped would pass for merely the natural curiosity any mistress would have about a thrall's talents.

Brendan rested his hands on his hips and flashed a cocky grin as he replied, "I had no choice about joining a Norse pirate's crew, but had I not swiftly learned how to sail, I'd not be alive today. Tell your mother and aunt not to worry. We'll find their children and return them home safely."

Haakon owned three knarr, the deep-sea vessels used for trading. On his present voyage he had captained one, while Svien and Jørn had each been in command of one of the others. The boats he had left behind were far smaller craft requiring only a few men to sail or row, and the missing children had taken one of those.

Dana found it far easier to survey the boats tied to the dock than to calmly ignore Brendan's wicked grin, but she didn't want him to think he was in charge of the rescue mission just because Erik lacked a captain's skills. "Soren is a fine sailor, and I'm confident he can find Thora and our cousins. Give him all the help you can."

The aloofness of Dana's manner as she delivered what he considered a totally unnecessary command didn't please Brendan, but he knew, with her mother and aunt standing nearby, she dared not speak to him in a personal fashion. The problem was, he doubted she even wanted to display the affection he craved. As they made ready to depart, he would have liked to have kissed her good-bye and whispered an enticing suggestion or two so she would be looking forward to his return, but instead he forced himself to hold his tongue and turn away.

He followed Erik into the boat Soren had chosen, and helped the boy raise the single square sail. While building Erik's house, he had been surprised to find that Soren worked as hard as any of the men, but because of the way they had met, they had continued to avoid each other. That tactic was impossible in the close confines of a boat, but as Brendan took a place at the starboard rail, he hoped their rescue voyage would be too short to strain the uneasy truce that existed between them.

Soren grabbed the tiller, and as soon as the sail billowed out, the sleek craft pulled away from the dock. As on the previous day, Brendan could feel the tingling heat of Dana's glance, and he could not resist turning for a lingering look at her. The gentle breeze off the water blew her long tresses about her shoulders, tangling the ends of the fiery curls just as he knew making love had. She was standing with her mother, comforting her with the sympathetic gestures he longed to receive himself, and he hoped they would have another chance to be alone together soon.

As he turned back to scan the horizons for a sign of the children's boat, Brendan found Erik had taken the place in front of him. The violet-eyed Dane was regarding him with so cold a glance that even though they had had no time to talk before beginning the voyage, Brendan was certain Erik knew about Dana and him. There was simply no other explanation for the hate-filled fury of the man's glance, but a boat was no place for another of their brawls, and he took care not to incite one. Instead, he chose the far safer subject of sailing. That Haakon had not taught Erik to master that skill as he had his other two sons disgusted him, but it was a problem that could easily be remedied.

"Sailing isn't difficult," he offered with an inviting smile. "If you've had no time to learn, I can teach you."

"I have no wish to learn anything from you," Erik responded with bitterly edged sarcasm.

The insult hurt more than Brendan had thought possible, for it clearly showed the mutual respect he and Erik had been gradually forming was at an end. Even if they had not shared the warmest of friendships, he had been shown more consideration than most thralls ever received from a master. That he had threatened to betray Erik by revealing his love affair with Berit to Grena now struck Brendan as foolhardy in the extreme.

He had never been the type to carry tales, and that threat had merely been a desperate ploy to win Dana's acceptance of the affection he had been determined to show her. He had never expected to have to carry through on it. When she had been late for their rendezvous, he had been too angry to realize what he was doing, but he knew by the time he had ridden to Grena's his temper would have cooled sufficiently to allow him to think more clearly. Erik had made his life not merely tolerable, but often pleasant, and not even a Dane deserved to have his kindness repaid with treachery.

How much had Dana told her half brother? Brendan wondered. Whatever it had been was obviously damning enough, and he couldn't help but question Erik's reasons for letting him on board the boat. Did Erik plan to shove him over the side and watch him drown? Brendan was confident he was too strong a swimmer for that. There were several islands nearby, so he was certain he could reach one even if he could not return to the shore of Fyn. No, he would not drown, not unless he had a knife wound or two to slow him down, and from the violence glowing in Erik's glance, that was a distinct possibility.

"We must think only of finding the children now," Brendan suggested firmly. "We can settle our differences later."

Even staring at the handsome Celt, Erik found it impossible to believe Dana could care for him. He was not only a thrall, but as arrogant and hot-tempered as any of the young men who had courted her without success. From what he had seen, Brendan possessed every trait he knew his beloved half sister abhorred in a man. How could they have become lovers? She had not been battered and bruised, so he knew she had not been forced to submit to the lust Brendan had never made any effort to conceal. She had to have been willing, but why? That was the question that tormented him. Why had Dana wanted this man when he was the worst choice she could ever make?

"Is it agreed?" Brendan prompted when Erik did not respond.

"Agreed," Erik replied, but his expression was still filled with loathing.

While Brendan could force aside thoughts of what would surely be their worst confrontation yet, he could not dismiss Dana from his mind so easily. It was as though she had cast a spell on him, for he was filled with the same gnawing pangs of desire as he had been before dawn, when he had carried her into the woods on Sky Dancer's back.

There was no sign of the boat the children had taken yet, but Brendan hoped they would overtake it soon. Surely Dana would be impressed if he were somehow instrumental in Thora's rescue. With that hope in mind, the sharp-eyed Celt doubled his efforts to be the first to sight the lost children.

Erik's thoughts were also focused on his half sister and cousins, for he knew Grena would be favorably impressed if he were the one who brought her twins home safely. Not that one brave deed would be enough to sway the woman's feelings in his favor, but it would be a start. The problem was, they had not been on the water long and already he was beginning to feel seasick. He couldn't let that news get back to Grena, though, as she would only laugh at him and think him a fool for not being as at home on the sea as her sons were.

Despite a brave effort, Erik could not hide his queasy stomach for long, but when he leaned over the side so as not to vomit in the boat, Brendan grabbed for the back of his kirtle to make certain he did not fall overboard. That made Erik feel all the worse for he didn't want to admit he needed help from anyone.

"Breathe as deeply as you can," Brendan advised the suddenly pale young man. "It will help to clear your head."

Erik jerked free of the Celt's hold the moment he had straightened up. He glanced at the boat's other occupants and was relieved to see all were so busy keeping a watch for the children that none had noticed how poor a sailor he was. He was badly embarrassed, however, and doubted he would feel well enough to make any contribution to the rescue effort.

"Sailing takes awhile to get used to," Brendan offered sympathetically. "And in foul weather nearly everyone gets sick. I'll wager even Haakon knows exactly how you feel."

At the mention of his father's name, Erik was sorely tempted to slam his fist down Brendan's throat, but he didn't feel up to making the attempt. He just propped himself up against the rail and hoped they would be able to return home before he made a complete fool of himself. When one of the field hands on the port side of the boat began to shout that he had sighted what might be the children's boat, Erik breathed a deep sigh of relief.

Thora and the twins had been playing down by the docks when the thought of going for a boat ride had captured their imaginations. Borrowing Haakon's smallest craft, the boys had taken the oars while Thora had simply sat in the bow and enjoyed the fun. The trio was laughing happily, and before they realized what had happened, the swiftly flowing current had carried them out of sight of the low coastline of Fyn.

While badly frightened, the boys bravely attempted to

row their small boat back to shore, but they quickly discovered they lacked the strength to successfully battle the current. The excitement of their outing was replaced with terror, for none was used to the numbing isolation of the open sea. Even though there were islands in the distance, none was home, and rather than trying to reach one, the three hapless voyagers complained bitterly about their lack of luck and remained adrift.

At twelve, Olaf and Hrolf were considered adults, and Thora quickly lost patience with their whining. "I should have known better than to come with you," she scolded, blaming the peril she found herself in on them.

Insulted, the boys shouted back a few taunts of their own, but with a haughty toss of her bright red curls Thora ignored them. By the time Soren's boat came into view, they were all miserably unhappy, not only to be stranded, but also with each other. To make certain they were seen, they moved close together to wave and shout, then realized too late what the result would be, for in the next instant the narrow boat capsized and they were all plunged headlong into the sea.

Both Olaf and Hrolf could swim well enough to reach the side of the overturned boat and hang on, while poor Thora, who had never been taught how to swim, splashed about screaming. The weight of her flowing garments pulled her down, and while she shrieked in terror the twins looked on, too frightened by their own plight to risk letting go of their hold on the boat to save her.

As they sped through the water, Soren and his unseasoned crew watched in horror, terrified they might not reach the children in time to avert the tragedy unfolding before them. They shouted to the boys to join hands and reach out for Thora, but the sound of the wind buffeting the sail blurred their words into a mournful howl, and the twins could not understand their helpful advice.

With Thora's frantic efforts to remain afloat growing feeble, the distance between the two boats decreased with maddening slowness. When at long last they drew close, her situation was desperate, and without waiting for one of the others to act, Brendan tore off his kirtle and boots and dove over the side. With long, sure strokes he swam to the little girl, arriving just as the exhausted child slipped beneath the surface of the water. Grabbing for her hair, he yanked her back up and held her securely until Soren had brought his boat in close enough for Erik to pluck her from his arms. Olaf and Hrolf were pulled aboard next, while Brendan was left treading water until the would-be rescuers' excitement died down enough for them to notice he needed a hand to help him scramble back up over the side. As soon as he had replaced his discarded apparel, Thora climbed into his lap and, sobbing pathetically, refused to release her hold on him.

With Soren shouting directions, the field hands slipped into the water to right the overturned boat. Once that feat was accomplished, they grabbed hold of the bow and started kicking. As the boat began to move, they pushed down on the bow to raise the stern, and a large quantity of water poured out. By repeating that process several times, they succeeded in emptying half the water from the slender vessel. Conscientious bailing took care of the rest, and once the boat was empty, a line was attached to tow the small vessel home.

Erik wore an exasperated frown as he remained in his place and watched the others work. It was clear Erik wanted to be of help too, but Brendan easily guessed why he had not taken an active part. "Even if you won't let me teach you, you should learn how to swim. While emergencies like this can't be foreseen, they are bound to occur when you live on the water."

"Is there anything you can't do?" Erik responded with a tone as harsh as his glance.

Brendan frowned slightly, giving that question careful consideration before he shook his head and smiled. "Not that I can think of."

Although she was thoroughly drenched and shivering with cold, Thora ceased crying and looked up at the confident Celt with an adoring gaze. With a soft sigh of contentment, she knew she was in love.

When the four women left behind had grown weary of standing on the dock, they sat down in the nearby meadow, for none wanted to return to the house where they would have to rely on a servant to bring word of the boats' return. Dana tried to keep her mother's and aunt's spirits up, but she was not only as badly frightened as they, but desperately tired as well after a near sleepless night.

Never silent, no matter what the circumstance, Grena had at first complained that her lively sons were impossible to control and then had had to fight back tears of fright when she realized they might come to some terrible harm. Berit did her best to console her by making her brothers' voyage seem the childish prank it was, but she was also acutely aware of the danger they were in.

A sad and restless group, the distraught women were lost in thought until Freya gathered her courage and tried to lift her companions' spirits with conversation. ''Soren has always watched the children when you come to visit, but with him away working on Erik's house, we should have kept a close eye on them ourselves. The boys are old enough to be of some real help to Erik, and when they return, I think we should send them with him to work on his house for a week or two. That will keep them out of mischief.''

After drying her eyes, Grena welcomed her sister's efforts to distract her from the problem at hand. Because she had only learned of Erik's efforts to have his own home that day, she was curious about the young man she usually ignored. ''Erik is young to begin such a project. Most men do not build their own home until after they have saved the profits of several years' trading.''

Dana glanced at her mother, and when she saw the dear woman was too embarrassed by the implications of the comment to speak, she answered for her. ''As a falconer, Erik has never had the desire to go trading, and probably never will. He has all the skills to become a successful farmer, however, so there's no reason why he shouldn't build a house and begin working on his own land.''

''And how is he managing such an expensive project without the wealth it requires?''

''Even without a great deal of money, he is hardworking and will succeed,'' Dana assured her aunt.

Grena thought that unlikely, and her skeptical expression

clearly displayed her doubts. "A man, even a young and strong one, cannot maintain a farm on his own. Does he have plans to marry?"

Freya broke into a delighted smile at that question. "A month ago I would have said no, but now I think that he must, although he hasn't revealed the young woman's name."

Dana did not dare glance toward Berit, but she knew exactly how uneasy her cousin must have become and swiftly defended her half brother, since she knew the pretty blonde could not. "Erik is both handsome and bright, and extremely industrious. He'll make some lucky young woman a fine husband."

As could be expected, Grena scoffed at that opinion. "Freya, you must teach your daughter that no matter how many admirable qualities a man possesses, if he lacks wealth, he is not a fine candidate for marriage. She'll be marrying soon herself, and I shouldn't want her to be mistaken about so vital a matter. Of course, with Jarald courting her so eagerly, that is scarcely a concern."

Dana found it impossible to return her aunt's insipid smile, but she could not abide being talked about as though she were not seated right across from the woman. "I doubt it is wealth that makes the marriage bed warm on a long winter's night," she remarked pointedly.

"How very young you are!" Grena responded with a throaty laugh. "A wealthy man is far easier to love than a poor one any night, winter or summer. What a man requires of a woman is the same, rich or poor, so it is in a woman's own best interests to choose wisely."

Dana knew from experience all men were not the same in any regard, and most especially not in the way they bestowed affection. She could not reveal she had the experience to back up that opinion, however. "I do not even know a poor bachelor, so I doubt I am in any danger of marrying one," she commented instead, hoping to put an end to her aunt's unwanted advice.

Freya was too sensitive a woman not to see Dana had been deeply disturbed by her sister's remarks. Thinking her daughter's defense of Erik quite noble, she joined her. "We were talking about Erik's prospects, not Dana's, and I agree with her that he is a wonderful young man who will be successful in whatever he undertakes. The woman who marries him will undoubtedly share that view and be an enormous help to him. Now I know none of you wishes to give up our vigil, but will you go inside and see we are sent some refreshments, Dana? I think something warm and sweet will make the time pass more quickly for us all.''

Grateful for any excuse to escape listening to her aunt's opinionated views, Dana rose and started for the house. As she passed Berit, her cousin looked up at her, but her expression was more wistful than confident, and Dana couldn't help but wonder if Grena's comments hadn't been meant more for her daughter than her niece.

Soren's boat was not sighted until late afternoon, and the weary women broke into delighted peals of joy when they saw he had the children with him. Olaf and Hrolf hung their heads in shame, but Thora, who was still snuggled in Brendan's arms, was smiling radiantly.

Dana stood back as the thrall carried her sister from the boat. The pretty child's damp and wrinkled clothes, as well as her tangled hair, gave clear evidence she had survived a terrible ordeal, but she seemed more pleased with herself than frightened as Erik described how Brendan had pulled her from the sea. When Erik reached for her, Thora left the slave's arms reluctantly and only after she had given his cheek an enthusiastic kiss.

Wanting to get her sons into dry clothes, Grena scolded them crossly as she hustled them toward the house. High-spirited boys could be forgiven any mischief if things ended well, but not when their pranks resulted in near disaster. Freya and Berit walked on either side of Erik, patting Thora affectionately as they followed the path, but Dana remained behind. First she complimented Soren for being so fine a sailor. Then she promised the men who had accompanied him a reward for aiding in the rescue. Last she turned to Brendan and with a nod drew him away from the others, who had begun to secure the boat to the dock.

While she would never admit it to him, Dana had been every bit as thrilled to see Brendan return safely as she had been with the children's rescue. As always, the sight of him was enough to make her heart skip a beat, but, as usual, that was a weakness she fought rather than attempted to understand.

"You've charmed Thora, but I don't want you to think my mother and I are not as grateful as she is that you were the one to rescue her. I will see that you receive twice whatever amount my mother gives the others."

As a thrall, Brendan had never been paid for his work, and he had not expected to receive any money that day either. Feeling his motives were being questioned, he was insulted and began to argue. "I didn't do it for a reward. Thora is a sweet child and I wanted to find her and the boys as badly as Erik and Soren did." It pained him to think Dana believed he had volunteered only in hopes of earning an ample reward, but he could tell she doubted the sincerity of his words even as he spoke them.

"You have impressed me as a man who does nothing without reason, Brendan, but even if you wished only to be helpful, you still earned a generous reward and I'll insist that you take it."

Brendan looked over his shoulder to make certain Soren and the men working nearby were not listening. Unfortunately, he saw that they all were. "I'll walk you to your house," he offered in a commanding whisper. While he dared not take her arm while they were being observed, he was grateful she did not resist, but instead started up the path.

Because there was something far more pressing than money on his mind, he decided they could argue about his reward later. He was not proud that it had taken threats to bring Dana to him, but he was still too uncertain of her feelings for him to admit he would not have carried them out. That was a secret he would have to keep until she came to him willingly, as he hoped she soon would. "What did you tell Erik?" he asked softly.

"I did no more than confirm his suspicions about us and beg for his silence. He will not tell my secrets any more than I will reveal his."

Brendan nodded, pleased her half brother had not learned of his stupid threats. "Talk Erik into staying here for the night. Then you can meet me somewhere close by later. What about the storehouse for furs?''

Dana waited until they had reached her door to reply. ''No, I'm much too tired to meet you tonight. Last night I meant to take only a brief nap but overslept. Tonight I'll not be able to wake at all.''

The delicate lavender shadows that marred the creamy skin beneath her eyes attested to her fatigue, but Brendan was too startled by her excuse to accept it. ''That's why you were late last night—you fell asleep?''

''Yes. I had intended to meet you on time. I had given you my word on it, remember?''

Brendan couldn't believe his ears. He had nearly gone mad imagining she hated him too much to ever take him as a lover. It infuriated him anew to learn that while his frustration with her tardiness had pushed him into a near blinding rage, the prospect of meeting him had held such little excitement she had fallen asleep! He looked away for a moment, attempting to gain control of the tumult of emotions that churned within him each time he looked at her. Before he succeeded, she reached out to touch his arm and spoke to him in a persuasive whisper.

''Don't be angry with me, because I do want to see you again. It's imperative, in fact, but not tonight. Meet me at the edge of the woods tomorrow night, and come early enough so that we'll have plenty of time to talk. We've something of great importance to discuss.''

The request struck Brendan as every bit as absurd as her reason for being late, but the red-haired beauty's manner was so insistent she stirred his curiosity rather than the streak of defiance that was so much a part of his character. His temper now under control, he finally noticed how tired she looked and accepted her suggestion, but with an important stipulation.

''Tomorrow night it is, but no matter what you wish to talk about, we'll make love first. Is that understood?''

Because that was the last thing Dana wanted to do, she countered with the subject she thought he would be unable to resist. ''No. You will have to keep your passions under control, for we will need all our wits about us to decide how best to arrange your freedom.''

Brendan's eyes narrowed slightly, for he thought she was merely toying with him, and that was something he could not abide. "Must I remind you again that you do not own me?''

Glancing past him, Dana saw Soren coming up the path. "I will explain tomorrow night.'' Then, in a louder voice, she continued, "Your breeches are still damp. Go to Erik's house and look for others before you grow chilled.''

Brendan heard the sound of approaching footsteps and understood her sudden change in tone, but as always, to be dismissed like a servant disgusted him clear through. He stepped out of Soren's way and started for Erik's, but he doubted the man would lend him any of his clothes now and thought he better just build a fire and dry the ones he wore.

Rather than follow his sister inside, Soren called out to the Celt. "You're a better man than I thought, Brendan.''

That unexpected compliment brought a smile to his lips, and Brendan turned back to face the boy. "I think the same of you,'' he replied sincerely, for what he had seen of the young man lately had impressed him very favorably.

Pleased that the Celt could see he was fast becoming a man, even if no one else did, Soren dismissed him with a wide grin and a wave and went on into the house.

When Grena was invited to stay the night. Erik quickly seized the opportunity to spend time with Berit and decided to sleep in his old house rather than make the trip through the woods to the new one. While he had not told Brendan he could stay there again, he wasn't surprised to find him there, since the man had always been able to think for himself. He saw by the scraps remaining on the slave's tray that, despite a trying day, Dana had not forgotten to send him a hearty meal. Her consideration for the thrall still amazed him, and as he tossed him the kirtle that had been found in the stable, he made his feelings clear.

"The next time you meet Dana, don't leave your kirtle behind. Freya mistook it for mine, and while Dana came up with a story her mother believed, it won't work more than once. Why Dana loves you I'll never understand, but—''

Springing to his feet, Brendan clutched the freshly laundered garment to his chest. ''She loves me? She actually said that to you?''

The unabashed joy with which Brendan had greeted that remark not only startled Erik, it made it obvious Dana had never spoken those words to him. But if she did not love him, why had she met with him secretly? More confused than ever, he stared at the well-built Celt for a long moment and then rephrased his statement. ''No, she did not. It was merely something I assumed when she asked that I continue to treat you well. I'll admit I neither understand nor approve of her behavior where you're concerned, but she knows her own mind and I'll not try and influence her.''

His hopes that he had won at least a tiny portion of Dana's heart dashed, Brendan tried not to let his disappointment show, but failed. ''You are her half brother, not her father, so it is not your place to tell her what to do anyway. Besides, she is the mistress while I'm but a thrall. I'm only doing her bidding.'' That was a long way from the truth, but when passion overruled her reason, he knew Dana wanted him as badly as he wanted her. What did it matter who was master and who was slave then? Nothing mattered then but the intense pleasure they gave each other.

Erik was certain Brendan was lying, for he simply could not imagine Dana amusing herself at a thrall's expense, and most especially not this thrall. She would never stoop to that. Recalling that he had been interrupted before issuing a warning, he provided it now. ''What happens between you and Dana must remain a secret, for your well-being as well as hers. Don't ever repeat your mistake and leave your clothes lying about so carelessly again. Now, it's been too long a day to stay up and talk, no matter what the subject. I'm going to sleep. Be ready to leave at first light.''

Following their former routine, Brendan helped Erik prepare his bed and then made up his own. He had expected a fight, and a good one. That Erik hadn't thrown a single punch, nor demanded he leave his house, left the perplexed Celt wondering how Dana had justified her request that he be well-treated. He was just as mystified by the man's remarks about the kirtle he had loaned her, since he had thought she had sense enough to hide it.

Brendan had no sister, but he knew, if he did, he would have torn a slave apart with his bare hands rather than allow her to sleep with him. Erik, however, seemed to have accepted the news that he and Dana were lovers with surprising calm. It was plain the man wasn't pleased about it, but he had accepted it. Strange. That was the only word that came to Brendan's mind. Everything these Danes did was strange.

It wasn't until much later, when he heard Erik leave the house, that he understood why he hadn't wanted to defend his sister's honor with his fists. Erik was undoubtedly meeting Berit, and he hadn't wanted to be bruised and bloody when he went to her. That thought brought a wide grin to Brendan's lips. Perhaps Dana had used the same threat he had, and had persuaded Erik to keep her secret as a condition for keeping his. With a low chuckle he rolled over to get more comfortable, but he couldn't help but wish Dana had been as eager to see him as Berit must be to see Erik.

CHAPTER XIV

As they retired for the night, Freya took Thora into her own bed. Berit again shared Dana's bedchamber, while as usual Grena had a room to herself. The bed was as comfortable as her own at home, but Grena slept fretfully, waking often, for she was still anxious about the fate of her twins. She knew they needed a father's guidance, and she lay awake mentally listing the wealthy widowers and older bachelors whom she might hope to entice to her bed. Confident she was more attractive than most women her age, she hoped to remarry soon now that she had made the decision to do so. Only the lingering warmth of her husband's memory had kept her from seeking a new mate sooner, but clearly her sons needed a father too badly for her to continue to mourn him.

Preoccupied by her plans, she rose, went into the hall, and sat down by the hearth, where the coals of the fire that had burned earlier still radiated a pleasant warmth and soft golden glow. Surely Haakon would help her, she thought with a smile. When he and his friends returned from their voyages, she would tell him of her hopes, and he would entertain his unmarried friends as often as it took for her dream to come true.

"Yes," she purred softly. Haakon was the key. He had always liked her, and he would do this favor for her.

With the subject of marriage weighing so heavily on her mind, Grena quite naturally began to think of her daughter. Berit would pose no competition for her because the charming girl would be seeking a younger man. Still, Grena feared Berit's remarkable prettiness might prove to be a distraction to the men she hoped to attract.

To avoid that possibility, Grena decided it was not too soon to find a husband for Berit. While she had never voiced her dreams aloud, she had always hoped her nephew Svien might have strong feelings for her daughter. As Haakon's son, he would inherit not only a large and prosperous farm, but substantial wealth as well. Yes, she mused boldly, a marriage between Svien and Berit was the best of all possible matches, and she would endeavor to win Freya's support for that plan before Haakon and Svien returned home.

That matter settled in her mind, Grena rose and stretched with a lazy satisfaction. A conscientious mother, before returning to bed she stopped by Svien's sleeping chamber to check on Olaf and Hrolf. The boys were sleeping soundly, their dreams, unlike hers, undisturbed by the perils of the day. Then, on an impulse, Grena looked in on her daughter. An oil lamp burned dimly in the corner, but even in the semidarkness she could easily discern that Dana was alone in her wide bed.

Grena pulled the door closed and waited for a long moment beside it. Could Berit have gone to the privy? While that was unlikely, she waited a while longer for her daughter to return to bed, and when she did not the obvious struck Grena with the force of a staggering blow. "No!" she whispered hoarsely. "No, it can't be!"

Berit's thoughts were still so childish when it came to men. Grena feared that despite her teachings a handsome appearance meant more to her daughter than the far more important consideration of wealth. Only that evening at supper she had noticed how often Erik had caught her daughter's eye. While she had never liked him, Grena could not deny that he had the dashing good looks that could easily melt a foolish young girl's heart.

Recalling that he had called at her farm twice recently, she grew increasingly suspicious and began to wonder if Berit hadn't spent some or all of the time she had gone riding lately with Erik rather than with Dana. Since Dana and the young man were so close, the possibility seemed a likely one.

"How could I have been so blind?" Grena moaned.

Bent on finding her daughter and ripping her from Erik's arms, if that was indeed where she was, Grena tore open the door and rushed outside. Before she could summon the breath to scream, the horrified woman slammed right into the amorous couple as they returned to the house, and it was only Erik's quick action in restoring her balance that kept them all from landing in the dirt.

When her worst fears were confirmed by Berit's kiss-swollen lips and wrinkled gown, Grena took her daughter's hand and yanked her from her lover's arms. Furious as much with her own stupidity in allowing such a thing to happen as with Erik, she began to rebuke him in a hysterical shriek. "My daughter is a silly child who'll not go unpunished for this, but when Jørn returns he'll kill you. Do you hear me? I'll see you dead for this. You had no right to touch my daughter. No right at all, and you'll die for it."

"But Mother, I love him," Berit began to wail, and when

Grena attempted to pull her back inside, she reached out for Erik, desperately wanting to stay with him.

"Grena, please, this is not the tragedy you're making of it," Erik calmly beseeched the hysterical woman. He took her daughter's hand and stepped close to her side before continuing. "I want to marry Berit. She means everything to me."

"You're nothing but the bastard son of a slave," Grena replied venomously. "You're no fit husband for any woman, least of all my daughter."

Awakened by the sound of angry voices, Freya came rushing to the door. The cause of the heated argument was immediately obvious to her, but despite her shock, she refused to allow her sister to create a scene that would awaken every last person on the farm.

"Come inside at once," she ordered firmly, and when Grena did not immediately obey, she tried another approach. "If it is truly Berit's reputation that concerns you, then this matter must be discussed in private."

Grena shook her head, fearing there was nothing left of her daughter's reputation to salvage. "Did you know Berit was the one Erik planned to marry? Did you know?"

"No, I didn't," Freya assured her, and with a calm born of years of experience in managing a large farm, she continued to encourage her sister to come with her to the hall, and finally succeeded in getting her there. She had hoped that, once seated, they could talk in a more reasonable manner, but that proved impossible when Grena continued to bemoan the terrible tragedy that had befallen her family.

"Yesterday my twins nearly drowned, and today I learn my daughter is ruined. Don't you understand what has happened? You have shown Haakon's bastard a true mother's love, and this is how he repays you. He has seduced your niece in your own home."

Dana came into the hall then, Grena's piercing shrieks having finally penetrated the depth of her slumber. She hung back, listening to her aunt sob and wail as her mother tried in vain to silence her bitter complaints. Berit was wrapped in Erik's embrace and weeping as pathetically as her mother. Dana easily guessed what had happened. When Erik shot her a pleading glance, she came forward and stood by his side.

"Grena," Dana began with a soothing sweetness. "There's no need for you to carry on so. Berit and Erik love each other deeply, and will be very happy together."

"You knew about this?" Freya asked in dismay.

"I know they're in love," Dana replied, refusing to admit more.

"Love?" Grena cried. "How can you speak of love? If Erik loved Berit, he would never have touched her. He would have realized she was raised to be the bride of a man who would make her proud, and not for the likes of a slave's son."

Erik straightened his shoulders proudly, but he knew Berit had never thought of him in such humiliating terms, even if her mother always had. "I am my father's son as well," he pointed out shrewdly, although he knew Haakon would never help him win Berit for his wife. Displaying his usual confidence, he made a solemn demand. "Name what you want for Berit's bride-price, and you shall have it."

Enraged by what she saw as an arrogance he had no right to affect, Grena leapt to her feet and refused even to consider his request. "I'll see her dead before I'll give her to you."

Although blinded by tears, Berit couldn't believe her mother's ugly vow and fought to make her take it back. "I will marry no one else, Mother. Erik is the only man I'll ever take for a husband, so you'd be wise to let us marry now."

"Never!" Grena screamed. Then, searching her daughter's face for the truth, she thought she had guessed it. "What did you mean to do? Did you think if you were carrying his babe I would give you to him willingly? If so, you were not only incredibly stupid, but wrong as well."

Horribly embarrassed by her mother's hostile accusation, Berit shook her head as she battled a fresh torrent of tears. "It wasn't like that at all."

"Oh, really?" Grena responded sarcastically. "You're still a virgin then? Is that what you're saying? Well, speak up or I'll satisfy my curiosity about the matter right here in front of everyone. It will take only a moment.''

"That is enough, Grena,'' Freya commanded sternly, as shocked by her sister's behavior as she was to discover Erik and Berit's romance. ''I can understand your rage, but I will not allow you to behave in so shameful a manner in my home. I think we should all go back to bed and then meet to agree on some rational plan in the morning.''

"Rational plan?'' Grena scoffed. ''I already have a plan. Jørn will punish Erik for this disgrace. He'll make him pay for it with his life.''

Paling at so vile a threat, Freya found it difficult to catch her breath. Sinking down onto the nearest bench, she closed her eyes for a moment in an attempt to find the calm that had just eluded her. Frightened, Dana rushed to her mother's side and hugged her tightly.

"Must you be so hateful?'' Dana asked her aunt. ''Can't you see you're making your sister ill?''

"And who are you to tell me what to do?'' Grena hissed at her niece. ''You have been on Erik's side all along. Berit hasn't been out riding with you, has she? She's been meeting Erik while you were the one who appeared at my door to make me think she was passing the time with her cousin, not her lover.''

"Oh, Dana, that isn't true, is it?'' Freya searched her daughter's face, wanting to know the truth, but she was devastated when she saw it in Dana's averted glance.

That her mother clearly thought her incapable of tricking her aunt so shamelessly pained Dana deeply, but rather than confess her guilt she looked to Erik for help.

Seeking to put an end to a scene even more wretched than the one he had once imagined, Erik tried again to soften the harshness of Grena's mood. ''Let's leave Jørn out of this, Grena. We are close friends and I don't want to fight him for any reason, especially not for loving his sister. Now I mean to have Berit for my wife. There's no disgrace in that desire, nor the fact we are in love. Name whatever price you want. We can come to terms and arrange for the wedding right now.''

"Must I repeat myself endlessly before you will believe

what I say? You will never marry Berit," Grena vowed through clenched teeth. "I'll not stay here a moment longer either. I'm taking Berit and my boys home."

"I won't go," Berit protested instantly.

That Dana had not immediately denied being involved in Erik and Berit's love affair had shocked Freya so deeply that she was not merely stunned, but physically ill as well. Now more readily understanding her sister's feelings of betrayal and sharing them, she had to force herself to speak. "I want you to go home with your mother, Berit. We are all too upset to make any decisions about your future now. Perhaps in a few days we can meet again and decide what is best for us all."

When Freya looked toward Erik, her disillusionment was so plain it broke his heart. She had always taken his part, even when no one else would, but it was clear she felt he had violated her trust and had been deeply hurt by it. He had hoped to win her approval for his marriage to Berit, but now he feared that might be impossible. If Freya did not approve, then she would not loan him the sum he would need, despite her promise to do so. Realizing the woman he loved was out of his reach for the time being, Erik released Berit and stepped back.

"Do as your mother says, Berit. Go home, and I'll set everything right as soon as I possibly can."

"No, I don't want to leave you." The sorrow in Erik's eyes mirrored her own, but as Berit reached out for him, he brushed her hands aside and again stepped away.

"I think you better leave, Erik," Freya suggested in an attempt to separate the couple, and she was greatly relieved when the young man turned and left the hall. "Now, won't you please stay here until morning, Grena?"

"No," the distraught woman responded. "That's impossible after what's happened. We must go, and as long as Erik makes his home here, we won't ever come back."

Dana's glance followed Erik as he walked by, her heart going out to him, but when she saw Soren standing in the shadows at the doorway her spirits sank even lower. He was clever enough to realize what Erik's absence the other day meant, but would he recall that Brendan had been gone for a while as well? The cold light in his eyes as he looked toward her told her that he did, and as Grena gathered her children to depart, Dana could do nothing but hope Soren would keep still until she had had a chance to convince him their mother had more than enough problems already without his adding to them by revealing what he knew about her daughter.

When Brendan awoke, he found Erik seated by the hearth. There was no fire burning, and the young man was merely staring into the ashes with the most sorrowful expression the Celt had ever seen. Fearing some calamity had occurred during the night, he rose from his bed and went to him.

"What's wrong?" he asked, the softness of his voice promising sympathy, whatever Erik's plight.

While only the previous afternoon Erik had despised Brendan thoroughly, he needed to confide in someone too badly to recall his feelings for the man now. He admitted nothing but that Grena had found him with Berit and in the terrible confrontation that had followed had vowed to see him dead. "I can't predict what Jørn will do, but I'll not fight him if I have any choice. We've always been the best of friends."

The problem Erik had described was so much worse than anything Brendan had expected at first that he didn't know what to suggest. Then, taking a seat nearby, he offered what help he could. "I've never seen Jørn fight, but I know from experience how tough an opponent you are. If you'll trust me with a sword, I'll help you prepare."

"A sword?" Erik asked, seemingly in a daze.

"Yes, a sword. Isn't that the weapon Jørn will choose?"

"Probably. He's very good with a sword." Erik glanced toward the Celt. "But I've never even held one, let alone learned how to use one in a fight."

While Brendan found that difficult to believe, he soon grasped the reason why. "I suppose Haakon taught Svien and Soren how to defend themselves, but didn't bother to teach you?"

Glancing back at the ashes which so closely resembled his dashed hopes, Erik nodded. "Something like that."

"Well, Jørn isn't expected home for several weeks yet, and if you'll trust me not to hack you to bits, I can teach you to use a sword as well as you do your fists. In the meantime, what about Berit? Is her mother likely to beat her?"

The question made Erik wince, for he knew Grena had been angry enough to take out all her frustrations on the beautiful young woman he loved. "I'm afraid so."

"Do you want to go and get her?"

"What do you mean? Just ride over to Grena's and bring Berit back here?"

"Why not? It doesn't sound like Grena can get any more infuriated with you than she already is."

"Probably not, but Freya wouldn't allow it, and I need her help too badly to make her angry with me too. Or more angry, I should say."

"Freya is mad at you too?"

"She expected better of me," Erik revealed with a sigh.

"Better than what? Did she think you incapable of love?"

As Erik glanced toward his companion, he was surprised by his sympathetic frown. "None of this concerns you, Brendan."

Insulted, Brendan resorted to his own tongue for a bitter oath to express himself before replying in words Erik could understand. "I belong to Jørn, and yet I am here with you. If you two are going to battle to the death, then I'd say I'm right in the middle of it." That was a decidedly minor cause of his concern, but he knew Erik didn't want to hear him mention his regard for Dana as the reason for his keen interest in her half brother's plight.

"You're right. Perhaps I should send you back to Grena's now, before things get any more complicated."

"No!" Brendan argued forcefully, but Erik easily guessed why he was so adamantly against leaving.

"You ought to know Dana is as miserable about this as I am. Both Grena and Freya know she lied to them to help me see Berit. I don't think Dana has ever lied to anyone until now, and naturally Freya is deeply disappointed in her."

Bone weary, Erik closed his eyes for a moment, but instantly Berit's tear-streaked face filled his mind's eye. Tormented by her sorrow, he quickly blinked her image away.

"I fell in love with a woman I had no right to have, and not only have I made her suffer, but her family and mine as well. I would leave home today, but I'll not let anyone think I haven't the courage to face Jørn."

"Leave? Have you lost your mind?" Brendan rose to his feet and, taking a firm grip on Erik, hauled him to his feet. Keeping his hands on his shoulders, he offered what he considered much needed advice. "Grena is a selfish, conniving shrew, and from what I saw of Jørn, he's no better than an arrogant fool. How can you even consider leaving Berit with them? What if she is carrying your child? Would you leave her to face that disgrace alone?"

Erik was already so unhappy Brendan's hostile questions didn't make him feel any worse. "No, I'll not leave her. My only hope is that eventually Grena will allow us to marry. I'll use whatever chance I have to convince her it's her only choice."

"That's better," Brendan assured him with an encouraging grin. "What you need is some sleep. Go to bed. We can return to your new house this afternoon."

"The new house?" Erik could barely recall the high spirits in which he had begun work on the home he had wanted to give Berit.

"Go to sleep, Erik. Everything will look better when you awake." Brendan steered his weary companion toward his bed, and Erik was soon sleeping soundly while Brendan was wide awake and cursing the fact he would be unable to see Dana until she came to him. He wanted her to know he would do his best to help Erik, and he hoped she would understand he would do it to please her.

As he prepared his breakfast, Brendan couldn't help but think how lucky they had been that Dana had refused to meet him during the night. If her absence had been discovered during the row over Berit and Erik, then he knew he would be in even worse trouble than Erik. That Dana was sharing Berit's disgrace troubled him too, for he thought her loyalty to her half brother and cousin were commendable rather than shameful. He felt a twinge of guilt himself then, for he knew he had chided Erik for meekly accepting his fate rather than seeking to change it. Well, Erik had heeded his advice, with the worst of results, and rather than shoulder part of the blame, Brendan vowed to see the young man marry the woman he loved, although he had no idea how he would go about it.

When she retired to her sleeping chamber that night, Dana knew no matter how long she lived she could not possibly spend a worse day. She could not forget the ugly things her aunt had said to Erik. Knowing he did not deserve the abuse, she was glad the spiteful woman had vowed not to return as long as he lived there. That did not lessen her fears for Berit, however, for she knew her cousin must be suffering terribly as a result of her mother's vile temper.

As for her own mother, Dana had hoped to make amends with her, but after Grena had left, the dear woman had retreated to her bedchamber and refused to speak with her all day. Soren had gone back to work on Erik's new house without telling her good-bye. Even though she suspected he was mad at her too, she was grateful he was keeping his reasons to himself.

That night Thora was again sharing their mother's bed, and Dana couldn't help but regret that she no longer had her sister's delightful innocence. Thora had known only that her mother was unhappy and had wanted to be with her. As a contributor to that unhappiness, Dana had not been allowed the same privilege. That she had secrets far more incriminating than those concerning Erik and Berit only served to deepen her feelings of isolation.

Her one consolation was that Brendan could no longer threaten to go to Grena if she failed to meet him, but for a reason Dana couldn't begin to understand, she actually wanted to see him. She had thought of him all day, wondering what he thought of Erik's plight, and if it had made him more sympathetic to her own. The need to speak with him outweighed her fears, and certain her mother was too angry with her to seek her company in the middle of the night, when the house grew still, she left and rode her mare to the woods.

When Brendan reached the spot he now considered theirs, he was both surprised and delighted to find Dana already there. "I didn't mean to keep you waiting," he offered by way of apology. "It was only that I didn't expect you to arrive so soon."

"Did Erik tell you what happened?" Dana whispered anxiously as he drew her into his arms. The warmth of his embrace was so soothing at the end of a long and troubled day that she relaxed against him without considering that he would misinterpret the gesture as a sign of surrender.

Drinking in the exotic fragrance of her long curls, Brendan pressed her closer still, adoring her supple body as much as her engaging spirit. "Have you forgotten? I said we would make love first and talk later."

"But everything has changed."

Brendan slackened his hold so that he could see her face in the moonlight. "Between us, the only difference is that I want you more."

Dana found it impossible to think clearly when the rich timbre of his voice was so enticing. He was smiling at her, a slow, sweet smile unlike any expression she had ever seen him wear. Unable to fight the attraction that she feared would destroy them both, she lay her head on his shoulder and sighed softly.

"You don't understand. My mother is so upset about Erik and Berit she will neither leave her room nor speak with me. If she discovered that I'd been with you—" Dana caught herself then as she realized too late she had just given Brendan the means to force her to come to him again.

Brendan felt her stiffen and was too clever not to understand why. "I wouldn't have gone to Grena, and I won't go to Freya either. I don't want you to be afraid of me, or what I might do to the people you love. All I want is for you to admit that you want me as badly as I want you."

Unable to believe him, Dana placed her palms on his chest and attempted without success to push him away. "Don't lie to me, Brendan. You were already on your way to Grena's when I left the house the other night. You can't deny it now.''

Gripping her arms forcefully to hold her fast, Brendan repeated his promise. ''Don't make the mistake of doubting my word, Dana. Neither you nor your loved ones will come to any harm because of me.''

''I have already been harmed,'' Dana reminded him coldly.

''No, you haven't. You have only been loved.'' Just as he had anticipated, the mention of the word love startled her into silence, and before she could think of a reply, Brendan lowered his mouth to hers. With the gentleness he knew she craved, he caressed her lips lightly until he felt her lift her arms to encircle his neck. Rather than take pride in the fact he had again overcome her resistance to him, he continued to ply her with lavish kisses until he felt tremors of desire fill her lithe body with a beguiling weakness that left her clinging to him for support.

She was again fully dressed, but Brendan did not let that obstacle slow his relentless progress toward intimacy. Slipping one hand beneath her chemise, he ran his fingers up her thigh, then over her hip to satisfy himself that she wore only a simple linen shift as an undergarment. He wondered what she had done with the one he had torn. Had she taken the trouble to mend it with tiny stitches, or had she just thrown it away?

The state of her wardrobe was the farthest thought from Dana's mind as Brendan's caress grew increasingly more bold. To escape that torment she raised herself up on her tiptoes, then discovered that only made it easier for him to probe the soft recesses of her body more deeply. He knew precisely where to concentrate his touch to make her crave more, and when she leaned against him, she felt the hardened evidence of his desire pressed firmly against her belly. He was blatantly willing their bodies to fuse into one, but this time she wanted to make certain he removed his clothing as well as hers first.

''I want you nude,'' she whispered against his cheek. ''Surely I am worth the trouble it will take you to undress.''

He had not dared waste the time when they had first made

love, but now Brendan agreed. He pulled off her tunic before removing his kirtle, however. "Help me," he urged, but rather than seeing to her own clothing, Dana dropped to her knees to unlace his boots. Rather than explain that she had misunderstood his request, Brendan stood still to simplify her task. He doubted she had ever seen to a man's boots, and it was so touching a gesture he didn't know why she refused to speak the words of endearment he knew she had to feel. When she stood and reached for the button at the waistband of his breeches, he caught her hands.

"Remove your chemise while I do this. I don't want to lose another pair of breeches due to your impatience."

While the taunt would have infuriated Dana at another time, in the moonlight-drenched woods it seemed only the sweet teasing one lover gives another, and she did not object. Taking a step backward, she untied the bow at her neckline and let her silk chemise slide to the ground. Her shift followed, and she stepped out of them both, apparently unembarrassed about appearing before him in the nude as she removed her own boots.

While he lacked her grace, Brendan managed to cast off the last of his clothes without looking too clumsy. He reached out to Dana then, and drew her back into his arms. Her silken flesh felt cool as it brushed against his far warmer skin. The fullness of her breasts begged for his kiss, and he quickly lowered her to the grass where he could caress her with eager kisses as well as his seductive touch.

As he drew the firm tip of one lush breast into his mouth, Brendan slid his hand between Dana's thighs to again use a knowing rhythm to lure her toward surrender. Her slippery wetness was proof enough her body was ready to accept his, but he needed still more from her. That he wanted her so badly tore at his soul, for no woman had ever exerted the control over his emotions Dana did. If only to assuage his masculine pride, he had to know he affected her just as strongly. He gave her a lingering kiss, then used his knee to spread her thighs wide before shifting his position to lie comfortably between them. Instantly he felt her grow tense, but knowing this time he would cause her no pain, he summoned all his willpower and began with only a shallow penetration. Balancing his weight on his elbows, he looked down at her, silently willing her to beg him for more.

As she lay beneath him, Dana saw only the compelling light in Brendan's eyes. Her body had opened easily for him this time, and while she disliked feeling so vulnerable she did not understand why he had not begun the motions he had taught her would fill them both with indescribable pleasure. "What's wrong?" she asked, fearing her inexperience had presented a problem she didn't see.

Brendan moved slightly then, but still his thrust was so shallow he succeeded in his ploy to tease her senses. At the same time he had to fight the impulse to plunge into the warm, moist depths he alone had savored. "Nothing is wrong," he murmured softly, "but we needn't rush. There's time for you to admit that you love me."

"Love you!" That she was with him was bad enough, but to say it was out of love when surely it was not was something Dana would never do. She felt him move in response to her tacit denial, almost completely withdrawing the soft, smooth tip of his manhood before again barely sliding into her. The sensation was the most exquisite torture she could imagine, and she knew he would keep it up all night if she didn't think of a way to turn his trick back on him.

"Kiss me first," she begged in an enticing whisper. "Then I'll say whatever you want to hear."

While that was not exactly what he had had in mind, Brendan lowered his mouth to hers. Her tongue teased his, drawing him lower still as she opened her mouth to accept his kiss, and in the next instant she moved beneath him. Sliding easily on the grass, she took the whole length of him inside her, then wrapping her legs around his hips, she crossed her ankles to hold him tight.

The worst of insults leapt to Brendan's lips, but recalling how he had longed to have her wrap her legs around him the first time they had met, he could not be angry with her. All he could do was think her as glorious a partner as he had known she would be.

His body blocked the light and he could not see her expression, but he imagined it was one of triumphant satisfaction. She had robbed him of that same sense of pleasure, but he did not really mind her defeating him in so stunning a manner. Knowing she was all the woman he would ever want, he finished what he had begun with a joyous abandon that left them both drained of all emotion except the marvelous afterglow of perfect peace. He fell asleep with her cradled in his arms, her fiery red curls fanned out over his chest.

When Brendan awoke later, he found himself alone in the woods and more determined than ever to wrench a tender confession from Dana when next they met. Then he realized, in the heat of passion they had made no plans to meet again, nor had Dana spoken of her desire to discuss his freedom. She had not even mentioned the subject that she had claimed was so vital. He was thoroughly disgusted with himself for promising never to harm her or her family when she had given him no sweet vows in return. He had wanted her to take him for her lover, but not when she left him without a shred of pride. Cursing his weakness for her, he made his way through the woods, and when dawn broke Erik found him sleeping with the other men and never guessed he had been away.

CHAPTER XV

"Drink this," Grena ordered with a grim determination that discouraged argument.

Recognizing neither the pale green color nor the peculiar fragrance of the brew, Berit took hold of the tankard but did not take a sip. "What is it?"

"Merely one of Olga's herbal beverages to help you sleep."

Berit was still as thoroughly miserable as she had been before dawn when Grena had dragged her and the twins away from her Aunt Freya's. Since then she had been confined to her bedchamber, where she had repeatedly cried herself to sleep.

"I don't want it," she insisted, but when she tried to hand it back to her mother, the solemn woman refused to accept it.

"Do as I say, Berit. You must drink every last drop."

Instantly suspicious, Berit took another look at the strange liquid. She could see her reflection dancing on the oily surface and doubted the drink was as innocent as her mother claimed. Fearing it would do her more harm than good, she held the tankard away from her body and poured its contents out on the floor. Her expression as defiant as her action, she handed the now empty vessel back to her mother.

Grena knocked the tankard aside, then slapped her daughter with a vicious backhanded blow. "You little fool! That you have given yourself to a man who is so far beneath you is tragic, but we must do all that we can to prevent you from bearing his child. When I return with more of that potion, you will drink it willingly."

"You expect me to drink poison willingly?" Berit gasped incredulously. Her mother had never struck her before, but the resulting physical pain wasn't nearly so acute as the emotional turmoil she had endured all day.

"It is not poison," Grena informed her coldly, "but a medicinal brew."

"It is poison if it will kill an unborn babe, and I'll never drink it."

Grena was determined to put a swift end to Erik's influence over her daughter and again make her the considerate child she had always been. "Oh, yes, you will," she threatened convincingly, "because you'll have nothing to eat until you do."

"You would rather starve me to death than see me wed to the man I love?"

"Yes," Grena replied calmly, and seeing no point in again listening to Berit's childish protestations of love, she left her bedchamber and locked the door.

Berit felt as though she had never really known her mother, the woman had changed so greatly since finding her in Erik's arms, but she would never give in to her impossible demands. Stretching out across her bed, she focused her thoughts on the man she loved, not the mother who had treated them both so cruelly. It had been slightly more than two weeks since the first time she and Erik had lain together, so it was too soon to know if she had conceived a child.

Perhaps, as her mother insisted, she was barely out of childhood herself, but because there was a chance she might be carrying Erik's babe, she would never drink anything that would end its life before it had even begun. She loved Erik so dearly the mere possibility of a child was as precious to her as a living son would be. She wasn't at all frightened at the prospect of defying her mother, since she had no choice in the matter, but as she drifted off to sleep she wondered if starving to death could be any more painful than dying of a broken heart.

When Freya continued to regard her with a disappointed glance, Dana tried to be patient. She thought her mother would eventually adjust to the fact that Erik and Berit loved each other, but when several days passed without the slightest brightening of Freya's downcast mood, Dana feared she had seriously misjudged the depth of her anguish. Not in the least bit sorry for what she had done to aid her half brother and cousin, she waited until Thora was playing with some of their servants' children and her mother was alone in her room. She then took matters into her own hands.

Freya glanced up as Dana came to her door, but then looked away, unwilling or unable to speak with her. She appeared very tired, as though she had not been sleeping well, and while Dana had had a difficult time sleeping herself, she was ready to confront the issue that had divided them rather than to allow the uncomfortable silence between them to continue.

Entering her mother's bedchamber as though she had been invited, Dana closed the door, then sat down on the edge of the bed. "I'm truly sorry our deception hurt you. When Erik first confessed his love for Berit, I encouraged him to claim land and build a house, hoping it would make it easier for him to win Grena's consent for their marriage. We had planned to come to you when the house was finished. Obviously that wasn't soon enough, but it doesn't change the fact that Erik and Berit love each other and want to marry. Erik had hoped that you would help him convince Grena to allow them to wed. Has what happened made that impossible?"

As her daughter spoke, the tension in Freya's expression relaxed only slightly. "You simply don't understand," she replied sadly.

"I understand the fact we're all heartbroken over this, but we needn't stay that way."

Freya shuddered slightly, then took several deep breaths before she spoke. "Over the years your father and I have had horrible arguments about Erik, but I fear none will compare to his rage when he learns about this. He will undoubtedly say that had I not treated Erik as one of my own sons, he would never have dared hope he might marry Berit. Haakon will swear Erik would have known such a match was impossible, and he would never have created the problem he has. He will insist this is not merely an instance of a young man following his heart, but the natural result of the love I showed him."

Dana had never heard her parents raise their voices with each other, so she was understandably shocked to learn they had had heated arguments about her half brother. "Erik is as fine a man as Svien and Soren. That Father treats him with less respect than he gives our servants, rather than as a son, upsets all of us as badly as it does you. Counting Thora, there are six of us who think Erik is being abused. If we stand up to Father together, then—"

Freya refused to encourage such a foolhardy action. "No, you mustn't even suggest that to the others. You dare not risk increasing your father's anger when surely it will already be terrible. That will only make the situation all the more difficult for Erik, and none of us wants that."

Dana had never imagined their current dilemma would require her to choose between two men she loved dearly. It had all begun with Brendan, she mused silently. They had taken in a slave in defiance of her father's wishes, and their lives had failed to run smoothly ever since. Because thoughts of the Celt caused an entirely different type of pain, she struggled to push his handsome image to the back of her mind.

Thinking she had only one possible choice, Dana made her decision quickly. "Father is wrong. It's as simple as that. I'll do whatever I can to help Erik, and if Father becomes angry with me for my loyalty to my brother, then so be it. Things could not possibly get any worse here than they already are."

"Dana!"

The vibrant redhead shook her head. "Nothing you can say will change my mind. If you and Father were to plead Erik's cause, I think Grena could be persuaded to allow him to marry Berit. If you'll not speak out in his behalf, then he'll have to fight Jørn for that privilege. I think he'll win too."

Freya was astonished by the sudden change in her elder daughter, for while she had always spoken her mind, she had not once been openly defiant of her parents' wishes. "And if Erik is killed? Could you live with the thought he died for love?"

"Yes," Dana answered easily, thinking she saw the question far more clearly than her mother. "It's the only thing worth dying for, isn't it?"

Moira rapped softly, then peered in the door, interrupting them before Freya could respond. "Mistress, there's an old woman from Grena's here. She's begging to speak with you."

Freya welcomed the news with a delighted smile. "She must have brought a message from my sister, and I hope that it's a good one. Send her to me at once."

Dana recognized the woman immediately as the one who had taken care of her cousins in infancy. Quite old and frail now, she appeared exhausted from her journey. Rising to her feet, Dana helped the woman to a place at the foot of the bed. "Your name is Ulla, isn't it? Please, make yourself comfortable. Were you given something to eat and drink?"

"Yes, mistress, thank you. I did not think you would remember me," Ulla replied shyly, obviously pleased to learn her long service to Grena's family had not gone unnoticed. After taking a deep breath, she hurriedly explained her mission. "In the four days since visiting here, my mistress has given her daughter nothing to eat, and only a few sips of water to drink. They are in the midst of some terrible argument, and each is so stubborn I fear Berit will die before their dispute is resolved. That is why I came here. I trust you will be able to help Berit in a way I cannot."

When her mother appeared too stunned to comment on her sister's cruelty, Dana questioned their caller herself and soon came to the conclusion that her cousin's plight was genuinely as desperate as her former nurse claimed. Not wanting to discuss their personal business in front of Ulla, she thanked her for coming to them, then ushered her from the room before she spoke to her mother.

"You had suggested that we all meet again in a few days. Clearly Grena isn't going to be able to discuss Berit's future calmly anytime soon, but it's imperative that we help Berit now. What do you want to do?"

"There's only one thing we can do," Freya announced with the same determination that had always allowed her to stand up to Haakon where Erik's welfare was concerned. "We'll have to stop Grena from tormenting Berit in the only way we can. Tell Erik to take some of the men and go and get her before she has to suffer through another day of her mother's spiteful treatment. Grena has never had a bit of sense, not since she was a child, but I won't allow her to get away with this."

Before she had fallen ill, Freya had been the most self-reliant of women, and Dana was thrilled to find she had lost none of her former spirit during the long months of her recovery. "Try and rest a while longer. I'll take care of everything."

Dana hurried away without explaining the details of a

plan she had just begun to devise. First she asked Ulla to remain a little longer, for if they succeeded in bringing Berit home, she would need a maid. She then hurried to the stable, had one of the boys saddle her mare, and left immediately to tell Erik what she had learned. With any luck, they would rescue Berit and have the entire matter resolved before her father returned home. Then, if Haakon wanted to fume and spit over the fact Erik had taken Berit as his wife, they would all have the courage to survive it.

Urging her mare to a gallop, Dana followed what was becoming a well-worn trail through the woods, but as she neared the site of Erik's new home, she heard the unmistakable clang of steel clashing against steel. Fearing Grena had somehow gathered an armed force to attack her half brother, she dismounted and led Dawn's Kiss to the spot where she and Berit had observed the men working. When she finally had a clear view, she was relieved to find only a mock battle where the men watching the two participants were laughing and calling out good-natured jests.

Both Erik and Brendan were stripped to the waist, displaying muscular arms and torsos that were deeply tanned and glowing with a light sheen of sweat. Circling each other warily, first one and then the other would explode into action, swinging his long, broad blade with a force that would have done terrible damage had it found its mark. Because this was not her idea of lighthearted sport, Dana's heart was soon firmly lodged in her throat. Breathless with excitement, she watched each of the men successfully block the other's blows with a fierce masculine grace that made their deadly sport fascinating as well as frightening to observe.

It soon became apparent that despite Erik's vigor, Brendan was the far more skilled of the two, but rather than push that advantage, he was cleverly leading Erik through a series of maneuvers that allowed him to practice what prowess he had. For a thrall to give a lesson in the use of a sword to his master was a most unusual sight, but then Dana had always known Brendan was no ordinary slave. That he had a fine appearance and a warrior's skill was obvious, but she longed to know so much more about him. Thoroughly enjoying the swordplay, despite the anxiety it caused her, she was sorry when by mutual agreement the young men brought it to an end.

As Brendan slapped Erik on the back and offered a few tips for their next encounter, his back was turned toward the woods and he did not know Dana had joined them until she spoke. He wheeled around then, his expression changing from one of relaxed camaraderie to his old mask of aloof disdain.

Dana watched Brendan's smile vanish, not understanding what she had done to deserve such a hate-filled stare. Was it because they had not discussed his freedom at their last meeting? she wondered. She blushed as she remembered each nuance of his loving and her shameless response to it, but she could recall little of his conversation. There had been no time to plan how to set him free, but that had been his fault, not hers! While she was sorry he was upset with her, she couldn't spare the time now to worry about his feelings when she feared Berit's life might be at stake.

Not noticing the silent exchange passing between Brendan and Dana, Erik smiled widely, then grinned sheepishly as he saw his sister's glance sweep over his gleaming weapon. "Soren left home with two of Haakon's swords so I could learn how to use them. I hope they've not been missed."

Soren walked up to join them, and Dana assured him they had all been far too upset to take an inventory of the weapons their father had not taken on his voyage. She waited for Erik to tell his workers to return to their tasks before she explained why she had come. When Brendan remained by Erik's side, as though he had every right to be there, she thought he might prove useful and refrained from telling him to join the others. She reported the dreadful news about Berit, then waited for Erik to respond.

Instantly Erik's face took on the same look of fierce determination that Brendan's wore. Turning to the slave, he immediately began to make his plans. "You advised me to go and get her, and clearly that's what I should have done. I don't want to make things awkward for you, though. Grena doesn't have enough men to keep me out of her house if I want to walk in with this sword in my hand, so if you'd rather not come along I'll understand."

With his glance still firmly fixed on Dana's face, Brendan sounded eager for the chance to join in another rescue. "No, I want to go. You don't need to pay me either. I'll do this just for the sport of it."

Erik clapped the Celt on the back, "Did you get a chance to see how brutal Brendan can be, Dana? He told me he was traveling about Erin, gathering support to drive out the Norsemen, when the monastery where he had stopped for the night came under siege. The attackers admired his skill with a sword so greatly they took him prisoner rather than putting him to death, which was lucky for us both. I can certainly use his help."

Dana found the tale every bit as intriguing as Erik obviously had, but her reaction was not the one he had predicted when she spoke to Brendan rather than him. "Why couldn't you have told me that story when I asked about your past? Would it have cost you so much in pride?"

"I had a good reason for telling Erik what happened," Brendan protested scornfully.

"While I am merely a curious female with no right to know anything about you other than what is obvious to the eye?" To pay him back for his contemptuous gaze, Dana allowed her glance to travel slowly down the muscular planes of his partially clothed body until it came to rest on the inviting swell below his belt.

Soren stared first at his sister and then at the Celt. He could have sworn there was something between them, but obviously it was nothing more than hearty dislike, for clearly they despised each other now. "I'll saddle the horses. If we're going to get Berit, we ought to be on our way."

"You're right." Erik turned to wink at Soren as he walked by. Then he turned back to Dana. "You go on back home. I'll try and have Berit there before sunset."

"No, I'm going with you."

"Are you good with a sword too?" Brendan asked sarcastically.

"No, I have other weapons," Dana responded instantly, silently daring him to ask what they were, but wisely he kept still.

"I don't want you involved in this, Dana," Erik insisted.

"I am already involved. Find a kirtle and let's go." Returning to the spot where she had tethered her mare, Dana quickly climbed into the saddle, and riding out into the clearing, she waited impatiently for the men to get ready so they could be on their way.

Believing that hunger was her most powerful weapon, Grena had expected to win the battle of wills with her daughter in a day or two. When by the third day Berit continued to stubbornly refuse to drink the pale green potion, Grena was thoroughly incensed. By the end of that day the pallor of the girl's skin gave her hope she would soon triumph, but while Berit was too weak to leave her bed on the fourth day, she still refused to do her mother's bidding.

Even as he continued to defy her mother, Berit was terrified that she now lacked the strength to fight should her mother summon several servants to hold her down while she forced the vile brew between her lips. With that fear foremost in her mind, the day seemed endless, but strangely, after the hunger pangs of the first day had subsided, she didn't feel hungry at all.

She felt very alone, however. She hoped Erik was thinking of her and working out a way for them to marry, for she would never accept that desire as hopeless. She felt her beloved nanny Ulla's hand on her forehead, a fond and familiar touch, but she didn't understand the dear woman's whispered words of encouragement, or why she soon left her all alone.

When Erik and Dana took up the lead, Brendan reined in his mount and rode along beside Soren. That the boy had dared to steal two of his father's swords had impressed the Celt, for it showed a strong loyalty to his half brother. More importantly, the lad's considerable skill with the weapons demonstrated Haakon's ability as a teacher, and Brendan hoped he would never have to cross swords with the man.

A faint smile played across his lips as he recalled the day he had left Grena's. To be returning as part of the small raiding party amused him, but he had not the slightest doubt they could accomplish what they had set out to do. Rescuing attractive maidens was an enjoyable pastime, but he couldn't help but wish they were on their way to rescue Dana so she would be in his debt.

As he had been on the first day he had ridden behind her, he was fascinated by the sunlight's bright sparkle on her glorious cascade of fiery red curls. The memory of falling asleep with her silken tresses spilled over his chest was almost unbearably sweet, and his smile grew wide until he recalled his dismay at awakening to find her gone. Clearly she was ashamed of what they had shared, although he had gloried in it. If Berit could love Erik, who had little but ambition and good looks, then why couldn't Dana love him? he wondered. He scolded himself silently then, knowing he should not long for love between them when what they shared always proved deeply satisfying to them both.

With that tantalizing thought in mind, Brendan hoped they could complete their mission swiftly so he would have an opportunity to convince Dana to meet him again that night. Three nights had passed since he had last held her, and he did not want their separation to continue indefinitely. As they neared Grena's home, Erik and Dana came to a halt, and Brendan swiftly moved to take a place at her side.

"Dana will go to the door and ask to speak with Grena," Erik explained. "Then the three of us will circle to the rear of the house. While the women are talking, we'll go to Berit's bedchamber and bring her out. I doubt we'll get far before Grena discovers what's happened, but at least Berit will be safe from further harm."

Brendan frowned slightly, seeing a complication Erik obviously did not. "We shouldn't leave Dana unprotected, for we'll have gained nothing if we free Berit but leave Dana behind.''

After a moment's hesitation, Erik nodded. "You're right, of course. I'll not allow Dana to become a hostage. You stay with her, and Soren and I will enter the house."

Although her first impulse was to argue, Dana saw the wisdom in Brendan's suggestion as quickly as Erik had. "I have an idea," she suggested helpfully. "Give Soren that sword, Brendan, as he's more likely to need it. I'll keep Grena talking as long as I can, but if I have trouble, force your mount to misbehave. Create some sort of a disturbance that will kick up enough dust to keep Grena distracted until Erik, Berit, and Soren have made good their escape."

Dana's expression was such a sincere one Brendan wasn't even tempted to display his earlier sarcasm. After handing his weapon to Soren, he assured her he would do his best. "I won't disappoint you," he promised, but his inviting smile conveyed a far more intimate meaning than his words.

Choosing to ignore the suggestive comment, Dana turned her horse toward the path, while Erik and Soren split off in the opposite direction to approach Grena's house from the rear. With her usual confidence, Dana rode right up to her aunt's door, and when a servant appeared, she asked for her mistress. She sent Brendan a worried glance, but he was enjoying himself too greatly to share her fears.

When the servant returned with the announcement Grena had no wish to see her, Dana was at a loss for a moment, for she had been certain Grena would come out, if only to scream at her again for aiding Erik. When she glanced toward Brendan, hoping for a sudden inspiration, she instantly received one. Knowing she simply had to draw her aunt out of the house, she quite shamelessly used him as an excuse.

"I've come to buy this thrall from her. Tell her I'll meet whatever price she sets."

As the servant again disappeared into the house, the clever redhead dared not look at her companion, for she knew without having to see his expression just how angry he would be. "I told you I wanted to discuss your freedom. I might as well arrange for it now," she whispered encouragingly.

"This is not the time!" Brendan hissed, certain Dana had just made an extremely foolish mistake.

When first informed of Dana's visit, Grena was outraged, but when she had been told the purpose of her niece's call was not to plead her half brother's cause but to do business, she became too intrigued by the prospect of making an attractive profit to send her away.

"Brendan is not for sale," she said without bothering with a greeting, attempting to conceal her eagerness to strike a bargain.

"My father always says that everything can be bought if a person has the right price. You know that we do, so why must be haggle over him? He is strong but frequently disobedient, and I doubt anyone else would have him."

Brendan sat silently fuming as Dana and her aunt debated his worth. Even knowing Dana's purpose was a noble one, he couldn't help but be deeply insulted. He was not a piece of horseflesh, nor a fine bull that could be sold from one family to another. Holding his tongue was almost impossible, but he succeeded for a few moments at least.

Opening the rear door with swords drawn, Erik and Soren slipped inside. They could hear the voices of the women working in the main hall, but there were no sounds coming from the bedchambers. Soren pointed to the door of Berit's room, but Erik found it securely locked. Motioning for the boy to stand aside, he aimed a brutal kick at the lock, and with a loud crash the door went flying open. Erik rushed into the room, saw Berit lying pale and limp upon the bed, and hurriedly gathered her up into his arms. Returning to the passageway, he found Soren brandishing his sword to keep half a dozen startled servants at bay, and with a call for him to follow, he carried Berit outside to their horses.

"What was that?" Grena cried, certain she had heard a disturbance inside.

"Perhaps someone dropped a cooking pot," Dana suggested, "but what does it matter? My last offer was a good one. Will you take it or not?"

Before Grena could respond, a serving woman came to the door and tearfully exclaimed that Berit had been kidnapped. Flying into a rage, Grena reached out to grab Dana's mare's bridle. "You'll not leave here until Berit is returned! Brendan, you belong to my family, not Freya's. You must help me!"

"Yes, mistress. Let Dana go. I'll see that she doesn't get away." Instantly the Celt positioned his mount to block Dana's escape.

Dana's expression was one of strained disbelief, as with a mighty yank Brendan wrenched her mare's reins from her hands. She had known he was angry with her, but had he planned to betray her when he had insisted she ought not to confront Grena alone? That was so fiendishly clever a ploy she was stunned, for it made his hatred of her shockingly clear.

Grateful that Brendan had moved so quickly to assist her, Grena followed the thrall's instructions, released her hold on Dana's mare's bridle, and stepped back out of his way. She laughed as, having lost control of her horse, Dana had no way to fight Brendan. "It is you who is caught in your own trap now!" she shouted gleefully.

The terror in Dana's eyes inflamed his already boiling temper, but Brendan had had no intention of actually doing Grena's bidding. Instead, he pulled Dawn's Kiss alongside his mount and wheeled them both around in a tight circle. Then with a wild cry he urged his horse into a gallop that the dapple gray mare had no choice but to match. Leaving Grena choking in a cloud of dust, he and Dana rode out of the yard and continued at a furious pace until they were lost from sight.

Knowing there would be no way to escape the fury of Grena's wrath, Brendan swore Dana was going to make the daring risk he'd just taken worthwhile.

CHAPTER XVI

Rather than race all the way to Freya's, Brendan veered off down a path that ran beside a stone wall separating two grain fields. Once he was certain they would not be observed from the road, he drew both his mount and Dana's to an abrupt halt. Leaping to the ground, he pulled the shaken redhead from her saddle and forced her back against the wall.

"Is there no end to the ways you'll use to humiliate me?" he shouted rudely. "First you describe me as the most worthless of slaves, and then you actually believed I'd taken Grena's side against you!"

Dana had to grip Brendan's shoulders to remain on her feet, for she hadn't had nearly enough time to recover from the fright he had given her before they had fled Grena's. Hoping he would continue to vent his rage with words rather than his fists, she didn't interrupt him, but wisely waited until he paused to draw a breath to defend herself.

"I have never tried to humiliate you. Never. That is a completely ridiculous accusation, and as for my remarks to Grena, you knew I had to keep her outside until Erik had made good his escape. I would have told any tale, no matter how outrageous, to hold her interest, and there was no reason for you to feel insulted. As for thinking you'd decided to return to Grena, I knew you were mad enough to do it. Indeed, you were already furious when I first saw you today, although I've no idea why."

"No idea!" Brendan scoffed. While she was still too flustered to think of protecting herself, he grabbed her knife and tossed it aside. Separating her legs with his right knee,

215

he pressed her closer to the wall. His stare as menacing as his sneer, he slipped his hand beneath her flowing garments and ran his fingertips up the length of her thigh. His touch was hot, possessive, not the tender caress of a lover, but the demanding hold of a man seeking to sate his passions whether or not his woman was willing.

Dana's eyes widened in alarm. She couldn't believe Brendan would be so abusive, and struggled to break free of his confining hold, but her efforts proved futile. She twisted in his embrace as he began to taunt her with a touch of insulting familiarity, silently daring her to deny him what he had already claimed for his own. Her breath came in short gasps as he began to tease her most sensitive flesh, but she continued to try to break free.

"Stop it, Brendan," she demanded, not about to give in to him.

"Stop what?" Brendan whispered hoarsely as he lowered his mouth to her throat. "This? Or this?" he asked as he began to probe deeply into her warm, moist sweetness. He held her open, vulnerable, striving to create a hunger for fulfillment that would match his own.

Rather than being aroused, Dana rebelled as she always had at the first possessive touch of other men. Consumed with a violent loathing, she gathered all her strength and struck Brendan a fierce blow to his left ear. When he recoiled in pain, she succeeded in shoving him aside. Retrieving her knife from the dirt, she wheeled around, prepared to use it.

"How dare you treat me as you would a whore you despise?" she hissed. "How dare you?"

Brendan's ear was ringing so loudly he could barely make out her words, but he understood enough to reply. "Why not? That's how you treat me."

"It is not!" Dana screamed, her expression mirroring the depth of her disgust with him. Her hair flew about in wild disarray as she shook her head, adding to the ferocity of her pose. "I have never treated you badly, never, but you continually choose to show me your worst!"

Brendan leaned back against the wall rather than struggle to keep his balance and risk falling. He feared she had broken his eardrum, for he had never experienced such excruciating pain. "You come to me only when you must, and you cannot wait to leave. I would never have left you sleeping alone in the woods as you did me."

Still brandishing her knife, Dana stared at Brendan, unable to believe his complaint was sincere. "Is that why you greeted me so coldly this morning? Because I awoke before you did? Was it very inconsiderate of me to leave without awakening you? You'll have to forgive me, but you're the only lover I've ever had and I've no idea what is expected of me." Dana was bitterly sarcastic because she simply could not understand how something so insignificant as her early departure could have prompted him to treat her with such a shocking lack of respect.

"I thought it was your freedom that was the issue, since I had told you that was what we had to discuss. Everything is far more complicated now, but I've not changed my original intention to see you're set free. I'll not allow Grena to say you've run away either. I will insist that I forced you to remain with me against your will. She can't threaten to have Jørn attack me with his sword, so neither of us will suffer any harm for what happened today."

Dana paused, thinking Brendan would have something to say because he never kept his thoughts to himself, but he merely stared at her with a puzzled frown. He didn't appear to have any interest in resuming their fight, and feeling safe now, she shoved her knife into its sheath.

"How am I ever to understand you, Brendan? You tell me nothing about yourself, and you twist each of my actions into an insult. I thought it was your freedom that mattered most to you. I'll still arrange for it when Jørn returns, but if you ever repeat the mistake of treating me as badly as you did just now, you won't be alive to enjoy it."

As Brendan strained to hear her words through the haze of pain that filled his head, he wondered if it was his fault or hers that she understood so little about him. He longed to be free with a desperation that often threatened to wrench his soul in two, but his desire for her was an equally powerful force. "I can't bear for you to treat me as a slave," he finally admitted aloud, sacrificing a large portion of his pride in the effort. "For you to use me, then walk away."

"Use you? How can you say such a thing?" Dana asked. "Erik thought you should remain at home today, but you insisted on coming along. It was also your choice to stay with me. If you were insulted by what I said to Grena, it's your own fault, not mine, because you should have known I didn't mean a word of it. Erik got away with Berit, and that's all that matters. I'm not going to stand here and argue all day about how we did it, or apologize if your feelings were hurt. Now come on, we've got to go."

Brendan did not interrupt the volatile beauty, even though he had been referring to being deserted after they had made love rather than to the way she had belittled his talents with Grena. He leaned back against the wall, hoping the pain would stop if he just stood quietly for a while. His ear wasn't bleeding, so he knew his injury wasn't as severe as he had first feared. "You go on ahead. I don't think I can ride yet."

When she had struck him, Dana had wanted only to distract him for a moment, not to cause him lingering pain. "Oh, Brendan—"

Her pity was the last thing he wanted, and the proud Celt looked away. "Just go. You've humiliated me enough for one day, and I'd rather not take any more."

Her earlier fears of his strength forgotten, Dana's eyes filled with tears as she moved to his side and clasped his arm. "I didn't mean to hurt you, but you should never have been so rough with me. You've been so wonderfully loving, and that's what I expect from you."

"Loving?" Brendan repeated skeptically. "Why, Dana, you said yourself that there is no love between us."

Dana flinched slightly, as though he had struck her. She could not tear her gaze from his, nor did she wish to when she saw her own pain reflected so clearly in his eyes. Brendan had turned a peaceful summer into a maelstrom of forbidden desires, and she dared not even imagine what further dangers might lie ahead for them.

All she knew now was that he was hurting, and she was responsible for his pain. Reaching up on her tiptoes, she kissed his cheek sweetly. "I shouldn't have said that," she confessed hesitantly, "when what I really meant was that I wish we could love each other, but I know that's impossible."

She turned away with a touching shyness, but Brendan reached out to catch her wrist and drew her back into his arms. Words of love came no easier to his lips than to hers, but he allowed the depth of his emotions to fill his kiss with a devotion he dared not speak aloud. With a gentle caress he molded the lithe contours of her body to his, shamelessly pressing her so close she could not fail to notice it was not anger that had aroused him now.

Dana pulled away slightly so that she could look up at him. "I have never wanted to humiliate you, and you mustn't ever try to humiliate me again."

Brendan would have agreed to any request now, but because hers was so sensible, he murmured his consent between deep kisses. The spot he had chosen had been ideal for a hasty confrontation, but now that he longed to spend the entire afternoon making love, he realized Dana was too fine a lady to lie in the dirt. He looked up then, wondering if there might not be a secluded spot nearby where they could enjoy their passion for each other.

Sensing his unspoken question, Dana stepped out of his embrace. "No, Brendan, we've got to go home. Erik and Soren must already think we weren't able to leave Grena's, and they are sure to gather all the men they can to go back for us."

Realizing the truth of her words, Brendan moaned regretfully and drew her close for one last kiss. "Promise you'll meet me tonight."

Dana rested her head on his shoulder as she attempted to think of a compelling reason to refuse. Another midnight tryst would be dangerous, but she knew mentioning the danger would only make it all the more appealing to Brendan. Finally she had to admit to herself that she also longed to extend the delicious closeness they had just begun to explore.

"All right, I'll try my best, but if I'm late or if I'm unable to leave the house, you must promise you'll understand and not accuse me of disappointing you on purpose."

Brendan cupped her face gently between his palms as he questioned her request. "Are you asking me to trust you?"

"Would that be so impossible?"

Not knowing how to reply, Brendan considered her question for a long moment. Other than his mother, he could not name another woman he had known well enough to trust. Surely to trust so beautiful a young woman as Dana couldn't possibly be wise. She was also a Dane, which was most definitely not a point in her favor. A clever man, he turned her question back on her.

"When you do not trust me, how can you expect me to trust you?"

Dana knew exactly what he meant, for when he had been so quick to assure Grena he would assist her, she had believed him as readily as her aunt had. Blushing with embarrassment, she backed away. "You were very convincing. How was I to know you meant only to fool Grena?"

His ear no longer troubling him, Brendan took Dana's hand and led her to her mare. "That's what trust is, Dana. You should have known I'd not betray you, no matter what I said."

"Just as you should have known I don't really consider you a worthless slave," Dana countered smoothly. "It seems we are both to blame here, not just me."

His mood now a lighthearted one, Brendan chuckled as he helped her up into her saddle. They rode home in a companionable silence, but their frequent smiles revealed each was delighted to be with the other.

When they entered the yard, it was Brendan who noticed the black stallion tethered by the stable first, but Dana's shocked glance when he pointed out the horse immediately conveyed the impression that the owner of the massive beast was not someone she wished to see.

"Do you want me to come inside with you?" he offered considerately, thinking she must be afraid to face the visitor.

Too astonished to speak coherently, Dana just shook her head. Leaving Brendan with the horses, she started toward her home, but before she had reached the door, a fair-haired man came outside to meet her. Well over six feet in height, with a burly build and lumbering gait, he easily enveloped the startled redhead in a boisterous hug, lifted her clear off her feet, and swung her around twice before putting her down.

Brendan was as shocked by the enthusiastic greeting as he was by the fact Dana didn't respond by boxing the man's ears for taking such bold liberties with her. For an instant the puzzled Celt wondered if this could be Haakon, for the man looked old enough to be her parent, but his full mustache framed a wide grin that was anything but fatherly. Grudgingly, Brendan had to admit he was a handsome fellow whose deeply tanned skin provided a healthy accent to his sun-bleached hair. Dressed in fine woolens elaborately trimmed with braid, he clearly had wealth in addition to a commanding physical presence.

Praying what he was witnessing was a reunion with a close relative Dana had never liked, Brendan motioned to the stable boy who had appeared to care for their horses. "Do you know that man?" he asked quickly.

"His name is Jarald Frederiksen," the lad replied with a satisfied smirk. "He likes to think of himself as Dana's betrothed."

Jarald Frederiksen. Brendan let the name echo in his mind as he watched Dana nearly disappear from sight as Jarald hugged her again. He was a great bear of a man, and the wily Celt hoped he was also as dim-witted and slow as bears were thought to be. He had taken an instant dislike to Jarald despite his pleasing appearance, but he couldn't forget Thora had said Dana would soon marry him. Why had he never had the presence of mind to ask her about Jarald? he wondered, for now he was brimming over with curiosity.

Having more gossip to confide, the boy continued without stopping to contemplate how Brendan would take his news. "I overheard him tell Freya that Haakon asked him to stay here until he, Svien, and Jørn return from Erin."

Startled from his thoughts by the horrifying announcement, Brendan reached out to grab the youth by the front of his kirtle and lifted him clear off the ground. "You're lying! No one ever said Haakon had gone to Erin."

Terrified, the boy dangled helplessly in Brendan's grasp. "He's never gone that far before, and no one knew that he had this time until Jarald told us."

Thoroughly disgusted, Brendan set the stable boy down and released him. For three long years hatred had kept him alive, but after only a month on a farm where the people were kind rather than abusive, he had become so complacent he had forgotten what kind of men the Danes were. If Haakon had gone to Erin, then surely he had gone for what plunder he could steal. The man might not keep slaves, but he undoubtedly wasn't averse to trading them.

Brendan felt sick to his stomach, for he knew he never should have allowed Dana's radiant beauty to blind him to what bloodthirsty murderers her people truly were.

Dana did not have long to wonder why Jarald had chosen to visit on that of all days, for as they entered her home he hurriedly explained that her father had decided to travel to Erin before coming home and had thoughtfully sent him to be certain they lacked for nothing before his return. He was clearly delighted by the request, as it gave him a reason to take up residence in her home, but she was as deeply shocked as Brendan. Why had Haakon picked that summer to visit Erin? she agonized silently. Brendan would never forgive her for this, she was certain of it.

Dreading the moment when the Celt would learn of her father's whereabouts, she watched in a daze of despair as Jarald congratulated Erik on his brave rescue of the woman he loved.

Cuffing Erik on the shoulder, Jarald paid him a sincere compliment. "You are your father's son after all." He smiled at Berit then, his glance an admiring one as he noted she had grown up to be an exceptionally pretty young woman. "If there's to be a fight, count me in," he offered with a booming laugh. "Or will all your kin side with Freya rather than Grena?"

Nearly knocked off his feet by Jarald's playful blow, Erik had to regain his balance before he replied, "I've no wish to start the whole family feuding."

"It is far too late to consider that now," Freya pointed out. Jarald had already been there when Erik and Soren had rushed in the door with Berit, so there had been no way to keep him from learning the truth. That the man would welcome a fight with such obvious relish didn't please her, but she feared they might not be able to avoid one.

"Time is on our side," she mused thoughtfully. "Grena's late husband's kin are all away trading, as are our brothers. As for Haakon's family—" She fell silent, for none had ever given Erik any more attention than Haakon had.

"Well, I'm here," Jarald volunteered with a ready grin. "I gave Haakon my word that I would look after you all until his return, and I mean to keep that promise."

Erik had taken a great deal of pride in Berit's rescue, but a man of Jarald's size and skill with weapons would be such a valuable asset in combating whatever retaliation Grena might send that he didn't dare refuse his help, although he hoped he would not need it. "I appreciate your offer, Jarald, but I want this matter settled peacefully, not at the point of a sword."

"You may have no choice," Jarald warned. "And if that's the case, then you must be the one holding the sword and dictating the terms."

Until that day Erik had never needed a sword, but he nodded, seeing the wisdom in Jarald's words. Berit was seated beside Freya, sipping the broth the thoughtful woman had insisted she consume before attempting to eat something more hearty. The blonde he adored looked terribly young to him, but she was so lovely he could well imagine her being at the center of a feud that could easily last several generations. It would take him several hours to list all the relatives and decide whether or not they would take Grena's side, but he had never been more uncomfortably aware that he was an outsider in Haakon's home. He was not kin to Freya either, and suddenly he felt very alone.

"It is generous of you to want to help me, Jarald," he repeated. "I have no kin to stand with me."

"And just what am I?" Dana asked defensively. "Am I no longer your sister?"

Soren stepped forward then. "Svien and I are your kin too," he announced proudly. "Brendan will fight with us, and he is easily worth two men."

"Who is Brendan?" Jarald inquired.

Freya drew her hand across her brow as she realized

Brendan might present a complication she had not foreseen. "I suppose you took Brendan with you today?"

"Yes," Erik admitted. "He was there." He turned toward Dana, wondering why she had taken so long to return home. "Did you have trouble getting away?"

"Some, but we managed."

"Who is Brendan?" Jarald repeated in so loud a tone his deep voice reverberated off the carved paneling that adorned the dwelling's walls.

Dana waited for Erik to answer, but he seemed unable or unwilling to describe the Celt, so she had to do it herself. "He is one of Jørn's thralls, but he lives here with us and took our side against Grena," she explained rapidly, striving to keep her feelings for the handsome slave from showing in either her voice or expression.

Jarald frowned for a moment, then came up with what he considered a brilliant ploy. "Where is the man? I want to meet him."

Dana shrugged. "In the stable, perhaps, or Erik's house."

Seeking to impress Jarald, whom he greatly admired, Soren rushed to the door. "I'll find him."

Fearing Jarald and Brendan would despise each other at first sight, Dana moved away from the burly Dane and took a place at Berit's side. She was grateful now that she and Brendan had not made love, for she would never have been able to maintain her composure had his intoxicating scent covered her body like a second skin. She regarded their guest with an apprehensive glance, but clearly Jarald had no idea in which direction her thoughts had strayed, and, his usual supremely confident self, he smiled widely.

Brendan was in no mood to be summoned to the house, but when Thora came skipping up and took his hand as he crossed the yard with Soren, he gave her fingers a loving squeeze. He and the little girl followed Soren inside, and after glancing around the room, he forced himself to greet Freya and ask how me might be of service. But it was all he could do not to loudly protest what he was certain was Haakon's bloody invasion of his homeland.

He already knows where Haakon is! Dana realized instantly. It was clear in the rigidity of Brendan's posture as well as his insolent frown. She knew that defiant expression all too well, and certain the way they had parted could not have caused such seething rage as he now displayed, her spirits plummeted even lower.

Not fond of children, Jarald gave Thora only a hasty pat on the head before he began to look Brendan up and down. He then walked around him as if searching for faults that were not readily apparent. "Haakon has asked me to assist Freya in his absence, so you must show me the same respect that you would give him. I know that you helped Erik kidnap Berit. Dana says you will continue to be loyal to her family rather than to Grena's. Is that true?"

Not enjoying being examined so closely, Brendan took a step backward to put more distance between himself and the inquisitive brute. Still clinging to his hand, Thora remained at his side. He caught Dana's eye and held it before he replied, but there was nothing gracious about his tone. "Yes."

Jarald nodded, then tugging at the ends of his mustache, he continued to regard Brendan with a curious gaze. "How loyal?" he finally asked.

Brendan's unwavering stare remained fixed on Dana, who frowned slightly as if warning him of a trap, but he was already on guard. "You need not question my loyalty, for I have proven it several times."

"Is that true?" Jarald asked Erik.

While Erik hoped Brendan was referring to his rescue of the children, or to that morning rather than to seducing Dana, he would not dispute his word. "I would trust him with my life," he responded sincerely.

"You may well have to." Jarald continued to regard Brendan with a thoughtful stare, but then with an impatient shrug, he appeared to cast off his doubts. "We need you to return to Grena's. Convince her that you despise everyone here. Discover her plans, and then let us know what they are. Can you do that?"

Before Brendan could reply, Dana leapt to her feet. "You expect him to spy for us?"

"Why not?" Jarald asked. "He is only a thrall, and if he

is as loyal to you as everyone claims, he will gladly do it."

"That is no way to repay him for his loyalty," Dana insisted as she came forward to confront Jarald.

That Dana thought him incapable of speaking for himself angered Brendan as greatly as Jarald's request that he turn spy. Now that he had the opportunity to regard him up close, Brendan saw the big man's eyes were an icy green that glowed with intelligence. Jarald was no dim-witted fool, but a near giant of a man with a keen mind. That was a dangerous combination, and Brendan did not want to ever have to fight him hand to hand. Never lacking for confidence, however, he was certain he would have the speed and strength needed to slice him to shreds with a sword.

A slow smile hovered at the corner of Jarald's mouth, sending his mustache askew. "Does he mean so much to you?" he asked with a deep chuckle, apparently thinking such a thing an impossibility.

Suddenly all the eyes in the room were focused on Dana, and she knew she had to exercise extreme caution in her reply for not only were Brendan's feelings at stake, but her own reputation as well. "I would never ask anyone to prove his loyalty to me with treachery, not even a thrall."

Brendan was enraged now, for Dana was again discussing him as though he were one of her animals rather than her lover. Not about to stand there and take such an insult in silence, he joined in the conversation in an attempt to force her to speak to him directly. "If it will help Erik, I'll tell Grena whatever you want her to believe."

Aghast that he would make an offer in direct opposition to her stand, Dana instantly refused it. "You'll do nothing of the kind! I'd not ask you to spy on my worst enemy. I'd never send you to my aunt for such a despicable purpose."

Thinking it most unseemly for Dana to argue with a thrall in front of Jarald, Freya put an immediate stop to it. "Dana's right," she stated coolly. "We may have had no choice about going after Berit, but Grena is my only sister and I'll not stoop to filling her household with spies."

While she was grateful her mother supported her view, Dana continued to regard Brendan with a threatening stare.

His glance was equally hostile, and she dreaded the heated argument they would undoubtedly have the next time they were alone. There was nothing she could do about her father's travels other than reassure him about Haakon's purpose, but when his mood was such a belligerent one, she knew he would never listen. Unaware that Jarald was regarding them both with an amused glance, she was startled when his hearty laugh broke the uncomfortable silence.

"It is not easy to find so loyal a thrall. When Jørn returns I'll buy this man and give him to you for a wedding present. Would you like that?"

Dana saw Brendan flinch, but for once he held his tongue. Forcing herself to turn toward Jarald, she favored him with a near dazzling smile. "That's an intriguing idea, but one we'll have to discuss later privately."

Fearing Jarald would note the hatred in Brendan's expression and guess jealousy was the cause, Erik quickly dismissed him. For the time being he needed both men, and he didn't want them wasting their energies fighting each other.

Seeking an excuse to avoid Jarald's company for as long as she possibly could, Dana accompanied Berit to Svien's room when her cousin said she would like to rest. As always, the blonde was eager to talk despite her recent ordeal. "Your mother told me to regard this room as my own, but I don't think she'll allow Erik to share it."

"Most definitely not," Dana assured her. "This has all been very upsetting for her. You and Erik must not do anything to make her regret her kindness." How she could offer that advice so calmly when she had taken an obstreperous thrall for a lover, Dana didn't know, for surely that knowledge would kill her mother. "I'm sure there will be as many opportunities for you two to be together as before, but you'll have to be discreet and not flaunt your love."

"Flaunt?" Berit questioned. "I'm sure it's plain that I love Erik, but I'll try not to revel in it in front of Aunt Freya. Now what about you and Jarald? How are you going to send him on his way when he's so eager to help Erik?"

Dana had been pacing, but she stopped and turned to face

her cousin. Her problems were multiplying faster than she could keep up with them, but she was fully aware of what she would have to do about Jarald. "While I'm sure Jarald likes Erik, I think he's offered to help him mainly in hopes of impressing me. He's a proud man, so I dare not refuse his proposal now when it's so obvious Erik wants his help. I'll just have to continue to let him think that I'm considering his proposal, and just haven't been able to make up my mind. It's not fair to lie to Jarald like that, but if Erik will benefit, and I think he will, then I'll feel justified in doing it."

Instantly understanding Dana's dilemma, Berit nodded sympathetically. "You might even use Erik's dispute with my mother as an excuse not to accept his proposal. I mean, how can your family be expected to plan any sort of a family celebration until my mother agrees to allow Erik and me to wed?"

Dana saw the danger in that option immediately, and took care to explain it to Berit. "I know he'd believe me if I told him that, but I hope your mother will soon relent, and if that's the only excuse I've given Jarald, I'd be forced to start making wedding plans as soon as you had completed yours."

Berit shrugged slightly. "Oh, well, it was just a thought."

"Don't worry about Jarald and me. If I have kept him at bay this long, then I can surely do it a while longer."

"Dana?" Berit licked her lips slyly before continuing. "I rather liked Jarald's idea about having Brendan spy on my mother. Since you didn't, what about Ulla? I'll bet my mother hasn't even noticed she's gone yet, and she'd be able to find out a lot more than Brendan ever could."

Dana frowned slightly, for truly the idea of spying on her aunt did not appeal to her. "Ulla is your servant, so I'll not tell you what to do, but I don't think that's a good idea and you know my mother doesn't either."

"I've got to do something," Berit insisted. "Erik is such a good man, and he shouldn't have to begin each day wondering if it will be his last. My mother will surely do something dreadful to get even for my leaving her, and if

Ulla could just give us a warning so that we'd know what to expect and when, it might save his life.''

When stated in those terms, Dana had to go along with her cousin. ''If you really think Erik's life is at stake, then I'll bring Ulla to you at once. I think the choice should be hers, though. She is an elderly woman and shouldn't be forced to do something against her will.''

''You just ask her to come to me. I'll take care of everything.''

Berit looked so determined Dana wasn't at all surprised when after only a brief meeting, Ulla departed for home.

Brendan watched the sunset turn the sky from a vivid blue to a gold-lined crimson, but he was still so enraged over Haakon's voyage to Erin that the incredible beauty failed to fill him with any awe or joy. Dana had been slow to agree to his urgent plea that they meet that night, and that had been before she knew about Jarald's arrival, and before he had learned the reason for the man's visit. Just thinking of the arrogant oaf made his lip curl into a snarl. They deserved each other! he thought with still aching pride.

He was thoroughly disgusted with himself for ever becoming involved with Dana, and it was all too plain to him now that she was always going to treat him as a thrall because that was all that he would ever be to her. When they were alone she might forget briefly, but when they were with others she showed him so little warmth he had been a fool to think she might actually care for him. Clearly she liked the physical pleasure he gave her, if nothing else about him, but now that he knew where her father had gone, he wanted nothing more to do with her.

Searching for a way to repay her latest series of insults, as well as her father's sins, he vowed never to meet with her secretly again. He dared not, he realized, for the temptation was too great that he would seize just such an opportunity to choke every last bit of life out of her gorgeous body.

His depression as deep as it had ever been, the proud Celt soon entered the small house he and Erik had shared and went to bed. As he fell asleep, he hoped Dana would sneak out to meet him, catch a chill, and die within a few days' time. That sorry fate would not only save him the trouble of killing her, but it would also save him the torment of wanting her still, regardless of what he had learned about her father.

After spending the evening in Jarald's company, Dana doubted she could bear much more, even if it were for Erik's sake. As usual, the heavyset man monopolized every conversation. He missed no opportunity to reach out and touch her, and she had lost count of how many times she had had to suffer through one of his suffocating hugs. Other women might find his tales amusing and his manner wonderfully affectionate, but she most certainly did not.

Excusing herself when Freya and Berit retired, Dana hurried her little sister into bed, then had to wait for what seemed like half the night for the child to fall asleep. Despite the wretched scene they were sure to have, she was too anxious to see Brendan to feel sleepy and left the house without bothering to don her boots the instant she felt it was safe to go.

She was disappointed not to find the Celt waiting, but because she had asked for his patience, she tried to show him that same restraint in return. It wasn't until she had waited a very long while that she finally realized he wasn't coming to meet her. She had wanted to talk about her father's trip, to assure him that, no matter where Haakon went, his interest was always on peaceful trade, but how could she impress him with that fact if he failed to appear?

Was it possible he was also angered by her refusal to allow him to spy on Grena? Hadn't he realized why she wouldn't let him be used like that? He had asked her only that afternoon not to treat him as a thrall, and she had done exactly as he had asked. Was he grateful? Obviously not. Still, she had thought he possessed the courage to tell her how he felt to her face.

Discouraged clear through, she mounted Dawn's Kiss and rode home, but her earlier excitement had been replaced with a sense of betrayal so deep she made only slow progress. It was almost dawn when she returned to bed, and thoughts of seeing either Jarald or Brendan that morning filled her with dread. She had never lived through a worse summer, and now it seemed as though it would never come to an agreeable end.

CHAPTER XVII

Brendan and Soren made ready to return to the new house early the next morning, but Erik insisted they wait for Dana, Thora, Berit, and Jarald to accompany them. While he had no desire to see Jarald ever again, the Celt was so proud of himself for not having trekked out to the woods in the dark of night, where he was certain he would have had a long and fruitless wait, he could barely keep from gloating when Dana appeared.

After two ample meals, Berit was again strong enough to ride, and eager for a tour of the house she had only been able to glimpse through the trees. She chatted happily with her companions as they walked toward the stable, her spirits high now that she had escaped her mother's domination. She had found her Aunt Freya, while deeply distressed by her situation, so sympathetic and understanding that she knew she would be content in her home until she and Erik were allowed to marry.

For appearances' sake, Dana had greeted everyone happily that morning, but in truth, she was far from pleased with the prospects for the day. When she saw Brendan waiting with the horses, she sent him a questioning glance, for despite her painful doubts, she desperately wanted to believe he would have a reasonable excuse for not meeting her. His sly smirk merely confused her, though, and with Jarald constantly at her side she feared she would have a long wait before having an opportunity to question the Celt.

As Brendan led Dawn's Kiss over to Dana, he noticed the shadows beneath her eyes and concluded Jarald must have kept her up quite late. He then wondered if they had had that private conversation about him she had mentioned. He thought he might have a chance to ask as he helped her mount her mare, but Jarald cut in front of him and grabbed the reins. Rather than offer his hands as a convenient step, the solidly built man simply gripped Dana's tiny waist and swung her up into her saddle. Without pausing to draw a breath, or needing to, he thoughtfully plunked Thora on Rascal's back before striding over to his stallion.

Brendan knew that the demonstration of strength had been meant for the red-haired sisters' benefit rather than his own, but he couldn't help but marvel at the ease with which Jarald had accomplished it. The man was large, but obviously that was due to massive muscles rather than dense layers of fat. Cautious rather than envious, Brendan vowed once again not to cross the stocky Dane unless he had a sword in his hand.

Dana was as frustrated as Brendan when Jarald brushed him aside. She considered it merely another example of the possessiveness she abhorred. She had dressed in cream and beige that morning, the subdued colors of her attire chosen to match her mood, but now she wished she had selected garments of a brighter hue to lift her spirits. She had not been able to shake the painful anxiety her solitary midnight vigil had created, and being forced to endure Jarald's company when it was Brendan's she craved only deepened her depression. With Thora on her right and her amorous suitor on her left, she felt trapped in a role she had no wish to play, but for the moment she had accepted the sorry fact that she had no other choice.

Pride and a tinge of apprehension filled Freya's expression as she stood at the doorway of her home to wave good-bye. It seemed as though only yesterday her children had been small. Now Svien was grown, Dana was a lovely, young woman, and Soren had displayed more in the way of manly ambition of late than she had ever hoped he might possess. Only Thora was a child still, yet she had intelligence and insight far beyond her years.

Enjoying the warmth of the sun, Freya felt stronger than she had in a week. With hope lifting her spirits, she strolled over to the dairy barn to speak with the women working there. It had been awhile since she had seen them, and she didn't want them to think their work was not appreciated.

As they traversed the path to the woods, Dana paid scant attention to Jarald's conversation. It wasn't until he began to compare their fields to his own, which he claimed were not only of greater size, but also far more productive, that she became sufficiently interested to comment.

"I don't believe I've ever heard you boast to my father that you are a better farmer than he, Jarald," Dana remarked with a sweet smile that belied her scathing intent.

Taken aback by the challenge, Jarald relied on hearty chuckles to gain him the time to formulate a suitable reply. "I was not comparing myself to him, but merely my fields to his," he finally exclaimed proudly.

"Perhaps he would understand the difference," Dana replied smoothly, "but, alas, I do not."

Fearing he had insulted her, Jarald doubled his efforts to be charming. Rather than continue to discuss farming, he began a detailed and, in his opinion, fascinating account of his recent voyage. Dana made a polite comment here and there, and encouraged by what he mistook for rapt interest, he embellished the colorful description of his adventure all the more.

Brendan and Soren were riding behind Thora, Dana, and her talkative companion. While the Celt could not overhear their conversation, he also mistook Dana's frequent glances in the burly Dane's direction as an indication of her interest. According to Thora, Jarald was rich, and he certainly had the size and strength to protect the beautiful young woman he had given every indication he intended to wed.

Brendan kept reminding himself that from now on his only feelings for Dana would be the virulent hatred a slave naturally harbors for his mistress, but that did not prevent him from being curious about her. Finally he asked Soren what he knew about his sister's plans.

Too concerned with his own problems to have much interest in the men vying for Dana's hand, Soren shrugged as he replied. "Jarald is far more persistent than any of the others, so I think one day they'll marry."

"What others?" Brendan asked, inordinately pleased by the thought he had succeeded in becoming her first lover when apparently a great many Danes had failed in that quest. Knowing she would no longer be regarded as a great prize, were that fact common knowledge, also gave him a perverse sense of pride.

Soren supplied a rather lengthy list, and then after a slight pause added several more names. "Dana's a beauty, and our family is a proud one, so naturally she has received many proposals. Isn't it the same in your land?"

"Of course, I'm certain a woman of wealth and beauty is prized everywhere," Brendan admitted grudgingly. Still, he couldn't help but wonder if Dana had discouraged the attentions of other men because she favored Jarald. Or was Jarald merely the latest man to attempt to win her heart? "Probably an impossible feat," he mumbled under his breath.

"Don't you want them to marry?" Soren inquired.

Afraid he had been overheard, Brendan voiced his true sentiments with a sarcastic sneer. "Why should I care what they do?"

"Because Jarald said he would give you to Dana for a wedding gift, and I think she would see you got your freedom."

Not enjoying the turn their conversation had taken, Brendan's mood darkened even more. "Unless you know that for a fact, you shouldn't mention it, Soren, for I don't take lightly to being called Jørn's property."

"Well, it's plain to me you and Dana get along so poorly she would set you free just to be rid of you."

While he considered that an insulting opinion, Brendan was still eager to learn what the boy knew for certain and what was merely imaginative speculation. Unfortunately, Thora rode back to join them then, and the chance was lost.

"What's the matter, Thora?" Soren teased. "Don't you find Jarald's stories amusing?"

The little girl made a face at her brother, but clearly he had guessed the truth and Brendan hoped Dana found Jarald's company even more tiresome than Thora had. He wanted her to suffer in every way possible, and while he knew she would not actually die of boredom, he hoped it caused her considerable pain.

When they reached the new house, Jarald seemed genuinely impressed with the fine structure that was steadily taking shape. Grateful something new had caught his attention, Dana took Thora's hand and fell behind while Erik and Berit continued to walk with Jarald and explain their plans. Brendan and Soren had already pulled off their kirtles and joined the builders, but when Dana caught his eye, the Celt reluctantly responded to her silent summons.

"There are some pretty flowers blooming by the stream, Thora. Why don't you pick some to take back to your mother?" Brendan suggested with an inviting smile, and eager to collect an armful, the little girl bounded off.

"That was very clever of you," Dana complimented sincerely. "Couldn't you find any way to get away last night?"

"Last night?" Brendan asked innocently, as though he had no idea what she meant.

Dana glanced over her shoulder to make certain Jarald was still occupied with her half brother and cousin before she hurriedly answered Brendan's question. "Yes, last night. It was a matter of trust, as I recall. I said I would be there, and I was. I knew you were furious about my father's voyage to Erin, but I wanted to at least try and allay your fears. What happened to you?"

The first flames of anger already glowed in her violet eyes, giving her a sultry gaze Brendan still found appealing, but he forced himself to ignore it. He had been quite proud of himself for staying away, and he hoped Dana had been thoroughly miserable as she had paced the clearing with that restless stride of hers. He thought it a pity he had to keep an eye on Jarald while they spoke, so he wasn't able to gauge the effect of his words in her expression.

"We had made our plans before we knew of Jarald's arrival. That changed everything for me. You'll have to content yourself with his attentions from now on because I can't look at you without remembering where your menfolk have gone, and I'll not betray my own kind by lying with you. Sleep with Jarald if you're lonely. He's obviously eager to bed you." Brendan held his breath as he awaited her response, and when Dana didn't erupt in a shrieking fit of name-calling, he risked looking down at her.

A look of astonished disbelief filled Dana's expression as she replied in a bitter hiss, "I can understand why you would worry about the purpose of my father's voyage, but how can you be so incredibly stupid as to think I would ever stoop to inviting Jarald to my bed? Have you lost your senses completely?" Moving a step closer, she struck his bare chest with a tightly clenched fist. "You will meet me tonight, and you will not keep me waiting or you will spend the rest of the summer locked up with the furs with no more than bread and water."

Brendan's gaze was every bit as hostile as Dana's. There was nothing he could do to protect his people from Haakon, but the sudden realization that he had already disgraced the wealthy Dane's daughter by stealing her virtue prompted him to agree to her demand. "Yes, mistress," he responded sarcastically, not wanting her to suspect he had given in willingly.

Dana was certainly she had won an important concession from him, but rather than gloat, she merely nodded slightly before turning away to join Thora by the stream. Love was not supposed to hurt so badly, she told herself, but she knew what was wrong: she had fallen in love with the wrong man.

Brendan was an arrogant, thick-headed Celt who would cause her nothing but grief. That was so horrible a mistake she didn't think she could ever correct it, but she would not allow him to hate her out of the mistaken belief her father was ravaging his home when she was positive Haakon's riches had all been earned through honest trade. It was a matter of honor that she defend her father's reputation, and she would not give up until Brendan understood the truth about him.

Jarald glanced Dana's way in time to see the fierceness of her expression as she turned away from Jørn's thrall. He had always considered her a serious young woman, not one given to frequent bursts of giggles as Berit was, but he could not imagine why she would have been speaking to the slave or seem so desperately determined as a result.

Dana was delightfully complex, but that was precisely why he had chosen her for his wife. While he harbored no illusions that she loved him, he was confident that in time she would. She was affectionate with her parents and brothers and sister, if not with him, but he knew his loving would please her so greatly she would soon come to adore him as Freya did Haakon. His present problem was how to gain her consent for their marriage, however, and he didn't want to have to vie for her attentions with the likes of a thrall, even a passably handsome one.

A slow smile raised the ends of his mustache as he decided the Celt slave would suffer a horrible accident, and soon. Pleased by the thought, he realized that the more problems that developed on Haakon's farm, the more his helpful assistance would be needed by all who resided there. It would not matter if Dana turned to him for comfort rather than love. If she became dependent upon him for any reason, he would consider it a vital step toward winning her hand.

Dana rested all afternoon, and she was wide awake when she left the house to meet Brendan. For Erik's sake and out of regard for her father's friendship with Jarald, she had made more of an effort to entertain the man that evening, but she had not known what to do when he had responded by nearly smothering her with affection. He had been surprisingly gentle rather than rough, but it was all she could do to endure his frequent hugs and kisses on the cheek. She knew he had to consider her cold, and she didn't understand why that didn't dim his ardor.

The effort to hide her feelings all day had left Dana feeling deeply troubled, and she hoped their dispute with Grena could be settled swiftly so that she could tell Jarald the truth: she valued his friendship just as her father did, but there was no hope for a marriage between them. That Brendan could have suggested she sleep with the man still disgusted her, and she was not nearly so eager to see him that night as she had been the previous evening.

Brendan, however, had decided to take full advantage of every opportunity to enjoy Dana's favors, since that cynical view of their romance soothed his badly troubled conscience where she was concerned. She had a way of playing upon his emotions as no other woman ever had, but now that he was aware of the danger, he was certain he could overcome it. He purposely reached the clearing first, and the instant Dana had dismounted from her mare, he drew her into his arms.

Dana had thought the future as dark as the shadows that surrounded them, but when she stepped into Brendan's arms, nothing seemed to matter but the delicious excitement of his warm embrace. She had expected him to be sullen rather than loving, but she was wise enough to know that was a trick of passion rather than truth.

"You must talk with me," she murmured against his already bared chest.

Brendan saw no reason for a conversation that would surely lead to another argument. "Words only get in our way," he protested as he tilted her chin to recapture her lips for another near endless kiss. Her taste was delicious, with a uniquely flavorful sweetness that as always left him craving much more. *I am using her just as she is using me*, he reminded himself, not understanding why that fact was so terribly difficult to recall.

Dana's fingers slid through the coarse curls covering his chest, but her gesture was a caress, not an attempt to break free. Giving up as hopeless the effort to gain his full attention, she spoke as best she could between kisses. With frequent prolonged interruptions as a result, it took her a long while to convey the message that her father's sole interest was in trade and that her only interest in Jarald was in the help he could provide Erik.

"That's what I wished to tell you last night," she confided when next Brendan allowed her a moment to breathe.

"So that I'd not be jealous?" the affectionate Celt teased, preferring to discuss Jarald rather than Haakon.

"You have no right to be jealous," Dana scolded softly. "You have no more claim on me than Jarald does."

"Oh, really?" Brendan whispered against her temple. Deciding to prove his point, with an agile move he pulled her down on the grass. She was clad only in a cloak and a flimsy silk nightgown that he easily cast aside, hurriedly followed by his own clothing.

Brendan had vowed to enjoy himself thoroughly, and with an appreciative grin he thought the perfection of Dana's lithe body more splendid each time he had the good fortune to strip her nude. He moved his hands over her with an adoring caress, slowly tracing each luscious swell and inviting hollow, and all the while continuing an intoxicating barrage of deep kisses.

He knew her to be a wonderfully responsive woman, but he was seeking more than pleasure that night. He wanted to bend not only Dana's supple body to his will, but her defiant soul as well. He was a man who relished a challenge, and she always provided that. His fingertips created a tingling pathway along the elegant line of her throat, over her pale shoulder to the flushed tips of her breasts. He then repeated that graceful trail with light kisses he gradually deepened to sample her taste more fully.

While he could feel Dana's supple body fill with tremors of excitement as his tongue teased her budding nipples, Brendan's lavish seduction had only just begun. He cherished the lush fullness of her breasts at the same time his knowing caress slid down her thighs, then back up to follow the curve of her hip before brushing over the flatness of her stomach. At last his touch slipped below her navel to comb through the triangle of fiery curls nestled there. Moving lower still, he parted the tender folds which lay hidden from his view, marveling as before at how quickly her body created an inviting wetness.

His fingertips were slippery now, easing their entry as he lured the breathless redhead toward the vision of paradise he saw so clearly in his mind. She held him tightly cradled in her arms, her hands slipping through his curls and then over his shoulders as she pressed him close. That she accepted his affection so readily inspired him to give even more. The haunting fragrance of her perfume was now mixed with her own captivatingly feminine scent, and Brendan longed to lose himself in the sensual wonder of her.

When he positioned himself above her, Dana raised her arms to embrace him, but in an instant he had eluded her grasp. He stretched out between her slender legs and spread adoring kisses on the soft, white skin of her belly. His tongue tickled, and she responded with a throaty giggle that served to inspire him to produce several more. In the most charming fashion, he coaxed her with a playful abandon until she was totally relaxed. Taking a firm hold on her hips, he rubbed his cheek against her inner thigh, cleverly spreading her legs wide so that when he lowered his head to enjoy the first of the intimate kisses that would send her to the edge of madness, she had no way to escape him.

Exalting in that momentary triumph, Brendan tasted the salty sweetness of her and was instantly lost in his own desires. The need to possess her more fully than he ever had any other woman overwhelmed him. Dana was his! he shouted in his mind, and as the words echoed in his heart with an emotional truth he could no longer deny, he deepened his kiss to prove his possession would last into eternity.

At first Dana writhed beneath Brendan in a vain attempt to escape the shocking form his affection had taken, but she was soon floating upon an enchanted haze of wonder and surrendered completely to the generous rapture he bestowed. He did not simply give pleasure; he drenched her in a flood of erotic sensation that threatened to cause her heart to burst with the sheer joy of his remarkable devotion. The ecstasy of sharing so passionate an encounter swelled within her, finally cresting at a shattering peak and showering her with splendor.

Robbed of all thoughts save those of Brendan, Dana could only cling to him weakly when he at last sought to find his release deep within her. That their passion for each other could create feelings so intense both shocked and frightened her. Rather than being lulled into a contented sleep, she lay awake in his arms, unable to gather the will to depart nor the wits to fathom just what they had shared.

Brendan could not recall lovemaking ever being so exhausting, but he was completely spent. "Will you admit it now?" he asked in a slurred whisper.

"Admit what?" Dana asked, too confused to think, let alone remember their earlier conversation.

The days were long, the nights all too brief, and in the pale moonlight that filtered through the trees there was already the promise of the coming dawn. Brendan groaned sadly, unable to believe they might have to part before the stubborn beauty in his arms admitted her need for him ran deep.

"Admit what?" Dana asked again.

Brendan tried to raise himself up on one elbow, slipped, and had to try again. "Admit that you belong to me," he began with a sly grin. "Your body knows the truth. Don't you?"

When Dana sat up to face him, her long curls covered her breasts, and by bending her knees slightly, she demurely shielded still more of herself from his view. "All I know is that when I am with you, nothing else matters, but that's merely an illusion, not the truth."

Dismayed by the seriousness of her mood, Brendan reached out to take her hand and brought her palm to his lips. "What is the truth as you see it?"

Dana took a deep breath, and forcing her rebellious mind to be coherent, she hastened to explain. "You are too fine a man to be a thrall. I mean to set you free and send you home. It's what you deserve, although it means we'll never meet again.''

Until that instant Brendan had lived very much for the moment. Earlier that night he had been bent on taking his revenge on Haakon through his lovely daughter, but as Dana's eyes filled with a mist of tears, he knew he should never have attempted such a vindictive quest. He could not dismiss his feelings with Dana, and he had been a fool to try. He despised all Danes, with one lovely exception, and he would never again try to trick himself into believing he hated her.

He was certain no Danish girl ever wed a slave, and even if Dana succeeded in arranging for his freedom, he would have nothing but the clothes on his back to offer her. Surely Haakon would not regard him as a suitable husband for his elder daughter. That Dana wanted to send him home was remarkably generous, but there was no joy in that hope if he would spend the rest of his life without her.

Dropping her hand, Brendan reached over to pick up Dana's gown and handed it to her. He then rose and yanked on his breeches. To boast he was the son of a king seemed absurd to him when he had no way to prove that claim. What Haakon would demand for her would be chests of gold, precious jewels, and bolts of the finest silk, not the elaborate promises any beggar could make. He would never be able to convince anyone he was of royal birth. Furthermore, whatever status he held in Erin was completely irrelevant to the Danes. To them he was but a lowly slave.

''You're right. I am too fine a man to be a thrall, and the sooner I'm granted my freedom the better off we'll both be.''

Dana studied Brendan's pensive frown, stunned he could dismiss her so easily when imagining a future that did not include him was unbearably painful to her. ''You see, it's all an illusion. We can't escape the world for more than a night at a time.''

Brendan helped her up, then waited until she had donned her cloak before he drew her into his arms. She resisted him for an instant, then slipped her arms around his waist. He wanted to promise her a hundred things, but until he had his freedom and had regained his wealth, he could not.

"I didn't really think you would marry Jarald after knowing me," he remarked in a joking attempt to put an end to the discussion of their dismal situation. "I promise not to be jealous of him, and I won't give him any reason to be jealous of me either."

In no mood for levity, Dana issued a warning as she pulled away. "Better make certain that you don't. I think he might be more of a pirate than a trader, and I don't really trust him, although I know my father does."

He had not forgotten that Haakon was probably also a pirate, but Brendan wisely kept his opinion to himself. He helped Dana mount Dawn's Kiss, then gave her knee a loving pat. "Even if you are an illusion, no more than a dream, I still want to make love to you as often as I possibly can. Will you try to be here again tomorrow night?"

Had he said he loved her and would fight for her at whatever cost, Dana would have found it easy to reply, but because he had not, a painful lump filled her throat as she again promised that she would try.

Walking back through the woods, Brendan came to the swift conclusion he would have to return home, gather a band of men, construct a ship, and then return to Fyn for Dana. The Norsemen and Danes kidnapped beautiful women all the time, so why couldn't he? It was a bold plan, and perhaps an impossible one when so much of the voyage would have to be made through waters infested with not only Norse pirates, but Danes as well, but it provided the only bit of comfort he had as he made his way back to the clearing where Erik's new house stood.

It was still dark enough for his approach to go unnoticed, but as Brendan reached the edge of the woods, he felt the eerie sensation he was being watched. Certain Dana would not have followed him, he glanced over his shoulder quickly, then scanned the tents the men had set up for shelter but nothing looked amiss. Thinking that his lack of sleep was playing havoc with his imagination, he left the trees, but before he had taken more than a single step, he was felled by a fierce blow that caught him on the left side of the head.

Landing facedown, and immobilized by an excruciating pain that encircled his head and shot down his spine, Brendan had to endure the further agony of waiting for the unseen assailant to strike him a second and fatal blow. He could feel blood flowing down his cheek, forming a gruesome puddle beneath his chin and he tried to call out for help, but managed to utter no more than a hoarse croak that was muffled by the dirt in which he lay.

He was certain that death would swiftly overtake him. A vision of sunlight dancing on Dana's flame-red curls filled Brendan's mind. He had always loved her hair, and he reached out, his grasp feeble as he tried to catch the end of a curl to draw her near. When an intense heat seared his fingertips, he yanked his hand back, horrified to find the alluring flames were real.

At first there were only a few wisps of smoke. Then it billowed up around him in suffocating waves as the flames shot high into the air. The brush at the edge of the woods had ignited quickly, and now several trees were ablaze. Again Brendan tried to call for help, and this time, terrified he was about to be burned alive, he managed a shriek that echoed through the whole meadow. He heard an answering shout, and then another voice he recognized as Erik's, but the smoke was too thick for him to catch his breath. Unable to call out again, he was certain they would never find him in time.

He wondered if there would be anything left for Dana to bury, or if she would know to put a cross over his grave. He saw her face so clearly then, the red of her hair as bright as the flames licking his sleeve, and it pleased him that his last thoughts were of the only woman he had ever loved.

CHAPTER XVIII

Brendan had not expected to awaken, so he was doubly amazed to find himself stretched out on a bench in the expansive hall of Freya's home. He had regained consciousness slowly, and at first had only been dimly aware of the voices that echoed all around him. Gradually the words had become clear, and he realized the people clustered nearby were discussing him. His head ached too badly for him to join in, but as usual he was infuriated not to be given a say in decisions concerning his welfare.

Dana had been keeping a close watch over Brendan, and when she saw his eyes flutter open, she stepped in front of him to prevent the others from making the same observation. When Erik had brought the Celt slave to them at dawn, she had feared her feelings for him would be instantly apparent, but fortunately the controversy surrounding the mysterious cause of his injuries had captured everyone's attention and the depth of her concern had gone unnoticed.

"All we know for certain is that there was a fire," Dana stated calmly. "There's no proof that Brendan set it. Indeed, if he had, he wouldn't have been burned and surely he could not have struck himself such a brutal blow to the head."

A man who relished any sort of argument, Jarald was on the edge of his seat. "How do you explain the fact he was in the woods in the first place?"

Dana knew exactly what Brendan had been doing, but she dared not reveal he was returning from a midnight rendezvous with her. As she attempted to supply some believable alternative, the wily thrall began rubbing his heavily bandaged hand up the back of her thigh and she had to first reach back to catch his fingers in a light grasp to still his caress. "Perhaps he heard a suspicious noise and went to investigate. Whoever set the fire clubbed him and left him to die in the flames."

Jarald waved aside that assumption as unworthy of consideration. "I doubt there was another man involved. I think the thrall misjudged how quickly the brush would burn, then collided with a tree as he tried to dash for safety."

"Brendan has worked with me from the day I decided to build the house. He wouldn't try and burn it down," Erik responded, echoing Dana's staunch defense of the injured man.

"How can you be certain?" Jarald asked, keeping to the facts. "From what you say, the thrall was with Grena only a few weeks, and then he has been here a little over a month. How can any of you make a judgment about his character?"

"He is a hard worker," Freya said. "And when Thora and Grena's twins foolishly took one of Haakon's boats, he was among the first to volunteer to find them."

"It was to his advantage to do so, Freya," Jarald pointed out with a ready smile. "For the more you thought of him, the better his chances were to earn his freedom." When Freya appeared skeptical of that argument, Jarald took a different approach. "You know how greatly I value your husband's friendship, and I'm proud to think he appreciates mine." He paused briefly to allow the gracious woman the opportunity to make a favorable comment, and she did not disappoint him.

"You're one of Haakon's best friends, Jarald. Surely you know that."

"Thank you. It's because I'm such a good friend to your family that I've taken an interest in this matter, and I think I can see things much more clearly than you all do. Now the thrall was willing to return to Grena's and inform us of her intentions," Jarald continued persuasively. "When you refused to consider that plan, I think he went to Grena on his own to offer his services to her. She was undoubtedly the one who directed him to burn down the house, but the fool made the mistake of setting himself on fire instead."

"Brendan is no fool," Thora contradicted sharply. She

was seated by the slave's feet, and gave his ankle an affectionate pat for emphasis.

Correctly interpreting his mother's anxious glance, Soren took his little sister's hand. "Let's go outside, baby. There will be time for you to see Brendan later." The inquisitive child hesitated a moment, but knowing from experience she was excluded whenever the conversation got interesting, she followed Soren out the door without creating a fuss.

"I can't believe my sister would be responsible for such a violent act," Freya insisted. "I know she is angry, and perhaps she feels I have betrayed her trust by taking Berit in, but still, to set fire to Erik's house is an extremely hostile response."

Berit sat beside Erik, her fingers laced with his. "My mother was in the worst of moods when I last saw her two days ago. I think she would set fire to this house as well if she thought she could get away with it."

"Oh, Berit, you can't possibly mean that," Freya argued.

Berit looked over at Dana's troubled expression, and at Erik. "I do mean it. I had hoped that we would receive a warning before anything happened, but perhaps the person I'm depending upon was unable to get away."

"You have a spy in your mother's house?" Jarald inquired, astonished a young girl would be so skilled at intrigues.

"Not a spy, a friend," the pretty blonde explained.

"No, this could not have been Grena's work, I refuse to believe that." Freya rose and crossed to Berit's side. "I will send word to your mother immediately asking her to meet with me later today."

Also rising to his feet, Jarald was quick to offer a word of caution to his hostess. "She will deny all responsibility for the fire. The only way to get the truth is from the thrall."

"The man is barely alive," Erik remarked regretfully.

"That will make it all the easier to force the truth from him," Jarald replied with obvious relish for the task.

That was a suggestion Dana rejected instantly. "No one is going to touch Brendan. We'll ask him to tell us what he knows when he feels up to it and not before."

"The man is more thoroughly smoked than most hams,"

Jarald pointed out with a hearty chuckle. "He'll not live out the day."

"I'll thank you to keep such gruesome thoughts to yourself," Freya requested, summoning the authoritative tone she had frequently used before her lengthy illness.

"Forgive me," Jarald begged. "I'm only trying to help you with what is clearly a most difficult situation."

Taking him at his word, Freya entwined her arm in his. "Would you do me the favor of riding over to Grena's to invite her to come see me? She'll be reluctant, but she respects you as highly as we do, and I think she would listen to your advice."

Jarald had planned to spend the day with Dana. He did not want to do errands for Freya, but because there was no way he could refuse the fragile woman's request, he tried to sound delighted to be charged with such a responsibility. He then gave Dana a charming grin as he invited her to accompany him.

Dana found it easy to return his smile as she supplied a perfect excuse. "I would enjoy the ride, of course, but I'm afraid my aunt is as furious with me as she is with Erik and Berit, and the mere sight of me would ruin any chance you might have to bring her back here. I'm afraid you'll have to go alone, and perhaps we can go for a ride together another time."

Because he hoped to impress both Freya and Dana, Jarald was forced to accept the refusal without argument, but he wasn't at all pleased to be sent off with a message he was certain any servant could have delivered. "I'll do my best to convince Grena to return with me, but I fear it may take a very long while."

"I'll be here when you return," Dana promised sweetly, but she hoped he would be gone all day. As soon as Jarald had left the house, she turned around to face Brendan and sat down by his side.

"Can you tell us what happened?" she asked.

"He's awake?" Freya exclaimed. "Why didn't you say so?"

Brendan tried to make out the faces of those who came forward to surround him, but their features were blurred.

Dana was close—that he knew—so the other red-haired woman had to be Freya. He assumed the tall, dark-haired man was Erik and the blonde with him Berit. He relaxed slightly then, thinking himself among friends. He ached all over, but the pain in his head was almost more than he could bear.

"It hurts," he managed to gasp.

Dana reached out to touch his curls. Then, afraid she would only increase his pain, she dropped her hand to her lap. "You've a deep gash in your head, so it's no wonder you're in pain. Erik reached you before you were badly burned, so I'm sure it's only your clothes that reek of smoke, not you. Can you tell us what happened?"

Brendan tried to speak, and when Dana leaned close in order to make out his words, he longed to pull her into his arms but lacked the strength to do so. Over the last few years he had had several brushes with death, but none closer than this one. Because the story she had told was a plausible one, he repeated it. He had not actually heard suspicious noises, but it provided a reasonable excuse for being away from his tent. In too much pain to speak at length, he provided only the briefest details.

"I heard someone in the woods but got hit from behind before I found out who it was. I didn't see them," he concluded, and closing his eyes, he slipped back under the blanket of pain that enveloped him like a shroud.

Dana sat back, but did not rise. She was sorry now Jarald hadn't been there to hear Brendan's side of the story, since he had related it in so convincing a fashion. "It's plain he didn't set the fire, but I'm afraid the person who did might try to harm us again."

"Harm me, Dana," Erik corrected. "It had to have been Grena's doing. There's no reason for anyone else to want to see my new house in ruins."

Freya raised her hands in a graceful plea. "The house suffered no damage, so I want you to go on back there. Search the woods for whatever evidence you can find. Footprints of men, whatever. I will never believe Grena had anything to do with this without proof that leads right to her door."

"Who else could it have been, Mother?" Dana asked, her patience wearing thin. "Berit has no heartbroken suitors seeking to get even with Erik, and Erik has no other enemies. Only Grena would be pleased to see the house he'd built for Berit burned to the ground."

Freya sighed sadly, "I know how it looks, but perhaps Erik will find something to prove otherwise."

Erik hesitated to leave with Brendan such a sorry sight. "I'm pleased Jarald wants to take so active a part in finding the culprit, but don't let him near Brendan. I won't have him tortured."

Considering what he had already suffered, Dana found the threat of that possibility deeply disturbing. "Don't worry," she said. "Whether or not Jarald trusts Brendan, we do, and I'll insist he accept our view."

Erik's glance locked with his lovely half sister's, and what he saw was a silent reassurance that she would guard Brendan's life with her own if need be. He still did not approve of her scandalous liaison with a thrall, but because her feelings for the man were obviously sincere, he trusted her to see Brendan came to no further harm. "I know he'll receive the proper care from you. That's why I brought him here. Now come outside with me, Berit. There's something I want to say to you before I leave."

As Berit left with Erik to tell him good-bye, Freya went to find Thora while Dana remained seated beside Brendan. The weavers came in to begin work, and other women moved about the kitchen baking bread and attending to the many chores required to keep the family fed. The house was filled with its usual bustling activity, but Dana heard little and saw nothing but the face of the man she loved. A handsome face that even in sleep was etched with pain.

While she and Erik would have only a few moments together, Berit made good use of them. "My mother has several men who would do whatever she asked of them. When she learns our house wasn't destroyed, she may try again. You must post guards to keep watch at night so no one else is hurt."

A slow smile curved across Erik's lips before he leaned down to kiss her. "You'll make a wonderful wife, Berit. I don't know how I've managed to survive without you all these years."

Berit blushed at his teasing, but didn't give in. "You can laugh all you like. Just make certain you aren't caught sleeping again."

Erik nodded, for he didn't want to argue about anything when her kisses were so sweet. He had meant to savor only a few, but it wasn't until Freya and Thora walked by and bid him farewell that he forced himself to draw away.

After sending her youngest child into the kitchen to request something especially nourishing for Brendan to eat when he next awoke, Freya placed her hand on Dana's shoulder. She spoke softly so she would not be overheard, but her meaning was very clear.

"First, I want you to forget everything I said about your father and Erik the other day. I was overwrought and never should have spoken my fears aloud. Haakon is the dearest of husbands, and no matter what problems are here to greet him upon his return, he would never blame them on me. Second, I want you to leave Brendan's care to the servants. You are not to sit with him again, nor are you to feed him, change his bandages, or touch him in any way. Is that understood?"

Because she and her mother had previously discussed the dangers in the closeness of her relationship to Brendan, Dana did not need to ask why Freya wanted them kept apart. She understood completely. Her mother considered the slave's devotion to her something to discourage, so she most certainly would not allow anyone to gain the impression Dana was equally devoted to him. Dana was devoted to him, however, and reluctant to leave his care to others. She rose slowly and did not immediately leave the sleeping thrall's side.

"He didn't deserve this," she whispered sadly.

"Of course not, but some good might come of it. He and Moira will have a chance to get to know each other well by the time he's strong enough to return to work with Erik. It's possible a romance might still blossom between them after all.''

Dana forced herself to smile. "Yes, that's true." Obediently she stepped aside as her mother summoned her shy Celt maid to take her place. She hoped Brendan would understand, but because he misinterpreted all her actions, she feared he would think only that she cared nothing about him. The truth was it broke her heart to have to leave his side.

Disappointed not to have Dana's company as he rode to Grena's, Jarald was still pleased with himself. It was a pity Freya's family were all so impressed by the injured thrall that they hadn't readily accepted his guilt, but only Freya's devotion to her sister had kept her from believing Grena had been behind the fire that had nearly claimed Brendan's life. It was almost too perfect. No one had even suspected that the thrall had been the intended victim of the attack.

"I should have struck him again," Jarald mumbled to himself. He had been certain his first blow had shattered the thrall's skull. Still, he doubted the slave would survive more than a day or two after suffering so severe a beating, and while his burns were slight, there was always the possibility they might fester. The burly Dane swiftly convinced himself that Brendan was dying.

As Grena's farm came into view, Jarald began to plan how best to further infuriate the woman in an effort to prevent her from ever visiting her sister's home again. Of course, even if she came along with him and denied any knowledge of the fire, he doubted anyone but Freya would believe her. He would prefer she stayed away, however, just to keep everyone feeling anxious. As he approached the house, he feared his greatest problem might be in keeping his expression nonchalant as he spun what he assumed would be clever lies.

Not once questioning his motives, Grena was delighted to welcome Jarald into her home. He had been a frequent visitor when her husband was alive, and she had missed seeing him. She gave him the most affectionate greeting she could provide, then replenished his ale frequently as they talked.

Good manners required that Jarald not state his business until he had inquired about Grena's family, and having forgotten just how talkative the woman was, he found himself waiting a long while. She did not mention her daughter, and so as not to embarrass her, he pretended not to know Berit's whereabouts.

"It was thoughtful of you to come tell me about Jørn's voyage to Erin," Grena complimented with a girlish blush. She and Jarald were about the same age, and while she had not considered him among her original prospects for remarriage, the fact that Dana showed no real enthusiasm when she spoke of him made her wonder if he might not have to seek a wife elsewhere. She had always thought him an exciting man, even if her niece did not.

Jarald was no stranger to an appreciative glance, and because Grena was an attractive woman, he began to wonder if his visit might not prove more amusing than he had originally thought. "What I have to say does concern Jørn, but you're the one I've come to see." He paused a moment, and when Grena's blush deepened, he reached out to take her hand.

"Haakon has asked me to look after his family until he returns, so I'll be staying at his farm. Freya told me you and she have had a dreadful misunderstanding, and she asked me to escort you to her home so that you two might settle your differences."

Disappointed the man had come at Freya's behest rather than to pay a social call, Grena withdrew her hand from his. "I'll not allow my dispute with her to intrude on our friendship, but I can't think of anything she could possibly have to say that I would wish to hear."

Jarald nodded sympathetically. "I understand, and I assure you I've no wish to become involved in your quarrel. There is the matter of Jørn's thrall, however."

Grena responded with a particularly bitter oath, not caring whether or not her language shocked her guest. "Brendan has shown himself to be completely untrustworthy, and the instant Jørn returns I'll insist he be whipped soundly and then sold.''

''I'm afraid that may prove impossible. He was badly injured last night in an attempt to set fire to the house Erik is building. Because he belongs to Jørn, quite naturally there is the suspicion that you were behind his actions.''

''What?'' Grena shrieked as she leapt to her feet. ''Is that why Freya wants to see me? So she can make such wild accusations?''

Jarald rose to face her, his tone as well as his expression intentionally soothing. ''Do not upset yourself, Grena. When people are angry, they frequently say things they don't mean.''

''He only attempted to set fire to the house—he didn't actually do it?''

''No, I believe a few trees were lost, but the house wasn't damaged.''

Grena took a step away, and when she turned back to face Jarald, her expression was as vicious as her tone. ''I wish I had thought of burning down Erik's house, but I didn't.''

''Perhaps there will be other opportunities,'' Jarald offered slyly.

''You would approve of such violent tactics?'' Grena could already see that he did.

''I admire a woman who knows how to get what she wants.'' He stepped close then, and continued to smile. He thought her husband had been dead about two years. That was far too long for so appealing a woman to be without the company of a man. ''You said your boys had gone fishing. Will they be gone all morning?''

Grena's eyes widened in dismay, for she could scarcely believe her guest was asking what he appeared to be asking. ''Are you no longer courting Dana?'' she took the precaution to ask.

Jarald raised his hand to caress her cheek tenderly. ''Dana is a child. What I want is a woman, one who knows how to please a man.''

For a long moment Grena continued to stare up at Jarald. His eyes were a remarkably clear green, and she had always admired his rugged good looks. If what he wanted was her, she saw no reason to refuse him. There were servants moving about, but none who dared question her behavior or gossip about it to anyone who mattered.

Turning away, she glanced back over her shoulder to issue a seductive invitation. "We'll not be disturbed in my chamber." She left the hall, and made no attempt to hide her delighted smile when he followed.

Grena had never been with any man other than her late husband, and he had always treated her with a respect she had naively assumed all men showed their women. It took no more than a few moments of Jarald's abusive company to convince her that mistaken belief had been a grave error, but by then her composure was so completely shattered she could not even cry out for help.

Jarald did not stop to kiss the curvaceous woman before he hurriedly stripped her nude, and even then he showed no interest in bestowing any gestures of affection. Rather than endearments, his comments were all obscene. He used words so filthy that Grena was sure they would have insulted a whore, and yet they fell easily from his lips, clearly from frequent use. He preferred a savage slap to a gentle caress, and rather than fondling her generous breasts he bruised her pale skin with a brutal clutch before leaving the deep crescent imprint of his teeth embedded in her tender flesh.

Jarald took great pride in the fact that he had not only the hearty appetites of a bull, but a beast's stamina as well. His eyes shone with a lustful gleam as he dominated Grena's voluptuous body with a passion for violence rather than shared rapture. Considering her tearful sobs compliments to his sexual prowess, he used her body totally without regard for her feelings. He satisfied himself time and again before finally growing bored with his sport and rising from the anguished woman's rumpled bed.

Once spared the burden of his weight, Grena drew in a deep breath to clear a painful wave of dizziness from her head. She was grateful Jarald had forced her face down on the bed, for it meant she didn't have to watch him dress. She didn't want to ever see the man again, and she would never admit that she had invited his advances. She was certain that not even Loki, the master of evil, could have given her more pain. Indeed, Jarald had caused her agony in ways she had not even known it was possible for a man to perform on a woman. Filled with shame at her own stupidity as well as loathing for him, she lay still as he made ready to depart.

"I'm beginning to think your husband wasn't half the man we all thought he was," Jarald remarked snidely as he drew on his boots. "You've borne four children, and yet you're as shy as a virgin. I like my women to have passion, Grena." He paused for a moment, and when she failed to respond, he whacked her across the buttocks, leaving yet another angry red welt.

"A woman is nothing without passion. That's why I intend to wed Dana. She can set a man's blood to boil with no more than a glance. It's difficult now to believe you are from the same family."

Jarald continued his steady flow of insults until he crossed to the door. "I'll tell Freya you've no wish to see her. As I said, I'll be staying with her until Haakon returns home. If I get the chance to come here again, I will. Or," he lowered his voice to a seductive hush, "you could always come to visit me." He hesitated a moment, and then, certain he was the last person Grena would ever want to see, he strode out, confident she would not go anywhere near her sister's farm if there were the slightest possibility he might still be there.

Until Brendan could care for himself, Dana convinced Freya he should not be moved. That was a small victory, but at least she could glance his way occasionally even if she had been forbidden to care for him. Yet in the time it took him to regain his strength, he became something of a household pet. He was not only handsome, but also graciously thanked anyone who performed the smallest service for him, and Dana feared they would soon have the same problem Grena had experienced. Even Moira had swiftly overcome her shyness around him, and he was so well tended Dana had not the smallest excuse to speak with him. While that was a great disappointment to her, Brendan seemed not to notice, and he continued to thrive under the generous attention their female servants provided.

When he felt well enough to elaborate on his initial description of the night he had been injured, Brendan kept his story identical to the one Dana had fabricated. While he would have recognized any of Grena's men, he had seen no one, but he was convinced she had been behind the fire. They all hoped Erik might turn up some piece of evidence, but after several days' search of the woods, he could offer no proof for their suspicions.

Jarald had been surprised when Brendan didn't fulfill his prediction and die. He seriously considered smothering him in his sleep, but for the first few nights Freya had servants remain with the thrall, and their solicitous concern for the injured man prevented him from carrying out that plan. Then, when after several days' observation, he saw nothing untoward between the slave and Dana, he decided he must have been mistaken about them. He forgot the man and concentrated his efforts on winning her consent for their marriage. Always confident, he was certain his extended stay in her home was helping him make some real progress in that direction.

Brendan attempted unsuccessfully to hide his anger as Dana and Berit again left the house with Jarald. From what he had overheard, the three planned to ride out to see Erik and have a picnic. That, as usual, Dana had not bothered to inquire as to his health or to tell him good-bye left him feeling bitterly insulted. He knew she didn't care for Jarald. Each time the man enveloped her in one of his incessant hugs, she cringed so violently he could see it from clear across the hall, so he wished she would cease to worry about Erik and send him on his way.

Inactivity of any kind had always been difficult for Brendan, but to lie almost too weak to move while another man courted the woman he loved with an apparently inexhaustible enthusiasm was unbearable for him. Nearly a week had passed and the once excruciating headaches were no more than a dull throb, but he still felt far from well. He had lost weight despite the fine meals he had been served, and when he got up to go out to the privy he still needed someone to walk by his side to make certain he didn't fall. It was a pathetic situation, and yet he saw no way out of it save patience, which was unfortunately a virtue he had always lacked.

Moira followed Brendan's hate-filled stare, then leaned over to whisper, "I don't like Jarald either. He's not nearly good enough for Dana."

Brendan waited for the maid to turn back toward him, but when she did, her gaze was so innocent he knew she had no idea why he disliked the husky Dane so virulently. "Won't she choose her own husband?" he asked with little interest in the girl's response.

"Of course, but she can't say yes if the man she wants doesn't ask her." Moira flicked the crumbs from her apron. "Do you want anything more to eat?"

Surprised by her insightful observation, Brendan just shook his head. He thanked her as she took his tray, then closed his eyes and pretended to be asleep. Somewhere on the dim edge of his memory he recalled formulating a desperate scheme to make Dana his wife. Had the villain who had tried to roast him alive succeeded, those would have been among the last of his conscious thoughts. And Dana was not even mildly upset that he had nearly died. She had not given him more than a casual glance the whole time he had been in her home!

What a fool I have been, he thought angrily. He still might build a ship and come back for her, but it wouldn't be to make her his wife. It would be to make her his slave. He relished that possibility, for the thought of having her do his bidding for a change was immensely satisfying. He would not make her scrub floors or do any hard labor. He would just keep her chained to his bed until she finally admitted she loved him. Knowing Dana, that might take a very long while, but he was determined to enjoy owning her, even if she had never truly had the privilege of owning him.

CHAPTER XIX

Dana awoke the instant Brendan clamped his hand over her mouth. He had expected her to struggle a moment before leaving her sleeping chamber with him, but he was shocked when she covered his hand with hers and kissed his palm. He simply did not understand how she could respond with so loving a gesture after ignoring him for so many days.

Before releasing his hold on her, he leaned down to whisper in her ear, "Come with me quietly. We mustn't wake Thora." He rose, walked soundlessly to the door, then held it open for her.

Dana was so happy to see Brendan was finally well enough to walk about unassisted that she didn't stop to analyze his mood. All she knew was that she wanted most desperately to be with him and quickly followed him out into the hall. When he reached the hearth, he turned to face her, and she immediately slipped her arms around his waist and lay her head on his shoulder.

"It has been absolute agony having you so close and not being able to go near you," she whispered. He was fully dressed, and the softness of his kirtle was nearly as inviting as his bare flesh would have been.

Brendan had awakened Dana for one purpose only: to tell her what he thought of the abysmal way she had treated him since the fire. To find her clinging to him as though they had never been apart was only further proof of her duplicity. She enjoyed the abundant pleasure he gave, but how could she have had so little interest in his welfare and expect him to believe she cared for him? Knowing she must think him a stupid fool, he did not waste his breath in delivering the tongue-lashing he felt she deserved. Instead, he chose another manner in which to take his revenge. He lowered his lips to hers, and with savage abandon proceeded to ravage her mouth as though he intended to claim her very soul before he let her go.

Dana mistakenly interpreted Brendan's demanding kiss as evidence he had missed her as greatly as she had missed him. She could not bear to think how close he had come to burning to death. Had Erik not searched for him with such frantic haste, she was certain his burns would have been far more extensive, much more severe, and undoubtedly fatal. Shoving that ghastly thought aside, she lost herself in the beauty of the moment. She felt only joy in Brendan's arms, and the thrill of again being with him warmed her clear through.

While Dana's mind filled with soft-hued images of love, Brendan's anger burned on. He had had every intention of claiming the lovely body she had flaunted just out of his reach, but he had never expected her to welcome him so enthusiastically. He had envisioned instead the haughty aloofness she continually showed Jarald. He was not punishing her at all, his tortured conscience kept repeating, but his body responded all too readily to the soft, smooth swells her thin nightgown barely concealed while his senses betrayed him by glorying in the intoxicating fragrance of her free-flowing curls.

He was dimly aware that he had made a serious tactical error, for it was impossible to hold Dana in his arms and not long to possess her. The craving to feel the seductive heat of her bare skin pressed close to his own kept building until he could resist it no longer. Withdrawing from her embrace, he hurriedly pulled her to the wide bench that served as his bed. He peeled away her single garment, followed by his own clothing, and in the next instant he lay with her firmly clasped in his arms. It was lunacy to take her like this, with her family and Jarald asleep nearby, but rather than inspiring caution, such thoughts merely heightened his desire.

Equally obsessed, Dana could on longer think at all. She could only feel the cresting wave of desire that as always threatened to drown them in ecstasy. It swirled around her with a haunting warmth that lapped at her flesh like tongues of flame. Nothing mattered to her but claiming Brendan as her own. She had suffered far too terribly without him to consider the danger of their actions or the lunacy of sharing his bed when it lay under her own roof.

She would know Brendan only this one summer. Like a shooting star he would cross the sky of her life all too briefly, not only searing her flesh, but remaining in her memory with a brightness she knew would never be surpassed. How could fate have been so cruel as to have allowed her only a taste of love without the hope of a lifetime of devotion? Didn't she deserve more? Didn't they both?

Brendan had only a light bandage on his left arm now, and he felt not the slightest twinge of pain as he held Dana close. He covered her face with adoring kisses, then lingered at her mouth once again, delaying the moment he would possess her completely for as long as he possibly could. He was not teasing her, but attempting to prolong their stay in the paradise they had always created together for as long as he dared, until his need for her made further delay impossible. Nearing that point, he was badly startled and recoiled with her when they heard the sound of a door being pulled closed.

Hurriedly Brendan drew the quilt at his side up over Dana to shield her from sight, but he found it nearly impossible to lie still as though he were sleeping when his body was so closely aligned with hers. He was much too aware of the smoothness of her skin and the supple grace of her limbs to successfully feign slumber. He held his breath as he waited for the intruder to walk by. The faint echo of footsteps continued until finally he risked opening an eye and caught a glimpse of Erik stealthily sneaking out of the house. Because Erik could not reveal what he had seen, if anything, Brendan relaxed, but he dared not laugh as he wished he could, even when he and Dana were again alone.

"It was Erik leaving Berit's room," he whispered as he pulled the quilt away, at last giving Dana the opportunity to breathe more freely. "Won't they be allowed to marry soon?"

Not only too warm, but dizzy as well, Dana didn't want to talk about her half brother and cousin. Instead, she lifted her arms to encircle Brendan's neck and bestowed a kiss so full of loving passion he lost all interest in the answer to his question. She was far too enchanting a woman to punish for any reason, and he wanted her too baldy to punish himself by denying that fact. He had not forgotten how much her indifference had hurt him, but that sorrow did not begin to compare with the joy he found in her surrender.

Brendan did not attempt to dominate Dana even now, for she did not lie still and compliant beneath him. She met his deep thrusts not merely with a graceful acceptance, but with a wildness of spirit that demanded even more of him. His fingers woven in her tangled curls, he kept her mouth pressed to his, drinking deeply of her sweet taste as he increased the motion of his hips to speed them down rapture's path at an even more reckless pace. Using more restraint than he had thought he possessed, he held back until he felt her climax begin to throb deep within her before he abandoned himself to the soul-shattering fulfillment of his own release. It shuddered through his still mending body, but he felt only wave after wave of the most glorious pleasure and not a single spasm of pain.

Dana continued to cling to Brendan long after the blinding thrill of their union had diffused to a pleasant and lingering warmth. When he at last began to draw away, she complained immediately, "No, please, stay with me."

"It's nearly dawn," Brendan warned, but he kissed her one last time before leaving her to pull on his breeches. "I should have awakened you earlier. I wanted us to have time to talk," he mumbled apologetically.

"You wanted to talk?" Dana found that remark highly amusing. "I have often asked you to talk, without success, but you made no such request of me when we left my sleeping chamber." Rather than rise to don her gown, she remained languidly curled atop his quilts. "We've a few moments still. What did you want to say?"

Brendan yanked on his kirtle, then combed his curls off his forehead with a hasty swipe of his hand. He didn't want to fight with her now, not when everything had been so perfect between them, but the longer he considered her question, the angrier he got. "I know you don't love Jarald, so don't accuse me of being jealous, but in all the time I've been here, didn't you have a single moment that you could have spent with me?''

Unable to return his hostile gaze, Dana looked away, and seeing the spacious hall was growing light, she was instantly aware dawn was much closer than she had thought. While she was disappointed that Brendan would ask such a question, she was as anxious as he to avoid another argument. She rolled off the bench, plucked her gown from where he had dropped it, and hurriedly slipped it on.

''It's a matter of trust, I suppose,'' she began hesitantly. ''I thought you knew me well enough to believe my feelings for you could not possibly have changed, but my mother forbade me to tend you. I obeyed her because I knew if I sat with you, everyone would soon see how close we've become. It didn't occur to me that you would misunderstand.'' She was tempted to add he had had plenty of feminine company, so she had not known he missed hers, but with a valiant effort she held her tongue.

When she turned to face him, Brendan saw his question had hurt her far more deeply than any shouted accusations of neglect ever would. ''Trust?'' he asked hoarsely. ''Is it always going to come down to that?''

Dana nodded. ''Without trust, how can there be—'' She paused, not wanting to mention love when he still questioned each of her actions. ''—friendship, or anything more?''

Brendan did not want to discuss anything more, for as he saw it, admitting that he loved her involved far too many concessions on his part. As long as he was a slave, the only freedom he had was in his emotions. How could he give away the last of his independence by admitting he loved her?

Instead, he spoke only about trust. ''It will be impossible for either of us to trust the other until I am free and we are equals. I am well enough to go back to work for Erik, and I wanted to tell you good-bye. I won't demand that you meet me again at midnight, and if you care anything for me, you will not order me to meet you either. I think each of us would be wise to avoid the other for a while.''

''You meant to say good-bye?'' Dana asked in befuddled

wonder. "But only after, rather than before, you made love to me again?"

Brendan stared at her, his resolve wavering dangerously as he saw the sparkle of threatened tears brighten her gaze. She had such lovely eyes, and he hated to see her cry. He knew there had to be some way for him to salvage his own pride without destroying hers, but before he could think of it they were interrupted by a loud pounding at the door.

"Who can that be?" he asked, fearing an attack of some sort.

"I have no idea," Dana replied, too hurt to consider likely possibilities. At that early an hour, their servants where all in their own quarters, and the knocking was so loud and persistent she knew it would soon awaken everyone in the house. If she were the first to the door it would cause no comment. Welcoming any distraction when she feared Brendan was about to say something she didn't want to hear, she hurried to admit the early morning visitor.

Not about to let Dana open the door to what he imagined might be a grave peril, Brendan overtook her and shoved her aside. He swung open the door himself, then staggered backward as a man wrapped in a hooded cloak stumbled across the threshold and lurched into his arms.

Dana recognized the flowing gray garment immediately as her father's, but since the wearer lacked his stature, she reached out to yank back the hood. "Jørn!" she cried out in delighted surprise. Then, taking in his flushed complexion and glassy stare, she grew frightened. "What's happened? Where are my father and Svien?"

Brendan was equally shocked to see Jørn, and he quickly lowered his grasp to the man's waist to help him over to a bench near the hearth. He could not bear to call the young man master, but he was as curious as Dana as to the cause of his disheveled state. Once he had eased him down onto a bench, he brought wood to build up the fire. Jarald joined them then, swiftly followed by Berit and Freya. The latter two rushed forward, intending to hug Jørn, but, frightened by his alarming condition, the women drew back.

Dana was grateful everyone's attention was focused on her cousin rather than on her and Brendan, for the Celt's scent clung to her every pore, but she had yet to receive answers to her questions and demanded them at once. Taking a seat at Jørn's side, she tried to coax a response from him, but he seemed in a daze, and rather than speak, he covered his face with his hands and wept.

Seeing Brendan was dressed, Freya hurriedly gave him an order. "Go down to the dock and find someone from Jørn's crew who can tell us what's happened. Perhaps there was a storm last night, or—"

With a loud sniff, Jørn wiped his eyes on his sleeve and began to sob out an anguished tale. "What men I have left are coming. We have to collect silver to pay a ransom. We must hurry. Trom will kill them if we're late."

"Who must you ransom, Jørn?" When he again dissolved in tears, Dana reached out to touch him, and just as she had suspected, she found his skin radiating an unnatural heat. "You have a high fever. Let's get you into bed and you can explain everything to us after you've rested awhile."

"No, there's no time," Jørn insisted between racking sobs. He struggled to rise, but lacking the strength to succeed, he fell back to the bench in a clumsy sprawl. He tried to make the necessity for haste clear, but his pleas were incoherent ramblings.

Seeing another opportunity to ingratiate himself to Freya and her family, Jarald stepped forward, plucked the semiconscious Jørn from the bench, and lifted him into his arms. "We can put him in my bed if you like."

"No," Freya said. "Take him into Soren's bedchamber. He's not here to use it and you'll need yours."

Dana rose and motioned for her mother to step back. "I don't want you anywhere near Jørn. There's always the danger that those who tend him might fall ill, and we mustn't risk your health for any reason." She led Jørn to Soren's chamber, and with the husky man's help, got her cousin into bed.

Berit followed them to Jørn's bedside and leaned down to caress his cheek lightly. "He's never been so sick as this, never. We must send for my mother's servant, Olga. Her herbal remedies helped Aunt Freya last winter, and surely they would help my brother now.''

"You have no one here with the same skill?" Jarald inquired, disappointed that his plans to keep Grena away were being threatened.

"No, unfortunately none of our servants have such a talent,'' Dana hurriedly explained. Seeing Brendan at the door, she went to him. ''See what you can learn from Jørn's crew, then go and get Erik. I know he must have been dreading Jørn's return, but there's no need for him to worry he'll have to fight him now, and I want him here when we tell my mother what's happened.''

Brendan stared at the young man on the bed. If Jørn died, Grena would claim him as part of her son's property. Being a slave was a ghastly enough fate without having to belong to a vindictive bitch like Grena. That was a small problem at present, however. He knew Trom, and well, but he held back that valuable piece of information to bargain with later. "Whoever is being held for ransom is in grave danger," he warned instead.

Dana swallowed quickly to force away the fear that filled her throat. "Please don't say anything to anyone until we've had the opportunity to question the crew. No matter whose life is at risk, we'll pay the ransom, but I don't want my mother frightened unnecessarily.''

Brendan straightened his shoulders, thinking it had to be obvious to all that Haakon and Svien must be the ones taken prisoner, for Jørn would scarcely be in such an agitated state had he only lost a few members of his crew. ''I understand. Your mother's feelings are to be protected at all costs.'' He longed to pull the distraught redhead into his arms for a comforting hug, but knew such a display would only worsen her problems. With no more than a brief nod, he turned and left, but he couldn't imagine Jørn's crew having any news that would be good.

Jarald had observed the hurried exchange, and when Dana turned back toward the bed he scanned her expression for some clue as to what she and the thrall had been discussing, but she seemed interested only in Jørn's welfare.

Still, he did not like the fact Brendan had stopped to talk with Dana before running Freya's errand. Perhaps the striking redhead unknowingly encouraged the slave's attentions, but he had no intention of allowing that to continue. He might have failed once to get rid of the Celt, but he would make certain his second attempt succeeded.

In his haste to leave his bedchamber, Jarald had paused only long enough to yank on his breeches. As Dana returned to Jørn's side, her gaze swept over Jarald's powerfully muscled arms and chest, but she found his impressive physique not nearly as handsome as Brendan's, for the Dane's body was as hairy as a bear's. When she realized he had noted the direction of her glance, she tried her best to smile.

What difference did it make that Jarald's body did not delight her eyes and invite her touch as Brendan's always had? Brendan didn't want her affection anymore, and although she still did not understand why, she would not ask him to explain the reasons for his rejection when that would surely cause her further pain.

As Jarald broke into a wide grin, it was clear his interest in her had not wavered. While that thought brought absolutely no comfort, it forced Dana to take a realistic look at the future. She had not cared for any of the men who had courted her before Jarald, and she had to admire his persistence. Unfortunately, that was the only thing she admired about the man, but she had given him so little of herself she knew she had treated him unfairly.

"You are always so quick to help us, Jarald," she complimented him sincerely. "I'm sorry I haven't told you more often how much that is appreciated."

"It pleases me to be of service," Jarald was delighted to respond. Dana had always been polite, but this was the first bit of true warmth he had ever received from her. Maybe Brendan meant nothing to her after all. Thinking perhaps it was jealousy that caused him to see rivals everywhere, he decided to keep his eyes open to gather more evidence before doing away with the slave.

Brendan recognized several of Jørn's crew as men he had seen at Grena's farm before they had left on their voyage. Those who weren't racked with fevers as high as Jørn's were so exhausted he didn't see how they had managed to bring the others home. Sprawled about the dock where they had fallen, they begged for ale to quench their thirst.

He ran back to the house to seek more help, then returned to the dock and encouraged the healthy men to relate their story. After listening to several rambling narratives, he was forced to extract bits and pieces from each, but he finally had enough of the tale to be reasonably certain of what had happened. It wasn't until then that he saddled a horse and went for Erik.

Having spent an extremely pleasant night in the arms of his beloved, Erik was in high spirits as he greeted Brendan. When the Celt leapt down from his mount and pulled him toward the privacy of the woods, he realized the situation was an urgent one. "What's wrong?" he asked instantly.

"You just missed seeing Jørn this morning," Brendan began, but he continued before Erik could reply. "He and most of his men are too sick to stand, but from what I can learn from the others, Haakon, Svien, and their crews were captured by one of the Norse pirates who control all the ports of Erin. Jørn was sent back to raise the ransom for the others, but he and the majority of his crew are all too ill to stand, let alone sail."

Erik turned to look at the men working on his house. They were an industrious lot, but rescuing the twins and Thora had been a challenge to their seamanship, and Erin was a long way off. "Was Jørn's ship damaged?"

"No," Brendan assured him.

"Good, then we can leave as soon as we have a fresh crew."

"You can't swim a stroke, and you'll probably be seasick the whole way. Are you sure you want to go yourself?"

"I'll not leave my father, brother, and their crews in the hands of pirates," Erik insisted, clearly insulted by Brendan's question. "Besides, there is no one else who can lead such a voyage."

Brendan flashed a knowing grin. "Yes, there is. I'll do it, but I must have my freedom before I set sail."

"Isn't there something else you'd like as well?" Erik eyed the thrall with an accusing glance, surprised he had not had the audacity to come right out and ask for Dana.

Stung by the taunt, Brendan's eyes narrowed slightly, for while he would not deny that Dana was definitely a prize worth bargaining for, he wanted to rescue Haakon before he mentioned her. "No, there isn't," he answered coldly. "My freedom will be payment enough for the time being."

While Brendan had proven himself trustworthy in many respects, Erik considered this too much. "You must think me a great fool. Given a ship and silver to pay a ransom, you'd have no reason to save Haakon and Svien. I doubt you'd even make the attempt."

There had been a time when he would have killed a man for questioning his integrity in so insulting a fashion, but Brendan knew masters trusted their slaves no more than slaves trusted their masters. Each was forever trying to get the better of the other, and this situation was no different from any other.

"Call Soren and let's go home," the wily thrall suggested. "No decision needs to be made this morning, but I think you'll soon see I'm the best hope you have to set Haakon and Svien free."

Not about to debate the issue any further, Erik complied only with Brendan's request that they return home.

Once informed of Jørn's return, Grena and Olga hastened to Freya's, but the closer they rode to her sister's farm, the more frightened Grena became. She had the right to demand Erik be kept away, but she dared not insist Jarald be banished as well. As desperately worried as she was about her eldest son, she was even more terrified of the man who had used her so badly. When she arrived and found him sitting with Freya, she quickly forced her eyes away, but it unnerved her to know he enjoyed such a close friendship with her sister.

Not bothering with a greeting, she asked quickly, "Where is my son?"

Freya came forward to embrace her sister, and thinking

the coolness of her response only natural, she did not comment on it. "He's in Soren's chamber. Berit and Dana are with him."

Eager to flee Jarald's presence, Grena immediately pushed by Freya. Olga followed carrying a large basket filled with the dried herbs she used in creating her potions. A tiny woman with a nervous temperament and the darting gaze of a bird, she gave Jarald a cursory and highly disapproving glance as she passed by him. The two women swiftly made their way from the large hall to the bedchambers that lay beyond.

Too distraught over the state in which she found her son, Grena wasted no energy berating Berit for leaving home, but instead simply ignored the girl and gave her full attention to Jørn. When it became obvious to Berit that her mother's mood was not a conciliatory one, she drew Dana to the door.

"It's plain I'm not needed here, so I think after I dress I'll go see what I can do for Jørn's crew."

"I'll go with you," Dana instantly agreed, and the two young women changed from their night clothes to more appropriate attire and left together. They soon had tents raised beneath the oak tree nearest the house so the ailing men could easily receive the care they needed. Moving those suffering from the fever required several trips, but they pressed the stable boys and shepherds into service and soon had the feat accomplished.

It did not surprise Brendan to find Dana had organized everything so beautifully by the time he returned with Erik. She was used to running all facets of the farm, so it appeared even emergency measures came easily to her. He saw Moira hurrying by carrying water and towels. She had tied back her hair as he had once suggested, and he chuckled to himself at the thought she would never have a better opportunity to meet young men in need of a wife. He just hoped none that she took a fancy to died.

Erik caught Dana's eye, and motioned for her to join them. "What have you told your mother?"

"Nothing yet, although I think I've pieced together what's happened. I can understand how Jørn could be captured by pirates, or even Svien, but not our father. He's far too fierce in combat to fall prey to pirates.''

Dana was directing her comments to Erik, as though he were not also standing by her side, and while Brendan could understand why she would be upset with him, he did not think such rudeness was justified. "Pirates are a treacherous lot. You mustn't think less of your father for falling prey to them.''

Slowly and with deliberate effort, Dana raised her glance to meet Brendan's, but she found him regarding her with a cool detachment she had not seen from him in a very long while. Apparently he was interested in discussing pirates without regard to their talk before dawn, while she felt as though she had gone from one dreadful emotional blow to another without any opportunity to recover from the first.

"Nothing could diminish my love for my father,'' Dana informed Brendan with a cold indifference that mirrored his. "Now let's see if we can't break this news to my mother as gently as possible.''

Erik turned to observe Brendan's reaction to Dana's surprising aloofness, but he found the thrall's mood equally difficult to judge. Something strange was happening between them, but this was definitely not the time to inquire as to what. Taking his half sister's arm, he escorted her into the house with Brendan following closely behind. For Freya's benefit, he tried to appear supremely confident, but the prospect of embarking on a voyage to rescue his father terrified him, for he could not even imagine that he would be able to defeat the man who had gotten the better of Haakon.

CHAPTER XX

As Dana, Berit, Soren, and Brendan gathered around the hearth where Freya, Thora, and Jarald were seated, Erik bent down on one knee at his stepmother's side. Taking her hands in his, he tried to soften the pain his words would inevitably bring, but he had barely begun to speak when she interrupted him.

Freya pulled her right hand from Erik's fond grasp, then caressed his cheek sweetly. "It's Haakon and Svien, isn't it? Jarald has already assured me that if that is the case, then he'll not only deliver the ransom, but make certain they return home safely."

While he had been determined to lead such a rescue party himself, although he was well aware he was sorely lacking in the necessary skills to do so, Erik was relieved beyond words to hear Jarald had already volunteered. "How can we thank you?" he asked him.

"You needn't. Haakon would do the same for me," Jarald reminded Erik, but the glance he gave Dana readily conveyed it was the red-haired beauty's gratitude that he truly craved.

Knowing his father's love of adventure, Erik agreed with their guest's observation. "Yes, I know that he would. I want to go with you. I've little experience with either sailing or fighting, but I'm going with you. I must."

Readily understanding Erik's need to accompany him, Jarald had no objection. "Of course you may come with me. I'll need every man I can find willing to make such a dangerous voyage."

"Rather than outfight the pirates, we ought to simply outwit them," Dana interjected in an excited rush. "I want to go too. With Svien captured, the responsibilities of Haakon's eldest hair fall to me. It is not only my right, but my duty to deliver the ransom."

While Brendan's mouth fell agape at the ridiculousness of the idea, Jarald greeted it with enthusiasm. "If your mother will permit it, I'll take you," he offered with a grin that grew wide when Dana responded with a smile. He had no doubt he could outfight any Norseman ever born, and if Dana were there to be impressed by the sight, then so much the better.

Fearing that the opportunity not only to win his freedom but also return home was slipping from his grasp, Brendan pointed out what he thought ought to be obvious to Jarald. "You said yourself the voyage will be dangerous. To take Dana along will needlessly endanger her life as well as your own when you're forced to protect her from Trom. He's not merely an arrogant bully who makes empty boasts of his prowess. He's incredibly strong, and so mean he thinks nothing of killing men for sport, and when he captures a woman, her fate is even worse."

Jarald waited for Freya or one of her family to remind Brendan it was not a slave's place to offer advice, but when none did, he dared not insult them by handling the matter himself. "You know Trom?" he asked instead, for if the thrall actually possessed valuable information, he wanted him to share it.

"I know him," Brendan assured the burly Dane. "Your god Loki can't compare to him for sheer evil. Doesn't the fact he's captured Haakon and Svien tell you how formidable an adversary he is? You can't introduce him to Dana in hopes he'll be so distracted you can outwit him!"

Freya was terrified by Brendan's description of Trom and hugged Thora tightly, but Dana was too hurt and angry to believe him. In her view the crafty Celt was merely trying to present a compelling reason to be included among the crew. Because she had promised him she would see he got his freedom and returned home, she was disappointed to find he apparently did not trust her to arrange it. Of course, she reminded herself, he trusts no one but himself.

"Your knowledge not only of Trom's tactics, but of Erin will prove invaluable, Brendan. I'll insist that Jørn allow you to come with us. The voyage will provide an excellent opportunity for you to earn your freedom."

Not impressed by Dana's offer, Brendan rejected it immediately. "I must be set free first."

"You must?" Jarald asked, amazed a lowly thrall would make such a demand.

"Yes, I must," Brendan repeated proudly. "I can promise you right now that no matter what terms Trom has set for the ransom, he'll not keep his word. He'll let Haakon, Svien, and their crews live until he has the silver, but he'll never set them free. He'll kill them all then, and you as well if you make the mistake of trusting him."

When that gruesome prediction was met with stunned silence, he continued in the same persuasive tone. "I'll not only lead you to Trom, but once we reach Erin I can also supply the additional men to convince him his only hope to remain alive is to release his captives. With my help, you can set Haakon, Svien, and their crews free, but I must have my own freedom first. That's the condition for my assistance."

It was Freya who spoke what was also on her daughter's mind. "It appears you have a pirate's soul yourself, Brendan, or you wouldn't attempt to use our family's misfortune in such a selfish fashion. Had you offered your help out of regard for us, your freedom would have been given in gratitude. Now... well, now we'll have to wait for Jørn's decision on the matter."

That he had disappointed the dear woman didn't trouble Brendan in the least, but he was thoroughly disgusted with himself that he had chosen this of all days to end his affair with Dana. If only he had kept his feelings to himself, she would have thought him a hero for offering to rescue her father. Now each time she glanced his way, her eyes were so full of pain he doubted she would ever forgive him. To make matters worse, she had begun to smile at Jarald, and he could not abide that.

Taking advantage of a momentary lull in the conversation, Soren joined in. "I want to go too, and I know how to sail, even if Erik doesn't."

"We'll make that decision later," Freya responded firmly. "First Jarald will have to return home to gather his crew and prepare his ship for the voyage. There will be plenty of time for us to decide who will go and who will remain here."

When Soren opened his mouth to argue, Dana quickly pinched his arm and fixed him with so compelling a stare he fell silent. "You'll need to be on your way then, Jarald," she suggested when she was certain Soren would hold his tongue. "Brendan, see that Jarald's stallion is saddled so that his departure isn't delayed."

Dana did not look at him as she spoke, a fact that rankled Brendan as much as the order to see to Jarald's horse. "As you wish, mistress," he replied with a slight bow, as eager to leave her as she was to see him go.

That Jarald had generously offered to make the voyage to rescue her father and brother had impressed Dana very deeply. He was handsome in his own way, and even if his voice was often too loud and his manners lacked polish, he could be depended upon in an emergency, and wasn't that a far more important trait? she asked herself as he prepared to leave. On the other hand, had Brendan not had something to gain, she doubted he would have showed any interest in the desperate situation that faced her family.

She looked back on the times they had made love with a terrible sense of loss and shame, for it was all too plain now that Brendan had only been using her. He had sought to bind her to him with affection that was only a clever pretense. He had never said that he loved her, but that had been the way he had made her feel. His rejection had not simply hurt her pride, it had shattered her belief in her ability to make sound judgments about people. She had trusted her heart and fallen in love with a handsome thrall who thought of nothing but winning his freedom and going home. That she had merely been a means to that end hurt so badly she did not think she would ever recover from the pain.

As he left his bedchamber after packing his belongings, Jarald found Dana waiting for him just outside the door. She looked so miserably unhappy, he quickly took her hand and drew her back into the room he had occupied.

"The Celt is only trying to make Trom sound fierce in order to make himself appear brave," he began as he enfolded her in a sympathetic hug that for once did not leave Dana feeling crushed. "Trom is no worse than any enemy I've faced, I'm sure of it. I'll not let Haakon and Svien die. You must trust me to bring them home safely, for your mother's sake as well as your own."

Cheered by his confidence, Dana managed a faint smile. "Yes, I do trust you to rescue them. It's just that I'm so worried. Once the voyage begins, I know I'll feel better."

"Do you really want to come with me?"

Dana understood his question was a personal one, and while she did not want to encourage him when she was too numb to feel anything, she did not want to be unkind either. "Yes, I want to go," she assured him. When he tilted his head, clearly meaning to kiss her, she did not try and avoid him. His lips gently caressed hers with an adoring touch that only deepened her sorrow because she knew his affection was real while hers was not. Brendan's kisses had always sent a wave of desire coursing through her. Jarald's only made her feel lonely and sad.

Thinking there would be an opportunity on their upcoming voyage to win more enthusiastic kisses from her, Jarald was not disappointed by Dana's lack of response. He knew she could not be rushed, but he was confident he was making steady, if maddeningly slow, progress toward winning her as his wife. Taking her hand, he escorted her from the house before her stay in his bedchamber could cause comment.

Dana walked with Jarald to his horse, then remained by the stable to wave as he rode away. He had promised to return in a few days' time, and she knew he would hurry. There was so much to do while he was gone, but her first concern was for the welfare of Jørn's crew. Before resuming her efforts to tend the ailing men, she decided to pay Dawn's Kiss a brief visit. Like all pets, the beautiful mare gave unconditional love, and that was very appealing at the moment.

Brendan was waiting just inside the stable door, and when Dana entered he immediately reached out to grasp her hand and pulled her back into the shadows in the corner. "You didn't trust Jarald before. Why do you suddenly trust him now?'' he asked in an accusing whisper.

Dana looked around quickly, then remembered the stable boys were helping care for the sick. She and Brendan were alone, their words unlikely to be overheard, but she did not want to talk. "Jarald can be depended upon to rescue my father and brother, but that's all I trust him to do.''

"Why don't you trust me to save them instead?''

"Trust you?'' Dana did not understand how he could ask such a ridiculous question. "I did trust you!'' she exclaimed angrily. "I trusted you more than I have ever trusted anyone outside my family, and look how you repaid me.''

Brendan knew exactly what she meant, and again cursed his wounded pride that had made him think the only way to keep his self-respect was to end their affair. He could not recall ever wanting to apologize to a woman, but he gave the task his best effort now. "I was jealous. Can't you understand that? I was jealous and so lonely that I didn't realize what I was saying this morning.''

As his expression softened, so did his grasp, but rather than relax in his arms as he had hoped, Dana instantly wrenched free. "All you ever wanted from me was your freedom. It's been plain all along, and I was just too stupid to see you for what you truly are.''

She turned and bolted from the stable, but Brendan followed right behind her. He reached out, trying to catch her elbow, but his fingertips only grazed the silk of her chemise. As they broke out into the sun-drenched yard, he saw Soren walking toward the stable and had to come to an abrupt halt.

Soren hurriedly came forward to block his sister's way. "Is Brendan bothering you?''

"No, of course not,'' Dana insisted, fearing the hostility of her expression would give away the shortness of her temper.

Soren looked over his sister's shoulder at Brendan and noticed he appeared as upset as she. On several occasions he had suspected there was something happening between the two, something that ought not to be, but each time he had been close to drawing that conclusion, he had gotten the impression he was mistaken. Now he wondered if the angry glances he had so frequently seen passing between Dana and the thrall didn't mask emotions of a far more dangerous sort.

"Your sister is angry with me because I told her she should stay home with her mother rather than sail to Erin with us," Brendan declared as he walked to Soren's side. He had meant to tell Dana that too, but he had not had the opportunity. "She's needed here, and we certainly don't need her with us." He clapped Soren on the shoulder, as though the boy had already received permission to make the voyage.

"I don't care what you two are arguing about," Soren began with an ambitious show of pride. "All I care about is going with Jarald, and you two are going to convince Mother to allow me to go or I'll tell her things I'm sure you don't want her to hear."

Brendan's first impulse was to knock the cocky youth flat on his back, but Dana grabbed his arm before he could throw the punch. "There's nothing to tell, Brendan," she warned with a menacing glare. "You and I despise each other, and it would scarcely upset my mother to learn that."

The hatred glowing in the depths of her violet gaze was so convincing Brendan dropped his clenched fists to his sides. He had to admit Dana had good reason to despise him, for there actually had been a time when he had thought becoming her lover would be the swiftest way to win his freedom. That day was long past, however. He could not reveal that without admitting her reasons for hating him had once been valid, though, so he buried that secret as deeply as his love.

"I know there's nothing to tell," he scoffed, "but I didn't want Freya upset with lies when she's been so good to me." When Dana's eyes narrowed slightly, Brendan knew she thought him a poor liar. "Soren's proven himself to be a good worker this summer. I think he should come with us. I don't need to be threatened before I'll voice that opinion."

Dana folded her arms beneath her bosom to keep from slapping the obstinate smirk from Brendan's face. "I believe the voyage will be every bit as dangerous as you say. If we fail, none of us will be coming back. That's why Soren will have to stay here at home. At least one of Haakon's sons has to survive him.''

Never having thought it possible he might be the one to receive Svien's inheritance, Soren was taken aback when Dana calmly pointed out the consequences of a possible tragedy. ''We won't fail,'' he insisted stubbornly, but he was now torn by indecision. The rescue voyage would provide the adventure of a lifetime, but choosing to remain safe at home might make him Haakon's principal heir, with more wealth than he had ever hoped to amass on his own. It was an almost impossible choice for a boy of fourteen to make.

Seeing her brother's confusion, Dana considered him sufficiently preoccupied to forget his threat to gossip about her and Brendan. Slipping her arm through his, she paused to make a final remark to the thrall before leading her brother away. ''This is a matter for our family to decide. You'll say no more about it.''

Brendan watched Dana walk away, the pride of her bearing unmistakable as always. She might hate him now, and with good reason, but he most assuredly did not hate her. No, her spellbinding beauty had lost none of its appeal, and he feared that even after he had won his freedom, he would remain her slave.

Berit and Erik stayed with Freya and Thora for a while, fearing Freya's courage was merely a brave front and that she might soon dissolve into uncontrollable tears, but that was not the case. Freya had enormous faith in her husband, and even if he had suffered the indignity of being captured by pirates, she was confident that with the help Jarald would provide both Haakon and Svien would soon be coming home. At present there was a far more immediate problem.

''Grena hasn't left Jørn's side, Erik, but if she does, I'm afraid your presence here will upset her,'' Freya warned apologetically. ''Why don't you and Berit go for a walk? I imagine you have a great deal to discuss.''

''You'll be all right?'' Berit inquired considerately.

''Of course. Thora and I have lots to do today, don't we, baby?''

Thora nodded as she snuggled up closer to her mother. As the youngest, she and her mother had always shared a special bond. She sensed Freya needed her now, just as she had needed her comfort after she had nearly drowned. "Yes, Mother," she agreed softly.

After pausing to kiss both Freya and Thora, Erik led Berit out through the kitchen so they could go for a walk without passing by the ailing men. He took her hand and started along the path that led by the storehouses. Still warmed by the love she had given him before dawn, he was content to simply walk, but Berit felt a compelling need to speak.

"I don't want you to go with Jarald," the lively blonde revealed. "I kept still when we were with the others, but now that we're alone there's no reason for me to pretend I want you to go."

Erik stopped in midstride and pulled her around to face him. "How can you ask such a thing of me?"

"How?" Berit replied incredulously. "Haakon has never treated you as he should. Why must you risk your life to save his when you know he would never do the same for you?"

While the opinion stung, Erik thought it undoubtedly correct. That didn't matter, though. "He's still my father, Berit, and I must try to save him if I can. There's Svien to consider too. He's been the best of brothers, and I can't leave him in the pirates' hands. I doubt that they'd kill him as Brendan fears, when they could make a fine profit selling their prisoners as slaves, but I can't let that happen. I can't believe that you would want your cousin to suffer so humiliating a fate either."

Unconvinced, Berit tried again to dissuade him. "Of course I love Svien, but what of me? How can you leave me when there's a chance you won't be coming back?"

Thinking he understood her concern, Erik drew her into his arms. "You mustn't be jealous of my love for my father and brother, Berit. I would make a poor husband for you if I cared nothing for my family."

"I'm not jealous!" Berit insisted tearfully. "It's just that everything has gone so badly for us, and I'm afraid, desperately afraid, something awful will happen to you.''

"We've known all along that things could not possibly be easy for us. But the voyage to Erin has nothing to do with our marriage, so there's no reason for you to think it won't be a success.''

Berit slipped her arms around his waist and hugged him tightly. "Yes, I know, but still, I couldn't bear to lose you.''

Erik kissed her temple sweetly. "You will never lose me, Berit. Never.''

As Berit looked up at him, her eyes filled with tears for she knew he meant that his love would never die, even if he did. "Please don't go," she begged again. "Please.''

With a loving caress, Erik pressed her cheek against his chest and he felt his kirtle growing damp with her tears. He made no further attempt to reason with her while she was in such an emotional state, but no matter how badly it upset the young woman he adored, he was determined to be the one to rescue his father. If she did not understand why, then it was because she was still in many ways a child. In time she would come to accept his decision. She would have to, for he would never change his mind, and he hoped it would not cost him her love.

It was late afternoon when Grena finally emerged from Jørn's chamber. It had taken the better part of the day for Olga's herbal remedies to begin lowering his fever, but at last they had had an effect, and he was sleeping comfortably. Exhausted, she sent Soren to her home to summon several of her servants so that her son would have someone with him both day and night.

When she joined her sister and niece, Grena was at first too weary to think about Erik, but as soon as she was sufficiently rested, his name came readily to mind. "I'm grateful that Erik has been wise enough to stay out of sight.''

Freya had been helping Thora begin a new tablet weaving, for unlike Dana, her younger daughter frequently liked to sit with her and sew. Looking up, she thought she saw something new in Grena's expression, a hesitancy, perhaps, that she did not recall. "He was here earlier, but he's far too considerate a man to wish to upset you unnecessarily. He'll keep his distance until he leaves for Erin with Jarald."

Grena nodded as Freya related the rescue plans, but the mere mention of Jarald's name made her stomach lurch painfully. "Perhaps Jørn will recover his strength in a day or two, and he can make the voyage himself."

"While I also hope that he's well soon, I've already accepted Jarald's offer to deliver the ransom, and I can't tell him he won't be needed when he returns with his ship and crew."

"He's not part of our family, though."

"He wants to be," Thora pointed out with a teasing smirk.

Freya could not argue with her daughter's opinion. "Yes, he certainly does, but I don't believe Dana is ready for marriage yet."

A painful lump filled Grena's throat, for she had always loved her nieces dearly, and the thought of Dana marrying a beast like Jarald was more than she could sanely bear to imagine. Unfortunately, she knew Haakon thought highly of the man, so there was no way she could discredit his name without revealing the contemptible way he had treated her. How could she admit that horror to Freya, who saw only good in everyone? Thoroughly humiliated by the memory of the ghastly afternoon Jarald had spent in her bed, Grena could see no value in describing it to her sister.

Besides, what if she did tell Freya? If Jørn wasn't well enough to make the return voyage to Erin by the time Jarald arrived with his ship, Freya would have no choice about sending the ransom with him. Telling Freya about Jarald would merely be cruel in that case, as her sister would have no choice about depending on him. As much as she hated having to keep quiet about the man's true nature, she feared that was her only option.

It was unlike Grena to be so quiet, and after studying her preoccupied frown, Freya was prompted to inquire if something more than Jørn's health might be troubling her.

Startled from her reverie by the question, Grena was flustered only a moment. "This is all so terribly upsetting," she explained hurriedly. "What an awful summer this has been. We've never had so many terrible problems. I keep thinking things can get no worse, but each time they do!"

Freya felt foolish now for having shed so many tears over Erik and Berit when the complications their romance presented were insignificant when compared to the life-threatening situation that faced her husband and eldest son. "We've survived a great deal, Grena, and we'll survive this summer as well," she remarked confidently, her faith in her husband unshaken despite the desperate nature of his plight.

While Brendan rode with Erik back to his new house to bring construction to a halt, he kept up a steady barrage of arguments in a determined effort to keep Dana from accompanying them to Erin. "She's clever, but the fact she's an attractive female makes her more vulnerable than valuable. If you love her, as I think you must, then you'll leave her here where she'll come to no harm."

Erik eyed Brendan with a skeptical glance. "When Dana has more of a right to go than I do, how can you expect me to make such a decision?"

That question gave Brendan a moment's pause, for it was true that Erik took his orders from Dana, not the other way around. "You're close to Freya. Convince her to forbid it then."

"Is this another in your endless attempts to stir up trouble by taking my side against Dana?"

"No!" Brendan exclaimed in a frustrated sigh. "Trom is evil, truly evil, and I don't want Dana anywhere near him."

Erik gave a thoughtful nod. "Is it Trom or Jarald that you don't want near her?"

Brendan pulled his mount to a halt. "It's not my feelings which ought to concern you, but your sister's life. This voyage is no place for a woman."

Nearly as angry as his companion, Erik reined in Shadow so that they could continue their discussion. "Dana is no ordinary woman, as you well know. While she's never sailed herself, she has often been out in a boat, and she never gets seasick. Svien taught her to swim, so she's in far less danger of drowning than I am. She can wear Soren's clothes and cover her hair so her femininity isn't apparent. You must have been impressed by what you've heard of Haakon. Well, Dana is her father's daughter, and she has courage aplenty. There'll be no reason for her to fight, but I want her with us anyway."

When Erik turned away to urge Shadow on down the trail, their conversation obviously over in his view, Brendan continued to fume. He knew Dana and Erik were closer than most twins, but why the man needed to have his sister along on so dangerous a mission he couldn't imagine. There would be a few days before they sailed, and he vowed to keep up his protests until Erik finally understood why Dana had to remain behind.

"You've got to learn how to swim!" Brendan called out as he started after Erik. They had planned to gather up the tools and send the field hands home. The house was nearly complete and could wait until Erik came back from Erin to be finished. The sudden realization that he would not be coming back to Fyn himself was almost more than Brendan could bear, but just as he had said, it was not his feelings which mattered now, but keeping Dana safe.

Ulla was among those who came from Grena's to tend Jørn's crew. She was old and frail, but she preferred alleviating the pain of others to dwelling on her own. Because she had known many of the sick all their lives, she provided as loving care as their mothers would. She worked until night had fallen and all were resting comfortably before she sat down to rest herself. When Berit and Dana came to speak with her, she looked around first to make certain Grena was nowhere near before motioning for them to come close.

"I did my best," she assured Berit. "But I didn't hear your mother speak a word about either you or Erik, much less plot against him."

Perplexed by this report, Berit frowned impatiently. "I'm

certain she didn't attempt to set fire to his house herself, but she must have sent someone else to do it. Maybe she realized there were other servants like you who love me and would have warned us. She must have taken care that none of you found out what she planned.''

Ulla looked up at the two pretty young women, envying them even though she had beautiful memories of the days men had found her attractive too. "I don't think your mother knew of the fire before Jarald brought her the news. I was working nearby while they talked, and that is the way it seemed.''

"Just what did she say?" Berit pressed Ulla to reveal.

The elderly woman shrugged. "I don't recall. They talked only briefly.''

"Briefly?" Dana asked as she exchanged a significant glance with Berit, for they both remembered Jarald being gone the whole afternoon.

Ulla looked down, not wanting to admit all she knew about Jarald's visit with her mistress. That was not the kind of thing a daughter should learn about her mother, and Ulla loved Grena as well as Berit.

Too curious to let her servant pretend a shyness Berit was certain she didn't feel, the blonde knelt by her side. "What happened that day, Ulla? We'll not be angry with you, no matter what you tell us, but it's important for us to know. It's more important than you may ever know,'' she whispered dramatically.

Ulla remained reluctant to talk until she realized the cousins would pester her with questions all night unless she did. "Your mother is a widow, Berit. Widows often get very lonely,'' she finally said.

"You mean my mother and Jarald—" Berit was so astonished she didn't know exactly how to phrase the question.

Ulla nodded.

At first Dana wanted to laugh at the thought of Grena and Jarald being lovers, but then she became angry. Jarald had been courting her for more than a year. Did he frequently pass his afternoons in attractive widows' beds? As for her aunt, was she so furious at Erik she would stoop to seducing his sister's suitor? Neither explanation satisfied her, and she felt as though she had been betrayed by them both.

"Thank you, Ulla," Dana said sweetly, despite the darkness of her mood. "I hope our family's troubles will soon be over, but please tell us if there's anything else we should know."

"I will, mistress," Ulla replied, relieved she had not had to relate how battered and bruised Grena had been when Jarald had left her.

As they turned away, Berit took her cousin's hand. "I can't believe it. I just can't believe it."

"Why not?" Dana responded flippantly. "Jarald's a good deal older than I am. I'll bet he's near your mother's age. Frankly, I think they'd make a fine couple, and I'll suggest it to him just as soon as we've set my father and brother free."

Berit had seen Dana angry often enough to recognize she was livid now. "That's very generous of you."

"It has nothing to do with generosity," Dana was quick to point out. "We need the swine's boat and crew or I'd tell him to spend his time elsewhere right now!"

While preparing for the voyage, Brendan and Erik were again sharing the small house on Haakon's farm. The thrall had been watching Dana move in and out of the tents pitched under the oak tree in hopes he would have a chance to speak with her alone. Berit had always been at her side, however. As he saw the pair walking toward the house, he knew from the savage length of Dana's stride that she would be in a most unsympathetic mood. What she had to be so angry about he couldn't guess, but he had had more than enough of her temper for one day and made no effort to approach her. He could wait until tomorrow or the next day, but before he left her home, he was determined to tell her good-bye in a way that would make her long for his return. That he still hadn't figured out how or when he could return didn't matter as long as he had the hope she would wait for him.

CHAPTER XXI

In the next two days, Brendan's efforts to speak with Dana were frustrated at every turn for she was never alone and he knew her moods well enough to be convinced sneaking into her house to again awaken her before dawn would yield the worst of results. She spent a great deal of her time tending the sick, and he was certain it was her sympathetic concern that speeded the men's recovery as much as Olga's healing herbs. The health of all the ailing men was improving steadily, and some felt sufficiently well to be up and about. It was plain, however, that they would not be strong enough to make the return voyage to Erin, and neither would Jørn.

Brendan had to rely on the information Erik passed on from Berit for news of his master's progress. Despite the fact the young man had received more individual attention than his crew, Jørn's recovery was progressing slowly. Because nothing about his master had impressed him in the brief time he had known him, Brendan would not have been surprised if he had succumbed to the mysterious fever that had felled so many of his crew.

At other times Brendan tried to be optimistic and hoped Jørn would soon recover the strength to enthusiastically welcome Jarald's offer to captain the rescue voyage, and also to send him along as a free man. He was fairly certain that approach would appeal to Jørn rather than having to attempt to rescue his uncle and cousin himself so soon after a serious illness. Whether or not that would actually happen, Brendan had to wait and see. He had never been the patient sort, and the delay left him feeling anxious and out of sorts, especially so when he had to spend his nights alone longing for the sweet company of an irresistible beauty who would no longer even speak to him.

Dana was pleased with herself for effectively hiding the pain Brendan had caused her. It had been no small effort to avoid him when he was frequently passing nearby, but she had stubbornly pretended not to see him. Berit had been with her almost constantly since Jørn's return, and while her cousin had a curious nature, she did not suspect Dana was deliberately avoiding Brendan, or the reason why she did so. They spoke frequently of the coming voyage, Dana with eager anticipation, and Berit with dread.

"Your mother is going to let you go, isn't she?" Berit asked with an impatient toss of the honey-blond mane she still wore falling free. That prospect was so frightening she had not even considered demanding the same privilege for herself.

"Yes, and while Erik won't need it, I'll look after him for you. He'll not only return home safely, but as a hero as well, and that will undoubtedly influence your mother to treat him more kindly."

"She might still expect Jørn to fight him," Berit reminded her cousin.

While Dana had not apologized to her aunt for the part she had played in Berit's kidnapping, Grena had not appeared angry with her. In fact, while her aunt had been more reserved in manner than usual, she had not been unfriendly. She hoped the woman felt guilty about sleeping with Jarald, but she had vowed never to let her aunt know she was aware of the indiscretion.

"I don't think so, Berit. Your mother seems to have changed somehow. My mother was always the calm, reflective sister, but now I see those same traits in Aunt Grena too."

"I've not spoken with her about anything except Jørn's health. I'm afraid to," Berit admitted sadly. "I don't want to upset her when she's so worried about my brother."

Influenced by Freya's confidence, Dana assured Berit the future could not help but be far brighter than the present but she was thinking only of bringing her father and brother home, and didn't allow herself to dwell on what might lie beyond that happy day.

The third morning after his return, Jørn finally felt well enough to relate in more detail how Haakon and Svien had become Trom's prisoners. While Grena had been reluctant to allow Erik to be present, Freya insisted that Jørn's story was far too important to the rescue effort for him to be excluded. Using the same reasoning, Erik brought Brendan into the small bedchamber with him. With Freya, Grena, Dana, and Berit already present, the room was so crowded that Soren and Thora had to listen from the doorway.

Unaware of the undercurrent of hostility that flowed between many of those surrounding him, Jørn gathered his courage, but his voice was still no more than a hoarse whisper as he began to speak. "The English have accepted us, and our position in the Danelaw is now secure. This summer we heard talk of Danes settling in Erin as well. It seems the people there are eager to welcome us because they know we'll help them rout the Norsemen."

Brendan clenched his fists at his sides as he wondered if Jørn's story could possibly be true. Everyone despised the Norsemen, for they had ravaged his homeland for nearly a hundred years, but that his countrymen would ask help from Danes to defeat their enemy of long standing struck him as too desperate and dangerous a ploy to be believed. He did not speak up, however, but continued to listen without drawing attention to himself.

Jørn continued, but with increasing difficulty. "I wanted to visit Erin, to see for myself what the prospects for trade were, but Haakon and Svien were against it." He paused then, his lips trembling slightly. "I kept telling them, if we were among the first to establish trade, then untold riches would be ours. Haakon said we already possessed sufficient wealth, but I continued to argue. When I threatened to sail to Erin on my own, he said he had never seen me show so much ambition. Because he didn't want me to make such a voyage alone, he and Svien went with me. I had gotten the route from a man in the Danelaw. He told me it would lead me to a safe harbor, but it led only to Trom. I'm to blame for what happened, and I dare not hope that any of you will ever forgive me."

Fearing Jørn would be overcome with guilt and weep uncontrollably as he had on the morning he had arrived, Brendan spoke up to distract him. "Is Trom still camped at the mouth of the River Shannon?"

At first Jørn did not recognize the Celt, for his appearance and manner of dress had improved greatly since they had parted. Realizing the cause of his confusion, Brendan reminded him who he was, and the young man tried to smile. "Of course, Brendan. Had I known we would be going to Erin, I would have taken you with me."

Startled by that comment, Dana turned to look at her former lover and found his full attention focused on her rather than on Jørn. As one, they had realized such a decision would have prevented them from meeting, perhaps forever. The sorrow of that possibility jarred them both, but she was the first to look away.

Only Erik saw the silent exchange, and ignoring its significance, he quickly stepped forward to explain that Jarald would soon be arriving with his ship and crew. "I mean to help him deliver the ransom. You need only rest and regain your strength."

Greatly alarmed by the mention of the ransom, Jørn tried to sit up straight, but overcome with dizziness, he fell back into the heap of quilts that covered the bed. "It may already be too late," he mumbled despondently. "We were to sail home, gather the ransom, and begin the return voyage that same day, or—" Seeing Freya's anxious glance, the pale young man fell silent.

They had already learned from the crew members who had not been stricken with the fever that Trom had demanded a thousand pounds of silver. While that was a huge sum, Freya had readily supplied it. "We have the ransom, Jørn, and we'll leave as soon as Jarald returns," Erik assured him. "The good weather will hold and we'll make up whatever time has been lost."

"I must go too," Jørn insisted weakly. "Trom will deal only with me."

"Trom will be too eager to receive the ransom to care who delivers it," Erik predicted. "If you tried to sail with us, you would be far too likely to fall ill again, and you'd not be able to deliver anything if you didn't survive the journey."

Jørn winced, but not wanting to take such a grave risk, he readily gave in. "I'll tell you all I can about Trom before you go."

As her son closed his eyes, Grena recognized he was too exhausted to say more, and she motioned for everyone to leave. Because they all shared the same need to complete their plans, they gathered around the hearth in the hall to discuss them. When Dana sat down between her mother and Erik, Brendan chose to stand across from her. He was badly disappointed he had not been able to strike a bargain with Jørn for his freedom, as remaining a thrall put him at a great disadvantage. Thinking, if he did not acknowledge his status, it might go unnoticed, he was the first to speak.

"I can guide Jarald's ship to a secluded harbor above the Shannon. Trom will expect us to come from the south, not the north, so the advantage will be ours. Jarald and his men can wait in hiding until I have the men I'll gather in place. We can surround Trom before he realizes he's in danger."

"You really don't believe paying the ransom in a straight-forward manner is even a possibility?" Freya inquired.

While he thought he had made himself clear on that subject during their last conversation, Brendan did not react in a hostile fashion. "No, Trom has absolutely no sense of honor. He has often demanded tribute from towns in exchange for peace. Then when he has every last item of value the townspeople possess, he attacks them anyway, sets fire to every dwelling, and slaughters the men. The women are usually dead in a day or two, and the children sold as slaves."

Hoping that the gruesome story had sickened everyone, as it did him, Brendan continued in a softer tone. "We ought to have the silver to ransom your husband and son with us, though, because it's impossible to say how elaborate a trick we might be forced to play, but you'll not lose a single coin."

"The silver means nothing to us, Brendan. It's only our loved ones' lives that are precious," Freya said.

"Of course," Brendan acknowledged with a slight bow.

As he was speaking, Grena had entered the room. "How can we be certain you don't plan to steal the ransom for yourself?"

"You'll have to trust me," Brendan replied, his expression becoming one of open contempt.

Grena laughed as though that were a preposterous request, and knowing the proud Celt had been insulted, Dana immediately took his side. "Brendan is trusting us, Aunt Grena. He may know what sort of man Trom is, but he doesn't know my father and brother. What if they are worse?"

The question hurt far more than Grena's, for it forced Brendan to realize that by freeing Haakon and Svien, he might be putting his own people in jeopardy. What if they had no more character than Trom? What if, once freed, they turned on him and killed his friends? Trom would betray an ally he no longer needed without a second thought. Would Haakon and Svien do the same?

There had been more than thirty men with Jørn. Surely Jarald would arrive with that many. If there were sixty with Haakon and Svien, he would be turning loose nearly a hundred Danes within striking distance of his home. Was gaining his freedom worth such a risk? How he could have thought only of himself, and not his family and friends, Brendan did not understand, but he felt not only ashamed but exceedingly stupid for having been so trusting of his master's people.

"I have work to do," he announced as he turned toward the door, no longer interested in discussing the rescue effort and not caring if his hasty departure was rude.

When Erik turned toward her, obviously alarmed, Dana quickly rose to her feet. "Aunt Grena, whether or not you trust Brendan doesn't matter. He'll play a vital part in my father and brother's rescue. Please excuse me. There are several chores I neglected to mention to him.'' Lifting her flowing garments above her feet, she fled the hall in a most unladylike haste.

Although Brendan heard Dana calling his name, he kept right on walking. He went on past the tents, waving to Moira, whom he had noticed on several occasions with a slender red-haired man who seemed to be thriving with her care. The shy maid blushed, but she was pleased he had noticed her, while her companion frowned, clearly disgruntled that he had lost her full attention.

Knowing Brendan had to hear her, Dana ceased calling to him. She slowed her pace to her normal one and followed him down to the docks. When he finally turned to face her, she didn't rebuke him for ignoring her. He was wearing the same hostile scowl that had marred his features upon leaving the house, and she was glad there was no one nearby to overhear what could easily become a heated argument if she failed to calm him.

''I know you don't want to hear my thoughts on trust again, so I won't repeat them, but I was trying to convince my aunt to be still, not attempting to frighten you. My father will be grateful for whatever help you give us. You'll never be sorry that you set him and my brother free. Only good can come of it.''

Still fighting to control his temper, Brendan looked over Dana's shoulder, thinking her farm as impressive a place as he had when he had first arrived. The servants were as industrious as he had supposed, and he had yet to hear a word of complaint about Haakon from any of them. He should have realized long before this that the man had to be of good character, but unfortunately he hadn't. Erik had called Dana her father's daughter, and now focusing his glance on her troubled frown, he realized that he had come to trust her too late.

''I was determined to hate you all,'' he admitted with unusual candor. ''From the day Trom took me prisoner, hatred was all that kept me alive. I vowed to survive no matter what agony he put me through. To survive, return home, and one day give him the brutal execution he deserves. It's Trom I want, Dana. Don't think I offered to help out of concern for you or your family. Your mother was right. My goal is a purely selfish one."

"What are you saying? That you will steal the ransom if you can?"

"No, I'm no thief," Brendan assured her. "But I don't want to ask the help of Danes to rid my homeland of the Norsemen and then find we are worse off than before."

Dana searched her mind, seeking a means to allay his fears, and an idea swiftly presented itself. "You must put that worry aside for the time being, Brendan. Now the challenge is to free my father and brother. Once that is accomplished, you can deal with Trom in any way you choose." Taking a step closer, she raised her hand to sweep away a curl the breeze had blown across her cheek and then laid her palm upon his chest.

"I can't speak for what other Danes may do, but I can give you my word that, once freed, my father and brother will not return to Erin unless you invite them to do so. Despite our many differences, I know that your heart is good. You once promised that you would not harm those I love, and I'll gladly make the same promise to you. Erik and I need you to set our father and brother free. You need us to return to Erin and defeat Trom. Let's join forces and make it one quest, not two."

The touch of Dana's hand warmed Brendan clear through, but he successfully fought the impulse to draw her into his arms and foolishly pledge not only his love but his life as well. "How does Jarald fit into your plans?" he asked instead.

The coldness of his tone gave her the impression he must find her touch objectionable, and Dana dropped her hand to her side. She turned away for a moment and looked out over the water. "He'll be coming soon, perhaps tomorrow," she murmured more to herself than to her companion. "I'm going to tell you something. I don't want you to confront Jarald with it, just remember it."

Intrigued, Brendan reached out to touch her shoulder and turn her back toward him. "What is it?"

Dana quickly related what she and Berit had learned from Ulla. She had not told anyone what conclusion she had drawn, but it troubled her deeply. "Grena and Jarald may have been lovers for a long while. If so—"

A clever man, Brendan instantly understood what Dana was hinting at. "Then he could have been the one who set the fire and nearly killed me! No wonder Erik found no tracks leading back to Grena's house. He and his men would have covered Jarald's trail when they brought me here."

Dana nodded. "That seems likely. We need him, though, Brendan. We need his ship and crew to reach Erin and free my father and Svien. Once that's accomplished, we can force him to tell us the truth about the night of the fire."

"We?" Brendan asked with the first smile she had seen from him in several days.

"I'll not forgive him for trying to kill you. Did you think I would?"

"That's he's slept with Grena doesn't insult you?"

"That scarcely compares to what he did to you," Dana scoffed. "I care not at all in whose bed he sleeps, but I'll not allow anyone to mistreat you."

She looked so adamant that Brendan could not suppress a laugh. "Why won't you admit that you love me, when it's so obvious that you do?"

That he would tease her again about so vital a matter hurt Dana badly. "I'm not the one who wanted to end what we've shared," she reminded him with an accusing stare.

She had put the blame squarely on him, where he knew it belonged, but before Brendan could find some eloquent way to beg her forgiveness for what had surely been the worst mistake of his life, he saw Erik hurrying toward them. "Does Erik know what you suspect?"

"No, I've told only you."

"It will be our secret then," Brendan replied.

"One of many," Dana whispered as Erik reached her side.

Seeing Brendan's smile, Erik assumed Dana had succeeded in winning his cooperation. With an embarrassed stammer, the dark-haired young man asked for a swimming lesson.

Dana left them, and the opportunity to ask her to meet him that night was lost. While that dampened Brendan's spirits considerably, he gave his full attention to teaching Erik how to swim, and because the young man was so eager a pupil, he did not find the task disagreeable, but he did not waste the chance to again insist he be given his freedom before the voyage to Erin.

Wisely, Freya had not asked Grena and Berit to share a sleeping chamber, so Berit still had a room of her own. Just as she had on previous nights, she waited anxiously for Erik to join her, and he did not disappoint her. He slipped through her door as soon as the house was quiet, drew her into a fervent embrace, and covered her face with adoring kisses. When he felt the dampness of her tears, he held her all the more tightly.

"It will take less than a week to reach Erin," he whispered. "No more than a day or two to free Haakon and Svien, and then another week to return home. We've known each other all our lives. Don't you think our love will survive if we're apart three weeks?"

The reassuring words did not help Berit overcome her fears. "I'm not afraid for our love, only for you!" she replied.

Brendan had taught him how to float, but Erik knew it would take many more lessons before he could actually swim. He also had Brendan to thank for whatever skills he had gained with a sword, but they would need to practice each night when they put in to shore. He was not yet a warrior of any merit, but he had taken the first steps and was confident his courage would not fail him when it came time to apply what he had learned.

"I'm no coward, Berit. I'll not ask Brendan and Jarald to save my father and brother. I want to do that myself. If you're going to continue to weep and beg me not to go, then I'll leave you now. If you have no faith in me tonight, perhaps you'll have some by the time I return."

Not about to let him leave, Berit refused to release her hold on him. "I have enormous faith in you, but that doesn't mean I won't be afraid."

Seeing they were getting nowhere, Erik led her to the bed. "This is what I want you to think about while I'm gone, Berit, only this," he murmured as he loosened the tie at her throat and slipped her nightgown off her shoulders. "With your love, I can do anything. You mustn't doubt that, for I never will."

Responding to what she knew was only the first of many delicious kisses they would exchange, Berit did not speak again of her fears, but that did not mean that they were forgotten, only suppressed for the night, if not forever.

Jarald arrived at dawn and not with a knarr, the deep-sea vessel he had captained for trading, but with a dreki, one of the sleek warships with which the Danes had not only crossed the seas, but also challenged Europe's rivers and conquered her people. Called the *Seahawk*, its ornately carved prow and stern gave the ship a majestic elegance that belied her deadly purpose.

At the first glimpse of the *Seahawk*'s diamond-patterned sail in the distance, Brendan's mind flooded with memories of death so intense he was certain he could actually smell the sickly-sweet scent of blood. He did not think he could stand to go near the ship, let alone sail it home. When Dana slipped her hand in his, he was so lost in his own thoughts he was badly startled.

"Jarald must not suspect that we know of his alliance with Grena," the stunning redhead warned in a hushed tone. "Do no more than watch and wait. The time for revenge will soon come."

Dana smiled when he glanced down at her, but the light in her eyes danced with a chilling gleam. That morning he had made another fruitless attempt to convince Erik to leave the beautiful young woman at home. Now he was forced to accept the fact that Dana had a natural talent for intrigue and would undoubtedly be the asset her brother had repeatedly insisted that she would be.

Overcoming his own stubborn resistance to taking Dana along, Brendan realized that, once in Erin, he might somehow find the means to convince her to stay, and suddenly her presence became extremely desirable. He gave her hand a tender squeeze, then released it before the others standing on the dock noticed how close they were standing or, indeed, suspected how close they truly were.

Dana welcomed Jarald with a friendly smile, then had to suffer through one of his boisterous hugs before she could speak. "We'll soon have your boat loaded with our things, but we need to speak with Jørn one last time before we sail."

Brendan and Erik followed close behind as Dana and Jarald started for the house, but not before they had gotten a good look at Jarald's crew. To a man they were as well-built as their captain, and their expressions showed them to be a determined lot. "Were Haakon's crew anything like these men?" Brendan inquired softly.

Erik glanced back over his shoulder. "Fit, you mean?"

"Fit?" Near giants was closer to the truth, but Brendan did not argue. "Yes. Are they able to handle themselves in a fight?"

"Obviously not or Trom wouldn't be holding them for ransom, would he?" Erik was quick to point out.

"It isn't like Trom to give anyone the chance to fight." Quickening his pace, Brendan entered the house, hoping Jørn would swiftly set him free so they could be on their way. Unfortunately, despite Erik and Dana's encouragement, Jarald advised against it, and clearly Jørn had greater respect for the older man's judgment than he did for his cousins'.

Still pale and weak, Jørn had neither the strength nor the initiative to argue and wanted the matter settled. "When Brendan returns with Haakon and Svien, I'll set him free. Not before."

Infuriated, Brendan moved closer to Jørn's bed, but Dana stepped in front of him to block his way as she continued to argue with her cousin. "You've admitted that it's entirely your fault that my father and Svien were taken captive by Trom. Because you can't return with the ransom yourself, a ransom which by all rights you should have been the one to raise, the very least you can do is send a freeman rather than a thrall in your place."

Jarald was too startled by Dana's impassioned plea to contradict her, while Brendan's heart swelled with pride.

Dana cleverly played upon Jørn's guilt over his uncle and cousin's plight until he lay cringing in a tearful heap. Then, taking Brendan's arm, she drew him forward. Her whole family had filed into the room, and she included them all in her glance. "You have witnesses aplenty here. Now set this man free so we can be on our way. Your illness has already cost us too many days."

Thoroughly humiliated, Jørn immediately granted Dana's demand. "You are a free man, Brendan. I have no further claim on you."

Elated, Brendan wanted to shout with joy, but before he could, Erik spoke up in a tone every bit as confident as his half sister's. "I intend to wed Berit," he informed his bedridden cousin. "Your mother says I'll have to fight you to the death for that privilege. Be ready for that battle when we return."

"What?" Jørn gasped. He turned a frantic glance toward his mother, whose hate-filled stare readily confirmed his worst fears. "No, wait, we must discuss this!" he pleaded.

"I have no time now, Jørn," Erik replied with a careless shrug. Taking Berit's hand, he led her from the crowded room, with Dana and Brendan following close behind.

While he would have taken a perverse pleasure in listening to Grena attempt to convince Jørn he had to fight Erik when clearly the fearful young man was loath to do it, Jarald was too eager to be on his way to tarry. He slid his arm around Freya's waist and escorted her from Jørn's bedchamber.

"Family arguments are best left to those involved," he confided with a warm smile. "I may not have another opportunity to assure you I will make our voyage a success, but I do want you to know that I will."

"I have every confidence in you, Jarald," Freya replied, delighted he had provided her with a means to leave her nephew's chamber at so embarrassing a moment. She was glad Erik had made his plans clear, however, as it would have been a difficult secret to keep until his return.

Nearly overwhelmed with gratitude, Brendan had no opportunity to convey it to Dana when the keys she carried were needed to open the storehouse where Haakon kept his weapons. Once the door was swung open and Soren carried a lamp inside, the exuberant Celt was instantly reminded of how dangerous their undertaking was.

While Haakon and Svien had taken their favorite weapons with them, there were still dozens left behind. There were long swords with gleaming blades, whose wavy patterns showed how they had been fashioned from iron bars twisted together and then pounded flat. Battle-axes lay along another wall, with spears whose graceful leaf-shaped blades glowed in the dim light. There were also bows and arrows, shields, helmets, and shirts of mail known as byrnies.

One glance convinced Brendan that Haakon could easily outfit a small army, and thoroughly disgusted, he turned and walked away. Before he had gone ten paces, Dana overtook him.

"We've far finer swords than the ones you and Erik have been using for practice. Don't you want to choose one?" she asked.

"Your father's interest is in commerce—is that what you still expect me to believe when it's plain a man who collects so many weapons must use them!"

Dana had not expected Brendan to get down on his knees to thank her for winning his freedom for him when she had merely kept her promise, but she had expected him to at least be civil. "I doubt my father has more weapons than any other wealthy Dane. Our men enjoy battle and take great pride in their prowess as warriors. I'll not deny that, but I've already given you my word your people will not be harmed for helping mine. What more assurance do you need?"

Brendan stared down at her, captivated anew by her violent glance, but her exotic beauty no longer clouded his thinking as completely as it once had. She was a woman, not a goddess, and she was mortal like any other. "If your promises prove to be clever lies, Dana, I'll make you pay for them with your life. This is the only warning I'll give, so if you had planned to trick me, you'd be wise to remain here with your mother."

"You arrogant swine!" Dana screamed, her temper ignit

ing instantly and flaring out of control. "You have made this the worst summer of my life, and I can't wait for the day when I finally bid you good-bye. You'll be on your own soil, surrounded by your own selfish kind, and if any are lost rescuing my father and brother it will be due to their own stupidity! Don't bother to take a sword if you don't want one, but I'll always have one at my side, and I'll welcome the chance to use it on you!"

Dana turned and walked back to the storehouse, her glorious red hair streaming out around her shoulders like golden wings. Brendan debated with himself. Then, knowing he would need a fine sword to kill Trom, he followed her. He relished the thought of again standing on his own soil and being surrounded by his own kind, but he had no intention of ever telling Dana good-bye.

CHAPTER XXII

Erik waved until Berit was no longer in sight. She had wept openly as they had said good-bye, but he was too excited about the journey to be affected more than momentarily by her tears. Soren's decision to stay behind had amazed him, but he knew the boy's presence would be a comfort to both Freya and Thora. That Soren had been so eager to look after the falcons had convinced him his beautiful birds would have the best of care in his absence.

Grena hadn't even glanced his way as the *Seahawk* had prepared to depart, and Erik had not been surprised. The woman was still fuming over the way he had spoken to her son. Remembering Jørn's panic-filled gaze, Erik began to laugh, and those around him turned to stare.

"I think you're lucky Berit can't hear you," Brendan

said. "It would break her heart to know you're in such high spirits when she's miserable."

"I was just thinking about Jørn. I didn't realize the prospect of having to fight me would terrify him, but clearly it did."

Because Erik looked so pleased to have aroused his cousin's fears, Brendan chuckled along with him. "I'll be sorry to miss that fight, but I doubt it will ever take place."

"Not if Jørn has no more courage than he displayed today."

"Is Svien anything like Jørn?" Brendan inquired in a more serious tone, as usual seizing every opportunity to gather information he could later use to his own advantage.

"The three of us grew up together, and have many things in common, but no, Svien is nothing like Jørn. He's more like Dana than anyone."

Brendan winced at that thought, for a man with her temperament would surely be not only bold but tough as well. "I'll look forward to meeting him then."

The wind was brisk, so the warships' sixteen pairs of oars were stored in their frames at the rail. Relaxing in the sun, the crew were seated on their sea chests, while the carved chests upon which Erik and Brendan sat were filled with silver. Two other chests containing the remainder of the ransom had been placed across from them, so the weight of the coins was evenly distributed in the center of the ship where it could be most easily borne.

Dana would have preferred to be near Erik, but when Brendan stayed close to him, she chose to take a place in the stern instead. She had had enough of the Celt's ridiculous suspicions for one day. He always saw the worst and was quick to accuse her of a seemingly endless list of imagined crimes. Perhaps when he returned to his own people he would find it easier to see the truth, but she feared his distrust ran too deep. At least she would have the opportunity to see something of his homeland, maybe even meet some of his people. If they were all as suspicious of Danes as Brendan, it would confirm her opinion that they could never have found happiness together, but the sadness of the thought weighed heavily on her heart.

The day was a fine one to begin a voyage, and that it had an exceedingly dangerous purpose only made it all the more worthwhile in Jarald's view. Even in garments borrowed from Soren, Dana was still the most fascinating of women, and he gave another man the tiller so he could concentrate his full attention on her. They would find a safe harbor each night and sleep in tents, and as he watched the wind whip through her fiery curls and impart a rosy blush to her cheeks, he tried to devise some compelling way to convince her to share his tent.

On several occasions recently, Dana had mistakenly believed she had misjudged Jarald. Now she knew her first impression of him as a conceited braggart had been extremely complimentary. She thought him capable of the worst sort of treachery, but she doubted he would stoop to any underhanded tricks while they were on board his ship.

Because she did not want him to suspect she knew about him and Grena, Dana tried to treat Jarald as politely as she always had, but it was difficult. At least his size was an asset, for she could lean back against his broad chest and escape the constant buffeting of the wind. The warmth of the sun was so soothing, Dana was soon dozing lightly in the comfort of Jarald's arms, never suspecting where such carelessness would lead.

Perplexed, Brendan wondered if Dana was trying to make him jealous again, and he swiftly decided that she must be. What other explanation could there be for her to plot Jarald's demise with him that morning and now sleep in the villain's arms that afternoon? She was either trying to drive him mad with desire or she was attempting to lull Jarald into a complacency that would make him easier to kill. Because neither alternative held a shred of honor, he tried to look only at the way the *Seahawk*'s gracefully carved prow sliced through the water, rather than at Dana's antics in the ship's stern.

Erik noted Brendan's frequent glances in his half sister's direction, as well as Dana's pose. "You once accused me of meekly accepting my situation," he leaned close to confide.

''I could now say the same of you. You have your freedom Why don't you challenge Jarald for Dana? Are you afrai you'd lose?''

Brendan eyed Erik with a darkly determined glance ''No, but I'll choose a far better time and place to face hir than this.''

Erik nodded, content to let the matter drop for th moment, but he was not averse to turning his own sword o Brendan if the man didn't adopt a more respectful attitud where his sister was concerned, and soon. That the Celt ha far more skill with the deadly weapon didn't disturb hin He didn't want to kill the man, only to give him a goo fight in order to settle the matter before Haakon took it upo himself to do so.

That night the voyagers camped in a secluded inlet o the western side of the Jutland peninsula where neithe their presence nor their precious cargo would be discovered Despite Jarald's gregarious manner, he was strict with h crew, and they responded as a well-disciplined unit each of his commands. After a hearty supper, the me chosen to serve the first watch took up their position near the ship, while the rest set up the tents and went sleep.

Alone in the small tent placed beside the one Eri Brendan, and several other men occupied, Dana found impossible to rest. She had too much on her mind, a without the gentle roll of the ship and the relaxing warm of the sunshine, sleep eluded her. Distressed by her cramp quarters, she first listened for any sound that would reve that some of the men were still awake, and hearing non she felt safe in venturing out despite being clad only in linen shift.

Keeping to the shadows, she skirted the *Seahawk*'s guard then continued along the water until she came to a sp where she could rest comfortably. Content to watch t stars' sparkle on the water until she could no longer rema awake, she was lost in warm memories of her father a brother until her solitude was broken by a man swimmi toward shore. She rose, prepared to return to the safety

ier tent at a run, but curiosity made her hesitate. Was it
merely one of Jarald's crew, or was it someone else?
Uncertain, she waited until he drew close enough to be
recognized.

Equally preoccupied, Brendan had also found it impossible to sleep that night. He had walked in the opposite
direction from Dana, then had gone for a swim, remaining
close to shore as he had moved back toward the ship. He
had chosen a spot well past the *Seahawk* to leave the water
o as not to alarm the sentries, but he had never expected to
ind Dana waiting on the shore.

That Dana had once dreamed of just such a moonlight
encounter filled her with wonder. She already knew exactly
how magnificent Brendan's muscular form would look as he
walked toward her, and she was not disappointed. His body
glistened with the stars' enchanting glow, the heavenly light
sculpting each plane and curve to godlike perfection. While
t had been his handsome appearance that she had first
oted, it would be his stubborn refusal to love her that she
would never forget. A single tear escaped her lashes and
olled down her cheek as he reached her. She did not touch
im, for she was certain that, just as in her dream, his skin
would be as cold as his glance.

Brendan's first impulse was to issue a vicious taunt about
arald, but Dana's sorrow-filled gaze forced that thought
om his mind. Instead, he reached out to encircle her waist
nd pulled her close. He pressed her cheek to the damp
ollow of his shoulder and simply held her for a long
moment, thinking, as he always had, that words simply got
a the way when they were together.

Dana was surprised, and quite pleasantly so, by how
wiftly Brendan's warmth dispelled the chill of the seawater
iat dripped from his curls. He had been swimming nude,
id her thin shift provided little in the way of a barrier
etween them. She could feel the slow, steady beat of his
eart beneath her fingertips, and found it not only soothing,
it also wonderfully romantic.

They had had the most tempestuous of affairs, and yet she
d not want it to ever end. She reached up to nuzzle his
roat with playful kisses, and almost immediately he gave

her shift a tug, then drew it off over her head. He flung it o
the sand, then carefully lowered her to the discarded ga
ment. It was not as soft as the bed of grass they had enjoye
in the forest, but she shared his eagerness to again mak
love and felt no discomfort.

Not one to waste such a splendid, if completely unexpec
ed, opportunity, Brendan wound his fingers in Dana's cur
to hold her still but he soon realized by the intensity of h
kiss that she had no wish to escape him. He relaxed the
cradling her more gently in his arms and his demandin
kisses became openly adoring.

Dana felt the change in Brendan, and welcomed it. Sh
did not want to make love with fevered haste that nig
either. Instead, she longed to explore the limits of the lo
neither had ever admitted. The droplets of seawater clingin
to Brendan soon made her skin as slippery as his. The lig
film of moisture heightened her awareness of his masculin
strength, making the pleasure of being in his arms all t
more intense.

She licked a salty drop from his earlobe, and he respond
by rolling over to bring her up on top of him. His lips we
warm, inviting, and his kiss so delicious she would ha
been content had there been no more to making love th
that luscious exchange.

Brendan could recall each time they had been togeth
and Dana's mood had never been so delightfully relaxed
it was this night. That was his fault, he knew, and he s
cursed the pride that had kept him from meeting her t
night of Jarald's arrival. He still mourned the lost chance
be with her just as he would the death of a dear friend, f
the opportunities he had not wasted had been all too few. H
knew love should not be what they had made of it, not
painfully hurried when it deserved to be savored at leisur
and he vowed to make this night an especially memorab
one.

He could not even imagine bedding another woman no
when his mind and heart were too full of Dana to ev
forget her. His choice was made for him. Either with h
consent or without it, he was determined to keep her for h
own. That he would have to kill the most despicable

pirates to free her father and brother before he spoke of his dreams seemed only a minor hindrance to his goal. For the moment he longed simply to enjoy Dana's affection and bestow all that he could of his own.

Dana's fingers combed through the damp curls covering Brendan's chest, then traced their path as they narrowed over the smooth flatness of his belly. "You're a very handsome man," she purred softly, "very, very handsome."

"I didn't think you had noticed."

Dana had known he would not modestly deny that her compliment was deserved, but she was not offended by his conceit when his pride was a large measure of his charm. He was a fascinatingly complex individual, but a man she barely knew. She had never succeeded in winning his trust with promises, but she knew he craved the ecstasy she gave each time they had been together. An imaginative young woman, she moved slowly down his splendid physique, caressing him with the lush curves of her supple body and trailing kisses in her wake. When his breathing immediately quickened, his excitement fed her own.

To find Dana so giving a lover astonished Brendan, but he wanted still more. In an enticing whisper he made the most erotic suggestion imaginable, and the flame-haired beauty did not disappoint him. With a seductive abandon she made love to him as he had once made love to her, using her lips and tongue to lure him across the threshold of rapture into a paradise of sensation where he called her name in a grateful moan.

By mutual desire, this was merely the first of the many exotic delights each created for the other, for Brendan was not content to passively accept joy without returning it. He responded by giving Dana the same thrilling ecstasy she had given him. A wealth of experience had made him the most romantic of lovers, and yet with Dana, each of his gestures was spontaneous, and genuinely given to please.

Just when Dana thought she could bear no more of Brendan's masterful loving, he carried her into the sea, rocking her in his arms in time with the water's rhythmic flow until the joy that flooded his heart again crested within hers. He placed her on her feet for a moment, then lifted her into his arms so she could wrap her legs around his hips. She laughed and coiled herself around him with the sensuous grace of a clinging vine. For so passionate a couple, the ways to bestow pleasure were endless, but, alas, the night was not.

When Brendan suddenly realized he could see the clear violet of Dana's eyes, he sat up with a start. They had been lying at the surf's edge, exchanging lazy kisses and too lost in each other to notice the approaching dawn. He looked around quickly to make certain they were not being observed, then rose and gave Dana his hand. He led her to the spot where her shift lay in a crumpled heap, shook it out, and handed it to her.

"Return to your tent as though you had nothing to hide. I'll have to swim back to where I left my clothes."

When he turned away without adding any words of affection, Dana reached out to catch his hand. Brendan turned back, but his glance held only the hint of curiosity, as though he expected a quick reminder of something he had forgotten, and she dared not speak of love when he had not. "Be careful," she teased sweetly. "I'd be terribly disappointed if you drowned."

"So would I," Brendan agreed with a ready grin. He gave her one last kiss, then sprinted across the shore and dove into the water. With long, fluid strokes he swam back toward the ship, but Dana didn't take a step until he was lost from sight.

Looking down at her rumpled shift, she knew she must look as though she had spent the worst of nights when just the opposite was true. Her hair was filled with salty grit, and because there would be no way to explain this, she did not go straight back to her tent but instead went to the spring where the men had drawn water for their camp. There was no one about, and she knelt down to wash her hair. Then she hastily removed her shift and scrubbed her body as best she could without soap. The chill of the bubbling springwater was invigorating, and when she was ready to return to her tent, she felt as though she had enjoyed a long rest. It wasn't until she reached the camp and found several men already up and moving about that she grew frightened.

Jarald was standing beside the *Seahawk*, supervising the loading of his gear, when he caught sight of Dana. It had not occurred to him to look to see if she was inside her tent. He had simply assumed that she was. "I was going to let you sleep," he called out as he walked toward her. To find the elegant beauty in such scanty attire was a shock, but the sight of her slender limbs was so appealing he did not scold her. Her hair was wet and she had obviously used her shift as a towel. The damp garment hid little his imagination did not swiftly provide, and he licked his lips slowly, hoping he would soon get a taste of her delectable body. "You'll want to dress before we eat."

"Yes, of course. I'll hurry." Dana sped past him, grateful she had had to endure no more than his openly appreciative glance. As she ducked into her tent, she noticed the wet tracks Brendan had left leading to his. They had taken a terrible risk remaining together so long, but she would not deny that it had been worth it.

Meaning to wake Erik, Jarald followed Dana, but when he observed the footprints leading to his tent, he grew curious and angled off to inquire of one of his men if he had seen Brendan that morning. Upon learning the Celt had just returned from a swim, the burly man's expression grew troubled. Dana had returned to the camp from the opposite direction, and surely she had only been seeking the privacy a woman would need in the company of so many men, but why would the Celt be out swimming at dawn?

While he resisted the conclusion they had been together, combined with his earlier suspicions of Brendan's interest in Dana, Jarald could not shake the impression he was a threat. For the moment they needed the Celt's knowledge of Trom's tactics, but once that need was past, he was determined to be rid of the man for good.

The second day of the voyage Jarald set a course that took them across the North Sea. He had not expected to sight land before nightfall, and his crew did not complain as they ate a supper of dried fish and cheese. Dana could tell Erik was no more pleased than she to have left the coast for the open sea, but she bravely kept her worries to herself and so did he. It was not until the following day that they reached an isle off the northern tip of Scotland, and eager to again feel dry ground beneath her feet, she was one of the first out of the ship.

That he had not succumbed to the queasiness that had plagued him for two days gave Erik the courage to look forward to the voyage's end. He and Brendan had spent a great deal of their time devising schemes to outwit Trom, and after a hot supper that night, they involved Jarald and Dana in a discussion of their plans.

While Jarald listened attentively as Brendan described the arrangement of Trom's camp as he drew it in the sand, he still did not like the idea of the Celt bringing in men loyal only to him. Keeping the thought to himself, he knew in the heat of battle a good many men might fall. He planned to make certain that Brendan was the first of them. When he glanced toward Dana, he found her observing the man's illustrations with no more than thoughtful interest, but he could not shake the feeling he would never succeed in winning her hand as long as Brendan remained alive.

Dana was too tired to even consider leaving her tent that night, and Brendan was equally exhausted. Because they had had no opportunity to arrange another rendezvous, he stretched out on a sleeping bag made of hides and was one of the first asleep. He was still so excited about returning home he could barely contain himself, but that enthusiasm didn't interfere with his rest.

On the fourth day, the *Seahawk* continued under sail, skirting the islands dotting the northwestern coast of Scotland, then crossing to the northern coast of Erin. Brendan could not have managed the voyage any better himself, for it put them in a perfect position to attack Trom from the north, where he would least expect it. Again they chose a secluded inlet to camp, and after supper they made their final plans.

"Trom has sentries at the mouth of the river, so you'll have to take care of them before dawn." Brendan again drew pictures in the sand as he spoke, indicating Jarald and his crew would move upriver while he and his men would attack Trom's forces from the rear. "Deprived of a warning, Trom and his men will be asleep. They're used to attacking others, not to being under siege, and will be unlikely to have their weapons ready. By the time they realize they're surrounded, we'll have already released their prisoners. We may even be able to get them out safely without a fight."

"And if not?" Jarald asked.

Brendan looked up, his gaze steady as he replied, "Then we'll give them a battle the few who survive will never forget. We'll not fail in this."

"On that point we agree," Jarald assured him, but he had no intention of walking in and out of Trom's camp without the thrill of spilling a great deal of blood.

"Tomorrow we'll journey down the coast," Brendan continued. "Once the *Seahawk* is safely hidden in a secluded harbor, I'll leave for my home. I'll return with my men around midnight, move into place, and wait for dawn. We'll free the prisoners and—"

"How can you be so certain your people will help us?" Jarald interrupted to ask.

Brendan glanced toward the heavens, thinking the man insufferably dense. "They despise Trom as much as I do. You can believe me that they'll be eager to do this."

Jarald nodded, but he still did not trust the Celt to return. "We'll need a signal. I'll make the call of an owl three times. You'll answer, but with only two calls."

As the men continued to refine their plans, Dana grew increasingly uneasy. Brendan described the Norse settlement of Limerick as being well upriver, but it unnerved her to know Trom would be able to seek help should he escape them, while they would have to rely solely upon themselves.

"When are you going to kill Trom?" she asked Brendan.

The question startled him, for he had thought she was interested only in the rescue mission. "I'll take care of him after I've released your father, brother, and their crews. I'll not sacrifice them in my own quest for revenge."

"How noble," Jarald responded sarcastically, preferring

to kill the hated Norse pirate himself. Thinking their plans complete, he rose to his feet, and after exchanging wishes for a good night, he excused himself and went to speak with his crew.

Erik watched Jarald depart, but while he admired the man's confidence, he didn't think his attitude nearly serious enough for the task that lay ahead. "I think we should have several plans, in case the first doesn't go as we expect it to."

Insulted, Brendan stood up before responding. "I'll not disappoint you. I'll provide the men to set Haakon and Svien free. You needn't fear I'll go home and not return."

Erik shook his head. "You don't understand. It's not you I'm worried about, it's Jarald."

When Erik glanced up at him, his gaze was so trusting Brendan was ashamed for being short with him. He had several alternative plans in mind, but he didn't want Erik involved in any of them. "Forgive me, but you can't possibly understand how eager I am to see my family again, and I can think of little else. Let's all try to get a good night's sleep, for we'll get little or no rest tomorrow night."

Dana had hoped Brendan might say more about his family, but when he turned and walked away, she silently scolded herself for having such a futile hope. She might get to meet his people after they had defeated Trom, but she wasn't certain Brendan would bother to introduce her even then. She gave Erik a hug before retiring to her tent, but despite Brendan's advice, she again found it difficult to sleep. Knowing he did not want her to meet him, she remained in her tent, but all her thoughts were of him and the love they had shared all too briefly.

Early the next morning, the *Seahawk* sailed past the forbidding Cliffs of Moher. Captivated by the sight of the sheer wall of jagged black rock, Dana stared in rapt fascination. Birds flew in and out of their nesting places in narrow crevices, their excited calls echoing above the ceaseless crash of waves at the cliffs' base, but their lively chatter failed to dispel the atmosphere of overpowering gloom.

Appreciating the sharp contrast the cliffs provided to the flatness of her island home, Brendan moved to Dana's side. "The view is spectacular from here, but can you imagine what it's like to lie at the top, lean over, and look down?"

The mere thought of that gave her a fright that was almost more than Dana could bear. "You've done it?" she asked apprehensively.

"Many times," Brendan confided. "At the top there are rolling green meadows, as pretty as any you could ever want to see. Erin is a beautiful land, Dana, far prettier than your own."

The pensive beauty found it easier to observe the cliffs than to return her companion's level gaze. She did not know what he expected her to say. Did he think she would beg him to show her his homeland? She lifted her chin proudly, content to wait for him to issue that invitation instead.

Thinking the lovely redhead was too worried about her father and brother to want to talk about Erin, Brendan fell silent. There were so many things he wanted to tell her, to show her, but this was not the time. He gave his full attention to the shoreline, studying it intently, for it would be suicide to venture too near the mouth of the River Shannon, where like a giant spider Trom lay in wait, eager for the kill.

As soon as they reached the cove Brendan had chosen, he and Erik left hurriedly to scout the route to Trom's camp. When they returned, the Celt had tarried only long enough to assure everyone all would go well, and then he had again disappeared into the woods that bordered the shore. Dana tried not to allow her heartbreak to show in her expression, but she failed. She had not the slightest doubt Brendan would return as promised, but that did not lessen the pain of his hasty departure. She feared he had a woman awaiting him. Knowing Brendan, she thought it far more likely there were several beauties who would be eager to welcome him home. "Home." She murmured the word softly to herself. Returning home had been all that had ever mattered to him.

There was much to be done to prepare for the coming raid on Trom's camp. There were weapons to polish, helmets and shields to sort out, and heavy leather tunics and shirts of mail to unpack. While there was no need for silence in the deserted harbor, the men went about their tasks with few words. All thoughts were focused on the night ahead, and Dana wished with all her heart she had some useful job to perform to lift her spirits from the depths of dread where they had sunk.

She had not helped prepare meals, but she did so now, even though she had little interest in the taste of the food. When night fell, she was too excited to sleep, and argued when Erik walked her to her tent. "I want to go with you. I can stay down by Trom's docks until you send someone for me, but I can't bear to stay here all by myself. Not knowing what's happening would be torture for me."

Exasperated by her request, Erik refused to give in. "You've made the journey, and you'll be there in the morning to greet Haakon and Svien, but there's no need for you to put yourself in danger by entering Trom's camp before it's safe. Brendan would be furious if he knew that you'd asked to go. That's why you didn't mention it to him, isn't it?"

"Let's leave him out of this," Dana insisted stubbornly. "It has nothing to do with him."

"It has everything to do with him!" Erik hissed through clenched teeth.

Instantly Dana raised her hand to cover his mouth. "Hush!" she implored him. "Isn't it plain that whatever there was between us is over?"

Erik grabbed her wrist and pushed her hand away. "And whose decision was that—yours or his?" When Dana lowered her gaze, he had his answer. "There will be time enough to settle this tomorrow."

"There is nothing to settle," Dana replied sadly. "It's over."

"If you think I'll allow some swaggering Celt to break your heart and get away with it, you're very wrong. With Haakon and Svien to help me, he won't stand a chance."

"You mustn't tell!" Dana grabbed hold of Erik's kirtle in a desperate clutch. "This doesn't concern you or them!"

"You won't change my mind, Dana. Now just go to sleep, and tomorrow when you wake up, it'll all be over."

Dana could not recall ever seeing Erik in so belligerent a mood, and while she continued to argue, her words made no impression on him. In his opinion, Brendan had treated her shamefully, and she found it difficult, if not impossible, to dispute that view.

"Just promise me you won't do anything about this tomorrow. You'll only endanger your own life if you're thinking about punishing Brendan when you should be concentrating on Trom."

Erik hesitated, but knowing she was right, he finally agreed. "All right, I'll do it your way, but I mean to confront him about this, Dana."

"Please, let's talk about it again before you do."

Reluctant to make that promise, Erik brushed her cheek with a hasty kiss, then turned away, eager to move Jarald's men into place for the coming attack.

Hoping to spend a few moments alone with Dana, Jarald had been waiting in the shadows nearby when she and Erik had approached her tent. He had expected them only to wish each other good night, but their unguarded conversation had swiftly confirmed his worst fears. To find that the beautiful young woman he had courted so diligently had slept with a slave, who apparently had tired of her, was so outrageous a happenstance his hand went immediately to his knife. He would kill Brendan, that much was certain, but Dana had wronged him too.

"Dana?" he called out as he stepped up to her tent.

Seated just inside, Dana leapt to her feet and came to the opening. "Yes, Jarald, what is it?"

He had not gotten used to seeing her in Soren's clothes,

and with her hair tumbled around her shoulders in casual disarray she had a childlike innocence he knew she did not deserve. "I don't want to leave you here alone. Come with me now, and I'll take you on ahead to a place where you'll be safe."

When he offered his hand, Dana took it eagerly. "Thank you. I tried to convince Erik to do just that, but he refused."

Jarald smiled, then put a fingertip to his lips to warn her to be silent. He led her away from the fire where his men were gathered, down past the ship, and then into the woods. Once he was certain they had gone far enough not to be overheard, he grabbed the knife she wore at her belt and pulled her around to face him. "I know all about you," he began in a low growl as he tossed her blade aside. "You've teased me for the last time, Dana. Tonight I mean to have what you've been giving so freely to your slave."

Terrified by the threat, Dana tried to break free, and failing that, she attempted to kick him, but Jarald was so tall and strong he simply held her at arm's length and laughed at her futile efforts to harm him.

"You're no more able to hurt me than Brendan will be tomorrow. I mean to kill him, Dana. You'll need him no more now that you have me."

"I don't want you!" Dana screamed, and Jarald responded by slapping her so hard her head snapped back with a force she feared had broken her neck. He shook her then, making her so dizzy that when he began to slap her again she could barely stay on her feet. Each time he struck her, he cursed her with filthy words she did not even understand, but still she refused to meekly submit to his superior strength.

"Did you ever fight Brendan?" the husky brute asked. "Did you ever tell him no when he hungered for you?"

"Never!" Dana shrieked, determined to fight him as long as she had the breath to do so.

Enraged by the insulting response, Jarald wound his fingers in Dana's flowing curls, hauling her close for brutal kiss that ended when she sank her teeth in his lower lip.

"Bitch!" he shouted, and unmindful of his own strength, he hurled her against a tree with a force that instantly rendered her unconscious. She went limp, slipping from his arms to the dirt at his feet. Disgusted, he sent his toe into her ribs. When she did not moan, he cursed her all the more loudly. He enjoyed her spirit too much to take her when she would not even recall what had happened.

"Slut," he hissed before spitting on the ground. "That's nothing compared to what Haakon will do to you when he learns you've been sleeping with slaves. You needn't worry, though. I'll offer to marry you despite that disgrace, and I know Haakon will be too grateful to me to allow you to refuse."

Chuckling at his own cleverness, Jarald scooped Dana up into his arms. With the same stealth with which he had left the camp, he carried her back to her tent, certain she would still be there when he was ready to hand her over to her father for another beating.

CHAPTER XXIII

Haakon heard a muffled thud as the guard at the gate of the stockade fell. Grabbing Svien by the shoulder, he gave him a shake. "Wake up, someone's coming."

Instantly alert, Svien peered into the darkness that surrounded them, but in the pale moonlight he could barely make out his father's face and could discern nothing in the shadows beyond. He heard the gate being pulled open slowly rather than being flung wide as it usually was. Whoever was coming carried no lantern, and the oversight perplexed him. "Who can it be?" he whispered.

Haakon shook Per, who lay asleep on his left, then clamped

his hand over his mouth before he could speak. There were more than forty men inside the stockade. Shackled together in groups of three, they were as restless that night as on all others, and like a silent wave, they awakened and leaned forward, to a man straining to see who was moving toward them through the darkness.

From bitter experience, Brendan knew the captives would be huddled against the wall of the sturdily built log enclosure, but he stepped carefully so as not to trip over any outstretched legs as he slipped through the gate. "I have come to set you all free," he promised in a hushed voice. "Where is Haakon?"

Suspecting a trick of some kind, Haakon hesitated a moment, but then thinking his situation could be no worse, he called out, "I am here."

"Come to me," Brendan ordered, unwilling to risk making his way to him. "I've come with Erik. Hurry, it will soon be dawn."

After nearly a month of captivity, Haakon, Svien, and Per, who was shackled with them, had learned to coordinate their motions, if not smoothly, then without frequent mishap. In the darkness, however, it was no small feat for the men to shuffle their way to the gate. Also eager to go, their companions struggled to their feet, but none dared dispute Haakon's right to be the first to leave.

"Where's Jørn?" Haakon whispered anxiously as he reached Brendan.

"Erik will explain everything later," the Celt replied, determined to see that Erik received the major portion of the credit for his father's rescue. "I have the key. As soon as I remove your leg irons, walk through the gate, then wait just outside for me." As Brendan bent down to unlock the iron cuffs encircling Haakon's ankles, he recalled vividly the humiliation of wearing chains. That was only one of the many crimes for which he intended to make Trom pay.

It was too dark for him to make out Haakon's features or those of the men with him, but even so, Brendan got the distinct impression not only of height, but of strength as well. He assumed Haakon's crew would be as well disci

plined as Jarald's and understand the necessity for stealth
without being told, and he was not disappointed. Placing the
key in an outstretched hand, he instructed the man to free
himself and then pass on the key. Soon the key was moving
from one shackled trio to the next with a steady rhythm,
with each newly freed captive following the man ahead of
him through the gate.

When the last man had cast off his chains, Brendan led
the Danes in a silent procession up the river and around a
bend to where he had left his own men waiting. It was not
until Haakon moved into the light of their lanterns that he
realized they had been rescued by a group of total strangers.
While Haakon surveyed the Celts with a confused mixture
of relief and suspicion, Brendan took the time to study
him.

All he had heard of Dana's father had led him to expect
someone of Jarald's robust build, but while Haakon was
well over six feet in height, he was lean rather than stocky.
His kirtle and breeches were ripped and stained, but his
stance was still a proud one. His blond curls where touched
with gray, as was his beard, but his blue-violet eyes were
alight with a youthful curiosity. He was one of the handsomest
men Brendan had ever seen, and he now realized that
despite the difference in their coloring, Erik resembled him
closely.

"Who are you?" Haakon demanded, not pleased at being
observed so intently.

Readily understanding the man's confusion, Brendan again
introduced himself as a friend of Erik's, then continued, "I
am Brendan, a prince of the Dál Cais, and these are some of
my people. We have come to put an end to Trom and his
evil band. You and your men may either wait here to stay
out of our way, or if you want to join us, we can supply you
with the weapons to do so."

"Erik would have mentioned a prince had he met one,"
Svien announced as he stepped forward to regard Brendan
with a decidedly skeptical stare. "He has no friends that I
don't know."

Svien was blond like his father and, like Soren, had
inherited his mother's blue eyes. He was also a handsome

man despite his filthy attire. His challenge brought a smile to Brendan's lips, for it reminded him of something Dana might say to a stranger. "He does now," the Celt assured him with an engaging grin. "At dawn he and Jarald will move into Trom's camp from the river, while my men and I will enter the way we just came. What is your choice? I know Trom has treated you badly. If you lack the strength to fight, none of us will think you cowards."

That comment was greeted with such loud protests Brendan had to raise his hands in a plea for silence. "How many men does Trom have with him now?"

"No more than a hundred," Haakon replied.

As they talked, Brendan had hurriedly counted the Danes. Including Haakon and Svien, there were forty-two. He was certain they had left Fyn with more, but knowing how cruel Trom was, he thought it remarkable so many had survived. He had found nearly that many among his people eager to fight Trom, and counting the men with Jarald, it would be nearly an even match. Jarald and Erik would be surprised to see he had freed the captive Danes without waiting for them, but he had feared a bloody brawl where many might lose their lives if the prisoners were not free to fight at the outset. Besides, having Haakon's men on his side at the start of the attack greatly improved his chances of killing the pirate who had caused him so much torment.

"Trom's men are like vermin," Brendan said, and there was an outpouring of far more insulting terms from the Danes. "Without their leader they'll swiftly scatter. It's only Trom I want. What you do with the others won' matter, but you mustn't set any fires. We don't want to make any of the Norsemen in Limerick curious enough to come downriver to find out why Trom's camp is in flames."

As they continued to plot how best to surprise the sleeping pirates at dawn, Haakon eyed the confident Celt with growing admiration. Brendan impressed him as a man of his word, and he did not doubt that he would fight Trom to the death. The outcome of such a match was by no means certain, however. "I'll give you the first chance to kill

Trom, but if you're wounded, I'll push you aside and finish him off myself. Now where are these weapons of which you spoke?''

"He'll not harm me," Brendan replied, but rather than argue the issue further, he distributed what weapons they had to share. "We mean to open the storehouse where Trom has your belongings, so do not complain if these swords and axes are not as fine as your own, because you'll soon have them."

Just as Jørn had predicted, Brendan had found his people eager to welcome the help of Danes to defeat the Norse pirates, and none had shared his fear that they might prove themselves to be every bit as aggressive and abusive once the Norsemen were gone. While Brendan still harbored that worry himself, it was a risk he was willing to take to rid his homeland of Trom.

Once everyone was armed, Brendan led them back to the pirates' camp. There was not a sentry left alive at his post to sound an alarm, and moving into position, they waited for the dawn to provide enough light for them to discern friend from foe. As they had planned, when Jarald gave the call of an owl, Brendan cupped his hands to his mouth to make the reply. He went forward then, intent upon slaying the villain who had sold him into slavery.

Had Trom not been a clever man, he would not have survived in such a dangerous profession for as long as he had. Awakened to the unmistakable sounds of an attack, he grabbed up his sword and ran to the door. When he found Brendan standing on the other side, his blue eyes aglow with a demonic gleam, he let out a piercing howl and with a savage lunge made a wild attempt to hack him in two.

Brendan had never expected Trom to surrender meekly, for he knew the man relished a fight, but he was determined to end this battle as the victor. He had been a fine warrior at twenty-three, but three years of hard labor had given him a physical toughness as enduring as the heavy steel blade he swung with both hands. He had seen the light of recognition in Trom's pale blue eyes, and knew he now regretted sparing his life, but the pirate's resulting anger only served to feed the Celt's determination to see him dead.

The clang of their swords resounding with the force of their mighty blows, Trom and Brendan moved in a tight circle, leaving the front of the house for the open space in the center of the camp. All around them other men fought, for the Danes wanted every Norseman responsible for their capture dead, while Erik, Jarald, and his crew advanced from the river, blocking all hope the pirates had of escape.

Relentless in his pursuit of satisfaction, Brendan fought with a deadly precision. When Trom began to tire, the fierceness of the Celt's craving for revenge gave him the stamina to increase the tempo of his attack. He watched terror fill the pirate's eyes as he realized he was beaten. Trom continued to fight, for he possessed a tenacious streak that would not allow him to beg for mercy from a man he already knew would show him none. Attempting a retreat, he staggered backward, but clumsy with fatigue, he tripped over his own feet and fell. Without the slightest hesitation, Brendan drove the point of his sword through the fallen man's chest, and the hatred that had consumed him for three long years finally found its release. There was no time to savor that joy, however, with blood and curses flying all around him.

Erik had fought beside Jarald, moving from the docks toward the center of the pirate's stronghold, but when he saw that the burly Dane intended to swing his sword into Brendan's back, he slammed into him hard enough to make his blow go wide. He then shouted a warning to Brendan, who whirled around in time to block Jarald's next blow.

Brendan had expended a great deal of energy defeating Trom, but he despised Jarald and welcomed the opportunity to fight him. This battle was nearly as fierce as the one he had waged with the pirate, but fortunately Jarald had already fought several men too and he wasn't able to summon his full strength either.

When he found no one left standing to fight, Haakon joined those watching Brendan and Jarald, but he could not understand why the two men would want to kill each other. When Erik stepped to his side, obviously worried about the outcome of the match, he tried to ask him about the bout, but he could not be heard over the din of the crowd.

Finding Brendan to be a far tougher opponent than he had imagined, Jarald used Haakon's arrival to a quick advantage. Moving back out of Brendan's reach, he shouted to the man he had come to save. "This slave is Dana's lover, and he doesn't deserve to live! Help me kill him!"

"A slave? He called himself a prince!" Haakon raised his blade, trusting a man he knew well rather than one he had just met, but again Erik stepped forward to protect Brendan. The bravery of that move so impressed Haakon that he lowered his sword to his side.

Svien pushed his way to the front then, shoving the men who stood between him and his father aside. "We have gained our freedom. What is the point in fighting each other?"

Jarald had to take several deep gulps of air before he spoke, but he then denounced Brendan as an arrogant slave who had seduced Dana and then abandoned her. "I've already punished Dana," he declared proudly, "and I meant to punish him as well."

Both Erik and Brendan went after Jarald at that taunt, and dodging their bloodstained blades, Haakon and Svien summoned several men from their crews to pry the combatants apart. "I want the truth," Haakon demanded when he gained control of the volatile situation. "Now who knows it?"

Thinking that as a neutral party his word would be believed, Erik attempted to explain his half sister's involvement with Brendan, but he could not deny she had taken a slave for a lover. When he saw he had succeeded only in infuriating Haakon, he quickly gave up the effort to champion his sister's cause. "Dana can speak for herself. She'll be thrilled to see you and Svien are safe. Let's go and tell her that you are."

Haakon was astounded to hear Dana had accompanied the men on their rescue mission, and he wanted to see her, but he first ordered his crew to search the pirates' lair for valuables of any kind. "Divide them with the men who came to help us escape, for the rightful owners of anything Trom had here are undoubtedly dead.'' That matter out of the way, he took the precaution of disarming both Jarald and Brendan before he allowed Erik to lead the way back to the cove where they had camped.

Putting his time to good use, Jarald reminded Haakon that he had wanted to wed his eldest daughter, and insisted that he still did despite her indiscretions that summer. ''She is a delightful young woman and I love her still. When I'm her husband she'll have no need for other men,'' he boasted proudly.

Haakon exchanged a worried glance with Svien, for nothing anyone had said about Dana had made the slightest sense to him. When they reached the sheltered bay where the *Seahawk* lay at anchor, he called Dana's name, but she failed to appear. ''Well, where is she?''

Jarald went immediately to her tent, but finding it empty, he shrugged innocently. ''We told her to wait here for us.''

''How did you punish her?'' Brendan asked accusingly. ''Just what did you do to her?'' He cursed his own stupidity at leaving the woman he loved in the same camp with a man neither of them trusted. Erik had been there, but apparently he had seen nothing. Brendan was furious with himself for not sharing Dana's story about Grena with Erik so he would have kept a better watch on the man.

''How many women do you need, Jarald? Wasn't Grena enough for you?'' the Celt shouted when the man didn't reply to his earlier questions.

''What has Grena got to do with this?'' Haakon inquired. ''I thought it was Dana you wished to wed.''

Jarald regarded Brendan with a truly murderous gaze. ''Grena is a lonely widow who begged me to enliven an afternoon. It's Dana I intend to wed, and I'll not allow a slave to stand in my way!''

With a sudden flash of insight, Brendan realized how great an enemy Jarald truly was. ''You were trying to kill me, weren't you? The fire at Erik's wasn't meant to destroy his house at all, only to roast me alive!'' He lunged for Jarald's throat, meaning to choke the last breath of life from him, but Svien and Haakon managed to pull him back.

In the midst of the confusion, Erik spotted Dana at the edge of the forest, leaning against a tree, barely able to stand. "There's Dana!" he called excitedly, but even at a distance he could see she was seriously hurt. He ran to her, then slid to a halt, appalled by her bruised and battered appearance.

"Did Jarald do that to you?" he asked as he tried to find a way to gather her into his arms without causing her any additional pain.

Not wanting to risk another confrontation with Jarald unarmed, Dana had crawled into the woods to find her knife. She had the weapon clutched tightly in her hand, but knew she lacked the strength to plunge it into Jarald's heart. "Don't let Jarald near me," she whispered softly, and enfolded in Erik's arms, she gave in to the pain that racked her slender body and slipped back into the welcoming peace of unconsciousness.

When Dana awoke, she found herself lying on a bed of furs in a dimly lit dwelling, but unlike her home, this one was round. Hearing the sound of masculine voices, she turned toward them and found her father, Svien, Erik, and Brendan seated around the hearth in the center of the circular room. They were sipping what was obviously not their first tankard of ale, and she was annoyed to think they had nothing better to do than get drunk when she felt as though every bone in her body had been broken. She was about to call out to them, meaning to scold them for neglecting her so shamefully, when her father began to speak. Sensing that what he was about to impart was important, she held her tongue.

In all his life, Haakon had never had so many idle moments as those he had had to endure as Trom's prisoner. He and Svien had often passed their time talking of the loved ones they had left at home, and whenever his son had mentioned Erik, Haakon had cringed inwardly. An active man, and not one given to introspection, he had grown horribly uncomfortable with the memories Erik's name called to mind, for it was inexorably linked to the most tragic event of his youth.

As the days of their captivity passed in dreary monotony, Haakon found himself dwelling with increasing frequency on his eldest son. His conscience repeatedly reminded him that Erik was no longer a boy who could be brushed aside. He was now a grown man, and Haakon knew he should no longer deny to himself and others that he was proud of him. Unfortunately, his fatherly pride was not something he could easily demonstrate. He had never been ashamed of his son, but he was deeply ashamed of what had happened to his mother.

Now seated together, his mood mellowed with the ale Brendan had supplied in hospitable abundance, Haakon recalled what he had seen of Erik's bravery that day, and he was convinced a father's praise was long overdue. Clearing his throat, he instantly had his companions' attention. "Erik," he began hesitantly, the words still not easy to speak despite his conviction they had to be said. "I want to thank you for what you did for us today. I had scant trust in Jørn, but I knew once he reached home, you and Freya would send someone to rescue us. We were all confident of that."

While he was touched by his father's praise, Erik did not think it was deserved. "It was Jarald who supplied the ship and crew to bring us here, and Brendan who warned us against paying the ransom. Had we followed Jørn's advice and sailed into Trom's camp expecting to exchange your lives for silver, we might all be dead."

That his firstborn would modestly refuse to accept his gratitude was something Haakon had foreseen. He reached out and gave Erik's shoulder a hearty squeeze. "The less said about Jarald the better, and I'll have to speak to Dana before I forgive Brendan for what he's done, but I don't want to talk about that now. My concern is for you."

In all his life, Erik did not recall his father ever wanting to talk with him as he now seemed eager to do. Unaccustomed to receiving the man's attention, he was embarrassed and looked away. "Have I done something wrong?"

"No, I'm the one who's been in the wrong for more years than I care to count."

Brendan glanced toward Svien, wondering if they shouldn't excuse themselves so Haakon and Erik could talk privately. Svien was paying such rapt attention to his father, however, that Brendan decided not to make that suggestion. He was intrigued as well, and leaned forward slightly, intent upon hearing every word that Haakon cared to speak.

"I swear I have loved Freya all my life," Haakon stated with a wistful smile. "No other woman ever touched my emotions as deeply as she does, but I will freely admit to knowing other women while I waited for her to reach her sixteenth birthday when we planned to wed. I had the same appetites as every other young man, and like others I sought to satisfy them as often as I could. We kept slaves then, and one especially pretty one was always eager to amuse me."

Erik readily grasped the fact Haakon was talking about his mother, and he didn't want to hear it. "I understand," he said gruffly, but he still found it impossible to look his father in the eye.

"No, you understand nothing, and neither did I," Haakon insisted. "Your mother was lovely, but while she knew of my marriage plans, she could not accept the fact that it was Freya that I truly loved rather than her. When you were born, she expected me to not only give you both your freedom, but to marry her as well. I can still remember each word of our last conversation as though it took place yesterday."

Haakon paused, and after a slight shudder, he forced himself to continue. "You were a handsome boy, and I was proud to call you mine, but Sofia was not satisfied with that, nor with the gift of her freedom either. She wanted to be my wife. She ripped you from my arms, held a knife to your throat, and said if I refused to marry her, she'd kill you. She was like a wild animal, screaming insults at me. Terrified, you were wailing almost as loudly as she. None of the pleasure I'd found in her arms was worth the horror of that moment.

"I tried to reason with her, to assure her I would look after you and her, but that only served to enrage her all the more. When she finally realized I'd never marry her, she raised the knife. She was going to plunge it through her own baby's heart, but I was quick enough to stop her. We struggled, and not caring whether or not she cut me, I managed to wrench you from her arms. I meant to send her away where, no matter how long she continued to hate me, she would never be able to harm you, but she turned the knife on herself and cursed me with her dying breath.''

His mother had been a slave who had died soon after his birth. That was what Erik had been told. Now he knew it was merely a convenient lie to shield him from a ghastly truth. ''Why are you telling me this now?'' he asked.

''You still don't understand,'' Haakon sighed sadly. ''Each time I looked at you I saw a beautiful young girl whose obsessive love for me had driven her mad. The violence of her death left me more badly scarred than any knife wound could have. It was my own guilt that kept us from being close. I worried that you'd learn the truth from one of the servants and blame me for your mother's death. At the same time, I couldn't forgive myself for being so flattered by her possessiveness that I didn't foresee the danger in it. I had never asked for Sofia's love, and yet she died for want of mine.''

When Haakon fell silent, Erik spoke his most immediate fear aloud. ''You must have wondered if I'd be like her.''

Haakon shook his head. ''No, you've always favored me in temperament, but you're a far better man than I was at your age. I know it's very late, but I'll try to be a father to you from now on, and never punish you again for my own mistakes. I don't expect you to forgive me, but perhaps in time we can become friends.''

Erik had grown up idolizing Haakon, and he was relieved beyond measure to learn his father had not shunned him because he was a slave's child rather than Freya's. Her abundant love had kept his childhood from being the lonely one it might have been. He had always longed for his father's love, and he was too wise to refuse it because it had come so late. ''I need something more valuable than friendship now,'' he stated with just a hint of a smile.

''Name it,'' Haakon offered agreeably, ''but let me assure

you I've already decided to let you keep a good portion of the ransom. I want to give Brendan a handsome share as well. I think you both earned it.''

Knowing he could put the silver to good use building his own farm, Erik was enormously pleased, but wealth had not been what he had in mind. "That's very generous of you, but I want to marry Berit, and Grena refuses to allow it. I'd like your help to win her consent.''

Despite his initial surprise at so bold a request, after a moment's reflection Haakon broke into a wide grin. "That's the least I can do for you. When Grena understands that I'm in favor of the match, she will be too. I should have realized she's been lonely without Jarald having to tell me. I think we can find her a second husband, one who'll also help to soften her attitude toward you.''

That Haakon and Erik had ended their long estrangement so amicably delighted Brendan, and he got up to fetch more ale. When he noticed Dana was awake, he went to her side. "It took all four of us to do it, but we gave Jarald a beating he'll never forget. Had he raped you, we would have killed him, but he swore time and again that he hadn't. Was he telling the truth?''

Dana's head still hurt so badly she had considerable difficulty focusing her eyes, but even though she could not see Brendan's face clearly, she had no trouble understanding his words. "Yes, our argument was a violent one, but I wasn't raped. It was unfair of me not to discourage his company last spring. If only I had, then he wouldn't have clung to the hope I'd eventually grow to love him. He should never have hit me. I didn't deserve that, but what about you? Are you content to let him live after he nearly killed you?''

Brendan sat down on the edge of Dana's bed and took her hands in his. "I fought him once today, and I'd have fought him again if Haakon hadn't warned me that should I slay him his family would retaliate by attacking yours. That's not a risk I'm willing to take. I'm satisfied to let him go with a beating that will keep him hurting for weeks.''

"Why would Jarald's kin come after us for revenge? We aren't related to you," Dana reminded him.

"That's what we need to discuss," Haakon announced as he reached the bed. "Brendan has proven his worth today. As a prince of the Dál Cais, he hopes one day to become king of all Erin. Such an ambitious man needs a wife worthy of being a queen. He claims that you want him for a husband, but I want to hear those words from your lips."

Dana didn't know which of her father's comments was the most startling, so she began with the first. "Why didn't you tell me you were a prince, Brendan?"

Brendan chuckled before replying. "When I was dressed in rags, would you have believed me?"

Dana did not need to search her heart long for that answer. "Yes, I would have believed you, but you chose not to confide in me. As for being your wife, I don't recall ever saying that I wanted you for a husband."

Both of Dana's eyes were black and swollen, but Brendan thought her beautiful still. "Perhaps not in words, but nonetheless you've said it quite eloquently. I know I've always been reluctant to talk, but now that I'm home, I'll be happy to recount our history for as long as you're willing to listen."

When her only response was a skeptical glance, he provided a brief introduction. "The most powerful people in Erin are the Ui Néill, they rule from Tara in the north. The Eoghanachta rule the south from Cashel. The Dál Cais are here in the west. If we can unite as one, we can drive the Norsemen from Erin. That was what I was attempting to do when Trom took me prisoner. He had no idea I was anyone of any importance. He saw only that I was good with a sword, and because he respected my skill, he allowed me to live. I didn't return that favor."

Dana understood the sly comment. "A prince," she mumbled again, barely able to think above the painful throbbing in her head.

Kneeling beside her, Haakon spoke with an urgent haste. "We can't stay in Erin, Dana. We're all needed at home for the harvest, and there's a danger we'll come under attack in we tarry here. Brendan has already summoned a priest to perform their marriage ceremony, but if you don't want to stay with him, then I'll carry you to my ship and we'll sail on the morning tide.''

Dana was still clad in Soren's clothes, and she had never felt less like discussing marriage. "Surely a prince ought to have such fine manners he would know how to politely ask a woman to become his wife.''

Brendan bent down to plant a tender kiss in the center of Dana's left palm. When he raised himself up, his eyes were alight with a teasing gleam. "I love you with all my heart and soul. I swear I have from the moment I first saw you riding up the path to Grena's. Your beauty was more blinding than the sunlight dancing on your curls, and I'll never forget that day. I was no more than a slave then, and although I am again a prince, I am your slave still. Please say you'll be my bride, and I'll give you a life every queen in the world will envy.''

Dana studied what she could see of Brendan's expression for a long moment, and while she was inclined to agree to his effusive proposal, there was still something more that she craved. "I want your trust as well as your love. Can you give me that now as well?''

Brendan nodded. "Willingly.''

"Then my answer is yes,'' Dana informed him with a smile that lit her battered features with a warm glow of happiness. Brendan leaned forward to kiss her, but Haakon immediately interrupted the show of affection.

"There is the matter of her bride-price,'' the tall Dane reminded Brendan. "Dana is an incomparable beauty, and I'll not simply give her away.''

"I don't expect you to,'' Brendan responded as he rose to his feet. After an absence of three years, he had no idea what his family might be in a position to offer, but he didn't want to waste the time to ask. "Keep the part of the ransom you planned to give me. That should be more than sufficient.''

"It is too much,'' Haakon argued.

"Not for a queen,'' Brendan replied smugly.

"Do you see why I love him?'' Dana asked her father. Haakon nodded. "I'll come back each spring to see that you always do. Now we'll have to find you something else to wear for the wedding. I doubt you want to be married in your brother's clothes.''

"This isn't my home," Brendan explained, "but the home of relatives with whom I spent part of my youth. I'll ask the women for a suitable gown.''

Dana reached out to catch his hand as he started to turn away. "No, wait, I brought a gown of my own to wear. It was in a silk bag in my tent. Did you bring it?''

"Yes," Erik assured her. "It's here.''

Brendan turned to find Erik and Svien shaking out a rose-hued tunic and matching chemise. Bordered with wide gold braid, they were even more lovely than the pink and rose garments he had always loved seeing her wear. "You mean you expected to marry me?" he asked in dismay.

It was impossible to see Dana's blush beneath her bruises, but it was an intense one. "I didn't want to ever have to tell you good-bye," was all she cared to admit.

Haakon cuffed Brendan on the shoulder. "Dana is clever as well as beautiful, but I can't believe you didn't know that.''

Brendan agreed, "Oh, yes, she has such a remarkable array of talents that I think it might take me a lifetime to get to know her well.''

"And for me to know you," Dana complimented him in return. When Brendan helped her to her feet, she assured him that she wasn't feeling too poorly to bathe and dress, but even if she had been, she would have denied it, she was so eager to marry him.

CHAPTER XXIV

Dawn found Brendan and Dana in the lush meadow atop the Cliffs of Moher. They stood arm in arm, yawning sleepily as they waited for her father, Svien, and Erik to begin their journey home. Thoroughly humiliated, Jarald had departed the previous day and would not be missed.

"Oh, look," Dana exclaimed, "here they come!"

Brendan joined his bride in waving excitedly as the two knarr Haakon and Svien captained came into view. They were accompanied by three of the more elegantly proportioned dreki which had once belonged to Trom. Seeing no reason to leave ships which could be used to pursue them, Haakon had taken the dreki he could spare crew to sail. Brendan's relatives had hidden another of Trom's ships in an inland lake and had sunk the rest. With Trom and his band of cutthroats dead, and his fleet either commandeered or destroyed, it would be a long while before another ambitious Norseman with evil intentions was able to take his place.

"They are such beautiful ships, aren't they?" Dana remarked wistfully. "Like living creatures, they glide through the sea so effortlessly."

While he had never thought he would see the day when he could regard a Viking warship as a thing of beauty, now that he had made friends with the men who sailed them, Brendan found that he could. That he now had such a magnificent vessel in his possession pleased him all the more. "If only we had discovered the secret of building such sturdy ships ourselves," he mused aloud. "Then the world might be at our mercy, rather than yours."

"What do you mean by 'ours' and 'yours'? Are we not of one family now?" Dana's gaze was still focused on the ships passing by the cliffs, but Brendan's answer meant a great deal to her.

Brendan took care to give her only a slight hug so as not to cause her badly bruised body any pain. "Yes, we are truly one. I was never even tempted to take a wife before I met you. I think you must be one of the bravest women ever born."

"Brave?" Dana denied with a sparkling laugh. "You are the one who fought Trom, not me."

Brendan recognized Erik by his dark hair as the final dreki sailed by, and waved to him. "You've left a loving family and a wonderfully pleasant life on a prosperous farm. And for what? To marry a man who will have to unite tribes that have been feuding for centuries before he can defeat his enemies."

Her good-byes made, Dana turned toward Brendan. "Do you think I'd be content to lead the placid life of a farmer's wife when I could be married to a prince with so noble a cause as yours?" Her teasing glance convinced him she thought the idea absurd. "I don't think I'm brave at all, merely very clever for loving you."

The sea breeze tossed Dana's fiery curls, and Brendan reached out to brush them away from her face before he leaned down to kiss her. "If what I hope to do proves impossible in the next year or two, I'll abandon the effort, Dana. I won't sacrifice our future to a dream that will never come true. The Norsemen hold the ports on the east and south of Erin, but Limerick is their only settlement on the west. Their interest is in trade, and they look to the sea. We can simply ignore them if we choose, and live our lives inland as we always have. It was a life not all that different from yours. I may have given up my portion of the ransom, but I'm certain your father gave me more than my share of Trom's booty. You'll never want for anything."

Dana thought Brendan wonderfully generous to think of her welfare rather than simply his own ambitions. She had married him in a Christian ceremony in which she had not understood a single word, and yet she had no doubts about the wisdom of what she had done. Their bond of love far surpassed whatever differences their backgrounds had given them.

"When my father returns in the spring with more men to help you, your countrymen are bound to be inspired to join the fight against the Norsemen. If they refuse, then they don't deserve to call Erin their own."

"I'll have to teach you to speak our tongue quickly," Brendan replied with an amused chuckle. "I think men will volunteer in great numbers to follow you. You won't even have to shame them into it."

"I'll do all that I can to help," Dana insisted proudly. "It's the least I can do for my husband."

Deeply pleased to have so devoted a wife, Brendan enfolded Dana in a tender embrace. "Had you not come here with me, I would have gone back to Fyn to get you. I swear I would have. For so long I've dreamed of nothing but coming home, but had you not been here, I would have been more lonely than when I was away."

While she was both touched and flattered by this admission, Dana was also intrigued. "Would you have told me you planned to return?"

Chagrined by the insightful question, Brendan nevertheless admitted the truth. "Probably not."

Dana's eyes narrowed menacingly as the temper which had once stung him so sharply began to flare. "Do you want me to shove you off the cliff?"

"No," Brendan murmured seductively. "I want you to make love to me until I beg you to stop."

"Is that a challenge?"

"You may consider it as such."

Dana glanced around the meadow. It was a rich, emerald green that invited a lengthy stay. "You said looking over the cliff was a thrill. Have you ever made love here?"

"Here?" Brendan looked around quickly, and seeing no sign of anyone, he grew as bold as she. He took the precaution of leading her well away from the edge of the cliff before abandoning himself to pleasure, however. "I think with you as my bride, my life is going to be filled with thrills."

"I'll consider that a challenge as well," Dana replied demurely, but as she helped him pull off his kirtle, her fingertips strayed through the thick curls covering his chest and her shy smile grew wide. "It's been a very exciting summer, hasn't it? The best of my life."

"Ah, my beloved, the best is yet to come."

They had become adept at removing each other's clothes. Once they were both nude, Brendan pulled Dana down into the feather-soft grass, and with the magical affection he had always bestowed, he made that promise come true.

Haakon spent every spare minute of the voyage with Erik. He not only taught him how to swim and sail, but he talked of other things that were important to him, and listened closely to the young man's replies. To his immense delight, he found Erik's mind quick and his judgment sound. He apologized more than once for his neglect, but Erik assured him there was no need to waste time on regrets now that they finally shared the closeness of a father and son. That Erik was so gracious a young man pleased Haakon all the more.

When they reached home, Haakon was so anxious to see Freya he leapt over the rail of his ship the instant it was secured to the dock. He raced up the path, and when Freya, Thora, and Soren came from the house to meet him, he first greeted his children with hugs and kisses, then picked up his wife and swung her around until they were both so dizzy he had to put her down. Freya held on to him tightly and laughed, for she knew he could not possibly be angry with her and still greet her so enthusiastically.

"Do you know about Erik and Berit?" she asked when she caught her breath.

"I think it's a fine match, and I'll convince Grena of it this very day," Haakon boasted proudly. "There's another wedding we need to discuss first, though."

"Another wedding?" Freya exclaimed in surprise. "Why only yesterday Moira told me she'll soon wed one of Jørn's crew. Who else is planning marriage?" She left his arms for a moment to return Svien's kiss as he reached her. She then waved to Erik, who was coming up the path with Berit. Th

lively blonde had raced by Haakon in her haste to welcome
home the man she loved. It wasn't until that moment that
Freya noticed Dana's absence. "Where's Dana?" she asked
anxiously. "Isn't she with you?"

Haakon's smile was so wide he instantly allayed his
wife's fears. "It's rather a long story, but the only thing you
need to know now is that Dana has married Brendan and
stayed with him in Erin."

"Brendan!" Freya gasped in dismay. "Why, I didn't
think she even liked the man."

"She liked him very well indeed," Erik announced as he
and Berit joined them. "They just kept it a secret, is all."

Berit was as astonished as her aunt. "Well, I wish you'd
told me about them. The next time you share in such a
delicious secret, I want you to tell me."

"It wouldn't be a secret then," Erik teased her.

Grena had followed Berit from the house, but thinking
Jarald would be with Haakon, she got only close enough to
overhear the tall Dane's remarks. She felt sick to her
stomach just imagining Jarald's lustful stare, but when after
several moments he didn't appear, she ventured forward.
"Is Jarald not with you either?"

"Jarald won't be coming here again," Erik informed her.
Then, thinking she would rather hear the story from Haakon,
he fell silent.

"Jarald is of no consequence," Haakon announced flippantly
as he went forward to give Grena a hug. "Come, let's all go
inside and have something to eat and drink. Then we can
make arrangements for a wedding between our children.
Erik has returned a wealthy man, but I'll warn you now that
if you ask too much for Berit I will argue all night to lower
her bride-price to a more reasonable one. My son is determined to wed Berit, but I'll not allow him to impoverish
himself to do so."

Both Berit and Grena stared wide-eyed at Haakon, for
neither had ever heard him call Erik his son. That he
seemed as set on the marriage as Erik impressed both the
women quite favorably.

"Mother?" Berit asked hesitantly. "Don't you think we
could at least discuss it?"

Grena's dreadful experience with Jarald had taught her a valuable lesson, and she would never again judge a man on his wealth alone. That Erik had managed to return home a man of means certainly worked in his favor, however. "Yes, I think we can discuss it," she agreed. "Jørn's gone home, but we needn't involve him. Now what of your men? Don't they need refreshments as well?"

"How thoughtful of you, Grena," Haakon responded with another broad grin. "Per is supervising the unloading of the cargo. Do you remember him?"

Grena nodded rather shyly. "Why, yes, I think that I do."

"Good, I invited him to have supper with us when he's finished. In the meantime we'll send something to eat and drink down to the docks."

When Haakon slipped one arm around his wife's waist and the other around Grena to escort them into his home, Berit gave Erik's hand an insistent yank to hold him back. "What's gotten into Haakon? I've never seen him in so relaxed a mood. And what's this about Per? Are they now as close friends as he was with Jarald?"

Erik was well aware of Haakon's plans for Per and Grena, but he thought that another secret he ought to keep for the time being. "My father is a remarkable man, but I'll have to tell you what I've learned about him later."

"Oh, Erik, must you keep more secrets?" Berit protested with such a bewitching pout Erik immediately leaned down to kiss her.

"If you're very curious, I could come to your room tonight and we could talk then."

"I want you to come to my room, but not to talk."

That Berit was so open about her desire for him pleased Erik as greatly as it had before he had gone away. "If you'd like to welcome me home with something other than conversation, that will be fine with me."

Berit's cheeks flooded with a pretty blush. "I love you and I missed you terribly. You shouldn't tease me about unless you would be happier if I hadn't noticed that you were gone."

"No, a wife ought to miss her husband, but unless w

hurry inside, we may never have the opportunity to wed.''

Trusting his far more practical nature, Berit laced her fingers in his and turned toward the house. ''Is what your father said true? Are you wealthy now?''

''Does it matter to you?''

Berit stopped at the door. ''You know that it doesn't.''

''Yes, I know,'' Erik replied. Suddenly the idea of remaining outside for another moment or two was extremely attractive. Longing to again savor the sweet softness of her kiss, Erik drew Berit close. ''I love you,'' he murmured softly before his mouth claimed hers in a lingering kiss.

Thanks to her love, his life had changed completely that summer. It was an exhilarating thought, but before it could fully take form, they were joined by Soren and Thora, who had been sent to bring them inside. Releasing Berit, Erik scooped the little girl up into his arms and gave her a loving squeeze. ''It won't be long before we'll be making marriage plans for you, baby.''

Thora's angelic features became quite forlorn at the comment. ''I wanted to wed Brendan myself,'' she complained. ''I'm sure there's not another man like him.''

Berit gave her cousin's golden-red curls a comforting pat. ''Somewhere there's a man for you, and whether or not he's anything like Brendan, I know you'll think him perfect.''

Thora considered that possibility a long moment and then nodded. She noted the affectionate glance that passed between Erik and Berit as they entered the house and hoped to grow up very quickly so that she could bask in that loving warmth too.

NOTE TO READERS

While the characters in *By Love Enslaved* are fictional, the historical setting is as accurate as I could possibly make it. In the summer of 1983, I had the opportunity to visit Scandinavia and visit many marvelous museums where artifacts from the Viking age may be seen. Particularly spectacular are the actual Viking ships which have been beautifully restored and are on display in both Denmark and Norway. These magnificent ships are more than one thousand years old, and provide a thrill I will never forget.

While Dana and Brendan did not really exist, their love story is an entirely probable one. In the 880s, Danes sought to establish a foothold in Ireland. Welcomed by the Irish, they had considerable success in their initial battles with the Norwegians who had occupied the country for more than fifty years. After three years of fighting, the Norwegians finally defeated the Danes, and no permanent Danish settlements were founded.

By 1002, a prince of the Dál Cais, Brian Boru, was the undisputed High King of Ireland. His defeat of the Norwegians at the Battle of Clontarf in 1014 marked the end of the Viking Wars in that country. A bold and courageous man, Brian Boru was widely regarded as an immensely effective ruler. While it would have been impossible for me to credit Brendan with Brian Boru's accomplishments, I can't help but believe ancestors with my hero and heroine's intelligence and bravery must have inspired them.

I would love to hear from readers who would like to comment on Brendan and Dana's love story. Please write to me in care of Warner Books/Popular Library, 666 Fifth Avenue, New York, New York 10103.

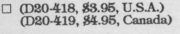